# CODE OF

# A DEBUT CRIME THRILLER

PHILLIP JORDAN

FIVE FOUR PUBLISHING

*Get Exclusive Material*

## GET EXCLUSIVE NEWS AND UPDATES FROM THE AUTHOR

Thank-you for choosing to read this book.

Sign-up for more details about my life growing up on the same streets that Detective Inspector Taylor treads and get some exclusive True Crime stories about the flawed but fabulous city that inspired me to write, *all for free.*

Details can be found at the end of **CODE OF SILENCE.**

## Chapter 1

*"...reports of a shooting in East Belfast earlier this evening. There are limited details at the minute, but the PSNI have cordoned off Risky's Nightclub. Initial accounts of the incident suggest one dead and one seriously injured. We'll update the information as it comes in..."*

Tyres squealed in the semi-darkness, echoing off bare and scored concrete walls as the lone vehicle descended into the underground garage. Overhead strip lighting strobed across the darkened windshield of the Vauxhall pool car overwhelmed by the mute blue flash of the internal strobe light.

*"...narrowly averting tragedy in a horrific collision and car fire following a high-speed pursuit in the city centre. The unnamed police officer has been hailed for their quick and selfless actions in rescuing a woman and her child trapped in the burning wreckage. A forty-one-year-old man has been arrested. Sources at the scene report that..."*

"...from Section Eight had the scene under control and signed me off... Thank you, sir. I appreciate that. I'm just glad they were okay."

The Vauxhall bottomed out as it descended into the lower parking area, a crash and grind of undercarriage sending sparks dancing under the chassis.

"I'm pulling into the car park now. Yes, Chief Inspector. Nothing on a motive for this one as yet and no one has stepped up to claim it... No. We have a witness being treated at the scene and they'll be brought to the Royal once deemed fit for travel. I'll do an initial interview there asap... Sir, I can assure you none of that will influence my investigation and I'll keep the DCI up to speed... No problem. Night, sir."

The car pulled in with a final screech of rubber on wet painted concrete and the whine of the electronic handbrake. The driver's door clunked open, the ping of a warning tone emitting from the dashboard, the engine ticking over as it cooled.

"Evening, boss."

Detective Inspector Veronica 'Ronnie' Taylor eased out of the driver's seat, bleary-eyed, a pen clamped between her teeth, and juggling an iPhone, car keys, parking ticket and a handful of loose change.

"Hi, Doc. Sorry, got here as quick as I could," Taylor mumbled through gritted teeth, offering a handshake.

"No bother. It's not like our boys got anywhere else to be. Good job up the road."

Detective Sergeant Doc Macpherson had the grip of a bear with a bone and the paws to match. Which was odd considering his moniker derived from his uncanny likeness to one of Snow White's famous friends. He reached past her, noticing body armour strewn on the back parcel shelf, a crumpled set of clothes stuffed in a Tesco bag for life in the footwell, and the stink of burning plastic. He shoved the door closed with a solid thump.

Taylor jangled the keys and change into her pockets and checked the screen of her phone. Missed calls and notifications. It followed the keys and change into the depths of her smart but wrinkled jacket. She pulled out a small tin of Clove Rock.

"Cheers. Here brought you a present."

"You shouldn't have." Macpherson accepted the token with a wide grin and clicked them open, offering her the first, which she accepted.

"ME here and all?"

"I think the creepy bugger hangs upside down in one of those lockers, to be honest."

Taylor delivered a tired but conspiratorial smile. She swept her chestnut hair up into a high messy bun and secured it with the pen. The movement releasing Eau de Burning Car Wreck into the surrounding air. She brushed a loose lock from her eyes.

"Who's holding the scene at the club?"

"Waller is SLO. He'll be fine," the DS assured her, noticing the sudden uptick of her chin at the mention of the new detective constable. "SOCOs are still there and half the night shift have the place cordoned off, but the punters are up for a riot. MSU are on standby to deploy and break it up. Reilly is accompanying the witness as soon as the paramedics give a fit to travel."

Taylor nodded, confirming she had received that brief.

Macpherson glanced at his watch.

"Last ETA one hour. We need to hold off until the doctor confirms capacity and consent."

Taylor raised an eyebrow in query.

"If this is who we think, we need to tick the boxes and make sure any testimony we get is solid."

"If it gets us our way back into the Firm, maybe I'll not end up in uniform after all," said Taylor.

Macpherson grunted and gestured to the nearby doors with their innocuous but ominous blue printed signage.

"We'll know soon enough. Don't be getting ahead of yourself. For one, this character's not in the position to be offering Queen's Evidence any time soon. After you."

Veronica Taylor blipped the Vauxhall's locks and led the way towards the underground entrance to the Royal Belfast Hospital Regional Forensic Mortuary.

The morgue wasn't a place that held a lot of fond memories for Taylor. Fragments of pain. Personal and professional. She had lost count of the times she'd stood in sombre vigil as a loved one identified a body, not that it was ever just a body.

Their footfalls clipped along terrazzo-effect linoleum until they were buzzed through into reception and received by a distracted middle-aged woman in washed-out green scrubs. She glanced up then returned to typing, the loud clackety-clack of keys under stubby red-tipped and chipped fingernails audible under her mutterings.

"Evening, he's expecting you. You can go on through. Sorry, we've another due for collection by the undertakers and someone who was in a rush to leave for the weekend misplaced the notes," she explained without looking up; a dark line between arched brows as she frowned at the screen then the clackety-clack as she remedied an error.

Like any normal establishment at half ten on a Sunday night, there was a quiet and stillness that preceded the flip into a new week and the madness of a Monday morning. As they walked the short distance along the eerie corridor, Macpherson, in anticipation, broke out the clove sweets. Popping one in his mouth he offered another to Taylor. Arriving at a familiar stainless steel door, frosted windows hiding the sights within, the sergeant, with a nod of deference, offered his colleague the first step over the threshold.

The sterile and clinical smell of the cutting room met them before the glass doors had fully swept closed. Tonight there was also a numb silence. No howl of dissection saw and no roar of the high-powered overhead ventilation sucking out the stench of decomposition and ruptured bowel. The faint odour of raw meat however refused to be overpowered by the scent of harsh disinfectant wafting from the plugholes of the stainless steel sinks that lined the rear wall. Glass-fronted cabinets above revealed instruments of horror that Taylor wished she had never seen used. The suite's once white tiles were now looking a little tired after years of soaking up spilt blood and gore. The centrepiece of the room was the four ominous steel tables atop one of which resided a formless mass hidden under a white sheet. Scales hung on meat hooks overhead, yet to be filled with human offal.

"Thanks for coming in, Professor Thompson."

"Never off duty, Inspector. Always hanging around here. You know what it's like in this caper."

Taylor ignored the splutter and flushed chubby red cheeks as Macpherson stifled his guffaw under a hasty cough, pantomime slapping his chest.

"Let it not be said I am one to let a lady down in her hour of need." Thompson gave her a theatrical bow, and a concerned look to the scarlet faced DS.

"You ought to give up the smokes, Sergeant or Irene will be writing up your certificate."

"Sorry, Prof. Choked on a sweetie there," said Macpherson, clearing his throat but grinning and shaking the man's hand.

The pathologist then offered his hand to Taylor, grip a lot more social than her sergeant's who had busied himself with searching out two disposable aprons and face-masks.

"Apparently, there's been a bit of a mix-up and Irene isn't a happy bunny. One of those weeks ahead, I fear. Shall we?" Thompson passed across a manila file containing the still-warm printouts the inspector had requested on the phone on her way in. Taylor opened and skim-read the details, taking in a few of the close-up facial pictures of the victim and the broad overview shots of the scene. Thompson, whilst scrubbing up, filled the two detectives in on what details he had; male, late forties, one hundred and eighty-five centimetres tall, weight eighty-seven kilos. Thompson's mortuary assistant loaded a tray with surgical instruments: scissors, rib shears, plastic tubes and hoses. The collection was then deposited into what was essentially an industrial dishwasher for sterilisation before the autopsy. As the assistant unscrewed the blade of a large surgical scalpel Thompson finished washing and gowning and then with help from Macpherson he snapped on a pair of latex gloves.

"Voila!"

The pathologist whipped back the white sheet with a flourish that a Parisian maître d' would have been proud of.

The photographs didn't do him justice. The corpse stared at the ceiling. He had died hard.

Drum and bass. Vibrations that outside began as a tinny bmm-tsk, bmm-tsk, bmm-tsk now thrummed underfoot and rose in tremulous waves that pounded through the organs and threatened to loosen fillings from their moorings. Heavy footfalls were masked by the music, yet somehow the knock was heard and the door to the inner sanctum opened.

A pair of eyes bulged from tear-stained sockets. Desperate for salvation.

Murder could never be easy. Quick perhaps, but never easy. A life ripped violently apart and not just in the physical sense. At a point, there was a sudden visceral realisation that all that had ever been and all that had yet to be was gone.

In the door's opening, she knew what was happening. Knew her time had come. Another scream ripped from blood-spattered lips, the sound obscured by the binding of cloth duct tape. She felt a broken rib snag sending shockwaves of excruciating pain through her body.

"Good job, Gary. You can fuck off now, love. Tell Raymond drinks are on the house for you tonight," said the newcomer.

"Ah, okay. Right enough, Mr Millar. Cheers now." Gary wiped the back of his hand across a sweaty and blood-dappled forehead, his breath laboured.

Millar patted him as he passed, hand lingering a little too

long on the younger man's bicep. The cheap Umbro tee shirt stuck to him, a wide inverted arch of sweat staining darker from throat to midsection.

"Now you know our arrangement, Gary. Not a word and maybe I'll call you in again for another wee job. Sound good?"

"Oh, aye. No bother, not a peep." Gary nodded. His eyes flashed back on his handiwork, then to Millar's hand on his arm. The sickening twist of guilt overridden by another craving.

"Erm, and my other gear?"

"In the back room with Rowdy. Don't be greedy and shoot it all up in one sitting now, will you?"

"No. No. Thanks again. I appreciate it."

Millar patted the boy on both his sweaty acne-scarred cheeks, his words warm, the tone cold, and his eyes devoid of emotion.

"No, Gary. Thank you."

Millar dragged the only other chair from the corner and across the bare floor, wooden legs scoring lurid marks as it skittered over the gaps between the floorboards. The space was illuminated by a single bare sixty-watt bulb dangling from a broken ceiling rose. Damp and mildew hung in the air. Detritus littered a space that had been commandeered as storage. Old plastic beer crates were haphazardly stacked and broken bottles lined a wall. Retired sound equipment, an old metal catering table, pitted and scratched with use, and a bowed rail of lost coats stood over an old, ruptured leather sofa. Discarded wraps of foil and the odd used condom wrappers were trapped in the seat cushions; the bouncers used it as a perk if they pulled a drunken clubber. Questions of consent closed with cold threats of something worse.

Placing the chair in front of his prisoner, Millar sat, one leg thrown over the other. He retrieved a pack of cigarettes from the inside pocket of his immaculately tailored suit and shook one loose then with old-fashioned aplomb, struck a match torn from a fancy embossed book and lit it; savoured the smoke and hissed a breath out.

"You might think I've brought you here because I'm angry, Lena, but I'm not. I'm just very disappointed."

A shuddering, heaving sob wracked the girl, her eyes screwed tight in pain. Millar reached out and tenderly touched her tear-streaked cheek.

He tore off the strip of cloth tape. It dangled from the left side of her mouth, the glue tearing a strip of skin from her lips, which bloomed fresh blood.

"Mr Mi-llar...!" Pleading. Her once pretty face, swollen, the eyes of a seasoned pugilist, lips split, one canine broken. Bloody and ugly with fear and pain.

"Shush, now, Lena. I don't expect you to say anything. The time for that will come later." Millar drew on the cigarette, tip flaring. He tapped dead ash into his palm.

"All this savagery Gary dished out is nothing to what's coming, my love. Downstairs there's a dozen coked-up horny wee bastards who are going to take turns with you. They'll not be gentle like I always insisted our friends were. No privileges of rank now, lady. There'll be no posh frocks or fancy apartment. No luxury hotel rooms and magnums of Bolly for you..." The words were spoken softly, soothing. No sharpness or edge. Almost a lullaby. Leaning forward, he put the lit cigarette to the girl's thigh.

She screamed, rocking in the chair but unable to writhe away because of the tight bindings. The screams died to whimpers and tears rolled down her cheeks.

Millar inhaled another long draw, then waved the red tip.

"That little tantrum has upset some very influential friends of mine. Generous friends. Your problem is you've gotten too big for your Jimmy Choo's."

Peeling the rest of the tape away, he gazed into her bloodshot eyes. He could still see beauty there amid the terror.

Millar exploded into motion, lashing out with a sharp backhand that drew an intake of breath from the woman. Before she could look up, his chair scraped back and he savagely punched her in the mouth. The force knocked the chair over. Her head slammed into the floor and she mewled a high whine. He snarled over her, face contorted in rage.

"That bloody scene lost me thousands! I'm going to have you broke back in, miss. It might teach you your place again." Millar was breathing heavily, enraged.

"You're going to be shackled to that table like a piece of fucking meat and when they've all had their fill, then I'm coming back in here with a broken pool cue and…"

"And you'll what?"

Millar spun around at the unexpected sound of the voice. His senses coalescing together in a blur to take in the image.

Male. Six foot. Athletic. The fabric of the black technical sweatshirt strained across broad shoulders. Narrow waist. Hiking trousers, black again over dark boots. Military boots. High over the ankle. Leather and synthetic mesh. No noise as he stepped forward. Slight limp.

Dark eyes below a black ski mask. Sawn-off shotgun trained in both hands. Practised tactical movement.

"Who the fuck are you? Have you any idea who you're…"

"Shut it and drop the gun. I know who I'm dealing with." Voice calm, a nod towards Millar's concealed weapon.

"You think I need to pull the gun? I'm telling you once more, sunshine, you can fuck off now and you might have a chance, but in about thirty seconds this room's going to be filled with boys who'll cut you to shreds very fucking slowly. That's after they give you a piece of what this bitch will be getting. They're not fussy, you see. I hope you like a bit of rough." Millar squared up to the stranger, chin jutted. The whining girl behind him was now silent; eyes wide at the intrusion.

Millar pointed a defiant finger.

"I'm going to give you the count of…"

BOOM.

The squeal was unnatural. It took the full second for Millar to realise it was his own. Lena's terrified screams added to the chaos as she rocked and bucked in the overturned chair.

Millar looked down at his right arm.

The close-up blast had shredded the hand to a broken twist of meat and torn the flexor and extensor muscles of the forearm to shreds; the white of shattered radius and ulna stark against the pulsing blood which was pooling on the floor at his feet at an alarming rate. Radial artery catastrophically severed by the broken bones. His useless lower arm now hanging perpendicular to its upper half. His chest peppered with dots of blood. White shirt beginning to bloom red in slow motion.

Shocked but moving from primal instinct, Millar reached for the revolver tucked into a speed holster concealed on the waistband of his trousers.

BOOM.

The room kicked out from under him. Unbearable pain as hundreds of tiny hornets shattered his kneecap and peppered through flesh to splinter the femur. The revolver skittered across the floor.

Senses dulling, Millar watched as the intruder dumped the shotgun and turned away to push two wooden wedges under the door and give them a kick for good measure. Millar recognised now the weapon was Rowdy's, the butt bloody, which meant aid may not be as forthcoming as first thought.

Groaning, he attempted to drag himself towards his own discarded gun.

A heavy boot to his shattered knee ended any ambition of retaliation in a gasp of howling agony. The figure loomed over him. Dark eyes stared into his own. Millar coughed, felt the coppery taste of blood in his mouth.

Hauled from the floor and dragged across the room, he was unceremoniously dumped on the old sofa.

"You're bleeding out. You don't have long so stop struggling."

Millar choked, blood in his mouth as he tried to raise his shattered arm and push back against the man.

"You need to focus on the next few minutes. It's over, Rab." A gloved fist twisted the fabric of his collar.

Rab Millar stared at the surreal form of his shattered limb oozing deep red blood into the filthy sofa. His lower leg twisted at an unnatural angle. A slap across the face. The man's eyes bore into him. Familiar eyes. A string of bloody drool ran onto his ruined two hundred quid shirt.

"You'll regret…"

The breath was blasted from his broken body as a flurry of heavy right-handed punches battered his solar plexus. Gasping, Millar flopped back onto the battered sofa, the masked face close to his own.

"You thought you'd got away with it, didn't you? That the truth was buried. Well, the game's up, Rab. For all of you."

Thompson snapped off his nitrile gloves and dropped them in a bin.

"Don't be distracted by the rest of the damage. He died as a direct result of blood loss from the gunshot wounds. Frightful mess it made too. Shotgun. Close range. Severed both the radial and ulnar arteries. It nearly took off his lower leg too. You have the weapon?"

"Recovered at the scene," Macpherson confirmed.

The assistant was bagging items of clothing that had been

cut off and was storing them away. Once the next of kin had been informed then the butchery could begin in earnest. Stainless steel trays would be filled with organs, and samples taken during the PM would be assessed to determine Millar's blood alcohol levels and any traces of drugs in his system, amongst other things. Not that it was likely to conclude anything different. A small silver dish lay heavy with its little load of deformed black pellets plucked from torn flesh; a gruesome caviar of bloody buckshot.

"We'll have the full report prepared and passed across to you as soon as it's complete, but that's the summation."

"Thanks."

"So, shall we call this one a happy accident?" said Macpherson. Taylor stood nearby, a frown focused on the corpse.

"I never thought I'd see the day it caught up to him."

"You know him?" Thompson's surgical gown and mask had followed the gloves into the trash. He beckoned them to follow him from the cutting room.

"Rab Millar." Taylor nodded.

The conversation was brief as they made their way to his office.

"If there was a villain of the year, then your man was a contender," said Macpherson.

"Live by the sword, die by the sword or in this case two point-blank, twelve-gauge, number five shot," Thompson philosophised, a hand holding his door for the officers to follow.

There was a whiteboard hung by the entrance. No messages, but a game of hangman underway. Little head and neck. One arm stencilled in blue erasable marker. Ten letters. _, _, _, _O, _, __O, I, _. The letters A and E already scratched out beneath the gallows.

His office was every inch the lair of the busy professional, and he gestured towards two chairs for the visitors. Clearing a rough space on his desk, he dropped his notes, fishing under a pile of loose papers for his phone and checked it for messages. A list of contact numbers and anatomy charts were pinned to the wall, and a bookcase sagged under the weight of medical manuals and periodicals. A mug declaring 'I'd find you more interesting if you were dead' sat beside a grinning skull, bookended by a photograph of a younger Thompson and an elderly woman, and framed diplomas.

"You'll have dealt with some of his handiwork in the last nine months," said Taylor.

"Is that so?"

"The Ballyskeagh drowning and the unlawful death in Brookvale."

"The one with the broken baseball bat?"

Taylor confirmed it was with a dip of her head.

"Couldn't get charges to stick. Slippery as an eel that one," said Macpherson.

"His chequered history has in very brutal fashion caught up with him then," said Thompson, as he put his phone away. "Do you think his death may connect to one of those?" The professor scribbled a ballpoint pen on the back of a legal pad, discarding it for another when it failed to write.

"I'm ruling nothing out. We know he had involvement not just in dealing, but also in the trafficking of drugs and young women which would automatically put him in the firing line of competitors and opportunists," said Taylor. "My gut also says Millar was managing affairs for Gordon Beattie during his absence."

"Gordon Beattie, the acquittal last month? The Concrete King?"

"That one. Yes."

"Slippery as an oily eel. Bought his way out of it more like," said Macpherson.

"We also suspect Robert Millar of making some of Beattie's problems disappear."

"Under the patio." The sergeant mimed a digging action.

"It's fair to say Millar had many a secret stashed away and we've just lost the chance to hear them," added Taylor.

"On the plus side though, perhaps a happy accident as Sergeant Macpherson suggests," said Thompson.

"One way of looking at it. The chief constable will want to avoid another feud flaring up over the head of it though," said Taylor. "Our superintendent is already having a coronary at the budgetary waste in failing to bring down Beattie without throwing more resources at keeping the firms apart."

"It was messy and has the hallmarks of an execution. You have a suspect coming into the main hospital for treatment?"

Taylor half nodded.

"Why look a gift horse in the mouth, eh?"

Taylor hesitated and shot a glance towards her detective sergeant.

"We'll be treating her as a witness," she said.

"I see."

"She's seven stone soaking wet and the initial assessment was she had been taped to a chair and beaten. She's in a bad way."

"Complicates things." Thompson's brows rose above a pair of half-moon glasses he had perched on his nose.

"There's every chance, any other day of the week, we would have found that wee girl spread out on some ghetto wasteland with a bag over her head and a bullet in her skull," said Macpherson.

Taylor was once again perusing the initial crime scene photographs that had been snapped, uploaded and printed out. Studying the level of ferocity. The efficiency of it. She couldn't put her finger on what troubled her exactly.

"We're going to need a fast track on any evidence left behind on the body, please. Diane Pearson and her team will be ripping apart the club for the same." Thompson's expression was one of accedence.

"Beattie has had a few more pressing distractions, which means he might not have as much of an iron grip as he would like. This could be as simple as someone making sure any of Rab Millar's recent antics were punished or a land grab by a competitor of Beattie. We need a lead because whoever did this and whatever group they're part of, we can't have reprisals and more bodies stacking up."

"Aye, no matter how grateful we are," mumbled Macpherson.

## Chapter 2

The black Audi Q8 swept down from the spartan hills into tree-lined avenues. Windows of the three and four-storey gentrified Edwardian townhouses flashed by in the dark. Suburbia gave way quickly to the roughneck of industry as they travelled past neon shop fronts, closed save for the Turkish kebab houses and Chinese takeaways and a twenty-four-hour convenience. No pause, engine gunning through a set of red traffic lights. Red, white and blue painted kerbstones marking out territory as sure as a stream of piss. Union Flags, St Andrews Cross, Israeli Star of David, and the dark maroon and masked figures of the UVF.

Into the sixties terrace streets. A working-class heartland strangling the sprawl of shipbuilding. Sodium lamps flashed overhead as the loom of cranes and huge bulk fuel containers appeared over chimney pots.

The Audi rattled off the sweeping tarmac road and into a gravel lane. Steel gates pulled aside at its approach. The compound was quiet save for two gatemen who melted back into the darkness as the SUV crunched to a stop.

"My condolences, Gordon."

Gordon Beattie turned from his vantage point overlooking the West Twin Silos and Milewater Basin. Belfast Lough was quiet. A Dutch freighter was visible on the horizon, the blinking white anti-collision lights of the superstructure visible in the inky blackness.

The newcomers' five-hundred-pound Tom Ford brogues scrunched the gravel as his driver closed the rear door of the SUV and took up watch at a discreet distance.

"I'm sorry to drag you away from your celebrations, but I expect this is better than me gatecrashing the grand affair."

Beattie nodded, incongruous in the industrial surroundings dressed in black tie and overcoat.

"It was wrapping up. Thanks. Appreciate that. We had our differences, but we went back a long way," said Gordon Beattie, taking the offered hand.

"Not going to be a problem? I'm informed there may have been a significant loss."

"I'm hearing the same. Not insurmountable if there was though," Beattie lied.

"Glad to hear it. I've been asked to remind you that a considerable amount of resource was put in play to ensure your liberty remained intact."

Beattie shoved his hands into the pockets of his woollen Crombie and turned his face back out to sea, the breeze flapping the hem of the overcoat and ruffling his hair.

"Is that someone's attempt to intimidate me, John?"

"No such thing, old boy. Call it a friendly reminder from concerned colleagues."

"Well, you can let them know there is no change to the deal from my end."

"You understand why there would be questions? The people I represent offer a means to bolster your operation at a time when, let's be frank, your financial position has become a little stretched."

Gordon Beattie glared at the man who looked back nonplussed.

"I just seek clarity that this unfortunate business is a wrinkle in developments and that you can still deliver."

"I, now is it?"

"You know what I mean. Word is you and Millar were not on the friendliest terms."

"I'd nothing to do with it."

"But you may have an idea who would?"

"I told him getting mixed up with those other bastards was

a mistake."

"Don't be getting too close."

Beattie swung round. Annoyed now.

"Are you telling your granda how to suck eggs, Johnny boy? Fuck sake."

From the corner of his eye, Beattie noted the stiffening of the bodyguard by the SUV.

There was no such change in demeanour of the man with whom he stood toe to toe, a vague smile on his narrow face, palms up, arms extended in mock surrender. Dull orange light reflected in the lens of tortoiseshell Cartier spectacles masked the glint in his eyes.

"We need to be sure you are insulated from any potential involvement. The investors will not indulge any more trips into the spotlight."

The man's tone made the threat implicit.

"Rab made a few poor decisions. If they'd come off different, we wouldn't be having this conversation." Beattie waved the thought away. "But that's not the point. Whoever did this will have to answer for it."

"You've moved on in the world. Try and keep it that way."

"Johnny, for fifteen years there's not been a door that hasn't opened for me in that city. No one operates without my say so and nothing moves without them digging deep to pay me for the privilege. The second I'm seen to let one upstart chance his arm, the next there'll be half a dozen at it." Beattie pointed out across the water at the distant glow of the city as he spoke.

"All the more reason to ensure that your position of dominance remains intact. For everyone involved. Just let your people handle the heavy lifting while you put things back on an even keel on the business front." Beattie stared out across the lough considering the advice.

"I went to war with Rab Millar at my side to build this

organisation. I owe it to him to see the bastard who put him down dead in a ditch." His words were a hiss through clenched teeth.

The man nodded, willing to be placated for the meantime.

Beattie turned to face him.

"You came to me with an offer, Johnny. I didn't come begging. It's obvious your people recognise a good thing when they see it. I just need a little time to sort this out."

"Just remember the timetable."

"The dates won't change. But this setback." Beattie shrugged. Took a punt. "The lost revenue might have some impact on cash flow. You'll need to tell them it's time to put their money where their mouth is and stump up."

"I'll advise the consortium of the request, but I suggest you find your own contingency," said the man, coolly. "There has already been significant investment."

"If the Assets Recovery Agency and the bloody taxman weren't still digging through my affairs with a teaspoon, I'd have a contingency and wouldn't be over a barrel to your mates for a loan," Beattie snapped.

"I'm sure you'll manage. In the meantime, keep your powder dry."

"There will need to be consequences. I can't be seen to have gotten weak."

"A necessary evil. Quite. Let's just not let pride come before a fall. Fair enough?"

"Fair enough. I'll appeal to their wallets and their better judgement. For a contingency fund." Conceded Beattie.

"Any assistance I can offer?"

"I'd be interested if the peelers have any leads. Nip it in the bud."

"I'll see what I can find out. On that front, it's come to our attention some members of the constabulary are not ready to accept defeat."

"Really? Stupid bastards. I'll be happy to pursue them for harassment. My brief says I'm in line for a decent claim already and that's before the TV stuff. Do you know they want to do one of those special reports on me? I reckon I'll have a bestseller by the end of this."

"Perhaps it would be better under current circumstances to let the dust settle. Recent events do not mean you are exempt from scrutiny."

"Which one of the bastards is it then?"

"Our resourceful DI Taylor."

"That frosty bitch." Beattie huffed a breath into the dead night air. "Perhaps she needs a visit in the middle of the night." His tone was icy.

"I think maybe a distraction would prove a lesser challenge. Perhaps your subordinate's unfortunate demise offers a convenient segue?"

"Aye. Do you know she was at my door every night checking that I hadn't broken the terms of the curfew? I know that cow. She'll be pinning this on me."

"If we can then we should offer up an alternative."

"I'm already looking into it."

The two men watched the progress of the freighter in silence for a moment.

"What about our administrative associate?"

Beattie scoffed.

"Struggling to keep his dick in his pants and enjoying the gluttony his position affords a little too much."

"Good. Keep him onside. A few more weeks, Gordon, and we shall have this all drawn up in a neat little bow, and for your efforts, you'll be more substantially off than can be counted in financial terms. If the next stage delivers as planned, then the path that's paved with gold stretches before us."

"Here's to a mutually beneficial arrangement." Beattie

saluted. The man named John offered his hand, and they shook in parting.

"A lucrative future." He agreed.

The gates rattled closed as the red glow of the Audi's taillights faded from view and Beattie paced along the broken concrete edge, peering into the black water where it lapped against the reclaimed strip of land.

What was going on, he thought? Why this out of the blue? Coincidence? Right when the most lucrative deal of his life was about to kick off. A veritable killing to be made. It wasn't every day the cartels opened bids for new and direct distribution lines. This was an opportunity to expand and open an end-to-end service that would stand him a man apart. With his own funds under scrutiny and usual credit lines cut off for the foreseeable, the consortium's timely investment meant he would remain in a position to honour his bid and soon preside over the single most valuable channel of illicit drugs into Ireland. North and South. One that could in a short time extend to Scotland and the North of England.

All he had to worry about was Rab Millar having offered up anything to derail or delay his plans in an attempt to pay off his own debts as he bid to flee the Reaper.

"Shall I bring the car round, Mr Beattie?"

"Aye, Tommy. I'm coming now. Give us your phone."

Beattie dialled, continuing to pace as he waited for the call to connect.

"Rowdy?"

"Nah. Harry. Who's this?"

"It's the fucking organ grinder, Harry."

"Sorry, boss. I didn't recognise the number, Rowdy's away to the hospital. Proper had his head carried off."

"What's happening down there?"

"Place is crawling with the cops. The wee lads are getting fidgety but DMSU aren't having it. Will I…"

"No. Let it fizzle out. Did you speak to Rowdy? What happened?"

"He was out cold when they took him. Hardly a tooth in his head. You know wee Gary? Aye well. He was doing a touch for Rab. One of the girls needed putting in order, and then some fucker just strolls in the back with a mask on, takes Rowdy straight out by the root. Took his shooter and smashed his teeth in with it."

"I heard this Gary fella is a fucking crackhead."

"Na, he hadn't scored. Your man barged in before he could get doled out."

"He just wandered in like the Terminator? Where were you and the rest of the boys?"

"There was a bit of a distraction, boss."

Beattie sighed, casting a look up to the black sky.

"Harry, what about the product? I'm hearing there was some lost." An awkward silence filled the line. Harry's breathing and then more silence, the phone dropping away from his mouth.

"That's what I'm saying…"

"Harry, the fucking product?"

"It's gone, boss."

"Gone fucking where? Barry's Amusements for a spin on the dodgems?"

"Up in smoke."

The silence stretched out as Beattie took a step towards the water's edge and hawked a gob of spittle into the dark waves, feeling the weight of the revelation.

"Amir has been on the phone. He says he wants the rest of his money." Harry delivered the news in an awkward cracking voice.

"I'm sure he does. Don't you worry. I'll deal with Amir.

You just start giving me straight information, son."

"The van came in as normal and the lads were squaring up inside, ready to split the delivery and she just went up. Just like that. I swear I don't know what happened. We tried to get the gear out, but it was roasting, we couldn't get near it. The next minute, your man's on the scene. Straight upstairs and night, night. By the time me and the boys got word, the door had been barricaded, and the pigs were pulling up. The fire brigade was hosing down the van before the whole place caught fire. I heard them say your man got out the fire escape."

"Where is the girl now?"

"Peelers took her away. Put her into one of their cars with one of those tinfoil sheets over her." Harry laughed nervously. "She's in a right state too."

"I want to know who did this, Harry. Are you capable of that?"

"Sure thing. I'll put the feelers out."

"You'll do more than put the fucking feelers out! Rab's dead and there's near a million quid's worth of product up in flames. For Christ's sake, it still has to be paid for," Beattie snapped, the pressure of the loss tightening around his gut. "You'll be cracking teeth and skulls until someone can explain who had the balls to hit me and do one of my people. After that, the bastards will really wish someone had scraped them into the abortion bucket for all their life's going to be worth."

"First class, Mr B."

"Bring in Gary for a chat and find out where they took the girl. We might need a word to see what she knows."

"Right enough."

"No hanging about, Harry."

Beattie ended the call before he heard any further reply.

He gripped the phone tightly, tension giving way to white-knuckled rage.

Eight hundred and five thousand pounds up in smoke. It was fine for the faceless moneymen sitting in their ivory towers, pushing demands of patient resolve and stoic restraint. But at what cost. He had already lost the last shipment when Millar had moved operations onto the Albanians as the police moved in on Beattie Holdings. While he was confident the import and distribution chain was buried deep the whiff of suspicion remained, and a well-directed forensic examination of the company had the potential to bring down the house. Gordon Beattie Holdings was worth more than its significant value. The concrete and aggregate business that was the backbone of the group offered legitimacy, giving him minor celebrity and the opportunity to sit with the heads of business and industry as a peer. The success of the group granted him the veneer of the wealthy philanthropists and soundbites from politicians, whose constituents benefitted from the cash and support GBH poured into their deprived communities, and the concrete needed to build low rent homes and community centres when they couldn't agree amongst themselves where to find funding to help.

There came a point though when it wasn't about money and appearance anymore. Power and wealth was just a way of keeping score. Twenty years of hard graft to get to this point. A lifetime of scraped knuckles and street fights, punishment beatings to kneecappings, and a stint at Her Majesty's pleasure. Who were they to say keep his head down? Especially now, when all he'd built was teetering. A familiar burning welled up in his gut. More than money was needed to fix this. There came a time when the hammer needed to drop, when people needed a reminder. This was his city. Every hour of every day he had worked to keep her British. He'd toed the line when needed, touted when it was necessary, squeezed every advantage from the duplicity. Rising inch by inch from the gutter to his grand gated mansion with its swimming pool, manicured acreage and Bentley at the door. The Bentley and half a dozen other luxury sports and vintage supercars were now languishing in a lock-up, still awaiting release by the Assets Recovery Agency following the case collapse. He'd get them back, and those who had fled the sinking ship would crawl back looking for forgiveness. He hadn't done too bad for a scabby-kneed dropout from the backstreet ghettos. He'd come from nothing and grafted to ensure the creep of his influence extended across the divide, insidiously reaching between the cracks of the peace walls and along the painted kerbstones be they green or orange. It didn't matter who was spending, he was selling through his select network of affiliates and taking his wholesale percentage and his commission in the dealing of grass, girls, or dodgy fuel. Shell companies covered every aspect from the manufacture and pouring of concrete to the bespoke furnishings of Belfast's growing number of luxury apartments and high-rise office space, paid for by complex and convoluted offshore accounts serviced by his narcotic distribution network. Not an ounce of heroin, cocaine nor a single pill made it into the Port of Belfast without Beattie taking his cut. His own ascension might not have been as fast as one of the glass and steel beasts that were getting thrown up at his behest but he wasn't about to see himself be accused of going soft because he had a cheque book in hand instead of an Uzi. The cops had cocked up more than once, the losses due to that insufferable, but for the moment, he was beyond reach, untouchable, and that grace offered the opportunity to recoup. To the others, this was his moment for reaffirmation after the recent blemish. Yes, it was a blatant exploitation of his current crisis, but it was a means to shore up lost revenue and cement his legacy. There would be no going back after this. His ascension was inevitable. As was his wrath.

He took a deep calming breath of the salty sea air as in the distance the freighter's horn blew a long, forlorn note. Beattie raised the phone and tapped out another number from memory, the recipient answering on the second ring. Beattie offered no pleasantries nor received any in return; his instructions were concise and clear. Closing down the call he launched the phone into the air and it disappeared into the blackness to be swallowed by the cold tide.

Tommy pulled up in the car and Beattie climbed in, Tommy waiting a beat for the return of his phone but then realising it wouldn't be forthcoming. Beattie motioned him on with a wave and settled back into the plush upholstery.

## Chapter 3

"Freaky Jackson."

Taylor stopped walking and took Macpherson's offered phone, assessing the Facebook profile he had pulled up on the screen.

Early fifties but physique of someone ten years younger. Shaven head. Thug. Backdrop of the Union flag and No Surrender. Macpherson skipped to another site. Grainy mobile phone footage. Corrugated walls. Makeshift pen and the snap and howl of dogs and the baying of a crowd.

"He's a fair bit further down the food chain than the characters you've been after. Nasty shite all the same. Aspires to make Belfast the dog-fighting capital of Ireland."

"I've a vague notion. Hatchetman?"

Taylor handed back the phone and continued walking until they arrived at the security gate and buzzed themselves back into the mortuary reception area which was unmanned and in dim light.

"That's the one."

"What's the connection to Millar?"

"They came up the ranks together, but where Rab took his opportunities in girls and gear and fancy suits, Freaky is a fair few degrees baser in his tastes and likes to get his hands dirty. Extortion with menaces. Violent assault. Home invasion. Arson. They call him Freaky because he gets off on inflicting the damage. He's twisted. Before Beattie began consolidating his empire the three of them worked hand in glove for Martin Coleman. Beattie had been Coleman's right-hand man for long enough and Millar was into the gear since he was in short trousers. Freaky, well." Macpherson shook his head.

"Freaky liked the kneecappings a bit too much, so when

Coleman met his bloody end the Monster fell into the empty niche. All was well as they made a name for themselves, stayed joined at the hip through the UDA feuds, after which Beattie saw the opportunity to move into the mainstream and got his celebrity status. Freaky was pensioned off, and it wasn't long after, Millar slid away into the background to manage things day to day, although the three always remained in loose touch. Beattie building the empire and the other two servicing the revenue streams."

"Let's see that again?"

Taylor inspected the profile. Jackson in various bars and clubs, with some trollop half his age hanging off his arm. In yards with scarred and aggressive dogs or holding up trophy kills. Blood smeared up his arm. Relaxing on an enormous bed, FREAK 24/7 spelt out in wads of cash beside him.

"Is that real?" Taylor passed the phone back.

"The hardware? Yes, it's big business."

The photo was of a balaclava-wearing and bare-chested Jackson proudly holding an AK-47 assault rifle in one hand and a Czech CZ 82 pistol in the other. He was identifiable because of the proud twin flags of Ulster and Union tattooed on his left breast and a Red Hand of Ulster on the other.

"Forty quid on the black market from Europe. It's a quare trade if you're up for it."

"Christ. I thought this was all behind us." Taylor despaired.

"Peace in our time, Ronnie. Peace in our time."

The car park was cold. Their breath fogged in the air. The howling two-tone of an ambulance pealing in the air once. Diesel engine roaring as it sped away.

"What has put Jackson in your head?"

"D'you know Pieterson? Whiskery sergeant on street beat. Works Queens and Library Quarter?" said Macpherson, continuing as Taylor shook her head.

"There was an altercation about a week ago at No Alibi."

"The nightclub. Yeah, I know it. It's another one of Beattie's."

"Aye. Gunge. Garage. Something or other. Kids have it packed out, and it's one of those four in the morning jobs."

"Grime," said Taylor stifling a grin.

"Whatever. It was one of Millar's. Pieterson was responding to an incident at one of the halfway houses in the area. You know the type, immigrants jammed in with parolees and the scum of the social ladder. Hotbed of nuisance. Anyway, some junkie had set fire to his dog and dropped it down the stairwell. Can you imagine? Poor wee craiter. If I'd been there, he'd have followed it."

"You're joking me?"

"Nope. When Pieterson got there, the poor soul was still alive."

"Jesus."

"So, end of that spectacle he was leaving and something kicked off down the street at the club. More than handbags at twenty paces because one bouncer had a broken jaw. Some punter was making a racket about debts, and Freaky was threatening to smash the fella into next week with one of those VIP barrier poles."

"Did they not lift him?"

"Wasn't worth the paperwork. Pieterson arrived as Millar made an appearance and it all died down. The bouncer didn't want to press charges. Quick win."

Taylor held a door from the stairwell open and Macpherson stepped through.

"Gives us an excuse to talk to him and see where he was tonight and what that was all about. Are you sure the two of them weren't still involved?"

"As far as I can be and to be fair, I haven't dug too deeply, just kept a weather eye on them over the years. Those two haven't been specifically linked with anything since the terrible trio went their separate ways. Millar was well known about town for procuring girls and supplying coke whereas other than the dogs, Freaky works the estates collecting debts and a bit of dealing. Weed. Ecstasy. Maybe heroin. I'm sure Beattie's acquittal might have been a cause for a celebratory get together but Pieterson never mentioned seeing him at No Alibi." Macpherson shrugged then continued.

"Freaky has indulged his sick tastes with no one to answer to and enjoyed making his own mayhem without getting anyone too riled up except animal rights and the RSPCA. He hasn't been dabbed for any of the usual paramilitary escapades you'd expect if he was still in the firm. He's a lowlife operating at the low end. Not the type Beattie wants to associate with these days."

Taylor considered her detective sergeant's assessment and decided.

"Still, considering the No Alibi thing, we pay him a visit. Nothing formal yet."

"Aye, aye, skipper." Macpherson knocked off a salute as they approached Taylor's car.

"I might swing past the locus on my way back."

Macpherson stretched his back out and the pop of cartilage was audible.

"To see what? A burnt-out wagon and a bullet-riddled room?"

"They might have missed something?"

"Don't let any SOCO hear you say that." He held up a hand as she protested.

"Look, I get it. When you've slogged for hours and a case gets thrown out, you're entitled to be pissed off, but you're going there for the sake of it, so you are."

Taylor half nodded her assent he was correct.

"Analyse Walker's initial scene report first thing. See if that will set your mind to rest. I'll arrange a meeting with SOCO and the crime scene co-ordinators and then if you still want to go after that I'll drive you myself. Leave it tonight. Tomorrow will be manic enough when news of Action Man's exploits hit the papers."

Taylor chuckled.

"It's a brave new world, Doc. It'll be all over the internet by now."

"Ach, you know what I mean. My advice remains, get your head down and we'll go through it all with fresh heads in the morning. It's what your da told me plenty of times and I'm damned sure he'd say the same thing to you now."

Taylor put her hand on the older man's forearm and squeezed. He motioned with his head back to the mortuary.

"Millar's not going anywhere. Thompson can do what Thompson does and if the wee girl improves through the night, she can be first port of call in the morning once she's signed off by the docs. Reilly will stay with her and Carrie was going back to help set up the incident room. It's under control for the night."

Taylor sighed. The multiple adrenaline spikes of the day's events had taken their toll, and she was feeling the effects.

"Millar have any other enemies from the old days?" she enquired. Mind tracking out more paths of enquiry.

"Plenty, and the Monster will have twice as many again. Although they might see him as Teflon now since they threw his case out. Now shut it off. That's another job for another day. Get yourself away home and sleep on it."

Taylor threw her bag onto the passenger seat and flopped into her car.

"I think I might. See you in the office?"

"Bright and breezy, Ronnie. Bright and breezy."

Taylor set her keys on the sideboard and gathered up a fat

wedge of unopened mail, which she sifted into order and placed in a drawer, then fastened the locking chain on her apartment door, shutting out the world and the sound of the odd car that still droned past the end of the street in the early hours of the morning.

She hadn't totally followed her sergeant's advice. Deciding to do a drive-by of the incident. Tired yet focused, her eyes were studious of the faces that still lined the painted kerbstones, searching for familiar faces. Tallying them against intelligence briefings and known offender lists, but no one was about. Even the odd random photographer hoping to catch a few quid for a shot appearing in the local rag's morning edition had the sense to be away in. The minor stone-throwing and catcalling reported earlier had long abated. Several windows were now boarded over with thin ply until the day dawned and the glaziers arrived. The line of officers assigned as a cordon, protecting the fluttering tape winding around lampposts and railings were either huddled into their neck warmers shifting from foot to foot waiting on the shift to end or taking their turn to sit in the cab of the livered Land Rover sharing whatever heat was blasting from the vents inside. Detritus from the paramedics' attendance littered the lay-by beside the club. The adjacent yard was dark, the flames of the torched van extinguished, the hulk burnt black, and the remaining water from the fire appliance now blending with the familiar drizzle that seeped into the bones of the city. It had been a fifty minute round trip, but she was satisfied.

Kicking her shoes off, she nudged them together as a pair and leaving the hall in darkness, she padded to the small open-plan kitchen, poured a glass of water from a filter jug in the fridge, and ignored the lack of anything else inside, mentally making a note that she needed to get some food in.

The last few weeks had been hectic with debriefs and a

post mortem on the Beattie fiasco, and now this new twist threatened to suck her deeper into the maelstrom. She made her way upstairs, dropped her blouse and bra into an overstuffed wash bin, and added detergent to her mental list.

Her weapon and warrant card were placed on a bedside unit. Flicking on a bedside lamp, the kindly face of her father smiled back from a silver-framed photograph, beside him an identical frame holding a picture of herself and her mother on graduation day.

Derek Taylor. Police Constable Derek Taylor, Deceased. Ripped apart by an under-car booby trap that left a daddy's girl fatherless at eleven years old. A killing that might as well have murdered her mother too, for Sheila Taylor had never recovered, dying ten years later. A slow decline of indeterminable cause that stemmed from a broken heart.

She sighed as she sat, tipping three cushions onto the floor and pulling off her suit trousers, which she jettisoned in the general direction of the wash bin, dressing in a tank top and cotton pyjama pants. The scent of a day's work and burning car escaped from her hair as she swept it up. The bed needed changing anyway. Shower in the morning, she resolved then dog-tired, she clicked off the light.

Gordon Beattie. Rab Millar. Freaky Jackson. Gordon Beattie. Rab Millar. Freaky Jackson. Flags. Guns. Girls. Coke. Cash. The gleaming riverside vista of glass towers and curving apartments, the dull strobing inside nightclubs.

The names, the faces and places blurred in her head like a nightmare carousel of some personal hellish ghost train.

"Is it even worth it, Dad?" she whispered into the darkness.

Sleep… She heard the strong, stubborn voice of Macpherson in her ear. Her father's tone lost to memory. Macpherson, her father's friend and colleague in those days, serving side by side during the dark days of the Troubles. He was the man who had stepped in and shouldered the role her father never again would. Holidays. School sports days. Concerts. Trips backwards and forwards to university. Someday down the aisle.

Taylor pulled a pillow over her face.

Who was she kidding?

Relationships were few and far between. Most times suffocated at birth by disclosure of her profession and tongue in cheek innuendo about handcuffs or truncheons. It was even harder to date within the confines of the job with gossip, rumour, and her obsessive pursuit of her caseload, and best of all now, her near pariah status.

Obsessions like Gordy 'Monster' Beattie.

Hardly a corner of the city was not tainted by his touch, yet it hadn't been a smoking gun that had almost brought him down but diligent research into his money and cash flows and a set of smouldering books. Not that she hadn't put in enough effort during her career in CID using more traditional means of bringing down the curtain on his activities. She'd diligently chipped away from the bottom up, but each success was lost as the sprawling web of his illicit activities became more tangled.

It was an obsession that started in her first year as a uniform PC when she was the first responder to the harrowing death of a pensioner. Bound to an armchair with his wife's tights. Ears cut off. Eyelids and mouth sewn shut with coarse black thread. Hear no Evil. See no Evil. Speak no Evil. Thirty silver coins scattered around his broken body. A complainant of the rising antisocial behaviour of the youths pushing drugs on the sink estate where he had lived for a lifetime. Terror weaponised and brought to bear.

It would be eleven years from that formative experience and three weeks tomorrow since Beattie walked past the flashbulbs and TV cameras set up outside the High Court leering his lecherous grin with his oily brief Solomon Reeves at his side. Expert witness testimony blurring the lines and distancing Beattie from ownership of three offshore companies that had seen him commit tax evasion and fill his coffers with illegally gained funds to finance a vicious drug and criminal empire hidden behind the facade of his concrete construction business.

Beattie's cobalt eyes stared into her own and then morphed behind a mask, the covered face finally replaced with the recurring dream of an old broken doll pulling at the threads which bound his eyes.

## Chapter 4

Father Michael Keane placed his stole upon a hook on the back of the vestry door and unbuttoned his cassock. The Monday morning service had been unremarkable. Not because he had delivered his message with any less fervour than usual, but that the lifeblood of the building seemed to have bled into the gutter to be swept away on a tide of apathy. The once vibrant and fervent community had passed on. The teeming streets were now either bulldozed or reclaimed by industry. Not the blue-collar work of old either. The hard men and women of the hand-built tenements who had devoted their lives and meagre wealth to see the church flourish had dwindled as the old was replaced by the new. This fresh blood was soulless. Gone were the tight-knit streets and winding entries; taverns and cafes' replaced by towers of glass and steel. Banking, insurance and media replacing shipping, rope and tea. The lions amidst the lambs, these showcases to modernity loomed in fearsome hunger over the remaining lowly weatherworn red bricks of the few remaining tenements and his own ancient stone bastion. The community that had served the borough had passed, his flock dissipated like ashes on the wind. Those who remained were as ancient as he was. The transition was many years before, but in his mind it was yesterday.

Keane, unburdened now of his vestments and secure in the knowledge his duties for the day were complete, followed his routine; replacing the gathered prayer books and hymn sheets in their trays and gathering the meagre offering and placing it in the safe that resided in the small cell that he used when the need to remain in the old building overnight arose. He checked the door to the loft and the sacristy, returning then to the nave where he would spend time in reflection and prayer before the altar.

Keane found to his surprise as he entered from the priest's door to the sacred space he was not alone.

"Sorry, son. I thought everyone had gone. Can I help you?"

When he received no immediate response, Keane stepped down the few steps from the altar to the front of the nave and faced the rows of old pine pews.

"Might I sit with you a while? I come in here after mass to get a wee appraisal from the boss, if you take my meaning." He gestured to the cross at the front of the church. The filtered beams from the stained glass windows set the polished wood of the altar alight. The musty smell of the old chapel was comforting. Polished pine and scraped stone walls. Motes of dust drifted in the shaft of light that shone like a beacon from a narrow window set high in the spire.

Keane smiled as he approached the seated figure.

"I've seen you in here regular enough the last few weeks. I'm Michael."

"Pleased to meet you, Father."

"May I sit?"

"It's your house. Please."

The man gestured to the space beside him.

"Well to be fair, I always say it's His house and I'm just the tenant lucky enough to be looking after it, so. What keeps you back tonight, son, you're usually out the door during the Creed?"

"Your homily resonated with me."

"Ah, I see. "

See he did. The man was in good enough order. Sturdy his old fella would've called it. A heavy woollen peacoat over dark jeans and work boots tried to hide the frame. Hands folded in his lap. Right thumb rubbing a gold wedding band. Keane could smell an aftershave he was familiar with but couldn't place. Dark-haired and heavily bearded, with a strong profile and a furrowed brow. Wreathed in chaos.

"Are you new to the parish?"

"I was here once. A long time ago."

"Right enough? Well, I've been here since before the country went to war on itself. When the wee streets outside teemed with big lads like yourself and they packed this place to the rafters every Sunday and most days of the week. Now it's fancy coffee and tower blocks and the poor destitute seeking an hour in out of the cold. Oh, mind me. I'm not talking about you, son." Keane placed a hand on the big man's shoulder. He could feel the hard, lean musculature beneath. Solid, like gripping the pew in front of him. Yet he could see in the grey lupine eyes that the soul was far from peaceful.

"You're welcome to stay as long as you like. Do you mind if I pray for you?"

"As I said. It's your house."

"I get the feeling you don't come in here for your own peace of mind?"

A weak smile broke the bearded face. Half nod, half shake of the head.

"You'd be right enough there. Brought up a pagan Protestant I was."

"The Lord have mercy." Keane crossed himself, his face aglow in a warm grin. He slapped his hands on the hard pew, then stood.

"In that case, rather than waste my time let's adjourn from here and you can join me in the scullery. If you've the time and the inclination I've a nice bottle of heathen whiskey, I've been needing an excuse to open."

For a fraction of a second, he thought his visitor was going to decline but then he followed suit. He was a good head and shoulders taller and half as wide again as the old priest who, although withered with age, still carried himself well. Keane led the way from the body of the chapel through a series of low doors and narrow passages until they arrived in a utilitarian scullery.

The room was small. A low stove burned, heat radiating from two hotplates and the thick oven door. Light came from windows set high above a deep Belfast sink and there was an old table and chairs next to a high larder cupboard. The priest gestured to the chairs.

"Do you mind me asking your name?" said Keane, opening a cupboard and removing two simple glass tumblers and a bottle of Bushmills whiskey. He placed them on the table, then followed with a small jug of water.

"Thomas."

"Ack. A fine Biblical name." Keane sloshed several slugs of the amber liquid into the glasses, adding a splash of water to his own and offering some to his guest who declined.

"In present circumstances, the connotations sit well. To your health, Father."

"Slainte." Keane clinked the offered glass. "A crisis of faith? If you don't mind me saying, you're wrapped in a darkness, friend."

Thomas sipped and offered no response.

"The companionship of Christ and the Father is a path to peace. If it's a route from your demons you're seeking, then I can offer the certainty that if you put your life in his hands your faith will be rewarded."

"There was a time before when I may have sought that, but it's not something I'd think was open to a man like me now."

"Ah, I see. That bad is it. I'll tell you this. Whatever the burden, as it says in the book of Matthew 'all ye who labour and are heavy laden, come to Me and I will give you rest.'"

Keane set down his glass and studied the younger man.

"Whatever you carry about in there that gives you the

impression you are incapable of redemption, or if you fear and are mistrustful of this Church and what it offers, then know now the true means of finding peace lies in your own heart. Not which bloody door you walk through on a Sunday." Keane smiled.

"My heart is dead, Father."

"Well now, that is a quandary we're in." Keane studied the man over the rim of his glass and was struck by a familiarity. Something in the lupine eyes. He felt a coldness slip along his spine even as the amber whiskey warmed his throat.

"If it's not your own salvation you're here for, then it must be someone else's. It's grief, is it?"

"I've passed beyond grief now. I'm ready for something else."

"Well, that's good is it not?"

Keane wasn't prepared for the response. Not harsh in tone or anger, but a quiet simmering malevolence.

"The book screams forgiveness, Father. The turning of the other cheek. It is love not hate that heals."

The man, Thomas, set his glass down. The liquid inside sloshed lip to lip like a heavy winter sea. His voice had the cold sharpness of Arctic winds.

"You've ministered to your faithful all these years, seen the chaos of this town. The barbarity, the futility, the pure wicked evil of man. How do you still believe in it? That God's love will conquer all? Just open your heart and let him in?"

"I believe it." Keane stared down the scepticism. "Unequivocally. It is a question of faith. I've seen wickedness first hand, son, and not only in this town. I've been across the globe in my day. South America, Sudan, Rwanda, Bosnia. I swallowed the grief of those left behind in more places, for more years than I care to remember. The Good Friday Agreement brought us a peace many would not have believed possible and many a widow or mother would give her own life for. It might have taken another ten years to get the politicians to work together but a whole generation only knows the Troubles through stories and old footage or what they read in a book. That's if they know it at all. Their heads are stuck in their phones these days."

"Peace in our time." Thomas half nodded, half shook his head and tutted.

"Well, I wouldn't go that far now," said Keane.

"No, nowhere near," agreed Thomas. "It's different but the same. It might not be about religion anymore but it's still about territory. Control." He sighed. "The same old guard who waged war the first time might have buried the hatchet and be up in Stormont or calling themselves community leaders and citizen representatives, but what about the rest of the lunatics? They're content for the suits to be raking it in from international grants, EU peace subsidies and even charities so they can scam some off the top under a bullshit recovery and reconciliation program to funnel it back to the organisations where it all started in the first place."

Thomas clenched his fist. The muscles of his jaw flexed and cracked. Grey eyes blazed. A cold fury.

"I've only been back a month and every night someone has been beaten for something. They're still at the kneecapping and you're lucky if you're just shot and it's not by claw hammer or a battery drill now. Businesses are burnt out for not paying protection. I've seen shooting through living room windows while folk are playing with their grandkids, and others intimidated out of their homes and livelihoods for complaining about it while everybody else turns a blind eye to avoid the same." He took a long swig of the whiskey and raised the glass. "Our twisted code of silence." Thomas looked at the old priest, who nodded.

"It's not perfect. I'll grant you that," said Keane.

"The same people are keeping the same people under the

same heel and the world is told it's progress," said Thomas.

"It's complex. But would you not rather bring your kids up in this society than the one you grew up in?"

"My boy is dead."

"I'm sorry," said Keane. "It must be a terrible time for you and your wife."

Thomas picked up the glass again and put it to his lips, then returned it to the table without taking a drink. Wiped a hand over his lips.

"They died together," he said.

Keane laid a palm across the younger man's forearm.

"I can't imagine."

Thomas nodded. His head remained bowed, thumb again working a beat across the wedding band.

"Do you mind me asking what happened?"

"They said it was an accident. It was a hit and run. Ran off the road. The fuel tank exploded."

"May the Lord hold them to Him until you might see them again."

The head rose.

"Nobody faced justice for it."

The old priest studied the man. Saw the weathered lines of grief around the grey eyes. Felt the weight of his own years. A familiar pain for all of those who had evaded their sins during the long bloody years. Felt his own impending mortality and the certainty he would soon face judgement for his transgressions.

"These things happen. Sometimes it can be explained, sometimes we have our own interpretation. The one thing in common is the guilt of those left behind in such tragic circumstances. Don't let grief define the rest of your life."

"They survived the crash, you know? The fire killed them."

"Is that what the coroner's report said?" Keane's mouth was dry with the horror of the thought.

"There wasn't enough to build a report on, but yes. That's how they died. In agony."

Neither man spoke for a long moment, the dappled sunlight throwing beams of golden light across the table.

"My wife was Cara Maguire," said Thomas.

Father Michael Keane stared hard at the man at his table. Searched the grey eyes and the features under the heavy grief-worn face. Outside, the dull throaty howl of a ship's horn shook screeching gulls from the rooftops.

Thomas scratched his thick beard and wiped his palm across eyes that had become dewy with unshed tears.

"Gene and Mary Maguire's girl. Eugene Maguire was my father-in-law."

"Dear Lord. That poor family."

"The last time I was here, they were burying the twins."

"I remember. Dear Lord, you must have been a child yourself?" said Keane.

"I was sixteen."

The priest nodded, the face slowly coming back to him.

"You left after. Joined the Brits."

"Soldier man and boy," confirmed Thomas.

"They fed you up well enough. You were a lanky streak. When you went away Gene said the only thing they'd be able to use you for was as a pull-through for a rifle. He liked you. For a Prod."

"Aye." A weary smile. "He said you weren't too bad yourself for a God-botherer."

Keane huffed a chuckle, his liver-spotted hand reaching for the bottle of whiskey. Sloshed a large measure into his glass. He raised it to his lips unable to hide the waver in his hand. The sweet, peaty fire failed to wash away the image of destruction at the mention of the family. In his mind's eye, he could see a confetti of newspaper falling from the sky, the billowing black smoke and orange flame. The burning husk of the delivery van glowing like a gateway to hell. A week later he had shooed gulls off the vestry roof only to discover they had been fighting over a child's hand.

"Broke that couple's heart when their only wee girl followed you across the water."

"She had a life. We had a life. Better than what remained for us here. They came to see that."

"Why have you come back, Thomas?" he breathed, knowing the true answer. He took another swig and set the glass down. Another image. Sterile, the bleep and hiss of medical machinery. A lifetime of comradeship, a long-buried promise.

Thomas reached into his coat and pulled out a faded, folded cloth. He laid it on the table and eased it open, the sunlight catching the polished beads and the small silver cross.

Keane sat back, easing himself away from the table.

"I told Gene to get rid of that."

"He kept it. It's kept me alive these past few years, but his last wish was to get it back to its rightful owner."

"Did he tell you about it?"

"The young fella? Told me he'd seen nothing like it."

"He always was the storyteller."

Keane reached out and lifted the rosary from the cloth. The silver cross spun and twinkled in the sun.

It had been a gift from a grateful mother.

"That wee lad should never have been there," whispered Keane.

"It's as well you were."

"He was seventeen. I wasn't for having him end up like those other two poor souls at Milltown."

The images of the fateful day flashed vividly. A dove grey sky bled a persistent mizzle. On the street, a half-stripped and spreadeagled soul lay in his own blood crying for his mother.

A routine traffic stop had resulted in a foot chase. Another classic lead-on and the young private chasing, too wet behind the ears to realise it, had led him into the middle of a vicious trap. Overpowered, stripped and beaten, before Keane, on a mission of his own, intervened and faced down the masked gunmen ready to end the boy's life in the name of the Cause. He had taken the boy by sheer force of will and then carried him half a mile to the nearest barracks, pelted with stones and a torrent of spittle the entire way by snarling youths spurred on by shadowy puppeteers. The youngster the Cross for his sins. Every step, his own walk to repentance.

"Did he tell you what I was doing for him that day?"

Thomas shook his head.

"I was bringing him information from an informant. To be frank, it was the last testimony of a dying man. I watched in the shadows as they tortured him."

"What information?"

"On the people responsible for the bomb that killed the twins."

The two men stared at each other. Each immersed in their private pain.

"His mother sent me it. After what I had done, I didn't believe I was worthy of her gratitude. Not when I'd just taken part in some other mother's grief. I told Gene to get rid of it when I told him I was done with his Cause."

"He understood, you know. He said you were the bravest man he knew."

"Aye, he loved to tell a story," said Keane, dropping the silver cross back into the cloth. "If you're back to bring me this, you've wasted a trip."

"I'm here to call in the oath," said Thomas.

Keane closed his eyes and exhaled. Even now, he was not beyond the reach of men like Eugene Maguire.

"Jesus, Mary and Joseph don't do this. Don't throw

another life away. Think about the memory of your dear wee boy," he said.

"My family. I know who did it. I know why they got away with it…" Thomas's voice was calm.

"You can't know for certain. What are you going to achieve? Has violence ever begat anything but more of the same? It will bring you no peace. I can assure you of that."

"Those twins died. Five years old and whatever information you had, it didn't see anyone punished for putting them in the ground."

"I didn't give him the information!"

Keane thought back to the raging Maguire, the threats and the agonising grief as his friend collapsed in his arms.

"Don't do this, Thomas."

"They deserve justice."

"Justice? It's justice you're calling it now? Call it the murder it will be." Fury rekindled the old priest's voice with past might.

"I have to."

"At what cost."

"At any cost! You were part of the struggle. Gene told me everything. You presided over it, saw in the end game. That's why I'm here. "

"No, there's no way." Keane stood up.

"You swore an oath to a dying man, Father."

Keane's mind rode back to a time past, snapshot images of Eugene and Mary, the devastation of the twins. His crisis of faith. A time off the rails. His oath. The path to peace. Facilitator. Overseer. Witness.

"I'm here to end this, Father. Those people who took my family, Gene and Mary's last child, their grandchild. The people who treat this place like their own kingdom. The people that covered it up. I'm going to war and I'm here for the artillery and you know where it is. So, you can fulfil a promise to a dead friend and help me or you can get in my way. It's up to you, but it's time to choose a side.

## Chapter 5

"So yes. I am very proud of my small part in the development of this facility. A community outreach like this is the cornerstone of protecting the vulnerable, threatened, and persecuted when they are in most need. It's a project very close to my heart. Thank you, I must get inside. Excuse me."

"Councillor Howard, have you any comment on the fatal shooting in Risky's nightclub and the subsequent street violence where several businesses were damaged and several people sustained injuries in clashes with police?"

Howard paused, neither inside nor outside the gleaming glass entrance of Sanctuary.

"It is my deepest regret that kind of violence still occurs in my constituency. One that I condemn, and I call on those who feel it is acceptable to resort to summary justice to desist and hand themselves in to the police. I am especially perturbed by the reports of youths and young children being involved in the disturbances against the security forces, who do a valiant job in protecting us, and I would hope this is not some wider orchestration of antisocial behaviour against our hard-working community. Thank you."

"Councillor, what do you say to those who deem you hypocritical for accepting financial assistance from Gordon Beattie, who is credited as one of the principal investors in this project?"

"Any transaction which has taken place in the provision of this establishment is on the record and beyond reproach."

"Yet you don't wish to go on record regarding Mr Beattie and his alleged involvement with the exploitation of vulnerable women through the sex trade and his ownership of several brothels in the city?"

Howard managed a chuckle at this.

"Mr Beattie is an upstanding member of the community. A celebrated business leader, philanthropist, and an employer in areas of economic deprivation. His generosity, not just in donations but in the supply of materials and labour to ensure this bastion of safety and security came into being should be recognised and applauded. Given the length of time Stormont sat in abeyance and with the dire needs of the people I represent, we should be grateful he put his money where his mouth is rather than raking over old coals." Howard looked round the gathered reporters with a frown of disappointment. "The High Court exonerated him of any crime, and any other historic charges are just that. Ancient history. Whatever groups Mr Beattie may have been attached to in his youth, he has abandoned them and should be praised for forging a successful career despite his early errors, and for encouraging others not to be coerced into that life. Thank you."

"Mr Howard…"

"How do you…"

"Councillor…"

The questions exploded from the group of reporters as Howard turned his back and breezed through the entrance and into the bright open foyer of the charity. Several tame journos from the print and television media loitered at the far end of the wide marble concourse, shepherded by a plain-looking but elegantly dressed young woman.

"Jane, my apologies."

"Nonsense. We haven't been waiting long." She took his offered hand in her own and gave it a professional pump. Howard placed his free hand over hers and drew her in conspiratorially.

"Breakfast briefing with the backers on more funding. Exciting for us, but they are numbers people and dreadfully dull. I hope everyone here is safe and well and the riff-raff outside is not being a nuisance?"

"We're all fine…"

"I could place a call and have some security brought round. Give you all a bit of peace?"

"Honestly, we are fine. It'll all die down following the announcement."

"Splendid. Splendid. Well, lead the way."

Howard appraised the woman as she strode ahead, imagining the lithe lines of her body beneath the tweed two-piece. Smiling that perhaps the plain-Jane exterior was an act and resolving to make some less than discreet inquires of her over a Buck's Fizz afterwards. His eyes lingered on her calves as she took the steps onto a raised dais and ushered him forward. Smiling, she laid a hand on his arm and spoke to the gathering press.

"Ladies and gentlemen, our sincere thanks for joining us at such short notice. I am Jane Richards, director of client services here at Sanctuary, and I am delighted to present our patron and sincere friend Councillor Malcolm Howard."

Richards eased aside and offered Howard the lectern with open arms and a wide smile.

"Thank you, Jane."

A smattering of polite applause rippled the crowd and Howard unbuttoned his jacket and leaned into the upturned faces and microphones.

"Can I just personally thank you for the warm welcome, Ms Richards, and the prospect of a fabulous breakfast. I know Director Richards will spoil us all with her hospitality today and hope you all will stay and indulge. While this morning's announcement will be an opportunity to glean some more facts, I know how much some of you enjoy a free breakfast now and then."

A wave of laughter rippled through the gathering.

Richards made a small bow and cast a directing arm towards trestle tables arranged with baked goods and tall urns of tea and coffee. Several aproned men and women busied themselves arranging cups, saucers and the paraphernalia of a well-arranged coffee morning.

"In all seriousness. The work Jane and her colleagues do here is an invaluable weapon against a rising scourge in our communities. Her organisation has led the way in putting the spotlight on the growing issue of domestic violence, the challenges facing those who endure such circumstances, and the fallout, especially for the children. This is a problem that does not discriminate across religious lines, nor is it dictated by gender or race. The fragmentation of families and that wider community is a peril that cannot continue. These issues, which some may put down as trivial, private matters to be dealt with within the confines of the family unit are misguided. These fractures stretch out across the community and divide neighbours. They widen and permeate the foundation of our society as these children suffer in the aftermath. Sucked into the void left by the decaying familial and community groups. Ignored. Exploited. Seeking a direction that those engaged in criminality and gangsterism are only too happy to exploit."

A smattering of applause as Howard warmed to his topic. A smile for Jane Richards, her hands clasped in her lap, cheeks flushed in rapt attention.

"Our current situation is one that cannot continue. The lack of devolved government has hampered the frontline response to these societal problems Sanctuary and other committed organisations are desperate to address. The institutions which should have had a cohesive, combined, and strategic approach have, in their absence, enabled a trickle to turn into a flood."

Howard paused and surveyed the crowd, which had

swelled. Flashbulbs popped on the periphery. He could see the gathering of press now pushed back to the kerb by yellow-jacketed NISEC security guards.

"There is no silver bullet, ladies and gentlemen. The work the team does here is a real and practical solution to a crisis that threatens to destabilise, disenfranchise, and drag us during these turbulent times back to a past which we all wish to avoid. What I am proposing today is a choice to embrace a positive future. These proposals would be best implemented by a united executive with cross-party cooperation but in the absence of this and following several protracted but positive trips to Westminster, I, alongside a select team of civil service advisers and with the blessing of Whitehall can announce the immediate release of significant funding to expand Sanctuary here in the city and widen her wings to three other cities desperately in need of resource expenditure. I'd also like to draw your attention to, and thank Frank Poulter, Chairperson of the Ethical Banking Trust who has aided in negotiations and the measures to ensure Sanctuary delivers those funds in the most effective manner and to Claire Laidlaw from Harper, Baxter, Brooke who have offered their services quid pro quo to those on the Sanctuary scheme who qualify and wish to avail of them. A prospectus and the press releases are available and will be disseminated. Now, if you will join me in welcoming Director Richards back to the platform she will run through where she sees this significant six-figure investment best going to work for all the people of our communities."

## Chapter 6

"My office, please."

It was an instruction. The tone disqualifying the polite request tagged on the end.

Detective Chief Inspector Gillian Reed's appearance exuded nothing but calm professionalism, considering the operations briefing room at the end of the corridor had all the outward signs of an out-of-control circus as detectives and uniformed colleagues alike clamoured for the limited seating ahead of the imminent update and assignments following events of the previous evening.

"Do you mind if I grab a wee coffee first, ma'am? I'm fair knackered after running around half the night. D'you want one yourself? Ronnie?" Macpherson queried, knocking off a jaunty salute as he made to scoot towards the team kitchen. Veronica Taylor shook her head. The DCI stopped Macpherson in his tracks.

"I can assure you, Sergeant, you were not alone in watching the small hours tick by. I've just been reading the overtime report. Now get in here. Libations can wait," said Reed, adjusting her thin horn-rimmed glasses with a manicured fingertip.

Immaculate in a designer skirt suit and matching heels, she looked more like an accountant than a tough detective, the guise catching many a crook and many a colleague off guard. A bean counter though, she was not. Reed turned on her heel, the scent of jasmine and orange blossom wafting in her wake.

Taylor shooed Macpherson in through the door. As she made to close it, Chief Superintendent William Law, resplendent in braided uniform, swept past without breaking stride. Two equally well turned out flunkies trailed behind.

"DI Taylor. Firstly, let me congratulate you on some exemplary work at that car incident last night. You were extremely courageous rushing in like that."

"No problem. ma'am. DS Collins at Eight is taking over after the arrest."

"Very good, and the shooting last night?"

"The victim was Robert Millar. Leaseholder and general manager of Risky's nightclub."

"Rab Millar. It all caught up with him then," said Reed. Taylor nodded in agreement.

"Formal identification and autopsy to take place this morning, and I expect our single eyewitness will corroborate," said Taylor.

"Risky's nightclub is owned by a subsidiary of GBH," Doc Macpherson added.

Gillian Reed wore an impassive expression. Her eyes betrayed no emotion, even if the acronym amused her. Gordon Beattie Holdings. Grievous Bodily Harm. She cast her attention between her two subordinate officers.

"We are treating the woman as a witness?" queried Reed, ignoring the input from the grizzled DS.

Taylor shared a quick look with her detective sergeant, then spoke.

"Witness. Victim. She was at the scene with injuries consistent with a severe beating. She's being treated at the Royal Hospital and given the situation, we hope she will have recovered sufficiently this morning to give a voluntary statement. Detective Constable Reilly is there and will confirm when she's fit for interview."

"Do we know who she is?"

"We got a hit back on her this morning. Previous caution for solicitation and possession of Class A. Nothing more significant but now we've established she was a sex worker, the hypothesis is that she was one of Millar's stable. Why was she in the room? At this point, given her injuries, we're thinking Millar had her card marked for something. Could be theft. Cash or drugs, maybe both," suggested Taylor.

Reid pursed her lips and considered the bare bones of what had been presented.

"This looks like an organised hit on Millar," she said. "Limited MO so should be straightforward to draw parallels with one of the other firms looking to take advantage."

"Nothing like this jumps out of my memory. Doc?" said Taylor.

Macpherson shook his head.

"It's a bit too personal," she added.

"Go on?" Reid toyed with her glasses, listening.

"There were a dozen places to hit Millar. Home. Gym. Any number of transits, or when he hung around the door of the club. Minimum effort, maximum impact. So why risk going face to face and hitting a hard target? The vehicle fire had to be a distraction to keep eyes elsewhere while our perpetrator enters the building." Taylor shifted in her seat, counting out a beat on the arm of her chair as she listed the potential obstacles. "An unknown number of hostiles inside. Access issues, locked doors, keypads, internal layout. He had all that to deal with on the fly unless he had the ability to case the place in advance. Points to somebody who knew what they were about or had prior knowledge. In and out, limited casualties, and clean as a whistle. Unless you wanted to stick two fingers up and advertise nowhere was safe for Millar and his crew, why that way?"

"You're quiet, Doc," said Reed.

"Oh, I'm just taking it all in. I'm holding my piece until the chief super asks for a wee pointer on ways he can improve the crime statistics this month and then I'll help him out."

Gillian Reed slid her glasses atop her head and rested back in her chair.

"You, my old friend, are a lost cause. Rab Millar was a nasty bugger and got what he deserved. That being said we are going to be under the microscope on this one and we don't need the grief considering with whom the recently deceased was acquainted."

Taylor had the grace to blush.

"With all due respect..." said Macpherson.

"I'm going to cut you off there, Doc. I empathise with the position you both are in. We've all had one slip the net but this case will have the ombudsman all over it. High-profile defendant gets acquitted and within a month one of his business premises gets rolled over and his old mucker is gunned down. Add to that your witness assault and the arson of a motor vehicle falling within this month's crime reduction strategy controls means someone will be on your case to make sure they are solved within the stipulated time guidelines."

"Hang on now. Some wee shite has been setting fire to wheelie bins, so we..." Macpherson raged.

"Do your best to control your language while the chief super is hovering about, please," Reed chastened. "I don't need another lecture like the one I got after you locked yourself in the gents."

"I didn't know he was in there," protested Macpherson. "And, it was the bloody lock's fault, not mine."

"Anyway, I believe the term you're grasping for is escalation, by the way. Be sure to include it in your report. Yesterday wheelie bins, today vans, tomorrow..." said Reed, a glint of amusement in her eye.

Macpherson threw his hands in the air, waving her words away.

"But..." Taylor sat forward.

"Go on. But what, Detective Inspector?"

"But this has nothing to do with Gordon Beattie."

"You're not naïve, Veronica. You and I know that one way or another this case is going to have us go cap in hand to Mr Beattie, either for assistance due to his ties to the business or because this murder is a message and somebody is trying to take advantage of his current situation. Problem is…"

"The bugger's out of bounds," huffed Macpherson.

"Look at it this way. So far we have the manager of a popular local nightclub shot dead in his place of work. Which, coincidentally, is owned by the investment vehicle of an influential member of the Belfast Chamber of Commerce who is also the owner of the largest concrete product supplier in the North of Ireland, CFO of a respected Charitable Foundation and someone we just tried and failed to put away for money laundering."

"That's putting some spin on it," grunted Macpherson.

"Has he been observed in or it even speculated he could be a patron of the place?"

Neither junior officer spoke.

"And am I or am I not correct that there is no evidence to consider any of this links to Gordon Beattie?"

"Correct," said Taylor.

"Therefore this is the investigation into a calculated murder, yes. A means to get hung out for police harassment. No."

"Just because the CPS got cold feet and dropped a bollock with a corrupt tax official."

Reed placed a dissatisfied glare on her detective inspector, and Taylor nodded an apology.

"Sorry, ma'am. Because they lost their nerve and failed to prepare a robust case against a hostile witness we ended up taking a savaging. It's common knowledge Beattie built his fortune on narcotics, prostitution, and protection rackets. Just because he's twisted those profits into cement, high-rise developments, and political donations doesn't mean he's not as bent as he ever was."

"As we have experienced; it is one thing knowing it and another proving it," said Reed.

"It wasn't the facts that got it kicked out of court, it was loopholes in procedure. Assign me Deputy SIO, I'm the best placed PIP3 officer in the department for this. I know Millar. I know the organisation and I know the connections." Taylor sat up straighter.

Gillian Reed nodded, then spoke candidly.

"If we, by which I mean you two, are spotted within a country mile of Beattie or his business operation," Reed held up one hand, raising fingers as she continued.

"One, the chief inspector will have you out of here as fast as your legs will carry you. Two, the ombudsman's office will be out of the starting gate faster than a buttered bullet, and three I'll be able to paper the walls with the harassment orders Slippy Solomon Reeves will be doling out like playing cards." Reed took a breath and then sighed. "You, miss, could still make something of yourself in uniform, your illustrious colleague alongside you there could not. Either way, it won't matter because you'll be both blind and arthritic from filling out the Regulation 15 notices to do the job."

The DCI stood and removed her glasses from their perch and tucked them in her breast pocket.

"We have already assigned a DSIO. I'm sorry. I really am. It's no reflection on you or your abilities, Veronica, but considering everything else, at the minute, I need you to play ball. Our priority here is going to be getting a quick result and pinning all our resources on finding the killer. I'll assign you to the case as I deem appropriate, but any side investigations on Beattie, GB Holdings or the deceased's links to either are shelved here and now. Clear?"

"Crystal." Taylor nodded.

"Doc?"

"Aye, loud and clear, boss."

❖ ❖ ❖

"Right now, settle down the lot of you. Take your seats and those of you who have none scoot round the back there."

Detective Chief Inspector Gillian Reed stood at the head of the briefing room, calling the chaos to conformity.

The sixty seats were full of staff in various degrees of order. While there were some fresh faces, there was an equal number who were red eyed and keyed up on caffeine following a long night. Dishevelled men with five o'clock shadow, their ties long since pocketed, and women with damp hair smoothed back into place or shoved up, their make-up reapplied in the station's WCs. Just another day at the coal face and the murmurs continued through the assembled team of uniforms and detectives until Reed drew them to a close with three sharp snaps of her fingers.

"Chief Superintendent Law," said Reed.

The imposing figure of William Law broke ranks, crumpling the polystyrene cup he held and tossing it in the vicinity of the wastepaper bin, which he missed.

"Thank you, DCI Reed. Okay, ladies and gentlemen. Less than twenty-four hours ago, this man, Robert Sinclair Millar, was shot dead."

Law stepped aside as one of his flunkies clicked a fob and a PowerPoint mugshot of a healthier Rab Miller loomed on the projection screen. Either side A0 boards displayed specifics and full colour renders of the scene within the building, the burnt-out van, the various faces of Millar in life and death, and the bruised and bloodied face and injuries of the girl discovered on site. Close-ups of her face, her wrists, and angry welts and cuts to ribs and back. There was another face only a mother could love. Richard 'Rowdy' Burns. Resplendent in a hospital gown with two shiners and no front teeth.

"Millar was no saint. That being said, an attack such as this is not just an attack on the individual but an attack on the community and a slap in the face to us all here today charged with upholding law and order. I will not tolerate any single murder or, God forbid, a return to gangland gun crime in this district."

Taylor and Macpherson scooched on a low bench along the side of the briefing room. Taylor flicked through a set of briefing notes issued by DC Carrie Cook and compiled by the scene liaison officer and most junior member of the team, DC Christopher Walker. He sat to her right making up the quadruplet by the side of Macpherson. The last member of her team DC Erin Reilly was still at the hospital. An earlier text had confirmed there was no update on the woman's condition.

"I'd like at this opportunity to remind you that the dubious honour bestowed on us last night means our one hundred and seventy-eight days without a reportable firearms incident has been reset and reported as per Codes of Practice, through the Policing Board Channels and the Home Office counting rules. With those revised reporting clarifications we here in District Nine are falling behind those of our colleagues in Districts Seven and Eight by a full seven per cent in direct comparison. The figures to hand show no correlation mitigating that discrepancy with any annual funding cuts to services. If anything, we are operating on a higher budget with poorer results. Pull your socks up, ladies and gentlemen. I expect a quick result on this one. I have appointed DCI Reed as senior investigating officer. She will continue the brief and issue assignments. Good day."

A murmur of contrite acknowledgement hummed through the gathering as Law replaced his cap and in a blur of shiny buttons, followed by his two henchmen, beat a retreat from the room.

"Hardly Mr bloody Motivator," grumbled Macpherson, eliciting a giggle from the sandy-haired Walker.

"Wise up, the pair of you." Taylor tapped the file against his thigh and motioned as Reed took up position to the side of the projection screen.

"Okay, folks. Keep it down to a dull roar. The chief super's points are valid, so bear them in mind. All regulation paperwork is a priority, and all crimes stipulated under the monthly crime strategy review are to be processed within the mandatory three days. Now before we start…" Reed paused and slipped her glasses back on.

"The collective we, have taken a kicking in the press and at the hands of the DPP in recent weeks. It happens. Get over it. Move on with the job at hand and try to remember you're all professionals." Her gaze seemed to linger a little too long in the general vicinity of Taylor and her colleagues, sitting as an island of their own amid the briefing. "Each of us has our role to play, and I expect complete cooperation and transparency across the teams." Reed let her eyes search for any sign of dissent or disparity.

"To the matter at hand, Detective Inspector Phillip McDonald will be DSIO with the incident room here at District 9, Musgrave Central."

The projector screen changed to a plan view of the streets around Risky's nightclub.

"This is the area of Watson Lane and Ballymacarrett Road. Last night at approximately twenty-one thirty hours one male, so far unidentified, proceeded inside and assaulted this man, Richard Burns. Rowdy, as he is known locally. Convictions for ABH, GBH, demanding money with menaces and armed robbery."

Reed clicked the fob which changed to the interior shot of the upstairs room.

"UI proceeded via Watson Lane side internal stairwell to

this room on the first floor. Bravo Kilo One Nine, first on scene, responding to reports of shots fired, discovered a vehicle on fire in the yard. Black, Ford Transit Connect, registration Delta Zulu Golf Nine Six Seven Eight. Risk assessment signed off by duty inspector; officers entered and secured scene. Image Foxtrot Zero One Seven in the briefing notes. Staff report this was a disused storeroom. Inside IC one female and IC one male, deceased."

Reed highlighted Millar.

"Detective Inspector Taylor identifies the victim as Robert Millar. Twenty-four Harcourt Way. Initial pathologist report states exsanguination by GSW. For those of you in the audience without the benefit of a medical degree, that means the vicious bugger was on the receiving end of a sawn-off and subsequently bled to death. Millar is known to us and under investigation for several unsolved crimes, and at this point, any of those could be a motive for his murder. DI MacDonald, can we communicate Mr Millar's demise and cross-reference to any open investigations?"

MacDonald nodded his assent. Raising an index finger to a tanned and immaculately groomed DC who, with a nod of acknowledgement, scratched in his notebook then replaced a chewed black ballpoint between white teeth. Sensing the eyes on him, DC Sam Simpson looked up, offering a brief nod to the gathered foursome.

"Ronald bloody MacDonald, DSIO? What a liberty, ma'am."

Taylor hushed Walker. Macpherson loomed across her lap.

"Detective Inspector MacDonald to you, son. You heard the boss lady. Team."

"Sorry, I'm just…"

"Detective Sergeant Macpherson. Have you anything pertinent to add at this point?" Gillian Reed's voice boomed.

"Ah no, ma'am. Apologies. Just ensuring my young

colleague here fulfils the appropriate data protection request before making any of our case files available for CIRS. Sorry, ma'am."

Macpherson glowered at the red-faced and now submissive Walker.

"Twat," he hissed, from the corner of his mouth, digging an elbow into Walker.

"Very good, Sergeant. Can you have your DC also make the approach to TICC and verify any route that may have been captured on CCTV of the assailant's access or egress to the site or the van on route to Watson Lane? Specifically, any flagged vehicles. NIFRS forensic officers will carry out a search and assessment of the vehicle this morning. That will need to be followed up too."

"Aye, ma'am." Macpherson grinned. Trawling the eighty cameras and the hours of footage that would be available at the Traffic Information and Control Centre would harden the lad for his misdemeanour.

"IC one female is undergoing treatment at RVH for injuries sustained prior to the murder. Currently, we are treating her as a witness and she will be interviewed in due course once signed off by the medical team."

Reed once again clicked the fob, and the projector displayed a high-resolution plan view of the locus surrounding Risky's.

"A list of the club's on-duty staff has been compiled and statements taken. The same for patrons. This will be updated to the case database in due course for review and follow-up. There will have been those who made a hasty exit when the shooting started, however, I'm told on good authority from noise enforcement that it's likely few punters noticed the shots at first so we may still get a witness. Sections Three and Four will resume door to door of houses and business owners in the immediate area up to and including the junction of

Brooke Street and I want a wider canvas on the egress road where Ballymacarrett Road meets the A20. Sergeant Harris will provide the brief for those involved. DI MacDonald will arrange family liaison for Mr Millar's next of kin and organise the search teams around the immediate locale for evidence dump sites. This is case number Golf, Six, Seven, Nine, One, three. Now, assignments…"

## Chapter 7

John Barrett rubbed the lens of his tortoiseshell glasses, more in thought than for any other requirement. The ribbon of traffic glowed as it threaded along the web of roads outside, the dull thrum of engines and scrub of brakes muted by the toughened blast-proof glass of his eyrie. Below, subordinates and colleagues hurried through a squall on the way back from breakfast meetings, trading weather talk and shrugs with the uniformed security guards on the gate.

Barrett watched the normality unfold. His eyes looked past the raindrops cascading down the windowpane and out over the swaying trees to where Parliament Buildings sat in splendour at the end of her mile-long manicured drive. Within the Portland stone edifice was the Assembly, the devolved legislature for the embittered North-East of the isle; seat of executive government and the grip of power.

He was the gatekeeper, the protector of democracy and the one who brought balance between the parties who still had no stomach to climb beyond their green or orange barricades.

Politicians came and went. Careers book-ended in success or scandal or, in the case of this current crop, wreathed in the ashes of failure. Failure to commit, to communicate, and to lead. Content to spout the same vitriolic bile that had accompanied their predecessors over his years. Climbing the greasy pole using the politics of division and fear. The veneer of unification had been tarnished and old masks were being replaced and old wounds reopened.

Barrett's tactic was as old as time. Divide and conquer and he was proud of its success. Another successful campaign in a lifetime of conflict, and now he sought the decisive victory.

He was the unknown face who wielded the power behind

the throne. A place where he was more than the sum of the legislature's collective capacity. As they all wrestled over the scraps, stepping on each other's throats, espousing one belief while condemning another; stymied by the only thing they knew, a belief that progress and success relied on the exclusion of the other.

Barrett had been a pragmatic man during the formative years of his career, cultivating a small fortune in the process. Those early days had been spent as intern, underling, and junior civil servant in both the hotspots and the low spots of the world where his apprenticeship imbued life lessons he learned and then assimilated, grease the wheels, money made the world go round and cash was king and that was how he came to the attention of the consortium.

The group comprised a number of shadowy individuals with vast wealth to invest in activities that offered excellent returns whilst avoiding excise duty, tax liability, and most of the laws put in place to stop those enterprises that offered the highest yield. They had been looking for an administrator and Barrett had fit the bill. There was no trickle. No crack in the dam nor build-up of pressure that released the floodtide. Barrett had decided he would play the game, and now he was playing to win.

Replacing his spectacles, Barrett returned to his desk. The desk was utilitarian, a typical civil service affair. Nothing ostentatious like his political charges had in their offices up the hill in the big house. From the surface he picked up a slim black and chrome headset and placed it on his ears, inserting an encrypted drive and shoogling his mouse to bring the screen of his PC monitor to life. As he launched several programs and a VPN he selected a call, busying himself with several of the ledger spreadsheets as the call tone pinged.

"Redcastle. Stewart Brokerage House." A clipped, professional English voice.

"Daniel Redcastle, please."

No reply, just professional efficiency as they routed the call.

"Redcastle." Home Counties. Plummy. Years of breeding and the best of schools.

"Daniel. John Barrett, I'm logged on and highlighting actions as we speak. I need the execution split and channelled into the usual funds. I also need six hundred thousand transferred to the Cayman account. Your normal fee applies."

As the broker enthused his greetings and thanks and made small talk with his generous client, he confirmed the dozen transaction requests and a powerful computer program launched, the stream of data originating from Barrett's PC spinning on its way in zeros and ones into the digital ether.

Four thousand miles away in a sweaty office saturated by sunlight on the seaward end of Cardinal Avenue, Georgetown on the Cayman Islands, a printer sprang to life and disgorged a sheet of confirmation. A few minutes later, the same tray received several embossed stock certificates. The secretary, a harried woman in her fifties, took them to her supervisor who nodded in satisfaction. Returning to her desk, she slid the certificates into thick airmail envelopes and printed off shipping labels to a bank in Abu Dhabi. They would be on their way within the hour. The certificates would be appraised and approved and a cheque to the value of six hundred thousand pounds sterling handed to a courier.

Within eight hours or less the cheque would be in the warren of streets off the Abadi Highway in the port city of Karachi, Pakistan. There, an eagle-eyed clerk, robed and bejewelled with skin like bark, fed an assortment of US dollars, British pounds, euros, and dirhams into a counting machine. As the day wore on and the Imams called their faithful to prayer, the cash would spread out like a web. From bribes to local officials and customs and border agents, to be lavished on health and wealth and many wives, to the arrangement of shipping and transport and the wages of the foot soldier with baser or more practical needs.

The cash would spread its way through the warrens, like venom from the city to the hinterlands and the deserts beyond; as far as the barren border regions, where tons of unrefined opium from Afghanistan slipped between checkpoints aboard covered diesel trucks, alongside their cargo of human misery bound East and West and all points between.

Barrett disconnected the call and closed the screens, his actions complete. Settling back into the comfortable, black, buttoned Chesterfield office chair, he contemplated Gordon Beattie. The former gangster had built a premier network of illicit procurement and distribution chains and had the logistics and contacts to service it to Europe and beyond. Finnrock, the backbone of Gordon Beattie Holdings, supplied concrete and concrete products to the North of Ireland and beyond. Their reach extended into the Republic of Ireland and Scotland with interest also now coming from a booming construction sector in London and the south of England; their star was very much in the ascendency. That veneer had to be maintained at all costs, as the real asset of Finnrock was its ability to ship and distribute massive amounts of cocaine across jurisdictions. Beattie had done his research and built an impressive end-to-end business.

Purchasing the drugs close to where they landed in El Jadida in North Africa, from there the cargo made the brief journey to a facility on the outskirts of Casablanca. The North African site set up by Finnrock offered cheap production and it was during the manufacturing process the contraband was secreted inside kerbstones, window lintels, precast floors, walls and staircases, then shipped by Beattie into the Port of Belfast.

The drugs were invisible to traditional search by sniffer

dogs and the unwieldy items, by their nature, put off a manual search. When the customs teams did have to address their quota Beattie's officials on the payroll had already issued a tip-off to the methods and means right down to the size of drill bit used to check the objects for their authenticity. Once they cleared customs, the products headed to a facility on the outskirts of the capital to be cut open, the drugs removed and then distributed onwards through the group's other various fronts from garden centre nurseries and car wrecking yards to builders' merchants. The scraps of concrete were then ingeniously, broken down and recycled. Discarded rubble was processed into aggregates that formed the sub-base for roadworks or ready mixed concrete for new building works and sold on. The ingenuity of the legitimate business alone had made Beattie a substantial fortune. Unfortunately, while the man himself was nowhere near on his knees, the smuggling business had stumbled. With charges filed and a prosecution deemed likely, there had been blood in the water and the sharks were circling. Competitors were testing boundaries and law enforcement agencies waited in the wings to pounce on the multimillion-pound assets they could feed back into the Exchequer.

A deal as lucrative as the one Beattie had negotiated with the Venezuelan cartels could not be kept secret, and it wasn't long before Barrett with his web of worldwide contacts caught the scent. Beattie's problem with the authorities proved a fortunate opportunity to become even more wealthy. Barrett along with members of the consortium manipulated Beattie's release by redistributing assets and diverting distribution lines, ensuring his exoneration and the survival of the smuggling routes.

Beattie had the potential to be the golden goose, with conservative estimates putting the street value of a single cargo shipment of corrupted concrete products at near three-quarters of a billion pounds. Not only that, but his shipping route offered another means of transport for any amount of the goods and services the consortium shipped across the globe. For all this, they would take a percentage, and Barrett would be well rewarded from that. All that remained was one more pressure test on the chain. The murder of his colleague had been unfortunate, but Barrett had grown to trust Beattie, had raised himself sufficiently and had enough expense and luxury bestowed upon him to be unswervingly grateful to his faceless masters. He could learn to be ambivalent towards such minor problems and realise collateral damage was an unfortunate event which one had to endure and best insure against.

❖ ❖ ❖

The hiss of hydraulics filled the warehouse as the crusher eased its mammoth pistons open. The ton of large rubble blocks inside had been compressed by the massive jaws of the machinery and now spilt out in a grating squeal of stone against metal. It was a place for the broken, a graveyard of smashed blocks and shattered columns stretching as far as the eye could see. Staggered staircases, huge plinths and reams of twisted metal rebar lined dusty grey aisles and everything was coated in dust.

Water, oil, and fluids drained from the crusher and pooled around the knees of the bound man beside the bright red control gear, his high-pitched protestations drowned out by the machinery.

"What is it you want? I swear to God I'll tell you, please. For Christ's sake…"

One huge hand shook him by the hair, the other jerked his arms, secured behind his back with cable ties, up higher. Tendons and ligaments reached their limits. The panicked shouts turned to painful howls.

"Mr Beattie doesn't have time for any of your shite,

Nobby." A rough shove pitched the man onto his face. A flurry of kicks to the ribs rolled him onto his side.

Freaky Jackson dragged the groaning man back up on his knees by the hair.

The hydraulic pistons slammed into their open position.

Gordon Beattie stood far enough back so that his elevenhundred-pound Lobb Oxfords wouldn't be soiled by the avalanche of crushed stone excrement or the blood of Nobby Riddel. A heavy-duty concertina coil of cable linked the bulky set of buttons in his hand to the machine.

"I swear, Mr Beattie…"

Beattie shook his head.

"Save your breath, Nobby. Did I not make myself clear last time? I'm sure I did. Freaky?"

"I heard you. Told him right to his face. One week, you said. Very generous if you ask me."

"I got your money. I did. You know I did. That was every penny I have, please… my ma…"

"Spare us, Nobby. Your ma wouldn't know you if you pissed on her. You know it's probably your fault, the dementia. They're saying now it's brought about by chronic stress. That's all you are to everyone. Unnecessary stress."

"No… no… no," he screamed as Jackson gave his arms another jerk. Tears were streaming now, words caught between sobs.

"But… I… paid."

"Aye, two grand. You've been sitting on fifteen for near six months."

"It's all I have," pleaded Riddel.

"Where did you get the money, you thieving wee toerag?"

The silence between sobs told a tale in itself.

"Did you think I wouldn't know? That I couldn't find out? Really. You robbed the same fucking chinky you use every weekend, you dumb shit."

"I'm sorry…"

"Taking a knife to a thirteen-year-old wee girl, scarring her for life? You're a waste of skin, son. A fucking cancer. Preying on working people, stealing what they've earned to pay for your debts and your habit. What gives you the right?" Beattie roared the last.

A dark stain bloomed at Nobby Riddel's crotch.

"You disgust me."

"I'm sorry, I'll give it back, I'll get…"

"Do you know whose money that was? My money. Who do you think they come to when they need a loan and can't get one from the thieving banks? Or they need protection from parasites like you? Who sorts their problems when the council tries to shut them down for skirting a few health and hygiene rules, eh? No germs survive two hundred degrees in a deep-fat fryer, do they? There's an idea. Maybe I should take you round to Willy and let him have a wee bit of justice for his girl? Get him to dip your hand in boiling oil? What do you think, Freaky?"

"Harden him for being a thieving toerag." Jackson licked his lips, leering at the squirming Riddel.

"I didn't know, please."

"Please, please," Beattie spoke in mock whining tones. "Save your breath, I've heard every excuse from you. You can't help yourself, this is a mercy, son."

A sour expression on his face, Beattie nodded at Jackson. The rest of Riddel's words descended into a garbled scream as he was lifted and hurled atop the hopper and onto the ragged concrete blocks within. Scrambling to find his equilibrium, he sank in the tangled miss-sized scraps of stone, blood seeping from a deep cut on his cheek as he desperately tried to find his feet.

Beattie handed the buttons to Jackson.

Freaky thumbed the green mushroom button, and the

compactor began to move, hydraulics hissing and the thick steel bin screeching as it slowly began the process of compacting the contents. Riddel's face was a mask of agony as his legs became trapped. The smashed concrete scraps now began to build up to waist height, his wails drowned out by the industrial cacophony as the pressure broke his ankles.

"Don't you worry. We'll see your ma is looked after, and that wee sister of yours too," shouted Beattie, although whether Riddel heard he couldn't tell, The man's face was a white mask, his tongue lolling out as the crush now ground down on his upper torso, the bones of his legs and pelvis long since broken and flesh pulped. As his head disappeared under the churning rubble, Beattie looked across to Jackson who stood with a rapt look of pleasure on his face.

"Bring your man over, will you?"

The compactor came to a final noisy crescendo and then shuddered with a final series of grating metallic clunks.

Jackson hooked the buttons to an upright and moved to seize a second wriggling man from the grip of two associates.

Beattie had moved away from the machinery as his two men, now absent their prisoner, began the unseemly task of scraping out the contents of the compactor and whatever remained of Nobby Riddel. The first man slapped back the steel bolt and heaved the hopper open and the other jumped into a small bobcat digger, the engine whining as he gunned it to life and put the shovel scoop to work.

Beattie stood beside a long metal-framed table. The oily scuffed surface held a number of screwdrivers, a cold chisel and club hammer, and a set of large bladed tin snips. In a plastic bread tray was a selection of other handheld drills and angle grinders.

"Bekim. I appreciate you coming."

"Fuck you, Monster. When Amir hears what you've done…"

"Shut your mouth, you nasty wee Albanian bastard." The man's belligerence earned him a slap round the back of the head from Jackson.

"This is my city, son. Amir is operating here by my grace. Whether I choose to continue to be so hospitable considering he lost me a ton of money depends on the next few minutes," said Beattie.

Bekim Nishani's struggle against Freaky Jackson's grip was futile as the bigger man shoved the youth onto a crate beside the table. The Albanian had the tight frame of a welterweight boxer and the broken nose to match. Clotted blood dried into the neat moustache and beard while tattooed arms strained against the plastic zip ties that held his wrists.

"You think I care about your threats? You think that show scares me…" Nishani hawked a gobbet of bloody phlegm and spat it at Beattie, but it fell far short.

Beattie smiled and picked up the tin shears. Nishani struggled, but Jackson forced him down.

"Now, are we going to conduct this like gentlemen or am I going to have to offer some incentives?" He pointed the shears at the Albanian.

"Amir will…"

Beattie reached down and grabbed the young man's right ear, Nishani trying his best to twist away.

Beattie snapped the jaws of the tool closed on the top half of the ear and the blood washed across Nishani's cheek. The inhuman howl echoed in the warehouse and his struggle ripped him from Jackson's grip, tipping him onto the floor where he writhed in pain.

"Get him up."

Jackson reached down and manhandled the grunting Albanian back onto the crate, Beattie throwing the chunk of flesh on his lap.

"Bekim, you've one good ear left so my advice is to use it

and keep your tongue in your mouth. I can tell by looking at him, Freaky there is getting a hard-on thinking about putting you into that crusher?"

"What do you want!" the Albanian screamed, stamping his feet, body juddering on the crate, the collar and shoulder of his shirt drenched red.

"I want to know who shot Rab Millar dead."

"I know nothing…"

Beattie placed the tips of the shears across the entrance to a nostril.

"Don't tempt me, Bekim."

"I swear. It wasn't us."

"Then why have you been running your filthy foreign mouth off about Rab."

"Me?"

Beattie tutted, took a step back, and leaned down into the Albanian's face, the shears now pointing at Jackson.

"Bekim, he'll tell you. I'm not a patient man. You've been slumming it around the town telling anyone who'll listen, Rab Millar stole from you and you were going to make him pay."

"He does fucking owe me money."

"Well you're not getting it back now are you?" Beattie roared, spittle peppering the Albanian's face.

"What for?" said Beattie, more calmly.

"I paid for his whores and the frigid bitch walked out on me. I demand my money back and then that fat tub of lard threw me out?"

"Rowdy?"

"Fucking Rowdy."

"Decided to take matters into your own hands, then?" growled Jackson.

"I complained to Amir, and he has words with Millar and then tells me to forget it."

Nishani spat another glob of bloody spittle onto the floor, his face contorted in pain.

"But you get the drink in and your balls grow a bit."

"He made me look stupid."

"I should've buried you the other night." Freaky shoved the Albanian's head forward.

"You couldn't…"

"Focus, Bekim, I swear I'm this close to letting Freaky have you." Beattie held a finger and thumb a half inch apart. "You got turfed out of the club the other night because you're a vicious wee bastard and you damaged the merchandise again."

"She needed a slap to teach her some respect."

Beattie reached forward and snipped the Albanian's bottom lip in half.

The Albanian writhed his head from side to side, blood pouring from the wound.

"What do you know about Rab's murder?"

Tears in his eyes, teeth grating together, bloody bubbles appeared as he tried to form words.

"Stop. Okay. Okay. I might have heard something…"

## Chapter 8

Elaine Weir pushed the button of the lift and despaired as her daughter wriggled out of the pushchair and gave her a gap-toothed grin.

"Come on. Come on." She stabbed the button again, knowing she was going to be late in dropping the child off at school and she for work. Again. It wasn't bad enough the school teacher gave her that superior look when she noticed the shiny elbows of her daughter's cardigan or the scuffed shoes but working for her father in his own small convenience store she got away with less than if she had been an employee he didn't know from Adam.

"Right, come on, Freya. We have to take the stairs." She did an about-turn, the wheels of the pushchair squeaking on the filthy floor and the protestations of her four-year-old ringing in her ears.

Fearon House was the usual hangover from the swinging sixties. An eleven-storey behemoth built at the end of a boom period to ease the pain of housing stress brought about by the slum clearances in the city, when row on row of red-brick terraces had been tipped over in the name of progress. The block loomed over the cramped post-war housing estate which sprawled in all its gory glory around its feet. The estate was marked out, like most, by the flags, the painted kerbstones, and the murals reaching up and shamelessly declaring its Loyalist identity; in the traditional sense with murals of King William of Orange upon his white charger and the fluttering flags of the loyal orders and then in the darker hues of maroon UVF banners, Red Right Hands and three-storey high murals of armed and masked men declaring No Surrender and the reminder they were prepared for peace, but ready for war. The sentiment was a sham, a throwback to a heyday long past. All that remained was a catch-all mask to cover gangsterism, criminality and antisocial behaviour.

Elaine wrestled with the door to the stairwell, hinges long-absent oil and swollen by neglect protesting as she forced it wider.

"Take your wee bag for me, Freya," she said.

The little girl clutched a pink satchel containing a meagre lunch to her chest and darted through the door as Elaine hauled the pushchair through behind her.

"Wait, Freya. Come here to me. Don't be running off down those stairs."

The little girl stopped. Her face screwed up.

"Yuk, stinks." She wafted a hand over her face.

"Aye, it does," agreed Elaine. The sour smell of spilt booze and urine was swept up the draughty stairs by wind howling through broken panes of glass on a mournful soundtrack of traffic drone from the motorway that skirted the estate.

"Come on, be a big girl, walk on ahead of Mummy."

As she fought with the off-balance pushchair laden with Freya's larger school bag and a change of clothes for when her sister collected her later, she heard a peal of laughter and the sound of glass smashing below her, sending a sliver of cold up her spine. A rough tirade of swearing and more laughter and a staccato blast of sharp barks. As she stepped onto the landing, she saw Freya, distracted by the sounds and ever inquisitive, skip ahead and then watched in horror as she faltered over her feet, the strap of the lunch bag tangling her step. Her daughter yelped in surprise as she tumbled headlong down the stairs.

Her fall was halted by the arms of a man.

"Are you alright, love? Freya. Come here."

Belongings abandoned, Elaine ran down and grabbed her

daughter as the man set her down.

"Sorry, thanks. What have I told you, lady?" said Elaine, as she fussed over the child in relief.

The girl's eyes were saucers as she stared up at the stranger.

"No harm done. Off to school are you?"

Freya nodded.

"Thanks," Elaine stammered, heart thumping. "Yes, running late as usual." She offered a weak smile. The man was tall, broad and bearded. He'd dropped a large olive green bag he'd been carrying and now stooped to retrieve it.

"Do you need a hand with that?" He motioned towards the pushchair and its cargo. Freya looked up at her mother and smiled.

"No, I'm used to it. Probably safer on these stairs than in those lifts any road."

"It's no bother."

"I'll manage. Thanks, though. Are you new here? I haven't seen you about?"

"Yes. Just a few days." He patted the bag now hefted over his shoulder.

"Still moving in the essentials. Sorry, I'm Tom."

"Elaine. You must have been desperate?"

"I'm sorry, I don't…"

"This dump. Cape Fear," she added, her eyes casting a resigned look about the grim stairwell.

"I've stayed in worse places…"

A sharp wolf whistle filled the air.

"Alright, Elaine. Who's your boyfriend."

"Hi, Billy." Elaine pulled the child closer and threw an offhand wave, shooting a glance at the man who stood beside her, unable to hide the nervous expression.

The newcomer strutted up the half landing to meet them. He was tall and skinny, with beady wet eyes in a milk bottle white face, and a fuzz of wispy stubble on his upper lip and jawline. His companion not far behind gripped a thin leather leash attached to a stocky Staffordshire bull terrier, its stubby tail wagging, tongue lolling from a panting mouth.

"Hi, is that it? Blowing me out are ya?" he said.

"No, just late. Got to go, school, you know."

"What do you want to waste her time on that shite for? Skipping it did me no harm, did it, Barney?" Billy Webster turned to address his companion doing a mock twirl. He was wearing the best of hooligan chic, a dark grey Canada Goose padded jacket, dark Lacoste tracksuit, and Armani trainers. On his wrist, a smartwatch flicked up a message, a clean note echoing in the grim stairwell.

"What you looking at?" he said, with a frosty scowl at the stranger's proximity to the girl and her daughter.

Tom appraised the pair, shifting the strap holding the bag on his shoulder to a better position.

"Cat got your tongue, big man?" said the smaller kid, fighting to keep the dog under control.

"Give over, Barney. He's just helping me down the steps with the buggy. If you're planning on any nonsense, your ma will be in the shop later on for her fags and I'll be telling her to have a word."

Elaine's hard tone softened as she thanked the man and began the hassle of descending the stairs and securing her daughter amid the fractious atmosphere. Tension filled her face as she tried to negotiate the pair of lads lounging along the rails and the proximity of the dog which strained against Barney's grip to sniff at the child's legs.

"She's gonna tell your ma, Barney. That's you for it," said Billy, a lecherous grin creeping across his pockmarked face. "In for her fags? In for her bottle of methylated spirits more like."

"Big Rhonda will be blootered later and scrounging a few

quid for a ten deal," said Barney. The boys cackled at the thought, joined by sharp barks from the animal.

"Shut it!" Barney bellowed, jerking the leash. He was a younger, less sophisticated, and more eclectic version of Webster with brand new Nike Air Max and dirty Kappa joggers under a Puma hoodie, pulled up over a red snapback.

"Rhonda the Honda," said Billy. Another fit of laughing died as he set his sights once more on the stranger.

"You trying it on with her, mister?" Webster pushed himself off the rail, looking the man up and down.

"Fancy your chances, do you?" Barney echoed. The dog began to circle his legs, a dull vibrato growl rumbling from it.

"We look out for her now her man's away. Don't we, Elaine?" Billy wasn't looking at her, instead eyeing the bulging canvas bag.

"He's not my man," snapped Elaine. "He might be Freya's da, but we're not together." Her eyes met Tom's, an explanation and a plea in the look. Leave.

"Maybe it's the wee girl he's after, Billy. You a paedo?" Barney Murray stepped closer and shoved the man who rocked back on his heels but quickly regained his balance. The dog responded to the move, straining against the grip and rising on hind legs.

"Lads, I don't need any trouble. I'm just going. The lady needed help with the stairs, so if you excuse me, I've been on the night shift."

"If you'll excuse me," mimicked Webster to hoots from his mate. "You're either a paedo or a poof, mate, and that slapper's no lady. You know what happens to the likes of your lot round here, do you?"

"For God's sake, Billy. Leave him alone. He was just giving me a hand. Now stop it, you're scaring the child."

Webster glared at her.

"You go on about your business, Elaine." He turned to the

child, "Uncle Billy just wants to talk to the man, Freya. Have fun at your wee school, sure. Daddy'll be home soon," he said, adding the last in a small, childlike voice before shooing them away with a dismissive wave.

"Don't be telling her that, Billy." Elaine Weir's defiance returned. "Graham won't be out anytime soon and even when he is…"

"You'll what?" Barney took a few steps towards her. Panic filled her eyes as the Staffy lunged, caught at the last moment by a vicious jerk of the lead. Barney Murray cackled in delight.

"You think you'll stop Graham Bell from seeing his wee girl? Aye right."

Tom Shepard took a step forward.

"Lads, I'm away on here. Sorry for the bother, miss."

Elaine hesitated. Shepard nodded.

"You'll go when… we… tell… you." Webster stalked up to the larger man, each quiet word punctuated by a stabbing finger.

"Go on, miss," said Shepard, taking a small step backwards to create a space between himself, the two youths, and the now agitated dog. He nodded a confirmation for the girl and her daughter to clear out. Violence with the locals hadn't been on his agenda, but he wouldn't sidestep any if it arrived.

Elaine Weir grabbed her daughter by the sleeve of her coat and pulled her away, pushing the child ahead and dragging the buggy behind. The clatter of their footsteps receded down the concrete steps in their wake.

"So?" Webster stalked back and forth, an agitated expression on his face and Murray with a sour sneer on his tried the best intimidation pose he could manage. The dog between his legs was a well-used and rehearsed prop.

"I don't want any trouble, lads. I just want to get home."

Adopting a submissive pose, he shrank back a little against the wall, arms held out to the side, palms extended.

"She's out of bounds, alright. You a problem with that?"

"No problem here."

Webster studied the man, confidence swelling as he sensed an opportunity.

"What's in the bag?"

"Look, I'm just off a night shift and I'm…"

"He said what's in the bag. Are you deaf?" howled Murray. He was pacing now too. The youths moving through their pre-fight routine, hyping it up, feeding off each other, and the dog, also sensing it, flattened its ears against its head. Shepard observed the display and plotted his actions. Webster was the closer, blocking the way up and his confidence was his weakness. Murray was edgy, his position at the top of the stairs an apparent strength, yet the dog was his saving grace. The kid would be hurt, at worst break something if things got heated.

"Moving in stuff," he explained.

"Moving in? You hear that, Barney?"

"Moving in. You'll be paying your dues then?"

"Dues?" Shepard watched the two circle.

"Insurance, mate. The House is a rough spot, so you need people watching your back."

"I think I'll take my chances."

"You're out of chances, mate. If you won't pay, we'll just have the bag."

Murray began the move; rehearsed or not he was the more aggressive, his gait swaggering and a practised expression of bravado as he loosed the leash and let the Staffy charge, claws rasping on the scuffed concrete floor. The animal was intended to both distract the eye and intimidate as Webster reached out and grabbed the shoulder strap. Shepard stepped forward, closing the gap. Murray faltered, the expected tug of war when he would lay into the distracted target now nullified. He jerked the dog back, the animal yelping at its arrested motion.

There was a shrill electronic explosion of sound. Bass. Blips. Rap lyrics.

Webster, eyeball to eyeball with Shepard, shoved the larger man in the chest.

"What the fuck, man?" snarled Murray, tightening the leash and giving the dog another harsh pull back to heel. Webster pulled an iPhone from his pocket and put it to his ear, staring at Shepard, who remained silent.

"Freaky! Man, what's up? Yeah, yeah… fuck man, I know it's all over Facebook. Bastards. Do you know who…" Webster used the same dismissive wave as he had earlier and jerked his chin towards the stairs. Turning away, he mimed a pistol with his fingers at Shepard.

"You'll keep, Paedo," spat Murray, guiding the dog away. "We'll be seeing you around."

Shepard watched the two retreat until they were out of sight. Webster's conversation animated, the kid full of himself.

"Aye, sweet. Fucking right I'm in. When and where… Dead on… Here did I tell you? I've this new bitch for next week. Wait'll you see her, she's a cracker…"

Shepard waited until the drone of conversation was inaudible, shifted the heavy canvas bag, and took the stairs up to his landing.

## Chapter 9

"Switchboard?" Macpherson stopped his pacing so abruptly Detective Constable Carrie Cook, who had been watching him started in surprise.

"Does she really think sitting here with our two arms the one length in the hope some tip lands in is the best use of resources?" Macpherson huffed a breath, then once again began pacing back and forth outside the DCI's office, the voices inside muffled by the closed door. His short legs pumped like pistons as he marched and seemed to drive blood in ever-increasing bursts up to his beetroot face. Five impatient seconds later he jammed on the brakes again, finger jabbing the air in protest and voice raised in frustration.

"Stuck in here while Ronald MacDonald and the burger boys are out cracking the case, don't make me laugh. They couldn't find their backsides in a blackout!"

"They aren't that bad, and it wouldn't be the first time a phone lead led to something," said Carrie.

She sat on a plastic chair with her briefing notes clasped to her chest, a shield against the fury rising from Macpherson, her knees jiggling in time with his strides.

"You're only saying that because Slick Simpson fancies you, Carrie."

"He does not," she said, slapping the folder but missing the stomping DS.

"Come on, Sarge. Will you flipping sit down? You're going to give yourself a heart attack and you're making me dizzy watching you," said DC Chris Walker approaching along the corridor. Macpherson paused, looked up and shook his head.

"Enjoy the phone lines, losers. That's me off to TICC." Walker beamed as he brandished his notice to search the

Traffic Incident Cameras while absentmindedly tucking in the shirt tail that perpetually worked its way out of the back of his trousers.

"What did I tell you about having a bit of respect for your superiors?" Macpherson, defeated, slumped in the chair next to Cook.

"Don't you mean my elders, Granda? Funny, I could've sworn I heard you question the DSIO's ability to…"

"You're a quare one to be calling anyone Granda. You must've had some paper round, son."

Christopher Walker pulled a face. Only in his early thirties, Walker had the complexion of someone much older, and what hair he had left he had given up on trying to style into anything resembling a contemporary cut. It rankled somewhat that the elder Macpherson had a full head of hair, even if it was snow white.

Macpherson stilled for as long as he could manage, bounced back to his feet, and thumped the younger man on the arm.

"Get yourself away and be grateful you've been let loose. Ring in if you find anything. We'll be needing someone to talk to other than the cranks that have seen King Billy and his horse roaming behind the Shankill baths."

"Sarge," said Walker with a firm nod.

"And none of that heavy breathing malarky when you do. Puts Carrie right off her cornflakes."

"Has the guv been in there this whole time?" asked Walker. Cook nodded the affirmative.

"At least there's been no sound of anything getting turfed about," said Macpherson.

The three detectives started as the door opened.

"I see the welcoming committee's all here," said Taylor, sweeping her briefing folder up to face them.

"I've got us the witness review and liaison with SOCO to

update the case database. Anything that comes from CCTV and the van we can chase up. We'll still have to cycle on and off the phones, though. Happy?"

"A pile of twisted scrap metal and a load of young ones off their tree?" Macpherson groaned, "Sure, we'll have this cracked by dinner time." His enthusiasm was gone.

They walked out of the corridor and Taylor badged them through a secure door into a stairwell lobby.

"Phones are that way." Taylor pointed down the stairs. Macpherson took the file from her hand.

"Aw, there's no need to be like that. Flip you for the van?"

"Carrie's getting the van." Taylor took the file back and sifted out several printouts, passing them across.

"See if you can trace the owner and recent history and while you're at it press forensics to release anything that might have survived the fire. Latent prints, trace fibres. Anything." Cook slipped the paperwork into her file with a nod.

"Chris, is that the paperwork for TICC? Good, when you get over there, check the camera at the junction beside the flyover and the ambulance station, the one behind the paint shop. Anyone driving into the yard had to pass it. See if it picked up who was driving and if we know them."

"Will do," said the junior officer.

"While you're at it, ask about the CCTV hard drive model at the club. We haven't got a password yet. They might know a way to bypass and get us in."

Walker nodded, adding a note.

"Did you tell the boss about Jackson?" said Macpherson.

"Come on, Doc. You taught me better than that. He's not on the radar yet, so we'll swing past him later. We've a few witnesses to speak to first."

"We're not doing the door to door in that weather, are we?" The DS had stopped by the window and was staring out at the bucketing rain.

"You can stay on the phones if you like?"

"You win. What's the story?"

"You and I are going to the hospital to speak to Rowdy Burns."

"Oh," said Macpherson, perking up. "Are we stopping for grapes?"

❖ ❖ ❖

"Thanks, Doc. You shouldn't have."

Detective Constable Erin Reilly accepted the offered plastic cup of tea.

"Aye well, don't be going all dewy eyed on me till you taste it. Don't know how people are supposed to get better drinking this pi—"

"Hi, Erin, you doing okay? You look knackered?" Taylor interrupted her sergeant's diatribe on the tea's merit and greeted the young DC.

"I'm fine thanks, guv," said Reilly. The DC looked barely out of her teens, but the sweet innocent looks and ruffled blonde bob were a deceptive veneer under which hid a tough and street-smart investigator. Macpherson emptied the remnants of his own tea into a stainless steel water fountain and jettisoned the crumpled cup into a waste bin tucked behind some blue anti-microbial curtains.

"Don't suppose you've a fresh pair of knickers there too, Doc? I feel like I've been living in these clothes for a week and I get the heebie-jeebies hanging around in here. It's all the acquired infection posters and those wee cardboard boke buckets. They creep me out."

"Ah, well…" The detective sergeant, caught out for once, stumbled for a reply.

"Leave him be, Erin. He's in a bad twist today. How's the patient?"

"The doctor isn't long away in. Her nurse told me on the

QT earlier she was doing better. Blood pressure is up and she took some tea. We should be able to see her once the doc's given the once over. You want me to sit in?"

"No, you get yourself off home. It's been a long shift for you. We'll see you tonight and bring you up to speed."

"Thanks, ma'am. Doc," said Reilly, giving Macpherson a wink as she grabbed her jacket from the back of a chair.

"Aye, nighty night, cheeky chops. Away and get your beauty sleep while the rest of us do the heavy lifting."

Reilly laughed as she walked away.

"Erin? What about Burns? No trouble? Visitors?" called Taylor.

"No. All quiet." She stopped and indicated over Taylor's shoulder.

"He's over there in the separate room at the end of a three-bed bay. Slept like a baby, but that might be because they drilled him with enough medication to coop a rhino."

❖ ❖ ❖

"Are you sure he's okay to talk, nurse?"

Taylor and Macpherson peered across the ward to where the hulk of lard that was Richard Burns lay sprawled on a bariatric bed. The man had been no oil painting to begin with, and the past twenty-four hours had done little to improve him, both eyes were almost shut and his upper lip had swollen horrifically, as had his cheek and chin.

"He's a head on him like a football but I can't tell if it's the rattle to his coupon or the fish suppers the bugger's been inhaling," said Macpherson.

"Nurse?" Taylor prompted the staff nurse who sat opposite, scribbling notes at her station.

"Oh, he's fine. It's all superficial. Soft tissue damage, cuts and abrasions. He has lost a few teeth and it will be a while before he's eating properly," she said with a shrug.

"That'll do him the power of good. No brain damage either

then?"

"You're happy he can be questioned?" said Taylor, glaring at her sergeant who continued to stare at the man-mountain.

"Doctor says to fire away but I think that's because she wants rid."

"Mr Burns has that effect on people. Thanks, we won't take too long." Taylor shook the nurse's hand and then mock shoved Macpherson towards the glum figure poking a crust of dried blood from his stubbly moustache.

"Alright there, Rowdy. Wow, you look like one of those tribesmen from the Discovery Channel. You know the ones. Keep a saucer under their lips. You ever see them? My missus is mad for those documentaries. If it's not the soaps, it's one of those National Geographicals or whatever. Jesus, that's a cracker. It's out to there, man!" Macpherson flopped down on the edge of the bed and pantomimed the swelling.

Burns groaned in pain at the vibration. He had been hooked up to paracetamol drip and the canular looked like a feasting insect against the size of his huge hand.

"Sorry, Officer? Can you not sit on the patient's bed, please? Infection control, thank you."

"It's detective sergeant, Florence," said Macpherson, with a smile and wave across the ward. "No bother, it's not like I'm an old man or anything."

"I think she's sweet on you, Rowdy." Macpherson winked, tipping a nod to the scowling nurse as he rose stiffly to stand by the bedside.

"Mr Burns, I'm DI Taylor. My colleague, DS Macpherson, I think you know well enough. We're here regarding the events of last night and would like this to be a voluntary interview so you are not being placed under caution. You are free to leave at any time. Do you understand?"

Burns' belly wobbled as he shifted in the bed which groaned under the bulk. "Hardly likely in thish ssshhtate," he said, the words lisped through swollen lips and exacerbated by the missing teeth.

"Think of the good all this hospital food'll do you, Rowdy. You'll have shrunk to a mountain in no time." Macpherson looked about, aghast. Sudden realisation dawning on him.

"Shite, I forgot your grapes."

"Can I call you Rowdy?" said Taylor. As he shrugged in reply she pulled a chair across, slipping off her jacket and retrieving her notebook from her bag. Rowdy Burns was in a side room of his own. From her position on the hard-backed plastic chair, the DI could see a uniformed constable now sat at the ward entrance replacing Erin Reilly. Taking her time she arranged the notebook on her thigh and gave Burns the chance to work out how he could see her without cricking his neck.

"Have you been at Risky's long?"

"Long enough. Is this is about the boy that did this to me?" It took a moment for Taylor to translate the slobbering speech but she caught up quickly.

"Aye, amongst other things. It's not like someone to get the drop on you, big man," said Macpherson, drawing up his own chair.

Burns shrugged and the bed creaked. The buzzer on the automated drip sounded and after a moment the nurse silenced the alarm and adjusted the flow. Taylor nodded her thanks as she made herself scarce.

"Did you know your assailant? See him before. Maybe had a run-in at the club?" said Taylor.

"He was wearing a mask."

"It looks like he tried to beat you beautiful?"

"I don't like the way he's speaking to me. Am I not the victim here, missus?"

"It's detective inspector, Rowdy. I'm sorry about my

colleague, you'll have to excuse his manners, we were up half the night and spent a good chunk of that with your boss."

"Should I have a brief here?" Rowdy Burns looked lost; in pain, uncomfortable and with none of his back-up in place to talk for him.

"It's a voluntary interview, Rowdy. About the man who assaulted you? We could arrest you and take you down the nick and then you could have a solicitor present but—" Taylor shrugged.

"What did Rab say about it?" interrupted Burns.

"Not a whole lot to be honest," said Taylor.

"Well then. No comment."

"Come on, Rowdy. Let's not be unhelpful."

"I want to speak to Rab."

Macpherson leaned in close to the patient.

"Rab's tattie bread, sunshine."

Burns, visibly shocked, gaped like a landed fish. The little red graph on his monitor upped a notch as did the flashing icons for his heart and respiratory rate. Taylor watched his fat face pale, one of the three chins sinking into the grey tufts poking from under the unflattering hospital gown.

"Anything you want to get off your chest now that might help us get to the bottom of your fat lip and why your boss is lying in a freezer across the road?"

Burns swallowed a few times. Pudgy fingers reached out for the jug of tepid water that sat next to an empty plastic cup on the overbed tray table.

Taylor stood and poured a large slug and handed it to him. He slurped, a good swig running down his bristled chin as he winced, the fluid bloody from damaged gums and teeth.

"Sake," he bristled.

"You're alright, Rowdy. Take your time." Taylor took the glass back off him then refilled it and placed it nearer his hand. Burns collapsed back into the pillows and Taylor returned to her notes as he composed himself.

"Nothing to tell. Was in the office and heard something kicking off outside. Next thing I was waking up here."

"What office?"

"The wee office I use. Out the back of where they take the cash off the punters."

"That's your office?"

"Yes."

"What time was this?"

"Not sure?"

"What time do you start at the club?"

"Seven. Eight?"

"So which? Seven or eight."

"Not sure, eight?"

"What were you doing?"

"Usual."

"The lady isn't a mind reader you nugget? What's usual?" Macpherson barked, raising a hand to placate the nurse who glared over before reaching for the phone on the desk.

"This and that. Shift some drinks up to the bar. Set up any sound gear that's needed and get the security sorted. Spread the word on any recent troublemakers. You know, general stuff."

"Was Rab Millar there?"

"Why?"

"Simple question, Rowdy. He was the organ grinder, wasn't he?" said Macpherson.

"What time do the doors open?" interjected Taylor.

"Ten."

"So were the punters in or not in when this commotion kicked off."

"Aye, they were in right enough."

"So Rab would have been there too, being the face and all?"

Taylor looked at him, pen tapping a beat out on the page, her expression that of a disapproving schoolmistress.

Burns pantomimed a long hard, think.

"Aye, he was right enough now you mention it. I remember because wee Gary told me. He came into the office looking for…" he said, nodding, then catching himself. "Hang on is this an interrogation? What about the shithead did me over? You've hardly asked about that? You want to be out there looking for him not harassing hospital patients." Burns picked up the water then put it back down abruptly, jiggling the drip line that fed into his canular as he wiped a hand across his mouth.

"Who's Gary?"

"Just some wee scrote. Sometimes does the bogs and reds out the bins for a few quid, he was in to be paid," said Rowdy.

"Gary who?"

"Wee Gary."

"Surname."

"Webster, I think. I don't know him that well."

Taylor's mobile beeped. She fished it from her pocket and read the incoming text message then handed the phone to Macpherson so he could be appraised of the information. He placed the phone back in her hand, stony faced.

"So Millar was in but you didn't see him, right?" said Taylor, frowning.

"That's what I said." A curt, confident nod.

"So was this commotion just before or a while before?"

"Before what?" Burns' expression was confused. "I'm tired. All these questions. Am I not concussed or something?" he protested.

"You'll be grand. Nurse says you're right as rain. Better to get this over while it's fresh in your mind. The commotion outside I mean, was it before or after paying this Gary fella?"

said Taylor.

"I didn't give Gary anything alright," retorted Burns.

"Thought he was looking to be paid?" Macpherson's tone now one of exasperation.

Burns sat in surly silence.

"Must have been a bit of a shock?"

"What are you talking about?"

"Black transit in the yard? Great big fire."

"I don't see…"

"Tell me how the van got through that big gate before spontaneously combusting. Assuming that's what all the commotion was about."

"We sometimes have acts on. Bands. Rappers. Guest DJ. Would have been one of them. One of the security lads might have let them in. There's an intercom to the office if I don't see it on the camera."

Taylor pondered and rat-a-tat-tatted her teeth with the end of her pen.

"The camera. It's set up to record isn't it?"

Burns nodded.

"We're trying to get the footage of the club's cameras from last night but no one seems to know the password."

Burns remained silent.

"So, you didn't see it arrive or let it in last night then? Security lads handled it?"

Burns nodded.

"Didn't see how the fire started?"

Another slack-jawed bob of the head.

"So you didn't see the girl either?" said Taylor as she flipped back a few pages in her notes, fixing Burns with a questioning look.

"I…"

"Tell you what it is, Rowdy. We are going to go through a list of employees and we will speak to them all. While we're doing that we are going door to door and canvassing the public. It won't take long to find out what time you were in, who you were with, and if you went for a piss or not. Contrary to popular belief, I'm short on patience so help us out, will you?"

Burns blinked, fat face turning to each detective.

"Why not save me a lot of time and paperwork and tell us the score with the girl? It will help you in the long run."

"No comment."

"Christ, Rowdy. You going down that road? Wind it in for your own sake, man." Macpherson growled.

"We'll be taking that room upstairs apart. What are we going to find?"

"You'll find nothing…"

"Abduction, false imprisonment. I reckon I'll be able to swing GBH with intent, maybe even attempted murder? That's a step up for you."

"No."

"Maybe you just drove. It looks like that, doesn't it?" Taylor turned to Macpherson who nodded.

"You're barking up the wrong tree."

"So put me straight?"

"No comment."

"Rowdy, we know there's more to this…"

"No comment."

"I've a CCTV still here of a van the same as the one burnt out at the back of the club outside a city centre apartment complex. Guess who gets out?" Taylor waggled her phone at him.

Burns shook his head.

"Not a crime is it?"

"What were you doing there?"

"Coming to work."

"Who was the other fella?"

Taylor swiped across. Displaying a new screengrab.

"Is it Gary 'I don't know him that well' Webster?" she said. A shrug.

"And who's this? Singer. Rapper. DJ? You the artist's chauffeur too?" She swiped across a third picture.

Burns looked at the image. Grainy as it was there was no mistaking his bulk and between him and another male was the slight figure of a girl.

"I'd advise you to talk, Rowdy, because now we have this I will dig and if your boss was still alive he would tell you, I'm like a bitch with a bone when that starts."

Burns blinked. Staring at the picture. He started to speak but it turned into a strangled croak.

"No comment."

"Do you hold a firearms licence?" said Taylor.

"What?"

"I wouldn't think so. I've your rap sheet here—"

"What?"

"Started early. Three burglaries and a dangerous driving with no insurance. Intelligence taken into consideration and return of goods saw the charges dropped. Three counts of assault later earned you a stretch inside, then riotous assembly, drunk and disorderly at a flag protest. Will I keep going with the drug-related offences?"

"That's me done talking without a brief."

"We recovered a weapon at the scene. Do you know how it got there?"

"I was out of it. I can't help you." Burns' fat hands slapped the bedsheets.

"Between us, we have your prints on it and it's looking a cert it was the one that gunned down Rab Millar," said Taylor.

"You see all this tells us you know more than you're letting on? CCTV quality isn't great, but there's you and that's the girl we found badly beaten beside the body of your boss. You see the problem?"

"Were you sweet on the wee girl, big man? Start having a wee fantasy you could be Richard Gere but she gave you the knockback or were you trying out for a transfer? Did someone else put you up to it? You after a wee change of employment?" said Macpherson.

Burns reached to his hand and ripped the canular out, blood spraying up the sheets as he wildly swung his bulk in a vain attempt to get out of bed. Alarms began to bleep and the nurse leapt to her feet.

"Pigs, you've got fuck all—" The drip stand crashed to the floor.

Taylor's seat clattered over as she leapt to her feet and shoved the big man in the solar plexus, momentum carrying him across the bed and into a heap on the floor. The warning alarms now rose to a wail.

Macpherson knelt, taking the bleeding hand and bending back the wrist joint. As he twisted the arm, Burns bellowed in pain, as the sound of rapid footfalls approached. The two uniforms arrived at the door as Burns writhed around in an attempt to stand. The PCs were pulling out extendable batons but Taylor waved them off.

"Don't make it worse, Rowdy."

Burns kicked out his feet like a petulant child.

Macpherson released him and the big man crashed against the bed, his breathing ragged and wheezy, his fight spent. Taylor reached out a hand and beckoned for the PC's cuffs.

"Richard Burns, I am placing you under arrest for possession of an illegally held firearm with intent to endanger life. You do not have to say anything but it may harm your defence if you fail to mention when questioned something you later rely on in court."

## Chapter 10

There was a vast contrast between the chaotic scenes they had left and the one into which they now walked.

The water, bedclothes, and patient monitoring equipment had been strewn across the floor and the warbles and hoots of disconnected systems added to the disorientated melee as they had hauled Rowdy Burns, in none too gentle fashion, from the floor and dumped him back onto the bed like a large sack of spuds.

The little nurse had launched into a tirade against the officers and in particular Macpherson, who drew the bulk of her ire as he tried in his own inimitable fashion to placate her.

Following the arrival of more staff, order had been restored and the two detectives were hustled out of the room with sharp words from the charge nurse following them across the floor.

Now they stood in a similar room, but with a vastly different atmosphere.

The air smelled of lemons, but the deodorant wasn't quite strong enough to remove the trace of the plastic bed sheets or the scent of antiseptic.

Midnight blue floor tiles and walls that the brochure would describe as Navajo White or Heavy Cream were scuffed where the door had rubbed and the back of the bed had agitated the plaster.

The overly made-up face of a television presenter and her seated guests mutely surveyed the scene from the set on the opposite wall with the ticker tape somewhat clairvoyantly announcing today's topic as 'Domestic Violence. When is it time to leave?'.

The girl on the bed was sleeping, carried off on a lullaby of soft beeps from the machines monitoring her vitals and the hiss of the radiators. She snored lightly. Snuffling, raspy breaths due to her nasal cavity being bunged up with bloody scabs. Her face had all the telltale signs of having taken a good beating. A tramline of paper stitches lay over a cut eyebrow, both eyes were blackening, her lip was split and thin faux-tanned arms lay atop the sheets, bruised, the skin marbling up like petrol pooled in a puddle.

"I'm not asleep."

"We're sorry to disturb you. My name is Detective Inspector Taylor. Veronica. This is DS Macpherson."

"Lena. Lena Borodenko."

"Do you feel up to a few questions, Lena?"

"I don't know how I feel. I'm sore, so I am."

The girl's accent was somewhere Eastern European, coupled with the flatter vowels and vocabulary of a local.

"I'm sure. Is there anything we can get for you?"

Lena shook her head, the movement making her wince. A hand searched down the side of the bed.

"Could you hand me that up?"

Macpherson traced the spiralled cable and passed her the small handheld controller that had fallen between the side rails of the bed. The skin of her hands was scraped and dried blood was ground into the crevices of her knuckles. Coral red gel tip nails were cracked with two missing on her left hand. She keyed a button and with the hum of motors and the hydraulic whine of pistons, she moved herself into a more upright position.

"We need to talk to you about what happened to you and Mr Millar."

The girl's head moved almost imperceptibly.

"Lena, the only address we have is care of Sanctuary Care and Refuge. Is there anyone else we can contact for you? Let them know you're safe?"

"No."

"Okay. Now forgive me, but I also have you recorded as being cautioned for possession of a Class A drug and contempt of court. You didn't show up for a hearing?"

"That was ages ago. I had to go home because my father was ill. I did community service like they asked and paid the fine. It got me my place in Sanctuary. They helped me after… after my troubles."

"I'm sorry to hear that. Is your father better now?"

"He died."

"My condolences. I know these questions sound mundane, but I'm just confirming details. Can you tell me why you left the care of Sanctuary?"

"It became unnecessary." She paused, looking awkward. "I was grateful for the help, it's just." Her brow furrowed, looking for the words. "I cannot explain."

"That's okay. Can you tell me where you have been living since you left?"

Borodenko seemed to shrink. Her black eyes welling with tears.

"Apartment seven oh six. Speakers Square."

Macpherson let out a low whistle.

"That's a nice spot. Are you riverside?"

"Yes, it was the penthouse over the square," said Lena.

"It was?" said Taylor.

"It is," she said in a small voice.

"But…"

"But I do not think I will live there anymore."

Taylor gave her a tight, supportive smile.

"We'll look at contacting the landlord on your behalf. Get you back in there to collect any belongings?"

"Go back?" The girl's bloodshot eyes widened a little further, the white of the left a dark web of broken capillaries.

"You wouldn't be going alone," said Taylor with a

reassuring nod.

The girl looked anything but happy at the thought. Even under the black eyes and cuts, Taylor could see the girl was pretty. Young, pretty, and vulnerable. It didn't take much to realise why Millar had sucked her into his orbit.

"That was quite a step up from sheltered living accommodation, Lena?" said Taylor as she scratched the address down.

"It was a perk of my employment."

"Which is?" Taylor hated making her spell it out.

"I was a hostess in the Thirty-One Club."

"I don't know it."

"No reason you would. It's a Gentleman's Club, isn't it, missy? Swanky one at that," said Macpherson, suddenly interested.

"You go there?" said Lena, eyes now suspicious.

Macpherson gave a short, derisory laugh.

"No, girl. I'm a brave few rungs down the ladder to be highfalutin in places like that, let me tell you."

"You know it though?" said Taylor.

"Oh, aye. Old school tie brigade, funny handshakes and roll up the trouser leg stuff. What! What!"

The girl smiled despite herself at the detective sergeant's plummy impression.

"How long have you been working there, Lena?"

"Eighteen months."

"Were you there last night?"

"I was supposed to be."

"So how did you up in Risky's nightclub?"

"Don't be telling us it was for a wee dance and a few Bacardi Breezers either," Macpherson added with a wink.

"Millar. Is he dead?"

She again avoided the question with one of her own, but with a resignation in her eyes that led Taylor to let the silence hang between them.

"I…" The girl looked at her hands, another tear bloomed and rolled down her cheek.

"Did you work for Robert Millar?" Macpherson prodded.

A slow nod as she wiped away the tear.

"After these things. Drugs. Court. I was low, you know? Desperate." She indicated the paperwork.

"I had my place in the scheme, and they had me on programmes to help me find a job. I cleaned some houses but it became… difficult."

"How so?"

"Sometimes the ladies of the house, they are not kind to girls like me."

Taylor could appreciate the narrow-minded attitudes the girl would have faced from the well-heeled wives club. She could also imagine the effect a lithe young girl may have on the more liberal husbands and why she, as opposed to they, had endured any ire.

"One girl, she knew I was unhappy with the situation. She introduced me to a man in a bar. I got hours there dancing and made some extra money. I felt I had found some independence, and I didn't want to go back to that place."

"To Sanctuary?"

Lena nodded, eyes on the television.

"When I met Mr Millar, he was good to me. Offered me job, good money and after a while nice place to live."

"This was while working at the Thirty-One Club?"

"Not at first. A little later."

"What exactly was your role there?"

"Robert Millar was a businessman. He had his contacts, and they done business. Afterwards, there were parties."

"At which you were encouraged to show his guests a good time?" said Taylor.

"I am young. Attractive. I show these men a fun evening.

Entertain them, flatter them, make them feel good about spending money on their deals."

"Did you have to sleep with them?"

"Not all of them, no."

"Forgive me for cutting to the chase, but to be clear, Millar had hired you as a prostitute for his business parties."

"An escort," Lena corrected, "It wasn't just sex. I am an adult. I have had lovers. So what if I made money from it?"

"Were these men from the Thirty-One Club?"

"Sometimes."

"There were others?"

Lena shrugged again.

"I've seen dozens of girls like you, Lena. Seduced by the glamour, the attention and the lifestyle. I've seen nearly every one succumb to addiction, abuse or worse."

Lena gave a resigned sigh.

"What kind of business deals were these?"

"I was not part of those. They talked in other rooms while myself and other girls made the party ready."

"So you know nothing of what went on?"

"I have suspicions, but what do I do. I am there to do my job."

"Look where that's got you. How did we get from these fancy parties to here, Lena?"

"Some of these people, they are not people of class. Foreign men. Men who Mr Millar had dealings with. I am only meat to them and when I complain and he tells me this business is important. He will compensate me for the trouble."

"He did that alright," muttered Macpherson.

Lena lowered her gaze, studying the scratched and bloody knuckles.

"What did you suspect was going on?"

"I know that sometimes there was gambling. Some other times, drugs."

"What happened to make Millar do this to you? Did something happen at one of these parties?"

"Millar did not beat me."

"Well, you didn't do it to yourself," said Taylor.

There was a prolonged silence in which the only noise was the machine's artificial beeps and Lena's raspy breathing.

"Lena, help me understand what happened last night. We know you were picked up because we have CCTV footage."

Tears fell again, and she didn't attempt to halt them.

"Can you tell us who they were?"

"One was Rowdy. Ricky Burns. He was Millar's minder. You know, never far away. I did not know the other."

"Just to make sure we are talking about the same man, can you describe him?"

"Younger than me. Twenty, maybe younger. Thin. Dirty fair hair. They called him Gary."

"Great, Lena. Tell me what happened as far back as waking up yesterday morning until the paramedics arrived."

Lena described in emotionless and stunted words how an expected cash call had turned into a forced abduction and beating, fists balling in the sheets as she described her pleas but receiving no explanations or recriminations. She broke off, Macpherson offering her some water and flinched as the act of drinking cracked her scabbed lips.

Taylor scratched notes and the tangents they raised to explore later in her neat sloping style, pausing, as Lena described Millar's dismissal of her abuser and then his subsequent torture and rape threats and the timely intrusion which may have saved her life.

Lena shrank back into the mattress.

"Have you any idea who that man was?"

"No."

"Did he say anything? Indicate why he was there?"

"Not really. He just told Millar to stop and then shot him. I just remember the blood." The girl put her hands over her face and the measurements on the monitors took a leap as her hands trembled.

"Lena, it's okay. You're safe now. There are officers outside. No one is going to come in here."

"You think I believe that! That man, he shouldn't have been able to kill Robert Millar. What if he comes back for me?"

"Have you any reason to believe that?"

She hesitated.

"If you have any idea, any inclination at all it will help."

"What if he thinks I can tell you who he was? What if he meant to kill me too?"

"Lena, please take a breath." Taylor slid closer on her chair and placed a hand on the bed. Macpherson cast a furtive glance at the ward bay behind. Disinclined to get into a second round with the charge nurse.

"Do you think it was any of the men who associated with Millar at these functions?"

"I can't say. He was wearing a mask, I tried not to look."

"Okay. Thanks. You've done well. I think we'll let you get some rest."

Lena blinked away more tears, sniffing painfully.

"Honestly, you are safe here. The officers will be outside. I'm putting my card here. If anything at all comes to you just ask the nurse to contact me."

"Yes. Okay."

"Do you have anyone we can call?"

A shake of the head. Vacant stare at the ceiling.

"Would you reconsider a return to Sanctuary? Once the medical team says you're fit to leave? I can have them make an approach."

Lena Borodenko dropped her chin onto her chest, hair falling across her face, shoulders sagging.

"I don't know…"

"I'm sure they will be happy to have you back considering, Lena. Look, I'll ask the ward social workers to make enquiries and I'll have someone pick up some of your things. Is that alright with you? Make sure you get some rest and if you remember anything else…" Taylor gestured to the card.

The girl bobbed her head in gratitude although to Macpherson, stood back quietly observing, the sincerity of the gesture didn't quite match her body language.

## Chapter 11

Malcolm Howard smoothed his sideburns and swept a parting in his hair. Regarding himself in the mirror, he smiled. The reflection staring back had the satiated glow of a man who had enjoyed yet another guilt-free indulgence. Not too shabby, he thought, appraising himself. Greying hair from a well-developed chest peeked from under his white shirt as he fastened the last three buttons. Approaching fifty-five, although his belly had not the tightness of his youth, it was still not the overhanging edifice that was the ruination of many of his peers because, with a voracious appetite for indulgence and gluttony, Howard also knew there was a requirement for balance and control.

He tempered fine wine and haute cuisine with his morning trips to a Cultra health club. The sweat and endorphin rush had thus far kept the spread at bay, although in recent months he was relying more on the sauna than the spin bike to keep trim. This afternoon's bout of sex was a far more enjoyable way to burn the calories off the morning's exquisite breakfast pastries.

Never judge a book by its cover, he reflected again. Jane Richards had proved much more than the plain exterior presented to the world. He could not remember their first introduction many months ago, but then the ordinary and under-ornamented woman was hardly his usual fare. Unsure just how she had inveigled herself to him, he looked across at her supine form in the reflection of a mirror as she slept off their exertions. The bedroom door was ajar. She lay on the bed, the severe sixties matronly updo of that morning unleashed, and long dirty blonde locks spread over her shoulders and down the naked curve of her spine. Perhaps he had just seen the inner sensuality and provoked it to the surface. Yes, she was certainly a find, he decided.

The vibration of his phone interrupted his thoughts of her straddling him. His car had arrived and, focusing once again on his reflection, he withdrew from his pocket the patterned silk Ferragamo tie that had been a gift from his wife and placed it around his neck. Tie fastened, he shrugged on his jacket and appraised himself one last time in the mirror.

As he was about to leave his phone buzzed again. He hesitated. Number withheld. Exiting and closing the door behind him without a second thought to the woman inside, he put the phone to his ear.

"Malcolm Howard, speaking."

❖ ❖ ❖

"Mr Howard? Veronica Taylor. Thanks for meeting us."

"Inspector, my pleasure. It's nice to put a face to the name." Malcolm Howard accepted the offered hand as Taylor introduced her colleague.

"Detective Sergeant Macpherson."

Introductions covered, Malcolm Howard presented the way into the gilded lobby of the apartment dwelling with a dramatic open-palmed gesture.

"We're sorry for troubling you personally. I had contacted the agency, and they said they would speak directly to the owner."

"My wife is Daphne Morrow. It's not the first time similar confusion has arisen."

"I see, so this is her property?"

"This building and the one next door are part of Morrow and Burke's portfolio. Well, old Jamie Burke is no more, but she kept the name. Ever the sentimentalist, my wife."

The large double-fronted door opened into a marbled porch, and then into the lavish lobby of the Speakers Square development. High ceilings and recessed lighting greeted them, the walls covered in rich mahogany panelling and dressed with gilt-framed mirrors and paintings. At regular intervals, small sconces with muted downlighters showed off their contents of elaborate objet d'art in tones of jade and gold.

"It's quite something, isn't it?" Howard smoothed his tie as he regarded the expressions of the two detectives.

"How the other half live, eh?" said Macpherson, stooping to regard a foot tall flame-haired nude.

"It's a tribute to Botticelli's Venus," said Howard.

"You don't say? My missus loved the other big lad, God rest him. Pavarotti, you know? Could never get into that classical stuff myself."

Macpherson stood back and puffed out his cheeks.

"I tell you what, I've no great eye for art, Councillor, but that's not half bad for a blind fella."

"Was Morrow and Burke, the primary developer, Councillor Howard?" said Taylor.

The bemused Howard took a second to draw his eye from Macpherson who, shaking his head in wonder, had strolled further along to appraise the other artefacts.

"Lord, no. This place went up in the height of the boom years. It wasn't until much later they began their own developments from the ground up. Back then the company acted as managing agents for the developers and the buyers." He paused, checking the lower lip of one frame with the tip of a finger, pouting at the thin trace of dust that came away. "It offered a ripe financial reward without getting your hands dirty, so to speak." He removed a pristine white handkerchief and cleaned his fingertip. "I can't recall who, but they appointed Morrow and Burke straight off the bat. They look after most of the prestige complexes in the city. I'm sure Daphne's office could check for you. You don't mind me asking why you're here exactly?"

"We following up on the assault of a tenant and we need access to the apartment?"

"My goodness. There was a break-in?"

"No. Nothing like that."

"So do I need to see a warrant or something?"

Taylor and Macpherson exchanged a look.

"We were seeking some cooperation from the landlord, Councillor. I could have a warrant arranged?"

"Of course you could. Of course. I'm sure it's fine without, I just thought you may have procedures to follow."

"We have the tenant's permission to recover some personal items," said Taylor.

"Well then, follow me. What number was it?"

"Seven oh six."

Howard's finger hovered over the lift call button for just a second, then pressing the button he turned and beckoned them forward.

"The penthouse suite. All the way up then. This way, please."

They stepped out on the seventh floor into a lobby of thickly piled walnut carpet, tastefully matching the walls, panelled in the same oiled wood as the lobby, and a crystal chandelier dominated the space. The lobby was four metres square; bulkheads with hidden lighting showed off several other works of art and two doors led off.

"There's two penthouses?" said Macpherson, taking in the high ceilings and nodding in appreciation at the woodwork.

"Just the one, Sergeant. During construction, the client bought up the two that were on spec and rolled them into one property. There is a rooftop garden, and the balcony wraps around the whole north-east corner of the building. Please, come in and see for yourself."

Howard had removed a key card from the recesses of his jacket and swiped it against the access reader beside the penthouse door. Taylor stepped in as he made for the handle.

"Councillor. Sorry, do you mind?"

Howard snapped into an awkward rigid posture with a horrified expression.

"You don't think…"

"Not at all, but if you could please refrain from touching anything that would be appreciated."

As he nodded his acquiescence, Taylor, having donned a pair of nitrile gloves, pushed the door open and paused in the opening. Silence but for the hum of the overhead spotlights and the occasional clack, whirr, ping of the lift.

"Hello? Police?"

No reply returned.

They entered a bright hallway of polished beech floors and immaculate ivory white walls. By the door was a coat rack under which were scattered several pairs of shoes, designer trainers and a couple of pairs of heels. A golf umbrella lay at an awkward angle against the wall. Taylor led the way with confident strides until they entered an open-plan living area. The panoramic windows allowed unrestricted views out over the city, south across the centre and west to the looming dark smudge of the Black Mountain and the supine face of the Cavehill, then east across the River Lagan, a dark green ribbon threading out to the lough.

The living area was tidy. A few magazines lay on a coffee table and a trashy celebrity tabloid was abandoned on one sofa, across the back of which a couple of faux fur throws had been draped.

It was homely. Lived in. A half-empty bottle of Chardonnay and one glass sat beside the sofa, a dribble left in the bottom suggesting the drinker had planned to return to it sooner rather than later. Taylor decided there was nothing to suggest what she was seeing was someone's sanitised version of Lena's home comforts.

"It's an incredible space, isn't it?" said Howard, peering out across the city.

"Quite the view," agreed Taylor.

"You've been here before, Councillor?"

Malcolm Howard watched the traffic, red tail lights stretching towards what had been the old Sailortown. Dilapidated warehousing was scattered between regenerated student accommodation and a burgeoning media city, high-end apartments, and office high-rises.

"Oh yes. Several times."

"In what capacity, sir?"

Howard turned to regard the two detectives. Macpherson was flicking through the magazines, gloved fingertips skimming the loose leaves of paper.

"Just as I've accommodated you today, I have carried out similar duties in the past to help out."

"Would any of those been lately?"

"Several months ago. I was here to let in a plumber. There had been a complaint about a drain blockage."

"Do you know the young woman who lived here?"

"I do not."

Howard shifted, turning his back on the panorama, arms crossed and a scowl on the edge of his expression.

"I thought you wished to view the property and collect some items. This feels a little like I'm being questioned, Inspector, and it's quite irregular."

"Any complaints from other residents over strange comings and goings? Parties? Arguments?" said Taylor, continuing to scan the room for any outward sign of things being out of place.

"Could you perhaps elaborate on that question, Detective Inspector?"

"We are trying to build a picture of the victim's background. If perhaps elements of her lifestyle played a part in her assault," she said.

"I see. Well, again, apologies, but I wouldn't know."

Taylor nodded.

"The property is quite secure, entrance PIN, key cards, intercom. I'd like to know if there were any means of access that hadn't been returned and see a copy of the CCTV."

"I could raise the query. Shall I call now?"

Taylor smiled and declined, removing a business card from her jacket.

"You'll get me on either of those numbers. It all looks in order in here. Do you mind if we look around the rest of the property?"

Howard looked at the card for several seconds and then in a nonplussed manner waved his agreement and flopped onto the sofa.

The polished beech floors ran throughout, as did the full-height windows and tasteful decor. The penthouse was spartan but not sterile with custom furnishings and artwork neatly arrayed in display cases and bespoke niches.

"What do you think?" said Macpherson as Taylor approached.

"Bit above what my salary would stretch to!"

"And the rest. So, excuses that we're being good Samaritans aside, what are we looking for exactly?"

"Anything that might be odd. This isn't just going to be home. Millar didn't have her shacked up here for nothing. We'll hit a stone wall if we try to get information on the parties he held at the Thirty-One Club, but it's not inconceivable that sometimes it drifted back here."

"Are you hoping for a wall full of photographs?"

"Or a little black book."

"Dear diary? Good luck with that," said Macpherson with a chuckle.

"Something happened to get Millar riled up. You never

know what might be lying around. Jesus, this is some place."

The two detectives peered into a double bathroom. It was exquisitely tiled in marble with a huge copper tub in the centre, double handbasin and walk-in shower. A mirror reflected the space was pristine in its cleanliness, and there wasn't a speck of dust on the gloss tiled floor either.

"Bedroom?"

"Lead the way," said Macpherson, finishing his search of the dressing gown pocket on the back of the door.

The corridor continued to circuit the apartment and then ended at a set of double doors that opened into the master suite.

"I think it's fair to say this is the office, then," said Macpherson.

The two crossed the threshold into what was an opulent suite, the centrepiece of which was a king size bed with plump pillows and plush sheets. A chaise longue divided the space between the bed and a door that she could see led to an en suite. The decor was dark and sensuous. Deep mahogany and reds. The walls, papered in an expensive damask, held elegant gold frames of nudes and couples in coitus.

"It's looks cleaned and staged," Taylor observed as they made a circuit of the space.

She opened the doors of a matching mahogany wardrobe.

"Have a look at this?"

Rather than the expected drawers, shelves and rails of clothes, the unit held enough paraphernalia of the world's oldest profession to make a Bishop blush. Shelves of sex toys and lubricants, a bowl of condoms. Eye masks, blindfolds and, supported by hooks across the back frame, various rods, crops and whips. Propped incongruously on an upper shelf between a long red wig and a pair of elbow-length black latex gloves was a nun's headdress.

"Take's all sorts," muttered Macpherson.

Taylor closed the door, and they continued to look around.

Another cabinet housed a temperature-controlled wine fridge and a collection of crystal decanters and heavy matching glasses. Half a dozen bottles of premium champagne were chilling. Macpherson nosed the neck of one decanter like a practised sommelier.

"Oh, that's the stuff alright," he said.

Taylor continued to explore.

The en suite was just as sterile as the bedroom. Another porcelain tub and double walk-in shower; the faint hint of jasmine and sparkling surfaces.

"It's a stone's throw from the courts to here. That and the big media and law firms down by city quays," said Macpherson.

Taylor gave him a warning look. They were well away from the lounge, but it wasn't a line of enquiry she wanted Councillor Howard to take away to entertain the local government lunchroom with. They left the master suite and continued their circuit around the other side of the penthouse.

"They didn't set her up here to cater to the readers of the back pages of a mucky magazine. Have you any contacts in vice we could lean on for background?"

"Maybe. Let me think," said Macpherson.

The second bedroom suite wasn't as grand but still comprised a generous space on the north-east corner with its own en suite. This time it resembled a well-lived in hotel room. There was a wheeled suitcase beached on its back in one corner with the lid closed down but swathes of material bursting from within, a sweatshirt sleeve, laces from a training shoe, one leg of ripped denim jeans.

A dresser and wardrobe held the rest of the owner's collection of clothes and shoes.

The bed in the corner was made up but messy. Scatter

cushions had been propped up against the headboard and the rippled duvet showed a telltale hollow from where someone had sat on it. The remote control for the flat-screen television and a handbag sized pack of tissues lay marooned in the middle.

The low afternoon sun streamed in through tilted blinds and dust motes floated in the air. With the years Taylor had under her belt, she could get a sense about people from their space. As an observer and an invader into their most private sanctuaries, her job was to piece together the fragile threads of a life. Who they were, how they lived, who they loved. This time she could confirm those observations with a living witness, but more often than not the person could never tell her themselves.

Taylor flicked through disordered clothing rails; casual wear and cocktail dresses mixed with gym clothes. Trainers, flats and skyscraper heels shoved in the bottom in no particular order creating a nightmare of organisation.

"Are you grabbing a few things?"

"Might as well. It's an excuse to ask her about down the hall and see if she'll give up anything else. Throw me that bag."

Macpherson reached down and passed across a black and pink Nike sports bag. Taylor hefted it, checking the contents which amounted to a towel, shower gel and a few elastic hair bobbles. She left the contents and added a couple of sweatshirts and sports leggings and a pair of jeans and training shoes. As she moved aside a pile of folded tee shirts, her knuckles hit something hard. Digging in, she slid out a thin laptop computer.

Macpherson busied himself checking the few books that lay by the bed and looking through the contents of the bedside drawer which held a couple of bills and the detritus of emptied pockets.

"Do you have an evidence bag?"

"What?"

"An evidence bag?"

"Ronnie, we don't even have a warrant. Put it back."

Taylor shrugged.

"She might want to check her Facebook or something."

"You're a terrible liar. Here." Macpherson pulled a folded ziplock bag from his inner pocket and passed it across. Taylor slid the PC inside and placed it in the holdall, then went to the en suite to grab a few more bits, leaving Macpherson to continue his search of the drawers and windowsills.

Toiletries, a collection of toothbrushes and some bottles of liquid make-up and powders dotted the rim of the sinks, and a huge mirror that reflected the space was dotted with dried water droplets.

Taylor opened the drawers of the vanities and had a quick rummage. Standard fare. Some similar brands to her own, some top end. She selected several small items. A face wash and wipes, a few bottles of make-up and a roll-on deodorant which she set to one side. Stepping on the pedal of a small bin, she peered inside. Disused wipes, a few cotton buds.

"Doc?"

"Did you find something?" Macpherson moved into the doorway, an expectant look on his face.

"Maybe."

Taylor dipped a gloved hand into the pedal bin and as she drew out the object, Macpherson let out a low whistle.

"Is it happy news?"

The pedal bin clanged closed.

"It hasn't turned out to be."

Taylor held up the pregnancy test to the light. No ambiguity of one stripe or two. Just one word.

Pregnant.

## Chapter 12

A persistent mizzle coated the windscreen in a haze of fine droplets, obscuring the view of the darkening street to a blur of smeared and streaked neon and diffused orange orbs as the streetlights illuminated. Window wipers heehawed across the glass in a juddering motion.

"Chinese or Indian?"

The speaker lifted a coffee cup from the centre panel and shook it for the twentieth time to find it was still empty. He sighed, craning his neck in search of relief from the hours coupled up in the passenger seat, observing precisely nothing at all.

"Are you listening to me? Come on, let's jack this in. It's pointless."

"We've at least an hour left. I'm not getting a flea in the ear from Rollins just because you can't be arsed finishing a shift."

Police Constable Johnny Beck tweaked the wiper baton and the juddering heehaw smeared the rain away just enough to see out the front window of the liveried Police Service of Northern Ireland Land Rover.

"What about last week when we had to babysit that old, dead girl until the funeral directors turned up?"

"What about it?"

"'Don't worry about booking in the OT, lads. Inspector's having a badger about the budgets. Sound familiar? Your super Sarge Rollins used the old swings and roundabouts one, didn't he? Well, come on. It's round about time we pissed off for a few beers." Adrian McNarry tapped on the gear stick.

"Aidy, we've only another hour."

"We've sat here all day and hardly a sinner has come or

gone. Waste of resources is what this is."

Beck shook his head and bit back a response. It had been a long and fruitless shift.

The two constables sat in the cab of the Land Rover parked up at the end of a typical Belfast Street. The road cut an arterial route through the estate of red brick terraces, some with gaudy garden furniture in their front passages and more than not flying the Union Jack or the variation of a theme of the Ulster Defence Association or the Ulster Volunteer Force flag.

A shop on the corner had done a roaring trade over lunch and when the kids kicked out of school, its windows now illuminated and misted with condensation. A little further up on the opposite side of the street, busier than the convenience, was a bookies that clung like a limpet to their target building, the three-storey corner premises dwarfed by the three high-rises that loomed a few blocks and a barren, scorched field away.

With its whitewashed walls dirty from traffic spray and neglected upkeep, 'the Corners' wasn't a salubrious drinking establishment. Instead, under the neon advertisements for Guinness and Harp Lager, it was proudly and resolutely a Loyalist drinking den. The mural on one wall was of a masked warfighter and the UDA banners hanging over barred windows clarified this wasn't the place for a quiet drink with a lassie or to watch the Monday night footie. That being said, the patrons of the place enjoyed both those pastimes, albeit they were just that. Patrons. Fully paid up and dyed in the wool members of the balaclava brigade and woe betide the stranger who walked through the frosted glass saloon doors.

"Ten minutes then?"

"Will you give over? I'm not here for the good of my health either, you know. You any idea the shit we'll get into if we rock away and something kicks off?"

"Catch yourself on. I heard that shooting was an in-house job, anyway."

"Really? You heard that?" Beck didn't bother to contain the sarcasm.

"I did, aye. Anyway, there's no chance this lot are going to start up over a waster like Millar."

"Why's that then?"

"You soft in the head? One reason only. Money. Have you any idea how much Stormont threw at them to stop killing each other. Millions. Millions. And what did they spend it on? Finest Columbian marching powder and as many dodgy business start-ups they could get the forms for."

"Piss off."

"You know Andy White from traffic? His missus works in the civil service and wrote the cheques."

"Were they running a sweepstake the day you got let into the police?"

"I'm telling you. Nothing kept those two firms apart like a river of free fifty-quid notes."

"Nothing to do with the threat of a bullet in the head sending the Mad Monk across the water?"

McNarry raised his middle finger.

Billy McBride, the Mad Monk, had been brigadier and chief of active operations in the UVF wing's notorious nutting squad. Outspoken, violent and self-serving, he hadn't baulked at the cold-blooded gunning down of Republican or Loyalist alike as long as it furthered his grip on the drugs trade in the east. The press and the politicians were in an uproar as his exploits grew in audacity and took the headlines away from the success of the Good Friday Agreement and the focus that was on ratifying a power-sharing devolved government. The situation had only been curtailed when fellow brigadier and quartermaster Gordon

Beattie had reportedly put a blowtorch to his balls and told him if he wasn't on the overnight ferry, a few singed pubes and the police would be the least of his worries.

"Charlie, Sierra, One, One. Control. Over."

Beck returned the gesture and keyed the receiver.

"One, One receiving."

"One, One. You are stood down, confirm receiving. Over."

"Charlie, Sierra, One, One. Received. RTB?"

"Roger, One, One. Return to Base. Control out."

McNarry slapped the dash.

"Get the boot down, boy," he smiled gleefully as Beck nudged the big beast into first gear.

"Someone's looking down on me at last. First pint's on me if you get us back before seven."

❖ ❖ ❖

The police wagon grunted out a gout of filthy black smoke as it roared past. Although partially obscured by the heavy, scratched Plexiglas windscreen, the man that walked in the opposite direction observed the two officers smiling and joking.

Fuck sake, he thought, what's the world coming to when the peelers are out and about like it's a Sunday drive. As he paced along the footpath, he reminisced on the old days when fear stalked the streets and barely a night went past when fresh-faced tossers like the two roaring back to barracks would be picking up body parts from bomb blasts or scraping up the remains of a punishment shooting. Now it was all grassroots engagement and proactive problem-solving. Policing in a new era. What a load of balls.

He smiled grimly, pace slowing as a figure exited the bar ahead and moved away from him up the street. A memory niggled in the back of his head. He had only the blink of an eye to register the man's profile, but still deep in his dead soul a nerve jangled. He pushed the thought aside and shoved his hands deep in his pockets as he looked up at the aged and worn signage of the bar. He remembered vividly the last time he was in. It hadn't ended well.

The door to the public bar squealed on crippled hinges, a banshees warning wail to announce the arrival of ill tidings. The old wooden floorboards were smooth and black by years of abuse, the ceiling still nicotine yellow. A familiar warmth in the atmosphere, the smell of stale beer and piney disinfectant from the open door of the toilets. A couple of televisions droned and a handful of punters watched a re-run of the weekend's old firm game or leaned expectantly over the long bar, eyes narrowed, brows furrowed in concentration as they tried to pick out their horse in one of a dozen track meets.

"Can I help you?"

The speaker was a young enough lad to be forgiven for not recognising the visitor, but age was no excuse for leniency.

"Fuck off, son," said the man, shifting his direction of travel to move around the youth.

He was a big lad, but soft through the middle. All show, hooped earrings and tattoos, not like the hard, lean scrappers of the eighties. He sidestepped and with an intimidatory expression put up a meaty hand to stay the visitor's passage.

"Are you deaf, mister? I said…"

Chairs clattered and at least one glass toppled to smash at the shock of the inhuman howl that reverberated through the bar.

Lumbering up to his full height, intent on using his bulk to discourage further disobedience, the young lad missed the hand that snaked out and struck him in the face. Two stiff fingers jabbed in the soft flesh of the right eye socket. A whip across the face and as the hand returned, thumb and forefinger grabbed a plated gold earring and tore it clean from the earlobe.

The big lad wheeled away, folded in two.

"Jesus Christ, Freaky. There was no need for that!"

The barman had placed his towel down and moved to raise the hatch.

"No manners, the youth of today."

"You're a vicious bastard."

"Now, now, Barry. Is that any way to welcome an old mucker?"

"You're no mucker of mine."

"You'll shatter a fella's heart. Is he in?"

Barry ignored the question and peered down at the writhing youth.

"Get yourself into the bogs and dry your eyes. You're embarrassing yourself. Jenny, get that mop over here and sort this mess." He raised a hand and snapped his fingers.

Stepping out from a small utility cupboard, hair scrapped back from a pockmarked and pale face, Jenny reached for a mop and steel bucket. Thin white hands took a grip, sinews popping from emaciated arms under the strain of the lift as she moved to clean the blood.

A ramshackle posse spread in a loose semicircle, blocking Freaky Jackson's exit from the bar. The racing commentary now forgotten.

"Sit back down, lads. Drama's over. I'll get you drinks in a minute." Barry returned to his position behind the taps.

"You've some cheek."

"Is he in or what?" said Jackson, tapping on the Guinness pump.

"I'll take one of these while I'm waiting."

Barry's skin had bloomed a hue of crimson. Before he could form a reply, the phone rang. A shrill warble. He plucked it from the cradle; placed it to his ear. An affirmative just audible on the line. Clunked handset back down.

"He'll see you."

"And they said hospitality was dead in here."

"He wants to know you're clean?"

"Tut, tut. What kind of man walks into a parlay with a weapon, Barry. Shame on you."

Barry shrugged as he opened the bar hatch and gestured to a spot against the wall festooned with calendars, football results and cut-outs from the local press.

He patted Jackson down from collar to ankle. Checked pockets and came up with nothing. Not so much as a set of car keys or a wallet.

"What about my drink?"

"Sure, you've no way to pay for it, do you? Up the stairs on the right." Barry Corrigan pointed to the narrow stairway, arms crossed. Resolute.

"I remember the way."

❖ ❖ ❖

"You might have just phoned?"

The two men faced off for a few seconds in silence, weighing the animosity and wondering if time had healed the bitter hate, or did it remain like the ugly disfiguring scars they carried?

"Harry has been trying to get you on the blower and you're unavailable."

"That numpty? I wouldn't give him the time of day. How's Rowdy?"

"Still an ugly bastard."

Duncan McCutcheon grunted and thumped back down in a leather executive chair positioned behind his desk.

"He's had worse."

"Haven't we all. You should've called ahead. You're lucky some of the old guard weren't in or they'd have topped you on sight."

"Now where'd be the sense in that, Chopper? You don't build bridges over the phone. Face to face, that's the way, so it is."

"Take your pick." McCutcheon nodded at the two-seater sofa or the smaller director's chair that sat opposite his own.

Jackson slumped onto the sofa.

"I'd like to say it's a nice place you've got here but it's a bit dated isn't it or are you going for the retro look?"

"You always were an obnoxious prick, Freaky. Sooner you say your piece, the sooner you can crawl back up your master's arse."

Jackson snorted a laugh.

"Beard suits you, by the way. Hides the scar."

McCutcheon didn't rise to it. The years had brought a temperateness to his idealistic passions. His meteoric rise through the youth ranks of the Ulster Young Militants and then with a well-documented career through the senior ranks of the Ulster Defence Association, he had proved himself adept if not exceptional in both modernising and galvanising the organisation after a wave of crisis, murders, expulsions and high-profile arrests. Duncan 'Chopper' McCutcheon had accidentally but not unexpectedly found himself ensconced in the inner sanctum, one of six divisional commanders. Making it to the high table had never been his goal, but it was a calling. To come to the defence of his country and his people. That threat more so now from factions within than enemies of old. He was a stalwart, a bastion of tradition versus the new wave of Loyalist gangster who traded on the name for the sake of instilling fear and intimidation to bolster their veneer of criminality. An everyman with no airs or graces, he was as at home dealing with the likes of Freaky Jackson as he was with the bespoke-suited representatives of the Loyalist political parties or ministers of state when the occasion called for surreptitious negotiation.

"What do you want?" said McCutcheon.

"I want to know if you and your mate the Monk had

anything to do with what happened to Rab."

"What's it to do with you? I thought you'd retired to the country?"

"Don't believe everything you hear."

"You're poking your nose in off your own bat?"

"I didn't say that."

"So the Monster has you back on the leash then?"

"Rab was a mate. So, are you going to play ball?"

"I didn't sanction it."

"That's a bit open ended? What about the Monk?"

McCutcheon held a poker face. Studied the man opposite. Close up, the intervening years were taking a toll on Jackson, that or the lifestyle. He'd noticed similar in himself lately. Maybe it was age, maybe the pressure of position. Heavy is the head that wears the crown, as the saying went.

"What makes you think Billy would risk coming back here?"

"He wouldn't have to come back, would he? He could just get one of his old nutting squad to pay a visit."

"You think he'd wait this long and not do the deed himself?"

"Exile does funny things to your head."

"Does Gordon Beattie still think so much of himself that I'd murder his mate out of the blue to make a point and risk another feud?"

Jackson shrugged.

"Think about it, Freaky. Why not have a pop at the organ grinder rather than go to the trouble of killing the monkey. Seems to me there'd be a bigger message made by topping the new statesman." Johnson snorted.

"You jealous?"

It was McCutcheon's turn to laugh.

"You know me, Freaky, I never wanted the limelight. If Gordon Beattie thinks now the spotlights are on him he's untouchable, he's more delusional than I thought."

"Horses for courses, Chopper. No skin off my nose if he wants to run for first minister. You're sure about the Monk though because I've heard with my own ears he's back in Belfast?"

"From who?" McCutcheon leaned his elbows on the table, interest piqued.

"One of the Albanians."

McCutcheon weighed up the potentialities of what that meant and what might come of the next few minutes. He sat back.

"I'd say I'm absolutely positive the Monk wasn't behind it."

"As sure as that? Has the mad bastard been in touch then?"

McCutcheon remained quiet.

"What are you not saying?" Jackson narrowed his eyes.

McCutcheon pushed his chair back and pulled open a drawer. Jackson stood quickly, taking a pace forward.

"Calm down. If I'd wanted you dead, we wouldn't have got this far. Sit down there." McCutcheon nodded at the chair opposite him. Jackson complied as the UDA commander shifted a keyboard and some paperwork out of the way and placed a brown jiffy bag on the desk.

"Go ahead."

Jackson reached out and lifted the bag.

"What's this? A fucking bung?"

McCutcheon shook his head as Jackson tipped the contents onto the desktop.

"Holy Christ," he whispered as the plastic baggie hit the desktop.

Inside was a single bloody digit. The third finger of a right hand. Not that he was sufficiently adept at anatomy to conclude that so quickly. It was the gold sovereign ring with the inset of a harp and crown that was the dead giveaway.

"Billy?"

"I've made the calls. No one in the know's seen him in a week."

"Fuck."

"Whatever is going on, Freaky, Gordon Beattie needs to know it's bigger than just him."

As the two men stared at each other over the dismembered digit of one of the most ruthless killers they knew, a barrage of gunfire tore into the pub.

## Chapter 13

"Barney, give us another toke on that?"

Billy Webster crooked a finger and reached out to take the joint off his mate. The two sheltered at a distance, in the shadows of an entry watching the Corners Bar. Webster had argued that they should stay in the van, but Freaky Jackson had told them they needed to be closer. He was confident but not reckless, and the possibility he would need them as back-up was on the high side of probability considering the last time he had ventured into the place he'd a hatchet in his hand and message to send.

Webster drew in a deep lungful of marijuana, the gun in his coat pocket a comforting weight as he paced,

"What's taking so long?" Barney Murray chewed a fingernail, this was a step up from keeping dick on street corner drug deals and marshalling dog fights. This was enemy territory, and they both knew strangers stood out like balls on a bitch.

"Billy, someone's coming," hissed Barney.

Webster puffed away. He had already noticed the three younger lads. It was hard to tell ages under the bum fluff beards and tracksuit chic, but they'd probably just left school. The trio swaggered towards the two trespassers with a confidence that belied their age. The street was quiet. No one outside the bookies and the shop just had a few old boys inside shooting the breeze and browsing the racing section of a red-top newspaper. Somewhere in the distance, the high-powered growl of a motorcycle echoed off the red brick walls.

Webster glanced at the Corners and then back towards the youths. He half cocked his head in greeting.

"Right, lads."

"You two lost?"

The ringleader stared down Murray, who without his beloved bull terrier and beyond safe territorial boundaries gave up nothing but a nervous cough.

"Just waiting on a mate, big man," said Webster. "Won't be long."

"Oh, aye. Who's this mate then?"

"Doesn't matter."

"I'll tell you if it matters or not, mate." The last word dripped with threat.

The three turned at the low throaty rumble of a motorcycle rounding the corner at the end of the road.

"You want a draw?" Webster held out the joint.

The ringleader batted the joint out of his hand, malice twisting his features.

"You dealing too? Bobby, teach these two a lesson," he said over his shoulder.

A small kid in a red Nike hoody that was drowning him stepped forward. His hand emerged from the front pocket holding a black four-inch folding knife.

"You want me to shank this prick?" he said, a psychotic glee behind his bright eyes.

Barney barely had time to register the knife coming towards him when the first shots went off.

❖ ❖ ❖

Glass showered McCutcheon; it glittered and pattered as it fell across his desk and the lampshade above his head exploded, swinging precariously to hang lopsided but still attached to the ceiling rose like a corpse dangling on the gallows. Gouts of plaster erupted from the wall above the chair where Freaky Jackson sat, bullets stitching across from left to right. Terrified shouts and sounds of panic rose from the bar below his feet as automatic gunfire raged outside and ravaged the bar.

The initial salvo lasted several terrifying seconds and the lull afterwards was sudden and eerie. From below he could hear the smash and clatter of glass, and scuffle of those seeking an exit or cover. Fits of coughing emerged amidst angry imprecations.

McCutcheon scrambled for the filing cabinet behind him. Freaky Jackson upended the desk sending paperwork, PC and monitor all crashing to the floor along with the Mad Monks missing finger. Kicking aside a jettisoned drawer, he shoved the piece of furniture towards the windows. McCutcheon spun around, pointing a pistol at him.

"Is this fucking your lot?" he snarled, his face beetroot.

"Don't be a daft bastard, Chopper." Jackson eased away from the barrel. "Get some rounds out that window for Christ sakes."

McCutcheon cocked the Browning Hi-Power.

"It's not us!" said Jackson.

As McCutcheon was considering the denial, the automatic rifle fire erupted again, splinters spraying the air and the impacts throwing up a choking dust. Jackson sidestepped in a low crab shuffle away from the windows.

"Chopper, you need to give me a…"

Jackson flinched as bullets zipped through the shattered glazing, peppering the already riddled walls. The furious hiss of a near miss drove him flat on his backside. Scrambling, he backed against the door frame. McCutcheon turned to speak, his face twisted in anger.

There was a dull crack and a puff from a concrete supporting pillar as another bullet struck.

Jackson watched in morbid fascination as the high calibre bullet ricocheted with a distinct waspish buzzzt. The impact and trajectory slowed the round but not enough to stop the tumbling piece of distorted metal tearing through

McCutcheon's jaw and exiting out through his mouth in a burst of blood and shattered teeth.

❖ ❖ ❖

The three youngsters bolted in a pantomime scramble of fear, arms flung over heads and eyes saucer wide in terror before becoming tangled in a scrum of panicked limbs. Bobby dropped his knife and sprinted, tripping himself and another boy as he went. The third didn't look back as the two scrambled to their feet to escape the gunfire.

Webster had ducked behind the wall, a frown of disgust appearing as Barney Murray belly-crawled past; his mate had pissed himself.

He peered around the corner.

Sitting predatory in the middle of the road, one bug-eye headlamp glowing and its throaty growl rebounding from the brickwork of the houses adjacent was a black Honda motorcycle. The rider, legs astride, body turned forty-five degrees towards the Corners, assault rifle shouldered was strafing left to right along the windows, the rounds juddering into brickwork and wooden frames. A sudden metallic clack as the magazine emptied and then in a swift practised movement, the gunman dropped the empty into an open rucksack hanging from his chest and slammed a new clip in place. A click clack ratchet of the bolt and then the muzzle barked again as he unloaded on the upper tier of the bar, spent cartridges spinning in the road.

Webster ducked back. The audible violence of the assault reverberated up the street. He looked at Barney sat hunched, arms around his knees, and then back up the street towards their van.

"Barney. Barney!" he shouted, trying to break into the boy's thoughts. "We have to get to the van."

Barney Murray shook his head sharply from side to side.

"Pull your fucking self together. We have to get out of

here."

"Freaky…"

"Fuck him, c'mon."

Barney's face was lily white, and his hands trembled.

"You need to get the van open and the engine running." Webster shook the smaller lad.

"I can't," Murray's words were sobs.

"You bloody have to."

Webster dug out the pistol Freaky had given him as insurance, hefting the weight and taking a glance around the corner where the rider continued to fire on the bar. So far no one had attempted to flee or returned fire which wasn't a good sign.

"When he reloads, you sprint for it. Do you hear me, Barney?" Webster grabbed his mate and shoved him up against the dirty alley wall. Barney acknowledged with a single, sombre nod.

Clack. Clack. Clack. Silence.

Webster shoved Barney out of the alleyway and the boy half ran, half scrambled along the line of parked cars before making a break across the road towards their van.

Sensing movement, the visored head at the other end of the street snapped around.

Barney fumbled with the van door, dropping the keys into the gutter in his haste. Cursing, he fell to his knees, hands scratching in the dirty gutter, feeling along the kerbstone and reaching around the tyre.

Webster stepped out and raised the pistol, his arm outstretched like he'd seen in all the movies, the scene in front of him like a video game.

Before he could shoot, the muzzle of the automatic rifle flashed and rounds walked up the pavement towards him. Splintered tarmac and shrapnel zipped past his ears, the fragments stinging his eyes. Webster pulled the trigger of the old Beretta 92. The shot went wild and Webster ran.

Dodging between parked cars, he fired blindly. Firing three shots and then diving behind the cover of an old Ford Mondeo, he winced at the dull thunk, thunk, thunk as rounds penetrated the flimsy bodywork and the sound of a harsh bang-hiss as a tyre was hit and the vehicle slumped on rusty suspension.

The van blipped as Barney got the locks open and Webster peeked out through the Mondeo's shattered windows. One last sprint to safety. Behind him, the engine roared to life and the gears ground in protest as Murray tried to find first and then kangarooed the van from its parking space. Webster stood, firing the remaining few rounds, and then spun on his heels and ran for his life.

## Chapter 14

"I'm sorry, Inspector. Maybe pull in up there. There's no way you're getting any closer, it's like the Alamo down there."

The police constable who leaned in to speak to Taylor pointed a hundred yards up the main road towards a bus stop and loading bay outside a shuttered delicatessen and home bakery.

An ambulance whoop-whooped as it drove out of the side street behind him and accelerated away, taking the main A20 towards the Ulster Hospital.

The scene was organised chaos.

The front door of the Corners Bar was open and a dozen uniforms faced out from behind red and white crime scene tape, their caps pulled low and Heckler and Koch G3 automatic rifles slung across their chests. The building facade bloomed in blues as another ambulance sat kerbside and Taylor could see paramedics working frantically on a patient.

"Who's here already, son?" asked Macpherson.

"DI MacDonald and his team arrived about fifteen minutes ago, and the crime scene folks have just pulled in. I think I saw the DCI duck under the tape a minute ago too."

"Thanks, Constable," said Taylor. He nodded, and she drove forward, bumping the Vauxhall up on the kerb as another liveried Land Rover had claimed the loading bay car parking space ahead.

"Detective Inspector Taylor. DS Macpherson." Macpherson held his badge up to the crime scene coordinator who studied it and then added the names to his clipboard.

"You can't go inside the premises yet. There's a briefing area to your left by the bookies but stay on the footpath," said the WPC, hoisting the scene tape.

Taylor nodded her thanks and ducked under. The two followed the taped access route to where she could see MacDonald with a phone clamped to his ear.

"Well, find out. We were supposed to have a bloody active presence... a few plus one dead, one critical... let me know when you find out." MacDonald hung up.

"Is your lad still at TICC?" he asked without preamble.

Macpherson glanced at his watch. "I wouldn't expect so. Problem?"

"Clusterfuck. Gunman on a motorbike. Eyewitnesses didn't get much. A black bike, khaki tank, no plates. He sped off up here." MacDonald pointed down the street. "The road feeds into at least ten others leaving the estate, so I'm clutching at straws as to where he went." He rubbed a hand over his face, "Best of it is we had uniforms in the street all day but they took an early bath."

"I'll get Walker back over to TICC." The DSIO nodded his thanks as Macpherson took a step away and pulled his own phone out.

"Did they get a stand-down or were they skiving?" asked Taylor.

"I'm trying to find out. Whichever, it's a balls-up."

"What's the low-down here?" said Taylor.

"About an hour ago, a single gunman targeted the bar. High powered automatic rifle, likely an AK-47 or similar. The ground behind us is littered with casings. Between out here and inside, it's going to take a frigging week to process."

"Did I hear you say there were casualties?"

"Yeah. One's away there in an ambulance, a nasty enough head wound. They think he might lose an eye. There's more walking wounded being triaged inside." He pointed to the bar and continued. "To be honest, we're lucky it wasn't a bloodbath."

"What about the unlucky ones?"

"One dead. The barman, single gunshot wound to the head. One other critical. Paramedics are working on him in the ambulance."

"You do know whose bar this is?" said Taylor.

"It's Duncan McCutcheon's place."

Taylor and MacDonald turned at the sound of Gillian Reed's voice.

"It is, and while he isn't the worst of them, I'd say it's a fair bet he won't take this lying down," replied Taylor.

"Well, it looks like he'll have to." Reed pointed at the ambulance. MacDonald filled in the detail.

"Gunshot wound to the face. He lost a lot of blood, but they got him stable and then he took a turn in the back of the ambulance and stopped breathing for a minute. They're trying to get him out of here now and over to the Royal."

"And nothing at all on the shooter?"

"I'd have thought you'd be lining up a prime suspect," said Reed. Hands on hips, she surveyed the street. She was still in her office attire but with the addition of a knee-length navy overcoat, an ID lanyard around her neck, and a Glock 17 pistol holstered on the waistband of her skirt.

"Ma'am?"

"Come on, Veronica. I can see the cogs whirring. What's your assessment?"

"About this being retaliation for Rab Millar?" said Taylor.

"Best guess on whether McCutcheon's lot were involved in that?"

Taylor looked at MacDonald.

"You know the firm better than me, go ahead," he said.

"I just don't see it," said Taylor "McCutcheon owes his position to the fact Gordon Beattie drove his predecessor out of post and over the water. Tit for tat escalated afterwards, but once McCutcheon established himself, the two came to a mutual understanding. McCutcheon was a true blue, and wasn't interested in the drugs game, just defence of the realm."

"Maybe he fancied expanding?" said MacDonald. Taylor shook her head.

"He's not the ambitious sort. Beattie tried to put him on a retainer a while ago to make sure he kept his nose out of that end of the business. McCutcheon rejected it, although he still toed the line and stuck to more traditional harbours. Doormen, protection rackets, illegal gambling, money lending. Old-school stuff."

"McCutcheon and Millar had a pretty spectacular falling out," said Reed.

"They did but they broke bread and have avoided each other ever since. Millar had plenty of clubs and liked a flutter though. I'll ask around in case there was something brewing behind the scenes," said Taylor, hoping that by agreeing to contemplate the possibility, it might go some way towards easing her superiors concern she was tunnel-visioned in her pursuit of Gordon Beattie and his accomplices.

The back doors of the ambulance slammed closed, and its Mercedes engine gunned to life. Blue grille and mounted roof lights illuminated the facade of the bar and the faces of the armed police protecting the scene. The siren warbled up in pitch then changed to a two-tone as it sped away.

"Locals are getting restless," said Macpherson as he arrived back at the kerb, putting his phone away and gesturing at the growing crowd.

Thirty people had gathered behind the cordon with a loose skirmish line of at least that number again further up the street. The second group was a younger mix, the hoody mob. Predominantly male but girls mixed in. Wide eyed and brandishing camera phones, they perched on garden walls or herded together in their tribal groups with the occasional bottle of Buckfast or can of lager doing the rounds. They remained spectators at the minute, but Taylor knew that could change as the simmering undercurrent of fury caught hold.

"Didn't take long for the vultures to arrive either," said MacDonald, following Macpherson's pointed finger.

Half a dozen print photographers were leap-frogging across the street, trying to get shots of the ambulance and the victims being brought out. Electronic flashes illuminated the scene as they snapped off sporadic shots of the police operation and the gathering crowd. Two television crews had also managed to push their way to the front of the melee. One cameraman and one harshly illuminated reporter were in the middle of the cordon filming a summary that would be rushed to the late news.

"Hey. Over there? Who's in charge? Is anyone going to tell us what's going on?"

The speaker was one of the group of thirty sandwiched between the small convenience store and the television crews. The woman, who may or may not have been in her late thirties had the puffed eyes of a boxer and the lined pout and hoarse accent of an eighty-a-day habit. Whoever she was, she held court over a smaller contingent of the crowd, responding to and throwing out questions.

"Philip, will you have someone deal with the nice lady and try to push that cordon back a bit? I don't need the chief super getting a debrief on UTV before I've put my report in front of him," instructed Reed, and MacDonald scurried off.

The sudden activity and the gruff questions had caught the attention of the camera crews who swept their halogen spotlamps and lenses across the cordon. Squeezing from between the shoulders and tangle of bodies, a dishevelled woman, make-up having seen better days and whose hair was an explosion of frizz, thrust a microphone across the barrier tape.

"Detective Inspector Taylor, have you any comment on the attack? Do you think it's retaliation for the murder of Robert Millar last night, and what are your thoughts it could be connected to the failed prosecution of Gordon Beattie?"

There was a raised murmur of voices in the crowd.

"Detective Inspector, can you give us any details?"

A line of uniformed TSG officers waded towards the cordon. The flash of photography and the harsh glare of the television cameras captured a stern instruction to move back from an equally stern-faced sergeant wearing rifle green coveralls and cap, and a Heckler and Koch submachine gun strung across his body armour. Another half dozen of his men in identical kit and posture moved up behind. The line of armed officers holding the crowd back would play out well on the late bulletin.

"Inspector, Gordon Beattie..." The reporter's words were drowned out as another ambulance blipped the siren and left the scene.

"What a mess," said Reed.

Headlights swept across them, illuminating the forensic officers in the road where they placed numbered flags and then took photographs of the area, flashbulbs adding a disorientating strobing effect to an already surreal scene.

"Guv?"

Diane Pearson the senior forensic officer and evidence team manager stepped under the tape and approached. She was clad in her protective suit with her mask in place and beckoned them over to a small makeshift processing station set up outside the bullet-riddled doors.

"What have you got?" asked Reed.

"It's a state in there, but we're working through it," she said. "It'll be for the medical examiner to confirm, but there's this?"

She placed a plastic evidence bag on the processing-station

worktop, slid across the clipboard and recorded the number and the contents.

"Small calibre bullet casing. We found it inside under a fruit machine."

"Okay?" said Reed, her tone suggesting she wanted more.

"The DB inside has a single gunshot wound to the forehead," Pearson tapped the centre of her own. Taylor bent over and examined the brass.

"Definitely different to the rounds that cut through this place. Are you thinking it was more than a gun and run?" she said.

Reed raised a hand before any of her subordinates could speak.

"Just to be clear, are we suggesting that as well as hosing the place down with an assault rifle, they had the audacity to go inside and carry out an execution?" said Reed, expression darkening.

"I'm not in the position to say that yet, but it does look like we have more than one weapon involved here," said Pearson.

"Assault rifle?" Macpherson butted in.

"Witnesses say the shooter on the bike had a military-style assault rifle. The casings type and sheer number of them lean Diane's folks towards something like an AK-47 assault rifle," said Reed.

Macpherson shared a glance with Taylor.

"Initial assessment, but based on experience, I'd say it's likely," said Pearson, nodding in agreement.

Before Macpherson could say anything else, Diane Pearson produced her 'pièce de résistance'.

"This was upstairs next to the critical."

"Are you fucking joking me?" said Macpherson as Pearson placed the package down, his other thoughts abandoned for the minute.

Reed sighed and looked to the black cloud-filled sky, the

lightning flashes of the crime scene photographers mirroring the growing migraine in her mind.

Taylor stared down at the pale hairy finger complete with a gold sovereign ring.

"Where's the rest of him?"

## Chapter 15

Elaine Weir checked her Facebook, skimming a few new posts and reading a text from her sister saying Freya had settled down. She smiled at the picture Janet had sent of the child's grinning face smothered in spaghetti sauce.

Elaine was eating into the last hour of her shift before locking up. The steady stream of teatime had petered out and now it was only the occasional local wanting cigarettes or the two camps that passed the evening needing a pint of milk for their tea or a six-pack of cheap lager.

She put the phone back in her pocket and shoved the basket of canned goods across the scuffed linoleum with her foot. Counting the goods remaining on the shelf, she marked them up on a printed list and restocked from the contents of her basket.

The chime of the door sounded as a customer entered. She finished a shelf of baked beans and moved back towards the till. Observing the aisles on the CCTV screen below the counter, she saw the back of a figure hunched over in the household aisle.

"Can I help you with anything?" she asked.

At the clatter of goods falling to the floor, she left her position and peeped around the display.

The customer had slipped and slid awkwardly along a shelf. One hand groping for balance as he struggled to support himself.

"Jesus, are you drunk? Come on. Get out!"

The shelf she had spent twenty minutes cleaning and restocking now listed to one side with the contents spinning on the floor.

"I'm alright, so I am."

She could tell he was far from it. The sheen on his face gleamed under the harsh strip lighting, and his pupils glared like spotlights. She'd seen them before. City slickers and suburban types, passing through to score their coke, crack or heroin from the graffiti-strewn maisonettes and abandoned terraces at the edge of the estate. They would use the lay-by outside the shop to park their company cars or SUVs to make the journey seem like a pitstop for a pint of milk.

"You're off your head. Out."

Leering he straightened himself up, jerking like a puppet being shaken on its strings.

"When do you get off? You want to party?"

"No, I don't. Let's go."

The leer broadened as he walked towards her. His face twitched, and he ran a hand across his nose.

"You're too pretty to be wasting the night in here, come on!"

Elaine glanced round the shop, but it was empty.

"Flattery will get you nowhere. Now, go on before—"

"Before what?"

He reached out a hand towards her. Elaine took a step back, and he laughed, veering away to pluck an energy drink from a promotion display.

"You can get to know me," he said, producing a wrap of gear from inside his jacket pocket and waving it back and forth. "What do you say?"

"No. If you're not buying anything, away on with you."

Elaine retreated behind her counter. He followed, gathering a few other things as he sniffed and talked to himself, finally dropping the half dozen cans of energy drink and cola onto the counter.

"Bottle of vodka," he slurred.

"Twenty-eight fifty," said Elaine, thumping the bottle down.

"How much? Fucking extortionate."

The entry chime of the door sounded, and as Elaine glanced at the CCTV, the man reached out and grabbed her hand.

"D'you hear me. I said that's fucking extortion."

"If you don't like it, you can leave it." She snatched back her hand but before she could take back the bottle he had lifted it, cracked the seal and taken a long swing. Pleased with himself, he pointed the bottle at her.

"Your health." He took another swig, burped and gave another manic cackle.

"Look at you, all dolled up to work in this shithole. The old fellas must love watching you bending over to fetch them up their paper." The combination of whatever narcotics he'd had and the alcohol were buoying the man's confidence.

"Out. Now."

"You going to make me?" he said, leaning in close enough that Elaine could smell alcohol and Indian food on his breath. "How much?"

"Twenty-eight fifty," she repeated.

"Not this. To take you out the back. How much?"

"Fuck you," she snarled, a tide of sickness rising in her stomach.

"Exactly. You look a lot cleaner than that last stinker in the estate." His chin dropped to his chest as he tried to focus and he grabbed at his crotch.

"I'm not telling you again…"

The vodka bottle thumped down as he abandoned it to make a grab for her. The display of gum and sweets on the counter was too close as Elaine tried to parry, and as she flung up an arm to arrest the man's momentum, the whole lot scattered to crash on the floor. She writhed away as his fingers snaked into the fabric of her top and he pulled her forward, the edge of the worktop digging into her hips. The other free hand sought a grip in her hair.

Elaine clawed at his face, her other hand fumbling below the counter.

Grunting with effort, he hauled harder, his weight advantage pulling her over the counter.

Elaine's fingers snagged the broken stair spindle kept for protection. It spun away, and she screamed as he drove a punch into the back of her head, rebounding her face off the counter. The spilt vodka stung her eyes and the fumes of it filled her nostrils.

Scrambling, her hand caught the improvised wooden baton, and she swung it, catching him a glancing blow.

He flinched as she tried to find purchase for a better swing. Grabbing the spinning bottle, he smashed it on the counter and wheeled to wave the jagged end at her face, whipping a hand back to strike, then yelped as the hand was twisted, then snatched violently in the opposite direction. The broken bottle flew from his hand into the open dairy fridge.

Elaine saw his eyes widen in surprise just as his body jackknifed. His face slammed on the counter, then he righted himself, inhaling a deep gasp as though breaking for air. Elaine instinctively swung the spindle in a two-handed backhand that caught him across the side of the head.

She roared and swung again. The blow was arrested and the spindle snatched from her grasp.

"Easy there. Stop. He's down. No, stop."

Elaine's breath came in ragged gasps, her chest heaving, and tears streamed down her face as she slumped back against the cigarette display.

"You're okay. Breathe."

Her vision blurred and her ears hummed with her own pulse.

"Elaine. It's Elaine isn't it?"

"Yes... I..."

"It's Tom, from the flats. We spoke earlier on the stairs."

"God, Tom," she sobbed.

"It's going to be alright. You stay right there, I'll be two seconds."

Tom bent over the groaning figure, now sprawled on the floor, and patted him down. No weapons. A set of car keys, a wallet with two hundred pounds in varied notes, a wrap of drugs, and a bag of pills. Each little green tablet was marked with a ragged M. He flicked through the debit and credit cards, also finding a driver's licence and business card. He pocketed the lot and then hauled the limp man to his feet, half carrying, half dragging him to the door and out into the street.

Thankfully, the path that led up to the convenience store was dark and the lay-by empty save for the poorly parked Audi SUV. Tom blipped the key fob, opened the rear door and shoved the man inside. A check to confirm he was in no position to attempt any retaliation, and then Tom hopped in the driver's seat. He gunned the engine and drove away from the shop, up into the dark area of low lock-ups that dotted the edge of one of the tower blocks. A set of temporary fences marked out half a dozen derelict garages with a large sign cable-tied to the front, 'DANGER – STRICTLY NO ADMITTANCE. SITE ACQUIRED FOR GBH'.

Pulling the vehicle up on the grass under the sign, he turned off the ignition. Dropping the keys in the footwell, he checked one last time that the owner hadn't stopped breathing or fitted. Satisfied, he walked the long way back to the shop.

The door chimed as he entered, and he flipped the closed sign around and snibbed the door.

"Elaine, it's Tom."

She sat slumped amid the carnage of scattered sweets and broken glass, holding a bag of frozen peas to her head. The tears had stopped. A pocket of wet wipes lay open at her side as she cleansed the smudged mascara and smell of vodka from her eyes.

"Let me see."

"I'm fine," said Elaine.

"Let me see."

Reluctantly she allowed him, and he gently parted her hair, checking her scalp.

"You're fine. It's just a bump," he said.

"Tom, thanks. I..." He waved the gratitude away.

"He's lucky I came in when I did." He hefted the spindle from the floor and smiled. "You should be at Wimbledon with a backhand like that. Do you want me to call anyone?"

"No. I'm fine." She took his hand and shakily stood.

"You don't look it?"

"I'll be grand. We get his sort in here all the time," she said, taking the makeshift baton.

"You might want to get rid of that," he suggested.

"He'll not be back with the police." She looked at the bloody end, then set the spindle on top of the counter.

"Really?" Tom's tone belied his belief.

"Really. He wouldn't dare and they wouldn't come. Not for something like this." She waved a hand around the mess.

"He was going to bottle you. Maybe worse."

"He was off his face."

"You're making an excuse for it?"

"What can I do? It's happened. He's gone. I'm grateful." Her top, torn in the fracas, hung loose off her shoulder and now the rosy blush of embarrassment and shame glowed on her face.

She walked behind the counter and grabbed a long-handled brush and dustpan. Tom picked up the bulk of what was salvageable and set it on top of an empty display case, scuffing the remains of the broken vodka bottle and sweets into a corner with his foot.

"You don't have to hang around, you know? This will give me something to take my mind off it." She stooped to lift a larger piece and dropped it into the pan, then continued brushing.

"You should get one of those buzzers to let people in at night."

"We're flush with cash for that right enough."

"Maybe this can go towards it." Tom fished out the two hundred he had taken from the evening's belligerent.

"I can't…"

"Call it compensation for lost earnings." Tom placed the wad of notes beside the till, and grabbing a loose pencil he took a piece of till receipt and scratched out a number.

"If he comes back and gives you any trouble, let me know." He slid the paper under the notes.

"You don't have to get yourself involved, Tom."

"You look after yourself, Elaine."

"I will. Oh, and here, those two wee hoods earlier, pay them no heed."

Tom nodded, giving a thin smile.

"They didn't, you know? Hurt you?" she said.

"No. They didn't. Handbags at dawn."

"They're just kids, really. Acting the big men, it can be like that around here."

"I've seen it all before. Night."

"Night."

He waved, the bleep, bleep and the scuff-slam of the door confirming his exit, Elaine put the snib back on the door and turned to look at the devastation.

"Where do you start?" she said, dropping baskets into a neat nest.

She took the dustpan and tipped the shattered glass into a black bin behind the counter. Moving to the till, she turned a key and tapped the cash drawer release as she lifted the money, dropping it on the counter when she noticed the bloody fingerprints across the Queen's face.

❖ ❖ ❖

"I'm telling you. I got him." Billy Webster slammed down on the brown charity shop couch, miming the action and sounds of two guns with both hands. "Call of fucking Duty, mate. You must've seen? Hundred per cent. Right in the guts too."

The flat-screen television showed the late news, and the lead story was the attack on the Corners Bar. The bulletin reported one fatality and several injuries while the police warned the perpetrator was still at large and appealed for witnesses.

"Maybe we should phone in?" said Barney Murray, sitting cross-legged on the floor with a PlayStation controller in one hand and a can of Special Brew lager in the other.

"Are you for real, piss pants?" said Webster, leaning forward to view the close-up shots of the bullet-riddled drinking den.

"Don't call me that."

"Don't be so fucking soft then." Webster knocked the lager from the other boy's hand, the remains draining out onto the floor.

"Crimestoppers is anonymous. We could snag a reward?"

"A reward for what?" said Webster.

"Information, mate."

"We have nothing to tell them and anyway, we had a frigging gun ourselves, dickhead."

Barney scowled and launched the now empty can into the corner with a dozen others. Curled up on a busted fabric armchair, the slumbering bull terrier gave a low grumble of complaint. Barney twisted round, searching under the couch for another beer.

"Do you really think you got him?" said Barney.

"Defo."

Webster had one eye on the television as he smoothed out cigarette papers and sprinkled in some tobacco. Satisfied, he lifted a thick nub of marijuana and ran the flame of a cheap lighter along it.

The rasp and clatter of the letterbox flapping as the front door to the flat opened and slammed startled the two. The brindle merely stuffed her face under the arm of the chair and let out a long snuffle.

"Freaky, man. Are you okay?" Webster jumped to his feet, spilling the joint onto the filthy floor.

"No, thanks to you two arseholes!" Freaky Jackson stalked into the room and grabbed the remote, turning the TV up. The same selection of images and brief clips from the scene continued to scroll.

"We thought you were dead!" said Barney.

"Is this my fucking wake then?" Jackson kicked over the pile of Special Brew tins and the dog snapped off a series of sharp, snarling barks.

Jackson drew a gun from his waistband and shot the animal.

"For fuck's sake, Freaky!" screamed Webster.

The Staffy whimpered in the chair, its bark silenced to short sharp wheezing breaths.

Jackson walked across and put a pillow over the doleful eyes. Another shot silenced the animal.

Barney Murray was hyperventilating, tears in his eyes as Jackson wheeled around, gun wildly gesticulating.

"You left me there!"

"You killed her. You fucking killed her." Murray knelt by the armchair, stroking the dog's paw, fibres from the blasted cushion drifting in the air.

"You left me!" shouted Jackson.

"We didn't mean to, I mean, we tried to…" said Webster,

backing up with hands outstretched.

Jackson jabbed the gun against Webster's forehead. "I've slotted boys for less."

He let a silence hang in the air. The two younger men looked at each other, Webster, for once, not so full of his own importance. Murray remained on his knees beside his dead dog, his face sheet white.

"Tell me what happened," said Jackson.

Webster cobbled together the attack and their escape, explaining, they had driven past every few minutes to see if they could pick up the older man but when first, the local firm had gathered and then the police arrived, they gave up and returned to the flat to lick their wounds and to work out what to do next.

"You'd of been better off following the bastard that tried to kill me than hang about," admonished Jackson. He jutted his chin at the television. "Any mention of Chopper?"

Webster shook his head.

"Just that someone was transferred to the Royal. They're saying it's serious."

"You're right there, son. Half his face came off."

The description didn't help Barney, who already looked ill. Webster's face, however, lit up.

"I got the bastard." He fired an imaginary shot into the room.

"Did he see your face?"

Webster and Barney shared a pained look.

"Of course he did," surmised Jackson. "And a wounded animal is twice as dangerous. What did you do with the gun?"

"It's in the van," said Webster.

Freaky Jackson shook his head slowly and without him seeing it coming, backhanded Webster across the face, knocking him flat on his arse.

"Barney, go get the gun and take that with you," Jackson motioned to the dog.

Murray remained frozen, mouth agape.

"Do you hear me? Wrap it in a sheet or something, just get rid," he snarled.

Murray, breaking free of his stupor, scooted into the hallway and began to frantically empty a small storage cupboard. A few moments later he appeared with a paint-stained floral quilt cover. He reverentially wrapped his beloved pet in the material and carried her out of the flat.

Jackson turned to Webster. His voice was icy.

"This isn't a game, Billy. What were you going to do if they pulled you over? Did a search and asked about the gun? You couldn't hold your piss!"

"I…"

"You two are going to clear off somewhere for a couple of days."

"Come on, Freaky, there's no need for that."

"Whoever is out there hasn't finished, I'll tell you that for nothing. I've no time to be fucking babysitting you two clowns as well."

"We can help."

"Aye, by getting out of my face. Go on, hurry that other retard up and then get that van away to fuck."

Jackson walked over to the chipped and battered sideboard. One door hung on a broken hinge and the other had a corner chewed off. He rummaged in a drawer until he found a phone and a cardboard sleeve containing a new SIM card.

"Are you still here?" he asked over his shoulder.

"Let us do something, we're not kids."

Jackson let out a sigh as he dropped the packaging to the floor and tried to boot up the phone.

"Charger?"

"In the wall there," said Webster, pointing.

Jackson plugged the phone in and then slumped into the nearby armchair, picking up a discarded beer tin as the phone slowly came to life. He drew out a packet of Lambert and Butler cigarettes, shuffling one out. The spark of the lighter was the only sound for a few moments. Drawing the smoke in, he flopped back, exhaling into the air.

"Right, tell you what. If you want to help, take the van up to the farm. Get it into the shed at the back and do not move it. Is the clear? If the peelers aren't looking for it, one of Chopper's mob will be."

"No bother."

"Sort the dogs while you're up there. It'll take soft boys mind off things."

He waved the cigarette in the general direction of the door then tapped ash into the beer tin.

"The dogs?" whined Webster.

"Unless you'd rather end up dead in a fucking ditch?"

"Okay."

"There's a load of smack. The two of you can get it split and packaged. Come back here tomorrow in the other van and get it set up in the crack houses like normal. Can you manage that with no balls-ups?"

Webster nodded enthusiastically.

"The big man needs all the gear away. Something's coming up, and he's leaning on us all to get the cash in," said Jackson.

"What about you?"

"Don't you worry about it."

"You'll go after your man?" said Webster.

Freaky shrugged. Took another draw as he thought about the last few hours.

"Sure, Barney can sort the dogs and stuff. I can help you hunt your man down. Be the wingman? What do you say?"

Freaky sat there in silence. In the distance, the flapping feet of Barney Murray sounded as he ran up the outside footpath, the kid's asthmatic wheeze hissing from the effort of carrying the dog's body and the stress of the night so far.

"What are you gonna do, Rambo? You think because you sit on that PlayStation, stoned and playing soldier…"

"I got him," protested Webster.

"You maybe got a lucky shot! So what, you think you're the big Sicario now? Too much TV and video games is your problem."

Jackson dragged on his cigarette then dropped it on the dingy carpet, stomping it out. When he got up from the seat, he had a softer expression on his face. He put his massive, tattooed paw around the boy's neck and squeezed, what passed for an affectionate shake nearly wobbling the youngster's head off. He had been a little older than the boys when he first pulled a trigger in anger, and he had been a lot younger when he was first shot at.

Billy Webster was his brother's boy. The dysfunctional reality of life in the estate meant Billy and his older brother Gary had been orphaned when their father, Raymond Jackson overdosed on the heroin Freaky pushed out. Their ma had died much earlier from cervical cancer. Not that Freaky was their guardian; the boys looked after themselves and he just threw them a few quid and gave them work from time to time, but he had to admit Billy had proved useful of late. Gary on the other hand was unpredictable, but that was a smack user for you.

"Look, son, this is big boy's rules now, no offence. Get the dogs and the gear squared away. We need to keep the crack house running and the money rolling in."

Webster looked at the carpet, Jackson noting the expression of disappointment.

"Look, between you and me, I wouldn't trust Barney with a set of scales and a bunch of bananas let alone all that powder. The punters will end up overdosing, and then I'll have another headache to deal with. I need you up there watching him. It's important. Business as usual, right?"

"Yeah, okay. I understand," said Webster.

"Good lad." Jackson patted him on the back as Murray slunk into the grotty flat. Reaching out a hesitant hand he offered the pistol, wrapped in a dirty yellow dust cloth, and Freaky took it.

"Away on with you now. Keep an eye on the phone. I'll ring you if I need you."

"Dead on," said Webster, nodding at Barney to move outside.

"Put the word out about that bike your man was on and keep your ears open too, yeah? Somebody might know something we don't," said Jackson.

The two nodded. Jackson dismissed them with a wave, muttering to himself as he stabbed a number into the phone.

"You never know what this bastard might try next."

❖ ❖ ❖

The vodka was coarse and the sharp bite of the first drink still burned in his throat as he sloshed another shot into a glass.

Tom Shepard sat naked on the edge of the bath, his silhouetted reflection staring back from the shower screen. Setting the glass beside the vodka bottle on the small sink, he grimaced, raising his right arm to check the wound in his side.

His nine lives had been used up long ago, so this he decreed must have been pot luck or the priest's offer of prayers for his soul had paid off.

Gritting his teeth, he poured a measure of disinfectant over the open wound, blood diluting and sluicing down his side and hip. He gasped at the sudden sting.

The bullet had grazed along a rib and opened a three-inch-long gash that needed attention and he had been fortunate not to have exacerbated the damage in carrying the dead weight of the prick from the corner shop.

He hadn't noticed the two boys from the stairwell until the last minute, and very much unlike himself, he had decided on restraint even as the mouthy one had taken a potshot.

He poured more disinfectant onto a cotton pad and swabbed the edges of the wound, thankful the rib wasn't broken and there were no bone fragments to tease out. It was just another war story marked out on the tapestry of similar tales that crisscrossed his body.

All in all, it hadn't been a bad day's entertainment. He smiled grimly, imagining the guy from the shop waking up from his sleep with a comedown and two black eyes after his run-in with Elaine's improvised wooden bat, although how the boys had been at the bar and tooled up played on his mind. Coincidence? They couldn't have known his plan? Had they somehow followed him? He was confident that wasn't the case, but he couldn't rule out the niggling thought he would have to pay them a visit to be sure.

Bringing attention to himself would have to cease, but events had highlighted that the decision he had made for entirely self-serving means may also have a complex but positive side effect. He had initially considered lopping the head off the beast but realised that another would just spring up in its place. The organisation was vertically integrated, each block symbiotic with the next piece in the stack and by dismantling it from the ground up he would not only irreparably damage it, but also let those at the top know he was coming and this was personal, their days of reigning with terror were numbered.

For the sake of the decent people going quietly about their lives and, for Elaine and her girl, he would see their ventures set up to bully and intimidate were dismantled permanently.

The current of tension that rose as the sun dipped behind

the barren black mountain was palpable. It wasn't that the hours of light put them off, the darkness just made them more brazen. As the moon rose, so did the crack of gunshots from alleyways. The scream of the punished and the sobs of their dearest forced to watch; judicial process brought to bear from behind a mask.

He had spent a week now observing the cars come and go, watching the swaps brazenly take place at the edge of the dilapidated park, beside the lock-ups and around the broken and abandoned maisonettes. Youngsters on skateboards and mountain bikes acted as couriers for the older lads while others loitered at the periphery watching for the police. Every few hours the quiet was interrupted by the bump, thump of a sound system as a car would wind its way up to the flats on a cash call or delivery drop. The estate was rotten, criminality burrowed to its core, and those who might step up were mute from fear of reprisal.

Tearing open a packet of wipes, he cleaned off as much of the blood as he could around the graze. The wound, red and angry, exposed flesh still oozing. He washed his hands, dried them on a clean hand towel, then sluiced more disinfectant over the wound and protected it with a couple of cotton pads under a broad X of duct tape.

It wasn't neat but had done the job. He took another vodka shot and three paracetamol to celebrate the end of the ordeal. Finally, he dragged on a clean pair of jogging pants.

Shepard put his soiled clothes and the bloody rags into a bin liner and then poured what remained of the kettle onto the linoleum floor, mopping up the worst of the mess. He took his time to cleanse the place with several refills of the kettle and most of the bleach he had under the sink. Doubling up the bin liner, he set it aside. He would drop it in one of the large trash bins beside the lock-ups when he went to check the Audi had gone. As he finished drying off the floor, he realised he had other priorities.

The smell of the baked dough, melting cheeses and pepperoni filled the small open-plan living area and his stomach rumbled. Although an awkward operation to lean down and remove the pizza, he managed, sliding it onto a wooden chopping board to cool before fetching the remaining vodka and glass. He sighed, slumping into an armchair.

Pizza had always been his craving. When he was cold, half starved, filthy and hungry, no matter what shithole of the world he was in, no matter who he was deployed with, the conversations soon turned to food and the first bite of the return to civilisation; a discussion to pass the hours of stress and darkness and a distraction from the cold MREs that they tucked into, whether on the hoof up some godforsaken shale peak of the Hindu Kush or under a tarp in the baking heat of Ramadi or Baghdad.

He didn't know of any reason other than it had been the go-to as a child on a Saturday evening when his mother had enough of cooking all week. It also evoked his earliest memories of Cara when they would drive up the coast in his battered old Fiesta during their dating days. The awkward fumble of new love in the backseat before a shared takeaway in the car with the cool night air and sounds of the shore a soothing symphony compared to the crump of distant car bombs or crack of shooting from the bitter, sectarian enclaves during the eighties.

As he sat, his mind drifted a world away, the vodka tasting like cool Pinot Grigio. Across the table, Cara's auburn hair tumbled in the Venetian breeze, her hand reaching across to his as they enjoyed food and wine in an outside street cafe, the Campanile of St Mark's Basilica soaring over the open aspect framed by clear blue sky.

Shepard pushed the thoughts away and rose, munching a mouthful, then hawing out air as it burned the roof of his mouth. He blew on the melted cheese to cool the piece and dragged a coffee table over. Wiping greasy fingers on the leg of his joggers, he reached out for the thin dossier that lay on its surface.

He didn't need thoughts of Cara or Adam now. The same way he didn't need them on operations. While teammates would revel in the nightly phone call or twenty minutes of FaceTime, he abandoned all thoughts and contacts of home. His mind had to be on the job, not worrying about bills or the petty arguments that could crop up being stationed three thousand miles away from normality. Neither had he ever written a death letter. Why tempt fate, he had argued when the company sergeant major had done the rounds in advance of deployment.

The irony of that was, he was the one who hadn't known.

It was almost a week before Cara's death had been relayed to him. He remembered the adjutant's grim face when he delivered the news. Shepard was dripping sweat in the corner of a hangar, burning off the stress and hours cooped up under a barbell. It was after a behind-the-lines incursion to evacuate oil workers and their families during the heat of another civil war threatening to destabilise the Middle East.

The CO had been apologetic but blunt. There had been an accident. His wife and young son had died. Take a period of compassionate leave.

The next months were a blur as he rode the stages of grief. He had returned to Belfast briefly to lay their ashes with her parents and siblings. A few weeks later he returned to Poole where he was assigned to the directing staff for the next intake of recruits.

He couldn't fault the firm, they had done all they could to help. Offered him time away from active operations and a chance to get his head together, regular contact with occupational health and endless calls of support. He had no horror story to tell. Nine months later he was back in the arid deserts of Southern Syria doing what he did best.

It was almost the fifth anniversary when his world uprooted again.

He flicked through the photographs laid out in front of him, chewing but not tasting, and slugged a shot of vodka from the bottle, wiping his hand across his mouth.

He'd first heard the story in the desert from a gobby, malingering Scot who was drunk on a spicy homebrew and lamenting the state of the country. When Shepard intervened, he had pulled him up on the state of Ulster, regaling him with how an operation to remove the head of a vicious paramilitary gang was botched and the fallout covered up by Special Branch. The details were stark enough that when he returned to Poole, he had an old acquaintance from 14 Intelligence corroborate the tale while gathering a few more of the salient points from other contacts in the intelligence service.

The dossier had been the catalyst, and Shepard shuffled it out once again across the coffee table.

There were several shots showing the scene of the accident. A couple of classified and copied post-mortem renders and notes. Thankfully, the contact had spared him photographs. Contained also was a police report, a redacted court summary, several mugshots, and a scanned email print.

'…that due to the clandestine nature of the operative and their intrinsic value to the security service and ongoing operations at this time, the recommendation of the arbitrator is that any detail of REDACTED participation in events of February twelfth be expunged from any and all records…'

Shepard stared at the faces and then sat back, resolute. The hard bit was over, he had taken the first steps. He had got their attention and now they would be scrambling to react, seeking a ghost and fearing the Reaper. With luck, they would soon turn on themselves, but in the meantime, he would continue to stick in the knife.

## Chapter 16

"McBride hasn't been seen for three weeks," said Macpherson offering the only remaining chair to Taylor, musing that all that was missing from the get together was a decanter of good malt and a pack of playing cards.

"Which confirms what precisely, Sergeant?"

Law was dressed in a navy lambswool V-neck jumper and matching slacks. Even in his casuals, the air of authority dripped off him. He looked over the top of his glasses at them, a stiff nod prodding for further detail.

"Sir." Taylor took over the update. "McBride is a registered violent offender. We know he fled Belfast under a cloud and we know from intelligence sharing he registered with Portswood Police Station with an address in Southampton, and for the first few months had trouble adjusting."

DCI Gillian Reed and Phillip MacDonald sat before the chief superintendent's imposing roll-top walnut desk listening quietly.

"Adjusting?"

"McBride got into the odd scuffle. He had his card marked for being drunk and disorderly a few times," interjected Macpherson.

"The locals were briefed on his background, but they didn't see anything that would suggest he was mixing with other felons or with paramilitary contacts from back home. In all, it didn't seem like an extension or expansion of his old operation. A fish out of water was how the detective explained it to us. McBride remained in contact with his police liaison and was following the terms of his licence," said Taylor.

"That is until three weeks ago? Pray tell why we only

know this now?" said Law.

"Unfortunately, no good reason. It slipped the net. He's been a resident of their jurisdiction for some time and was behaving himself. Granted he was to tell them if he was moving home or travelling abroad, but…" Macpherson shrugged.

"How sure are we that…" Phillip MacDonald pointed at the eight by six glossy evidence snapshot on the chief super's desk; a single middle digit, with hairy knuckle and nail gnawed to the nub.

"I'm at ninety-nine per cent sure that finger belongs to the Mad Monk," said Macpherson.

"We've seen your tabloid scrapbook, Sergeant," said Law. On the desk to his right was the book of cuttings that Macpherson kept. Snipped from the Sunday tabloids or the evening edition of the Belfast Telegraph he had, for as long as he could remember, filed away articles on the villains that he worked against. Taylor's teasing that it was all available on the internet now met with a gruff rebuke and a lecture on the failings of technology. The picture Law had prominently positioned was one of Billy McBride leaving court, middle finger extended and lips twisted in an insult at the police and prosecution service. There was a fat sovereign ring wedged on the finger.

"Is this the basis of your hypothesis?"

"Aye, that and my copper's gut."

Law drew in a slow breath and leaned back in his chair, pushing his glasses back up on his nose.

"Gillian?"

"We have the fingerprint away for comparison, so we'll confirm Robert's theory pretty quickly. The bigger question is one posed by DI Taylor. Where is the rest of him?"

Law slid several more pages of initial report across his desk and skim read, an occasional grunt or sniff in the ensuing silence as he found a particularly disturbing point.

"This," he tapped the photo, "doesn't directly mean Mr McBride is deceased."

"It doesn't, however, the forensic team did point out some dermis damage consistent with freezing so I'd suggest whoever sent his former colleagues that finger, they went to some trouble to ensure it arrived fresh. The ring also adds a degree of provenance it is him."

"Do we have any intelligence pointing to this being a kidnapping and extortion attempt?"

"None," said Reed.

"Links between this and the Millar murder?"

"Rab Millar would have been involved in the expulsion of McBride alongside…" said Taylor.

"I do not want to hear you say his name, Inspector."

"Yes, sir. But…"

"But nothing. What else?"

"With respect, sir, I think we should consider…"

"That's enough, Inspector!" boomed Law.

There was a silence in the room as Law considered his words.

"Let us be clear about this, again. Gordon Beattie was acquitted of all charges. Any historical crimes he stood accused of he has been punished for. He is not the bloody bogeyman, nor will he form any part of the current debacle because it is a PR disaster as it stands and," Law raised a finger in the air to still any protest. "Because it's highly likely another huge part of my budget will be ring-fenced for the charges of harassment and the subsequent compensation if we continue. I will not compound error after error. Are we clear?" Law stabbed the finger on his desk, punctuating the demand.

"I think it's a mistake." Taylor's voice seemed tiny in the large room.

"Veronica,' warned Reed.

"I'll tell you what was a mistake, acquiescing to the detective chief inspector's assurances that you could put aside your failure and move on. This department is not here to serve as the means for your own personal retribution or to encourage you, every time you find a sliver of coincidence to hook your hopes upon. Your career is hanging by the skin of its teeth as it stands and—"

Taylor made to speak, but a nudge to the back of her chair gave her pause. Law glared at the interruption.

"Sorry, sir."

"I should bloody well hope so. This is a complete disaster. The ACC is due here first thing in the morning and I have to explain to him not only why are we underperforming but how we let the wild west play out in the heart of the capital especially when it transpires that we had the building under surveillance."

"I've asked Inspector Connor to apprise me of the stand-down, sir," said Reed.

"Good, although God help us if it gets picked up because the conspiracy of collusion won't take long to surface. I already have the press clamouring for a briefing on Millar's murder, and now this is throwing chump to the sharks." Law was red faced as he spoke, his blood pressure rocketing.

"I made myself expressly clear this morning, a quick result was needed. Not an escalation to tit for tat violence. This," he pointed at the photo of the severed finger, "is a distraction. It's as likely the D company mob asked for McBride to be silenced themselves and this is their proof. Now we have a war zone in a city street, another corpse and a paramilitary godfather in hospital, all while our investigation seems to be clouded by the need for redemption over a poorly handled prosecution."

"We are all on the same page, Chief Superintendent,"

placated Reed, her composure as fresh under the onslaught as her appearance.

Taylor considered her reflection in the large window behind the chief super. What little make-up she had tried to conceal her weary complexion with had gone. Her lank hair was dragged back into a high ponytail that accentuated her pale face. The cuff of her shirt was smudged with God knows what, and there was blood on her jacket from tackling Rowdy Burns that morning.

"Inspector Taylor may be tenacious in her pursuits but that doesn't necessarily mean she is wrong to be so." Reed held her palm up to fend off interruption, "With respect, sir, we all are aware how delicate the situation is surrounding Gordon Beattie and while I agree we shouldn't be quick to put two and two together neither should we turn a blind eye to possible motives that while they may not implicate him, may still be in part due to his prior connections to these networks."

Law breathed in a deep nasal breath and pursed his lips.

"Granted. However, until I say otherwise, there is to be no approach made to Mr Beattie. Clear."

There was a resounding murmur of compliance.

"This other victim then. God forbid you're going to tell me he's related to this Beattie debacle too?"

"He's the barman of the Corners, Barry Corrigan." Phillip MacDonald spoke up.

"Execution?"

"Single low calibre shot to the head. We are appealing to the patrons of the bar but so far nothing." MacDonald shrugged, then continued. "The forensics team will be working through the night to get a picture of events and provide some assessment for the morning brief. Until then, we can only begin to speculate. Follow-up interviews are also scheduled and if need be, I'll have Inspector Taylor bring in some of the local toughs and get the lie of the land. As soon as we can get the approval of the medical team, we will interview Mr McCutcheon."

"I spoke with an acquaintance at the Royal this evening. I don't think McCutcheon is going to be speaking for quite some time. He is going to require reconstructive surgery on his jaw and is currently critical," said Law. "The locals have the torches and pitchforks out. They are hailing McCutcheon as some sort of Robin Hood. Generous community activist and voice of the people. The papers are already leading their website editions of the attack with pictures of Corrigan dressed as Father Christmas bouncing his infant grandchildren on his knee. None of this plays well, ladies and gentlemen."

Nobody had the foolishness to interrupt.

"I want a full report including eyewitness accounts and details on the attacker, sightings of the motorcycle, everything. I need a comprehensive breakdown of the events and a clear investigative direction by the time I have to sit down with the ACC."

There was another resounding murmur of acknowledgement as the chief super shuffled the documents together like a newsreader wrapping up.

"You're all dismissed."

❖ ❖ ❖

"Thank you, ma'am."

Gillian Reed slumped back in her chair and set her glasses on the desk.

"No need, Veronica. I agree with the chief super that Beattie is out of bounds, but I have a mind that closing off an avenue of investigation just because, is not the right thing to do either," said Reed. "That's not to say go running off looking for a way in, do you hear me?"

"Loud and clear."

"I mean it. You're a good detective so don't be backing the wrong horse here. I've seen people chase the one that got away before and it ruins careers."

"I won't," said Taylor, the promise in her voice but not in her heart.

Reed blew out a breath, shuffled through her messages and changed tack.

"You arrested Rowdy Burns this morning?"

"Yes. We have CCTV of him and another man bringing Lena Borodenko to Risky's. Forensic reports have his prints on the weapon used in the Millar shooting."

"He's in the custody suite?"

"Yes."

"Have you questioned him further?"

"No, ma'am. DC Cook did the preliminary earlier and it seems he's changed his tune and cancelled his request for a solicitor. He's content to sit and offer no comment."

"We'll hold off on phoning any for him. What about the other individual?"

"Gary Webster. We're looking at finding an address and picking him up."

Reed nodded and made a note.

"Did Carrie get anywhere with the van?"

"The van was registered to the business. No forensics yet."

"And progress in tracking where it had been?"

"We have footage of Burns with the girl outside her apartment at Speakers Square and travelling across town to Risky's. Prior to that, DC Walker got the vehicle on traffic cameras coming in from the north on the M5. Left the exit roundabout where it meets the A2 and followed it back on itself along the Shore Road where there's little in the way of coverage. Puts it near Rathcoole or Monkstown, but it could easily have come up over the mountain and back through Belfast."

"That's B company territory, isn't it?"

"Yes. There's no intelligence to suggest a linkup between the two groups, but you never know, they could be sharing resources or logistics."

"Have Walker go through it again. There has to be something we've missed."

Taylor nodded. Reed crossed her legs and peered across at her DI.

"Why are you sure McCutcheon isn't in the frame for Millar's killing?"

"I don't think it's his style, and it's been a while since they buried the hatchet. Pardon the pun."

"You're spending far too much time with Doc." Reed pointed a warning finger, a smile in the corner of her eyes.

"I'm not ruling it out. With bits of Billy McBride turning up, one of the old guard could still have been harbouring a grudge and put the blame on Millar," said Taylor.

She felt the day's tension flutter again across her forehead. The Loyalist feud that had seen the alphabet of UDA companies go head to head over territorial boundaries and drugs had ended when Freaky Jackson had walked into the old Corners Bar with a hatchet in hand and a score to settle. The result of the ensuing hand to hand duel had seen McCutcheon left with a facial disfigurement and Jackson expelled from the mainstream organisation. Gordy Beattie, bringing the pot off the boil, had gathered the clans and facilitated a truce.

Taylor shook the thought of Beattie away. Reed was right, her pursuit was borderline obsessive and yet his face emerged again into her subconscious.

The truce had worked out well for Beattie. That was perhaps his single most important action and had validated his position and given him a veneer of virtue that the politicians could hang some hope on, a facilitator within who could bring to an end to the unpredictable and violent storms that raged within the disparate groupings, mocking the ten-year-old peace agreement, and at a time when they were trying to form a cross-party executive. Although she had no cast-iron proof, that deal hadn't hurt Beattie financially either.

"You weren't buying the chief super's idea that D Company put McBride on forced long-term absence either?" said Reed.

"Again, it's not McCutcheon's style. I think there might be something else going on we can't see yet. Looking in, I'd say the whole umbrella organisation will be on edge after tonight. It's worth considering if this could be some kind of coordinated action against the broad UDA movement."

"Republicans?"

Taylor turned up her nose.

"They've enough on their own plate. An internal coup, perhaps? Look, don't shoot me here, but we know Beattie's organisation has taken a hit after the court case. What if somebody is gathering the troops and trying to regain a foothold? Killing Millar would be an obvious message. McCutcheon owes a lot to Beattie too, indirectly," Taylor shrugged.

"What do you know of this Corrigan character?"

"He was a steady Eddie. Probably knew more than he let on. Nothing significant in his jacket. A few cautions and a riotous assembly. Criminal damage charges from way back too, but then you couldn't throw a dart round there and not hit someone who'd been involved in a flag protest or a street disturbance. Go back far enough and their fathers and brothers were manning the barricades."

"Have a nosey around. If he lasted this long, then he's bound to have a few skeletons lurking. There's somebody that knows why he's taken a bullet to the forehead."

The door creaked open and Macpherson appeared,

juggling three steaming cups of tea and a selection of chocolate bars which he dropped onto the desk.

"Couldn't remember who took what, so I filched these." He dumped sugar and low-calorie sweetener sachets on the table beside the chocolate. Both women uttered their thanks.

"Where's Ron... I mean DI MacDonald?"

"He's gone back to the scene to coordinate the transfer of evidence and the follow-ups," said Reed, breaking up the squares of a Dairy Milk bar.

"Billy McBride. May he rot in hell." Macpherson toasted the air with his tea.

"Have you updated Southampton Constabulary?"

"Yes, ma'am," said Macpherson through a mouthful of KitKat. "I asked them to put out a request to local hospitals for amputations or for DBs missing a right middle finger. The DS on duty said if it was a gangland hit, he's as likely to have been taken out to sea and dumped."

"Do we go wider with this?" said Reed.

"If a body washes up somewhere, we'll hear soon enough," said Taylor.

"If he hasn't been chopped up for chump." Macpherson snapped a second finger of his KitKat in half.

"So what now?"

Taylor sipped her tea and leaned over to flick through her notes.

"At the minute we still have no one claiming either attack, which is unusual so that may rule this in as being something out of the ordinary. Corrigan might be the easier of the two. He's low key. It should be easy to find out if he's pissed anyone off lately."

Reed nodded.

"To focus on Millar, we have Borodenko's initial interview, which places him having regular business meetings, which reading between the lines, involved less slick partners than was the norm. We need to establish who these foreign boys were and any potential motives they might have. A deal gone sour or a double-cross. Borodenko isn't fully forthcoming about why she was beaten either."

"Then there's the baby," said Macpherson.

"She's pregnant?" said Reed, surprise showing in her expression.

"We found a positive test in the apartment. I'm planning on challenging her about it in case she's been stupid enough to extort a client and Millar got wind," said Taylor.

Reed tossed her chocolate wrapper into the wastepaper bin and drained the rest of her tea.

"Okay, we have Burns in custody. We can charge on possession of an unlicensed firearm, with his history he'll do time. See if he'll trade and give us something on these meetings that puts names and faces to the participants. If Burns gives anything up, have the girl corroborate. Offer her pictures if we can get any and then get to the bottom of her story. Is she still in the hospital?" said Reed as she made notes.

"She is. Health and Social Care was trying to get her a place back in Sanctuary on her release."

"They were on the news this morning. Some big new investment," Reed observed.

"Aye, we met the big cheese dishing out the cash earlier," said Macpherson.

"Malcolm Howard?"

"Aye, he let us into the girl's apartment. What?"

Reed looked to Taylor, who summarized the afternoon's events.

"Was he aware of our interest?"

"No, I told him the tenant had been the victim of an assault and we were picking up some items and checking security."

"I think we should tread lightly until we get some detail on what was going on there. If his wife handles that property and it's highlighted that not only does Millar have connections to it, but it's a brothel, the press will have a field day let alone the storm it will whip up in here."

Taylor had considered the possibility earlier. Malcolm Howard, pillar of the community, the man putting significant government grants to work. Placing him even tangentially at the scene of a battered sex worker and the crown prince of vice would put the scrubs on any good that might come from his hard-won investment.

"Right, away you go and see if you can shake anything out of Burns before you get off. We'll reconvene tomorrow morning at ten. That should give forensics some time to gather an initial brief on this evening's shooting and any other results from Risky's."

The two sounded their agreement and Reed swept their wrappers and cups into her bin.

As she pulled the door closed, Taylor watched Reed switch on her laptop and log in.

## Chapter 17

Interview room four was like any normal office environment in the world. It had the same dry, uncirculated air, and the slightly damp smell of mopped floor tiles and washed down walls. The hum of air conditioning did little to heat or cool, and there was a deodorant not quite strong enough to remove the fug of the occupants' sweat or the scent of stale coffee. The table was dingy and chipped where the door had hit, although the dent on the door proved which had come off worse. The black scuff of furniture and nervous feet had worn patches in the linoleum.

"You know you still have the right to request legal representation?" said Taylor.

The big man sat nursing a cup of coffee in a plastic disposable beaker, condensation prickling the inside rim. His hands were scraped, and dried blood was ground into the crevice of the knuckles. His face was a mess of paper stitches and blooming bruises. The swelling had abated a bit, but Rowdy Burns looked about as miserable as she had ever seen a suspect, while Macpherson looked positively gleeful.

"Would you like more coffee?" said Macpherson, his grin widening and with an air of hospitality he reserved for his favourite villains.

Rowdy's hair jutted from his scalp in unruly tufts and ignoring the offer he stared unblinking at the Formica desktop.

"Rowdy? What about a couple of paracetamol?" said Taylor.

"You wouldn't have anything stronger, would you?" he said, perking up, a weak smile breaking through.

"I'm afraid not." Taylor smiled and pinched two

paracetamol from a foil pack and dropped them on the table.

As Rowdy swallowed the pain relief, Macpherson signed in to the digital recording software, entering the authorisation code and then the two disks issued by the custody sergeant. The speakers hummed and then warbled.

"Interview commencing eleven forty-five pm. Officer conducting Detective Inspector Veronica Taylor. Also present Detective Sergeant Robert Macpherson. Can you confirm your name, please?"

"Richard Burns," said Rowdy.

Taylor ran through the rest of the preliminaries and then gave Burns a reassuring nod.

"Mr Burns continues to defer his right to representation, correct?"

"Aye," Rowdy shimmied back in the chair, wriggling to find some comfort which was difficult given the size of him.

"You know that your friend Robert Millar was shot dead last night?"

"So you told me."

"You also claim you have no knowledge of the killing."

"If you mean was it me then no, it wasn't."

"But you don't deny the unregistered firearm that killed him was held in your office?"

Rowdy picked at a fingernail and pursed his lips, which caused a grimace as the scabs cracked. He glanced up at the overhead bug-eye CCTV camera mirroring the tape recording with full high definition video image.

"It was only for show."

"For the avoidance of doubt, you're saying you kept the weapon there as an intimidatory measure?"

"In case any dickheads thought the place was an easy touch, yes."

Taylor shuffled a PC mouse and clicked on a folder displayed on the large split-screen monitor attached to the wall.

"If you could look at the images, please." Taylor drew up two pictures up on the screen.

"These are images taken during our search of Risky's. Specifically, this is the filing cabinet in your office. On the right, there are at least three boxes of ammunition for the weapon and on the left a significant amount of ketamine, GHB and a large amount of cash."

Rowdy continued his fascination with the tabletop, his eyes avoiding the images.

"We swabbed the inside of the cabinet, and the results came back positive for gunshot residue. Now, you can talk or we can wait until the ballistic results come back from the lab and we can compare that gun to details we hold on the database for its use in any other crimes," said Taylor.

"Come on, Rowdy, do yourself a favour, will you?" said Macpherson. "I'm not enjoying seeing you sat there struggling, it's not fair, big lad. You need to be recovering, not getting the third degree. We know you're up to your eyes in this, but cooperation goes a long way."

Rowdy leaned forward, twisting the plastic coffee beaker in circles on the table.

"You'll not have anything," he mumbled.

"Do you think we came up the Lagan in a bubble?" said Macpherson.

"No, seriously. You'll not have anything on the shotgun. I mean yes, it was fired and all but only at a few tins up the quarry. A bit of craic with a few of the lads. I swear it was just for protection."

Taylor weighed up the sincerity in his words.

"Protection?"

Rowdy nodded.

"From who?"

Burn pushed the beaker away and blew out a breath.

"Rab Millar wasn't exactly a saint, Inspector."

"You're telling me."

"Rab said it would put off anybody that came asking awkward questions."

"Convenient that he can't argue his version," said Taylor.

"What kind of questions was he expecting that needed a sawn-off to answer them?" asked Macpherson.

Once again, Rowdy clammed up. Taylor knew the dance. He'd drip-fed a little and now the gears would spin as the guilt kicked in. It wasn't dissimilar to fishing. She heard her father's words, often echoed by Macpherson. Give them a pull, let them run a bit, then reel them in. Neither she nor Macpherson filled the silence for a long minute.

"We'd like to help, Rowdy," she said finally.

"You want to cut a deal, yeah?" he said, a faint flutter of anticipation in his face that his ordeal may soon end.

"No, you misunderstand me. Chances are better than fair you're doing time." Taylor shrugged an apology as she saw the man's shoulders deflate.

"It's up to the DPP but with your history, the firearm, drugs, procuring the girl. You're stuffed, Rowdy. I'm sorry, it's just how it is."

"Doesn't sound like you're much of a help to me then."

"I don't know. There's always a chance any cooperation can help mitigate against a stiffer sentence, but you're going to be doing a stretch in the jail. So with that in mind, who's going to find out who put Rab in a box with you stuck in there?"

Rowdy made to speak and then thought better of it.

"Seriously, you don't want justice for your mate?" said Taylor.

"Whoever did this will get theirs," said Rowdy, a veneer of bravado creeping over the bruised shell.

"You sure about that? Because from what I'm hearing,

there's not too many tears being shed out there."

Rowdy's bloodshot eyes burned. His long breaths gave a wheezy whistle as he stared at the detectives.

"You've nothing to help us ID the man you say took your gun off you and shot the boss man?"

"It wasn't my gun."

"Whatever you say. But you're still saying you can't identify this mystery attacker?"

"No, if I could I would, alright. I didn't see a face."

"They didn't speak."

"Not a word. I heard a commotion and then I remember that I saw the balaclava and I hesitated for God's sake. Next thing he hit me like a mule and I was out, bastard."

"And there's nobody you can think of who would have had it in for Rab?" said Taylor.

"You know the kind of man Rab was and the business he was in. You don't move in those circles without the risk you'll rub someone up the wrong way."

"He's done that alright," said Macpherson. Rowdy flicked the condensation from his cup and huffed a breath.

"Look, it was all handbags, mostly. More about being seen to be seen, you know? Never back down, don't look like a soft touch. Dog eat dog."

"Jesus, did they give you a book of cliches to read in the cell or what?" said Macpherson, leaning his chair back on two legs and frowning.

"He must have had something in the back of his mind if he was arming you at the club. You're sure he didn't mention he was expecting trouble?" said Taylor.

"Rab? The man's a fucking trouble magnet." Rowdy looked at Taylor and then the tape machine.

"Enough trouble to get himself killed over?" she said.

"That's what I'm trying to tell you about the shotgun. It only takes one nutter."

"Like Billy McBride?"

"The Mad Monk? Flip sake he's over the water away with the fairies," scoffed Rowdy.

"So you know him well?" said Taylor.

"Where did you drag him up from?" Rowdy scowled, a look of sour distaste on his cut-up face.

"Well, did you?" Taylor prodded for an answer.

"Not especially, I knew what he was about and what he was up to. Good riddance to him."

"What do you mean by that?" said Taylor, Rowdy's animosity towards McBride growing with every mention of the man.

"A lot of people were glad when he was shipped out."

"So it wouldn't have been him that Rab was worried about?"

"Look, they put the Monk out and told not to come back. Whether or not he's held a grudge, he's had more sense than to do anything about it. Anyway, he's down the south of England somewhere playing 'Hello, Sailor' and enjoying retirement as far as I know." Rowdy tipped a wink and a nod of the head.

"Are you trying to tell us Billy McBride is a homosexual?" said Taylor, realisation dawning on what Rowdy's problem with McBride was.

"Christ, no. He's just a vicious psychopath who liked to rape the wee lads who looked up to him. Told them it was initiation the dirty bastard. I heard he's still at it."

Taylor sat back and took a second. A glance at Macpherson, who gave the smallest of shrugs and a twist of the lips. She took that as confirmation Rowdy's revelation was more than a rumour.

"Rab knew this?"

"Course he did. There was a wee clique back in the day decided to put a stop to it. Your man's antics were putting the lot of us in a bad light."

"You mean aside from the drugs, the prostitutes and the sectarian murders?" said Macpherson.

"I never did time for any murder."

"Aren't you the clever one," said Taylor. "Gordon Beattie did though."

Rowdy looked uncomfortable at the mention of the man's name.

"Don't you mean manslaughter, Inspector," said Rowdy.

Taylor gave a thin smile.

"Rab was pretty good for stepping in and doing a bit while Beattie's been under pressure, wasn't he?"

Macpherson sniffed and looked at her, his eyes flicking to the CCTV and the tape machine, but he said nothing.

"Can you shed any light on that relationship?" said Taylor.

Rowdy made to speak, then stopped and cleared his throat.

"I don't know what to tell you, they were like brothers, but you know families?"

"They fall out?"

"Sometimes, then they come back like nothing happened," said Rowdy.

"They fall out lately?"

Rowdy shrugged. "I used to tell Rab it was like The Beatles."

"The band?"

"Aye, the Monster leaves to do his own thing and the rest fall apart."

"Gordon Beattie is Paul McCartney. I've heard it all now, son," said Macpherson, dropping his seat back onto four legs, grin beaming.

"The Monster was always the driving force and Rab hung onto his shirt tails. Not that I'm ungrateful, but a spade's a spade."

"Why did Beattie leave his mates behind when he climbed

out of the gutter?" said Taylor.

"You'd need to ask him that."

"But you'd have an opinion. Rab's bound to have mentioned it."

"The Monster's a shrewd bugger. He was smart when he was inside, looked at the books when all them other bruisers were doing nothing but lifting weights. He saw the writing on the wall with the ceasefires and then the Good Friday Agreement. Rab always maintained he knew more about what was going on behind the scenes than he let on."

"Rab thought Beattie had a snitch?"

"Rab swung from paying off peelers and blackmailing ministers to being an MI5 mole himself for fuck's sake. But then Rab liked to dabble a bit, you know," Rowdy mimed a finger closing off one nostril.

"Did paranoia drive a wedge too?" said Macpherson. Rowdy pulled a face and then gave a half nod.

"Maybe."

Taylor considered what Rowdy had said. It wouldn't be a stretch to think Gordon Beattie was organised and capable enough to garner inside information to further his own ends. He had studied in prison, gaining a degree in building engineering and business studies, and built the foundations of Finnrock shortly after his release. If he had similarly developed his post-prison contacts just how much had the intervening twenty years benefitted him now he was on the other side of the divide and the politicians needed him to build their vision of a future Belfast.

"Beattie trusted him enough to keep running some of the businesses though?" said Taylor. It was an open secret in the right circles that the two remained steadfast friends.

"He didn't give a shit who it was as long as he got his dough at the end of the month," said Rowdy, offering her confirmation without directly saying so.

"And Rab still traded on the friendship?"

"He liked people to think he was in with the boys on the hill through Beattie, but Beattie needed a man of Rab's reputation to keep things going too."

"You'd testify to that of course?"

"Fuck off, Inspector."

Taylor smirked.

"Might it be that connection that got him killed?"

"Your guess is as good as mine."

"What did Freaky Jackson make of Rab's paranoid theories?" asked Macpherson.

"You're pulling out all the nut jobs the day," tutted Rowdy.

"Any hassle with him?"

"Not this long time. He tortured Rab early on mind you, shortly after he had me take over security. That man's not stable."

"In what way?"

"In the way he lets frigging dogs tear themselves to shreds for sport."

"Wouldn't have you down as an animal lover, Rowdy?"

"I'm not to be fair, but that's a close second behind the Monk's sick kicks."

"You'd be sure the assailant in the club wasn't Jackson then?" said Taylor.

"Ninety-nine per cent.."

"Even with the mask?"

"He was too big. Freaky's a thug all right, but that boy was like a barn door."

"What was the ruckus at No Alibi about?"

The big man did his best not to wince as he raised a stitched eyebrow.

"We're the police, Rowdy," said Macpherson in answer to the surprise etched on the big man's face.

"Something over nothing."

"Tell that to the boy with the busted jaw."

"He's alright. He got himself a compensation package."

"I bet he did. So why was Freaky back on the scene?"

"Rab drip fed him a few quid here and there. He was sympathetic to an old mate, and he needed a favour. Freaky done the deed."

"What was the favour?"

"He arranged some entertainment for a group of boys Rab was wheeling and dealing with."

"Freaky did? Were the girls not enough for these cowboys, then?"

Rowdy gave Macpherson a sour look.

"He took them a trip to the dogs."

"Do you know who they were and what the deal was?" said Taylor.

She could feel the turmoil. Rowdy had given an insight into his relationship with his employer, but dead or not, the loyalty remained.

"Come on, Rowdy? You were Rab's right-hand man. We know he's been a regular lately at the Thirty-One Club and he'd been entertaining a few fresh faces. We'd like to know what that was about?"

Rowdy rubbed his eyes and tried to wiggle his bulk into a more comfortable position. He didn't comment.

"We talked to the girl this afternoon. Lena?" said Taylor.

The up to this minute talkative Rowdy stuck out his bottom lip and spread his hands on the table.

"She told us about these get-togethers. Said Rab had started to scrape the bottom of the barrel? Do you want to have your say?"

"Bitch wouldn't know what she was talking about."

"So enlighten us? Who were they?"

"Albanians," spat Rowdy.

"Albanians?"

"Rab was drumming up some new business. He was looking for investors." The expression on his face told Taylor his prejudices didn't just run to homophobia. It was looking like xenophobia and racism were running close for second place.

"What kind of business?"

"I don't know," said Rowdy, agitation creeping into his tone. "He'd been looking at some old, run-down warehouses and derelict shops near the Westlink and down off Corporation Street."

"Bit of a swing away from running night clubs?"

"More money than sense, sometimes."

"He was looking at buying into property? For what?" said Taylor. Her mind was tracking what she knew of Millar and the new Albanian fraternity in Belfast, her knowledge of them limited to some minor racketeering and cigarette smuggling.

"I don't know the whole story. He was a wild man for doing a deal. He tried to buy one of those old mills up off the Springfield Road a while ago."

"I can't imagine the locals loving the idea of a UDA gangster being a landlord up there?"

"That's what I said, but he thought it was a hoot. He said if the Fenians burnt him out, the insurance would more than cover it. I think he liked the idea that it would be win, win." Rowdy chuckled at the memory.

"How did he get in with them?"

"Introductions. Word of mouth. I just made sure the security was running tight. Edgy sort. I always expected aggro when they were about. They thought they owned the place. I'd just get the nod that there was going to be a wine and dine at the Thirty-One or a wee bit of the other at one of the apartments."

"Like Speakers Square?"

Rowdy again looked uncomfortable. "Yes. Like there."

"Some spot. We were in there today too," added Macpherson.

"If you say so."

"Do us a favour, we have you on CCTV. Fifty to one says I'll get one of your dabs from the dusting?" Macpherson tapped a finger on the desk and gave a wink.

"Aye, okay. Rab arranged a few after-parties and card nights there. Big deal. He paid enough for the privilege."

"Did he not own the place?" said Taylor.

"No."

"Beattie's too?" said Taylor.

"You'd need to ask him."

Seeing something in her expression, he smirked.

"The Monster's on the back burner now isn't he. Read about it all in the Sunday World. That's got to piss you off?"

"You win some, you lose some," said Taylor, drily. Rowdy continued to smirk.

"So what's the deal with the girl? Why did Rab have her brought to the club?" said Macpherson.

"Stupid cow's delusional."

"Seemed okay to us apart from the booting you gave her." Macpherson gave a glare, Rowdy brushing the look off.

"I never touched her."

"If you say so. Why did Rab want her in?" The DS leaned back in his chair again.

"She was shooting her mouth off."

"What about?" said Taylor.

"She's a whore. Who cares?"

"I do. I care when I speak to a young woman who's been beaten, threatened with gang rape, and then has to watch someone get shot dead in front of her. She's only twenty-four, Rowdy. Have you any kids?" Taylor slid out of her chair and leaned in, elbows on the table, finger pointing.

"I do, aye. But they don't earn their money on their backs."

"No, they don't. But any pocket money you might throw them comes from peddling the misery of girls like Lena and the shite you shift out of those clubs so I wouldn't be taking the moral high ground here."

"My kids…" Rowdy began, but Taylor cut him off.

"You might tell yourself it's nothing to do with you, you're just security, whatever helps you look them in the eye and justify a night's sleep but you're as culpable as Millar."

Macpherson coughed. Taylor sat back, hovering on the edge of her chair.

"Rowdy, give us a line on what the craic was and we can take a break here," said Macpherson.

The tension hung in the air, bleeding off Taylor, who stared coolly at the big red-faced lump opposite.

"She thought she was a bloody shop steward or something. Made a scene about one of the Albanians and Rab had to put her straight."

"It must have been some scene." Taylor's tone was bitter.

"When was this?" said Macpherson.

"At the apartment. About a week ago. She got a slap for it but then Rab heard she was still gobbing off and decided she needed to be put in line."

"What did he tell you?"

"Not very much, but it pissed him off big time. I'll tell you that."

"Nothing about what she said or to who?"

"Nope. She's not as innocent as she looks, that one. She was Rab's prize filly. That's why he'd her shacked up in that palace playing Queen Bee. Stupid bitch."

"Why do you say that?"

"She led the high life, had all the perks. All she'd to do was party on and spread her legs from time to time. It wasn't as though it was difficult."

Taylor bit back a retort and Macpherson sat forward.

"What about the Thirty-One Club?"

"Fuckin' place, if you think Beattie's crooked you should get a juke into that place."

"Not your kinda circles, Rowdy," said Macpherson with a smile.

"Aye, something like that. I prefer a good honest class of criminal. At least Dick Turpin wore a mask, you know?"

"How did Rab get his feet in the door?" said Taylor.

"How did Rab get in anywhere? He saw an opportunity and exploited it. What do you think rich, old farts want after their cigars and brandies on a Friday night? I'll tell you what, not back to the frigid wife. Not that they give a flying fig either, as long as hubby is keeping them in diamonds and Moet."

"Is that all it was, a captive audience to peddle his stable?"

"Give him a bit more credit. Why do you think…"

A single, soft knock on the door interrupted them. Rowdy went quiet and Taylor glanced at the monitor showing the image from the security camera outside.

"Interview suspended at…" Taylor clocked the time on the machine, "twelve twenty-three am. Detective Inspector Veronica Taylor leaving the room."

"Sorry, Rowdy. Hold that thought," she said.

Taylor rose and made for the door. Exiting the room, she was greeted by one of the station uniforms.

"Ma'am, apologies for the interruption."

"It's fine. What is it?"

If the sound of his gravelly voice raised the hairs on the back of her neck and put her teeth on edge, the sight of him brought a bitter taste of bile. Flashbulb snapshots of him on the steps of Court One with a grinning Gordon Beattie at his side shot off in her mind's eye.

Solomon Reeves rose from the sitting area in a small alcove at the end of the corridor.

"Good morning, Detective Inspector. I believe one of my clients has been helping with enquiries? I'm here to ensure he is aware of his rights and responsibilities to your investigation."

The solicitor's oily grin beamed from a jaw that was smooth of shadow. He was immaculate in pressed suit and tie, his white shirt gleaming under the harsh corridor lighting.

Taylor glanced at her watch. She knew she looked wretched; acceptable given the length of her working day, and following on from a poor night's sleep and the events of the previous day. Reeves offered a hand. Taylor looked at it as though it would bite her. She should have known it was only a matter of time before someone turned up.

"I apologise for my tardiness however, I wasn't notified until very late in the game." His expression was one of cool professionalism with an underlying glint of steel.

Taylor swallowed her distaste of the man and shook. His grip was soft but firm.

"He's under arrest," she said.

"As I see." Reeves extracted a copy of the charge sheet from his inside jacket pocket and gave it a flutter.

"All the more reason to ensure he has adequate advice on hand. Some of my clients aren't blessed with the intellect to understand their predicament. Certainly not when they are already suffering from such a recent traumatic experience and being withheld medical care and attention," said Reeves, his throaty rasp like pebbles scattered over concrete. "I'd be most grateful if you'll grant me a few minutes alone with him before we might continue your interview?"

❖ ❖ ❖

Macpherson's yawn threatened to swallow his own head, and he rubbed his grumbling stomach.

"Sorry, I'm famished," he said, a wave of apology at the

continued groan of hunger. Taylor empathised. She was on fumes herself, having had little more than a stream of coffee, a day old filling station sandwich and the occasional square of chocolate Macpherson produced from what must have been at one time Willy Wonka's jacket.

"Well, that's all but put the scuppers on that," muttered Macpherson as the door opened and Sergeant Forsythe appeared, escorting the battered and red-eyed Rowdy Burns to the lift that would take them back down to the holding cells. How long he would remain incarcerated was now in question. Rowdy's feet scuffed the floor, and Taylor felt the weight of the day press down on her own.

Legitimately they had another eighteen hours in which to get him to fill in any more detail of Millar's recent past but given the slippery rat Reeves' appearance that was likely to dwindle to nothing. Charge or release had been his parting shot, and she knew the DPP wouldn't have the balls to go toe to toe with him.

The front doors buzzed as the locks disengaged and Reeves swept out in a cloud of Fendi aftershave and into the supple leather of his Aston Martin.

"Who do you think tipped him the wink?" said Taylor, rubbing her eyes as she slumped onto one of the reception area's plastic chairs.

"Does it matter?"

"It does if it came from in here." Taylor threw a gesture that dwindled into a despairing sigh.

"No, it doesn't," said Macpherson. "You know this place is like a sieve. Anyway, it could as easily have come from the hospital as from anywhere. Some sneaky journo following up Sunday's shooting, a nosey visitor, a porter with a big gob. Take your pick."

He was right, and she knew it, but the frustration was grating.

"Right, come on, I'll drop you home before there's no point in us going."

"Yeah, you're right." Taylor stretched out her back and dragged herself up.

Two in the morning.

No concrete progress on Millar. Burns who was just as likely an uncooperative witness as a suspect for anything and Slippery Solomon Reeves back to piss all over her. Why not ice all that with a dead barman, the Mad Monk; a finger anyway, and the Corners Bar in smithereens. It had been some day.

Six hours to get her head down, attempt to sleep, and then return for a reaming at the hands of the assistant chief constable.

She followed Macpherson back to the CID suite to grab her keys and bag. Living the dream.

## Chapter 18

*"…which we put to former MLA and Police and Justice spokesperson, Kevin Blackhall…*

*"I would like to take the opportunity to reiterate that this kind of behaviour should be resigned to our past and I would implore anyone with any knowledge of those responsible for these deplorable acts over the weekend or last night not to hesitate in either contacting myself or to come forward anonymously to Crimestoppers…"*

Veronica Taylor yawned and rolled her neck, popping cartilage machine gunning along the vertebrae as she flicked on the coffee machine and dug out a pint of milk from the fridge. It didn't pass the sniff test, so she put the rest down the drain and resolved to find the time to resupply later. Spooning the dregs of the Sumatran Mandheling into the filter, she added coffee to the growing shopping list too.

The television droned on, the interviewee not short of the answers he didn't have while in post. Taylor, only half listening, plunked a slice of white, grey bread in the toaster and a heaped spoon of sugar into a mug. Reaching over to take her mobile off the charger, she flopped down on an island stool, waiting for the toast to pop, and scrolled through her mail and messages. Her ears pricked at the mention of her name.

*"…the senior investigating officer into the failed prosecution against ex-paramilitary leader, Gordon Beattie last month. Detective Inspector Taylor, also seen here last night at the scene of a barbaric attack on the Corners Bar in East Belfast…"*

God sake, here we go again, she thought.

*"…to which Mr Blackwell had this to say. 'I understand that Gordon Beattie is a divisive figure however the work he has done to*

*steer former members of his organisation away from violence, and the number of local community initiatives he has launched off the back of his commercial success as chair of the IECFI should be applauded. I, for one, would welcome his input into any dialogue that might address this sudden increase in violence and tension that we are experiencing…"*

Saint bloody Beattie, she thought as the toast popped and her appetite disappeared. Chair of the Inner East Community Funding Initiative. It was like putting the wolf in charge of the sheep. She felt hungover from lack of sleep, her recent poor diet, and the weight of the past three weeks case review and the cut off conversations when she entered a room. Scraping butter on the more black than tan toast, she wolfed it down more for the calorie content than the taste. The newscaster had nothing more than speculation and gossip to add to the events at the Corners; a few soundbites with bystanders and the familiar-sounding hoarse rasp of a local community leader that turned out to be the woman from the cordon before moving on to other news.

*"…as we wait to see how this plays out in the coming days. In other news, the forty-year-old man arrested last night following an incident in the city centre has been named as…"*

Taylor clicked off the TV and padded to the shower. Ten minutes later, with towel-dried hair, she sat on the end of her bed and scanned her phone again.

A text from Macpherson to say he was running late and would see her when he got in. A couple of emails from Jack Collins at Section Eight asking for a return call and reminding her she needed to submit her statement regarding the Sunday night domestic that almost ended tragedy, and a brief initial synopsis from Diane Pearson regarding what she had gleaned from the Corners.

As Taylor scanned the brief, she paused, scrolling back up and then down, re-reading a paragraph and studying the diagrams on the small screen. A few clipped images attached and one significant finding. Rather than clearing anything up, the picture only made things muddier.

❖ ❖ ❖

"Guv."

"Morning, Chris. Morning, Carrie." Taylor strode into her corner of the CID suite, dropped her bag under the desk and booted up the PC.

"Were you here late?" said Carrie Cook in greeting. Beside her, Chris Walker was scrolling through a series of screenshots on his laptop.

"Late enough. Feels like I've only been away five minutes."

It was eight am, and she was pleased to see the team at their desks already and, although the cobwebs still clung to her, the maudlin mood hearing Beattie's plaudits traipsed out on the TV had subsided. The station cleaners were busy doing the rounds and there was a clipped energy from uniform. The imminent arrival of the ACC focused minds and motivations.

"Is Erin in?"

"Yes," replied Erin Reilly as she entered from the small kitchen space at the edge of their desk area. "Coffee?"

"I'll grab one in a minute. How are you after the other night?"

"I'm grand. Doc catching up on his beauty sleep, is he?" said Reilly, blowing on the surface of a steaming mug of tea.

"He'll be in shortly. Are you all up to speed on what happened last night at the Corners?"

They gave a resounding chorus of affirmatives.

"Good, what about Diane Pearson's initial report?"

"We all had a skim through just now." Cook pointed at her monitor, text and diagrams on display.

"Good, I'll get to Diane's findings in a sec." Taylor spun her own screen around and stood at the edge of her desk.

"Okay, so the overview on Rab Millar. I've confirmation from Prof. Thompson that cause of death was from the gunshot wounds. No surprise there. Blood alcohol was within normal limits, although toxicology showed signs of amphetamine use, probably chronic as opposed to recreational as there was significant damage to liver and kidneys. Doc and I interviewed Rowdy Burns last night, who was cooperative up to a point until Slippy Reeves rolled in after midnight to put the gag on him."

"You're kidding us?" Walker sat up straighter.

"He refused representation all day, I offered him the duty I don't know how many times. When did he change his mind?" said Cook.

"Burns didn't. Reeves got wind, and he's advised Burns to no comment from here on. He'll try to push the fact that his client wasn't medically fit and under the influence when he was arrested, which we all know is rubbish and have the discharge notes to prove but, Erin, I want every I dotted and T crossed. Arrest forms, custody reports, routine cell checks. Carrie, interview logs and transcripts. Reeves will look for anything to say we cut corners."

"Guv" the two women replied in unison.

"Chris, you got back to TICC last night?"

"I did. No motorbike matching the description though."

"Nothing?" said Taylor, a tone of disappointment creeping in.

"To be honest, the coverage around there is patchy. If someone wanted to come and go from the estate without being spotted, they could manage it easily enough," said Walker. "Might be nothing, but a Peugeot Bipper van was rubbernecking after the attack. Must have been on a loop around the area for twenty minutes then buggered off when armed response and the ambulances arrived." He gave a hopeful shrug.

"Look into it. See if you can get an address and registered keeper and while you're at it put a request out to Newtownabbey for a witness appeal on that burned out van. I want to know why it was in bandit country before coming back to the club. Carrie, any forensics back on that yet?"

"I'm expecting them later, fingers crossed. Last night will have put more pressure on them so it may take a bit longer. We've also received the CCTV recorder from the club but still no access," said Cook.

"Make a note to chase up the CCTV from the Speakers Square apartment building too. Let's see if we can pick up any other familiar faces who might have been visiting."

"Will do," said Cook.

"The last thing then is to look into Millar's communications data. Phone, email, social media if he had any. Before the gag went on, Rowdy Burns said he was dipping his toe in the property market. Look specifically for anything regarding a purchase on the Springfield Road and then any other real estate deals. I'm interested in the paper trail and anyone else associated with the deals. If you need to, put out a call to the Asset Recovery Agency and see if they have ever worked on anything."

As the team scribbled their notes, Taylor glanced at the clock. The second hand seemed to be moving at double speed and she wondered if the ACC had arrived yet.

"Have we anything useful from Sunday's witness statements?" she said.

Cook replied with a shake of her head. "Nothing jumping out yet, although they're still coming through."

"Keep an eye out for anything. Right, the Corners..."

"Sorry, I'm late."

Doc Macpherson manoeuvred his way into their cubicle section of desks, jacket in one hand and a plastic beaker of water from the cooler in the other.

"Hell of a night," he said, dumping the jacket on his chair. He turned, stifling a grimace, and burying a belch behind his hand.

"God help me, I'm putting you with Chris today if your guts are bad," said Taylor.

"Ack, I hadn't a bite yesterday, and then I spotted the Maharaja was still open on the way past."

"Well, I hope it was worth it."

"It was beaut at the time, now though…" Macpherson pulled a face as he dropped into his chair and hoked two Alka-Seltzer from a jumbled desk drawer. "So, what've I missed?"

"I was just filling in on where we got to last night and, lucky for you, we were just about to review Diane Pearson's preliminary on the Corners shooting."

"My timing is impeccable as always," said Macpherson, swirling the seltzer in the beaker with a big finger.

"By the skin of your teeth, as usual, you mean," said Taylor, Macpherson waved an apology. "Right, the Corners Bar, haunt and general habitat of pissheads and the wannabe gangster. It getting the treatment not twenty-four hours after Rab Millar winds up dead doesn't look like coincidence. Our heads of state want to talk retaliation and that's not a surprise, it's what the papers and the politicians are already harping on about however I think Pearson's report brings up some interesting points that we might need to look into. Firstly, Billy McBride."

"McBride's back?" Walker asked wide eyed. Macpherson choked on a sip of water.

"Not all of him, kid."

Taylor lifted a pen from her desk to occupy her hands as she talked.

"We are waiting to confirm that a finger found in the Corners belonged to Billy McBride. Where the rest of him is, we don't know. We will have to speculate seeing as Duncan McCutcheon is having reconstructive surgery this morning. This is where Pearson's initial findings come in."

Taylor stopped, shimmied her mouse and gave a few clicks. The screen showed a close-up of a dead man.

"Barry Corrigan. Long-term employee of the Corners and confidante of Duncan McCutcheon. He also ran the bar for the Mad Monk before McCutcheon came to power."

"Unlucky for him," said Walker.

"The powder burns around the forehead and the casing found adjacent suggest the shot came from a nine millimetre handgun at close range."

"The reports say high calibre rounds from an assault rifle," said Reilly, Cook nodding behind her, scrolling back through the email to the relevant section.

"As do the witness reports," agreed Taylor. "One assailant, agile, mobile and hostile directing a significant barrage of gunfire at the bar from the outside."

"You're thinking a second shooter inside?" said Macpherson.

"Three. I think," she said.

Taylor dragged a composite onto the screen showing a series of photographs. One of each end of the street, the intersection at the Corners and spent casings, and Pearson's handwritten notations.

"The main assault took place here, focusing on the bar from a stationary position." Taylor slid another composite across and zoomed in. "Here, we can see that several rounds were fired north towards this alleyway and the opposite corner of the street. Six rounds walk the footpath and another six impact the gable wall of the end house."

"Another target?"

"Another shooter. Pearson's people found another set of spent casings, three near the entrance to the alley, and another half dozen opposite near these parked cars." Taylor identified the vehicles on the composite. There remained a space between the last car, a red Hyundai, and the next a dark green Toyota Avensis.

"The cavalry?" said Macpherson, peering closely at the pictures and working an image into his mind's eye.

"Someone keeping dick," said Taylor, playing her own mental movie.

The team looked at each of the images and the wider plan view from Google street maps overlaid with positions and notations of what Pearson had collated.

"You might be bang on. Someone else was in that bar and it all went to shit when Rambo rolled up," said Macpherson.

"Maybe. Erin, when you're done with the custody material, get over to the bookies and get them to release their CCTV footage. Focus on the hours before and during the attack. See if we can get a known face hanging around making bets and killing time."

"Yes, guv."

"Questions anybody?" said Taylor.

No one had, each with enough to get on with in the meantime. Just as she was about to set them to their tasks, she noticed the pink and black sports bag beside her desk.

"Carrie, do me a favour? Run that down to the morning brief and see if anyone heading out past the Royal will drop it in. It's a few of Lena Borodenko's personal effects. Get them to ask if social services have got her into Sanctuary. Cheers."

Cook rose and collected the bag, and headed out to catch the tail end of the uniform brief.

Leaving them to it, Taylor mimed a drink to Doc, who was already on the phone. Receiving a silent acknowledgement, she headed for the kitchen. The place looked worse than the Corners after the gun raid. The printed paper signs spotted with tea and water stains, proclaiming it was a shared area and to clean as you go, were being blatantly ignored. After a good minute, she found a couple of cups that passed muster and as the kettle boiled, she leaned on the door jamb and stared into space, running through the prearranged list of questions she expected from the DCI and Superintendent Law in advance of their meeting with the ACC. While she remained the station's poster girl for fuck-up and failure, it was unlikely her presence would be required. Given Law's attitude the previous evening, it seemed she could keep her opinions to herself and follow orders or head on off to traffic or Tesco. If it wasn't so tragic, it would be comical how quickly he had distanced himself. One minute high on the anticipation of a big scalp and the next bitter in his recriminations. It wasn't so much that he had cut her off so quickly that annoyed her but rather the way in which he had gone about it. She was quite capable of understanding the need to circle the wagons but throwing her to the wolves rather than those in the PPS who had sleepwalked into the Solomon Reeves uppercut grated.

The kettle clicked off. Sloshing the boiled water over instant granules she recalled some of Macpherson's advice, *'Nobody's going to remember the dozen dealers you banged up when one walks because someone didn't read him his rights or made a handling of the paperwork when he was brought into custody.'*.

It was frustratingly true, and she tried to remind herself it was all likely temporary. Not that it made knowing Beattie was out there swanning around town any easier to live with. She reached into the fridge for the milk, a prayer for resilience on her lips. Wait for this storm to pass and then get on with the job and have another crack at Beattie.

The milk dribbled thickly into the first cup. She tossed the contents into the sink with a subdued groan and added a prayer for patience.

## Chapter 19

Assistant Chief Constable Kenneth Wallace sat at the head of the conference table and rose as they entered. Resplendent in his dress uniform and impeccable in manner, he addressed Gillian Reed first, thirty-five years in the province having done little to wear away his broad Glaswegian tones.

"Detective Chief Inspector, good to see you. Shame about the circumstances, how's David and the kids?"

Gillian Reed shook the outstretched hand and gave the standard preamble that one does when superiors ask about the family. William Law stood a metre behind, turned out for barrack room inspection, parade ground straight, cap under arm, peak polished to a shine that matched his boots. Detective Inspector Phillip MacDonald, another step behind Law, wore a pressed suit, buckled shoes and an expression that said he wished he was elsewhere.

"William." The two men offered each other professional nods and pleasantries.

"Assistant Chief Constable," said Law, one hand moving to introduce MacDonald, as Wallace looked over his shoulder.

"Detective Inspector Taylor. It's finally good to meet you in the flesh." The ACC sidestepped Law, whose throat reddened under his starched white shirt. Wallace consoled him with a pat on the arm and a polite smile as he passed and made the steps towards an equally reddening Taylor.

"Sir?"

"Ken Wallace. I've heard a lot about you."

"I'm sure it's not all true, sir."

Wallace laughed politely and ushered them all towards the conference table, taking up a position behind his seat.

"Please, sit and, before we get into this, we're all on the

same side here, agreed?"

Well, this is civil, thought Taylor, pausing as the others nodded and made a polite acknowledgement. When Reed had informed her she was sitting in, it was as unexpected as it was unnerving. She could tell by the look on Law's face, he wasn't one bit thrilled to have the district pariah aboard but Phillip MacDonald, to his credit, gave her a reassuring smile of encouragement as she tried to push Macpherson's analogy of lamb to the slaughter and his pantomime sharpening of knives out of her head.

"...and so I'll get straight to the point. The chief constable, myself and the other ACCs are coming under increased pressure to get this situation under control. The primary concern we have is the rising community tension because once these groups get a head of steam up, well, you don't need me to tell you what the potential is."

Wallace was the example of implacability. Sat at the head of the large conference table, his tone and presence exuded authority and commanded attention. In his mid-fifties and a keen amateur rugby enthusiast, he still had the broad-shouldered bulk and imposing physicality from his former days as a prop, the midsection perhaps running away from him, but his height helped carry it off. The son of a Catholic dock labourer and determined to leave behind the impoverished East Clyde tenements, he made the leap across the Irish Sea and joined the Royal Ulster Constabulary against his family's wishes. His proclamation of atheism was seen as almost worse than his birth religion, which itself was a burden to his progress from the first day on the job. Fenians didn't make good peelers, so the story went in those days. His tenacity and sheer force of will saw him rise from the rank of constable and claw his way up through the rank and file to his current position of seniority as ACC of the Police Service of Northern Ireland. Cocking an ear to rumour and service gossip, the expectation was he would be the next chief constable.

"As an organisation, we are agile and experienced enough to respond to a series of high-profile murders; we've dealt with enough of them. The concern here is the level of escalation."

He wasn't putting too fine a point on it either, thought Taylor, recalling her days in uniform, baton and shield in hand as the thin line of officers held apart hordes of rabid rioters, sectarian hatred hot for the blood of the other side. Like every officer around the table, she carried the scars of her own days on the frontline, the screams of her roommate as a petrol bomb lit her up like a piece of kindling and the limp dead weight as she helped drag the lifeless body of another colleague behind the cover of a Land Rover, his neck broken by a breeze block dropped from a high-rise.

"We aren't talking the good old days of the Troubles, either. Every one of us sitting here is aware of the sheer violence this new breed of firm doles out to their own, let alone each other. The attack last night could have been much worse. We don't need another Greysteel or Loughinisland massacre or more body parts in bin liners. Two murders in two days…" Wallace shook his head, letting the magnitude of the two deaths sink in.

"I can assure you, Assistant Chief Constable, the teams will work around the clock on this to ensure that…"

"William, I know they will, but can you save the platitudes for the press conference…"

Here we go, thought Taylor. Gumshields in, ladies and gents. She cast a surreptitious glance around the table, knowing Macpherson would have given his right hand for a look at Law's face.

"I'm confident each of you will try your damnedest to get this in hand. What I'm here for today is to hear how, and more importantly, how soon."

Law cleared his throat and tried to sit a little straighter, Taylor redirected her eyes front and centre, thinking that given he already had a rod shoved up his backside, that was an anatomical impossibility but credit where credit was due, Law was trying.

"We have several ongoing avenues of enquiry. DCI Reed is heading up the operation and DI MacDonald as DSIO is assisting. Obviously, the events of last evening add resource pressure, but we are confident we will have caught up within the next thirty-six hours."

"Where are the specific pressures, William?"

"DCI Reed, do you wish to appraise the ACC?" Law offered the floor to Reed with a wave of his hand.

"Sir, you'll be well aware both murder scenes have left us with an extensive amount of evidence to process. Add to that the external scene at the Corners where we need to ensure all trace evidence has been recovered before we open the area to the public again," Reed held up her hands, her tone resigned.

"Even if we wished to, we can't process this amount of evidence any faster. The teams in Seapark are doing what they can but there will be a delay on bullet comparison and given some cross-jurisdictional issues there is likely to be a delay on identification confirmation too. In terms of house to house and testimony gathering, it's just the time lag of procuring the statements and transferring to the database for review."

"I understand. However, if there remains an issue regarding cooperation from other forces, let me know."

"Sir," said Reed with a nod.

"We still have no one claiming responsibility for any of this?" Wallace looked around the table and Law confirmed the matter.

"As yet, no. In terms of motive, the strong supposition is a disagreement over territory or drugs led to the Millar killing and the Corners attack was retaliation."

"I see. DI Taylor, you know one party reasonably well. Do you concur with the assessment?"

Taylor swallowed, feeling the room shrink as Wallace and Law's eyes turned on her at once.

"I think it's likely that Robert Millar was killed because of his links to the drugs trade or one of his other illegal activities, yes."

"And the retaliation angle?"

"I think its early days to say for sure," she said. William Law's brow furrowed in a scowl for a split second, and then his attention returned to the ACC.

"Are we concerned that these may be attacks by dissident Republican factions?"

"Not in any sense other than again, I believe it is based in criminality rather than a sectarian motive. The attack on the Corners would suggest it's a Loyalist in-house disagreement playing out extremely violently," said Law, taking up the baton of addressing the ACC's questions.

"That's something, at least. This situation is bad enough without thinking it could spread cross-community. What are we proposing to mitigate any further escalation?"

"Mobile and foot patrols have been stepped up in areas where the intelligence assessments would suggest a high risk of reoccurrence or street gatherings. We have trained liaison and community officers reaching out to local representatives and activists to gain an understanding on the ground and to reassure them we are working to find the perpetrators and encourage them to make sure the people they represent do not make the job harder by involving themselves."

Wallace nodded approvingly.

"Good, it's a sound strategy. It seems to me, the key to both dampening down the tinder and procuring a reliable source for identifying the murderers is to appeal to these groups directly and offer any incentive possible. The resources and economic opportunities available since the ceasefires have kept these organisations at heel, and while the current climate isn't ideal, that avenue still seems our best bet for quelling this." Wallace nodded again, cementing his thoughts upon his audience.

"With respect, is that not an angle best served by bringing political pressure to bear?" said Gillian Reed.

"It is, Gillian, and it's one that I will pressure the justice minister with this morning. However, we've all been coppers long enough so don't tell me you don't have options that may incentivise some of these people to speak out on the QT."

Reed raised an eyebrow as she considered the words. Law spoke into the vacuum.

"For clarity, Assistant Chief Constable, are we to consider abandoning ongoing investigations and the potential for…"

"William, what I'm telling you is that getting control of a Loyalist feud that has seen two men die, two be critically wounded and almost a dozen others receive hospital treatment is the top priority for our political masters as it should be for us as the arm of law and order. We know how situations like this can descend into civil disorder. It's times like this when we must bring more than financial resource to bear."

Taylor remained silent as she felt Law's hackles rise.

"Apologies, it's just that…" Law began before being cut off.

"If you have the means to either reduce or place in abeyance potential prosecutable activities for the sole purpose of garnering information on those responsible for these outrages, then that is a bitter pill we will all swallow. Do I make myself clear?"

The skin of Law's jaw skittered over bone as he clamped

down and nodded.

"The chief constable endorses this, of course?" said Reed as she replaced the cap on her pen.

"Absolutely," replied Wallace with a firm nod. "All avenues are open to bringing this current chaos to an abrupt end, and on that point has anyone at a senior level reached out to Gordon Beattie?"

The air seemed to suck out of the room, and Taylor felt her ears pop. Wallace briefly made her the object of his gaze, and she felt the others' eyes look anywhere but at her. Law piped up, diverting attention and her growing unease.

"Considering his past relationship with Millar, and given the recent press attention the Service and of course Mr Beattie has had, the matter of engaging with him is delicate. I am taking the approach that he should have peace to put his disrupted affairs back in order," said Law. "I think it's only right we afford him the freedom to enjoy the liberty the courts have granted him rather than risk being seen to be engaged in some form of vendetta," he added with another brief look at Taylor, his hands folded beside his cap and elbows off the table.

"That seems a solid approach, Superintendent, however, Gordon Beattie has links to both the parties involved and I cannot overstate how significant his influence is in these communities. I would suggest that we make an approach through his legal team indicating we would be interested in putting the recent past aside and appeal to his better nature for any assistance he could bring to calming tensions before they explode again."

"Yes, sir," said Law.

"Are you on board with that, DI Taylor?" said Wallace.

Taylor hesitated, her heart rate jacking up in her chest and the uncomfortable feeling of her throat constricting. She swallowed back a reply, giving instead a curt nod, frustrated at just how futile her job could be. Months and years dedicated to bringing about the downfall of a man whose influence had shattered communities only to have to go cap in hand and beg for the use of those influences to avert more misery and no doubt have him lauded with the glory. She felt sick.

## Chapter 20

"Wait a minute, now. Am I hearing this right? Is he serious?"

Gordon Beattie leaned against the scaffolding rail and looked out across his city. All around him the noise of construction competed with the wind whipping at the high visibility jacket and hard hat that he wore. His vantage point was a slab of Finnrock bison floor, set eighteen stories high, that would eventually form the base of a rooftop terrace on yet another of his exclusive developments. Ten of the floors would serve as commercial lettings and the remaining eight as high-end apartments with the top floor split into two fifteen hundred square feet executive penthouse suites. As Beattie peered down at the men and machinery scuttling about the site compound below, he noted a pristine white Land Rover Discovery splashing through potholes and getting her twenty-two-inch alloys slurried in the brown muddy glar that constituted the current route into the site, but which would eventually be a pristine sweeping descent into a five hundred car underground garage for the exclusive tower block. But that was a way off yet.

"After all they tried to do to me. Is he serious?" Beattie moved the mobile phone to his other ear and watched as the Discovery was pulled over at the site entrance, tinted driver's window lowering as the gateman approached. Beattie shook his head in disbelief as he listened to the caller.

"Tell him if he has the Bentley, wait, if he has all the bloody cars back in my driveway by the end of the day, then I'll think about it. Cheeky bastards, wanting me to do their dirty work."

The Discovery having negotiated the security gate was pulling into a visitor parking bay. The driver exited to open the rear door. Beattie recognised the man who stepped out. He could see the consternation as his shoes sank a couple of inches into the thick, muddy ground.

"I'm serious, Solomon, tell him all the cars. Here, I've got to go, I'm at the White Lines Development for a meeting. Aye, it's coming on well. Listen, before you go, did you have any luck with that other thing?"

Beattie closed his eyes at the news.

"Keep trying. I need access to those funds. I've asked the lads to cash out all the other revenue streams. When the dough lands in, can you see to it getting lost? Okay. Good luck, speak to you later."

He cut the call and stepped down off the exposed balcony, walking through the bare open-plan structure of the incomplete apartment to the temporary service elevator. He could hear the whirr of machinery in the confines of the Finnrock concrete shaft.

As the lift came to a stop, he could hear muted complaints from within.

"Amir! Welcome to White Lines. You buying one of these or not?"

Amir Kazazi was a head shorter than Beattie but tapered from broad shoulder to narrow waist. The high visibility vest he wore drowned him, hanging near his knees, and he clutched the white safety hat under his arm like a football. He strode out on sturdy legs like a referee taking to the penalty spot, his face like thunder.

"You couldn't have found us somewhere else to park, eh? You know how much these shoes cost?"

Beattie laughed.

"It's a building site, Amir. What did you expect?"

"I didn't expect such a shithole. Anyway, how is your craic?" said Kazazi, scraping more mud off on the base of a firefighting station.

Beattie shook his head.

"How long have you lived here? 'What's the craic?' Come on, have a juke over here. Now is that not a view?"

Kazazi, an associate, and one of Beattie's site foremen followed as he led his way through to what would be the wraparound lounge.

"What do you think?"

"I think it's too high."

"Are you joking me? I've three others ready to go that will be twenty-five stories. Henry, why don't you take Amir's friend here across to Eighteen B and show him the mock-ups. We have a bit of business to chat about."

Henry nodded and presented the way with an outstretched arm. Amir waved his man's concerned expression away with a dismissive hand and then, obliging, he fell in step as Henry made off towards the lift lobby.

"You should be grateful I came after what you did to Bekim," said Kazazi.

"I wouldn't have needed to teach the wee sod some manners if you kept your boys under control, Amir."

"He was…"

"Amir. Listen, he was running about the town chatting about Rab. What was I to think?"

"You should have asked me to speak with him?" protested Kazazi.

"You'd have known what he was at, would you? Rab already told you to wind his neck in."

The Albanian glared.

"Anyway, I don't need to ask your permission," said Beattie.

Kazazi's eyes blazed.

"You should have asked me," he reiterated, "I was working with Rab to help you. I have just as much at stake and when you lose, I lose. The only difference is you can afford it." He waved a hand in a grandiose gesture around the large space.

"Aye, well. Let's hope things are getting back to normal. I'll tell you this though, there weren't too many people in the loop who knew about that shipment of pills."

"You are the one who has spent six months being investigated, Monster. If there's been a rat, you need to be baiting your own back yard, never mind digging in mine."

Beattie gave a curt nod. Pointed a finger.

"Just you keep an eye out on your side and I'll worry about mine."

"Agreed." Kazazi nodded.

"You never got to the bottom of how Customs came to finger the van?" said Beattie.

"Not a thing. Pot luck. I've had two tonnes of tobacco and thirty-five migrants through since then without any bother. They're up in the plant now, working off their travel costs. Well, most of them are, I held on to a few of the prettier ones if you want to call past the club later." Kazazi's broad face twisted in a lascivious smile.

"Maybe for a drink, but you can keep the skirts. Knowing your lot, they've been ruined getting them fit for work."

"You insult me again. All this business has made you sulk. Come on, Monster," The Albanian chuckled to break the tension and slapped Beattie on the back. "Why is it you bring me here? You don't seriously think I'm going to buy one of these from you?"

"Why not? I'll get Henry to give you a brochure for the car home. Come on up here."

Beattie led the Albanian up the concrete stairs and onto the roof terrace. The wind whipped in from Belfast Lough, vista extending all the way to the open sea where the green-grey water was capped in frothing white. In the distance, the vehicles on the M2 motorway looked like matchbox toys, and the vast dock and warehousing district on the north side of the lough was laid out like Lego blocks. To the south, a haze of steam from the exhausts of an eco waste and energy recycling plant smudged the skyline above the shipyard and huge industrial bulk fuel containers.

"I've good news and bad news for you," said Beattie.

Kazazi nodded, eyes darting across the panorama.

"What's wrong with you?"

"I don't like heights."

"Fuck sake. You're safe up here as long as you don't fall off." Beattie eyed the man.

"Constructions sites can be dangerous places, you know." He walked up close and took the Albanian's arm, walking him forward towards the rail. Kazazi resisted, but Beattie shoved him on.

"Look at that, will you. Beautiful isn't it. See all those cranes over there, I'm supplying all that. Over there too." Beattie swept his hand along the horizon. "The problem I have, Amir, is that after that whole balls-up I can't spend a fucking washer without them assets bastards wanting to see the receipt."

Kazazi stood his ground and swallowed. Gusts of wind rocked the two men.

"I've lads putting the word out around the wholesalers and the dealers. There's a bit of change coming," said Beattie, releasing his grip.

"What has this to do with me?"

"I wanted to tell you myself. I'm cutting your terms to twenty days and from here on out the rate will be forty per cent…"

The Albanian protested, a series of choked snorts.

"And, I want sixty per cent of your current liability by the end of this week."

"I cannot get that sort of…"

"Of course you can. I'm not asking you to fly to the moon.

Put in a few calls, lean on a few people. Dig some up."

"Monster, you are asking me to hand over the guts of three million in three days. That's…"

"That's business. Amir, call this an opportunity."

"The last opportunity I took from you cost me."

"These things happen," said Beattie with a shrug. "Look, I'm going to cut you in on something. Right now, at the ground level. It'll help ease the pressure of what I'm asking of you. Call it a sweetener. Rab was already trying to get you brought into the storage hubs, but now I need a new partner. I've a deal in the pipe, but I'm short on cash flow to service it. I have a safe shipment arriving in the next couple of days. I'll handle the import, but I'll need you to take delivery of the consignment and get it processed and out to wholesale."

"Collection only. I'm not set up for the rest."

"Collection and distribution. I'll make it worth your while. If you need resources to make it happen, I can put you in touch with the right people."

"You trust these people?"

"Of course I trust them. Look, I've been paying through the nose to keep this at sea for three months. Just you be ready to move on it when I give the say so. You do this right and you'll not look back and I'll think about extending your credit again. Okay?"

Kazazi took a step away from the rail and looked around the roof.

"I'll need to think about it. This could bring me more trouble than…"

"More trouble than I could give you?" Beattie grabbed the man by the arm again, his tone steely. "You're in business, Amir, because I say you can be in business. It's time to start remembering that. Don't be biting the hand that feeds you."

"I'm just saying…"

"Look, I know you couldn't give a toss about that pretty

wife of yours so I'll not waste my breath, but see the business that keeps you in Gucci suits and sets up the folks back home, the fancy house, the cars, the club, the girls, the gear. I swear to you I'll burn them down round your ears if you don't start bucking your ideas up. I need this to go ahead without a hitch. You do it and it'll be the making of you. All the shite you have now will be nothing to what you could have after this."

"Okay. I'll do it." Kazazi's eyes were wide as Beattie stood him against the safety rail.

"Good lad, Amir." Beattie grinned, releasing his grip and slapping the Albanian on the arm. Kazazi stumbled away from the edge.

"For fuck's sake," said Beattie, scowling. He beckoned the Albanian forward, motioning for him to look down. The smaller man tentatively took the half dozen steps back to the rail.

"What is it?" he stammered, at first resisting the urge to look but gradually after several peeks looked over the edge.

Below them, a large excavator was preparing the foundations of what would be a landscaped park and restaurant. A deep scar of earth had been opened and they could just make out the sound of the cement mixer beeping as it reversed towards the spot where the spoil was piled high to one side.

"Dangerous game. Construction," said Beattie.

Amir turned at the sound of footsteps scraping up the steps. Henry returned to the terrace, alone. He tossed across a hard hat to his boss.

"I'd put that on." Beattie pointed at the hard plastic helmet still tucked under Kazazi's arm. "We wouldn't want any more accidents today."

Below, Kazazi could see the body of his associate lying in the ditch like a broken toy. The huge barrel of the mixer spun slowly as the operator released the chute and swung it over the ditch. Ten thousand kilograms of ready mix cement slewed out, covering the body in a heartbeat.

"Call this a favour. Your man was up to his nuts in gambling debt, and he paid it all off in cash a fortnight after our shipment got lifted. Now how do you suppose he managed that?"

Kazazi didn't trust himself to argue.

"How come I know what your boys are about when you don't know yourself, Amir? If he spoke to the wrong person, it was over for you."

Below, the scene played out as innocently as any other day on any other site. Now that the corpse was buried.

"Do you want me to get someone to drive you back or are you alright yourself?"

The Albanian was mute as he watched the ditch fill. The last few cubic feet of concrete dribbled into the hole, and then a team moved to smooth the surface with large lengths of wooden baton.

Beattie tossed the hat off the roof.

"Money for Friday, Amir, and answer the phone when I call with the other details. Henry will see you out."

## Chapter 21

"I'm sorry again for your trouble, Mrs Corrigan. Thanks for the tea." Veronica Taylor offered the woman a compassionate smile. The widow Corrigan's small hand felt fragile as she shook it, the bones like a bird's but the skin calloused from her long days as a commercial cleaner. Close family and friends surrounded the woman. Her youngest daughter offered a feral smile of unabashed contempt, perhaps because she was here drinking tea and not out finding her father's murderer, thought Taylor. A couple of young children scooted about, oblivious to the grief. About twenty people had gathered in the modest two-up, two-down property and for the most part had distributed along traditional lines as clan gatherings went. Women in the kitchen and back room and the men meandering between the hallway, front room and out to the narrow front passage facing the road for a smoke.

Taylor returned to a few raised eyes from those gathered in the front lounge, her position granting her access over her gender. The furniture was shoved against the walls and a pasting table had been set up opposite the door, atop of which mismatched and chipped plates offered cakes, sandwiches and savouries, and pots of tea.

"It's not an all you can eat, for God's sake."

Macpherson turned at the hissed whisper, a third cup of steaming tea in one hand and a plate of dainty sandwiches, cut into crustless triangles balanced in the crook of his elbow. His other hand was occupied with fishing out a cocktail sausage roll from a bowl.

"I'm mingling," he said, popping the savoury in his mouth, chewing twice and then swallowing.

"It's not a flipping party," said Taylor, resisting the food even though her tummy grumbled at the sight of a fresh cream apple turnover. "That's bad for you and all, you're supposed to chew your food."

"I'm starving." Snatching up another sausage roll, he gave her an arch look. "I never had my tea break."

"You were dying with your guts an hour ago."

"Constitution of an ox. How is she?" His question was muffled behind a mouthful of pastry.

"She didn't say much. You?"

"Aye, come here." Macpherson wiped his fingers on the back of his trouser leg, edging away from the table and towards the window. "Jim. Jim, can I bother you again?"

Taylor followed to where a sombre suited, middle-aged man sat alongside a much older woman in the banqueted bay window.

"There you go, Mrs Baxter. Few wee sandwiches for you. You don't mind me borrowing your son for another wee second?" Macpherson handed across the plate and took a step back as the man stood.

"Jim, this is Ronnie Taylor."

"Pleased to meet you, Inspector. I knew your da."

"Jim was a gateman at Strandtown Station for what, ten years?"

"For my sins."

"You're Barry's brother?" said Taylor.

"Cousin. My mother is his da's sister. God rest him." He motioned over to the stooped old maid poking at the insides of a sandwich.

"I'm sorry for your loss, Jim."

"Thanks. Mess up there is it?"

"It is that. We've our work cut out," confirmed Taylor.

"We all know somebody killed in the Troubles but you're just never prepared when it lands on your own front door." He looked down, remembering her loss. Taylor acknowledged the clumsy observation and eased his discomfort with a nod and empathetic smile.

"You don't mind me asking you about Barry?" she said.

"No, fire on. Anything to help find the bastard." He lowered his voice as he uttered the invective.

"He was a stalwart in the Corners?"

"Man and boy. His first job was in there collecting the glasses. He'd touched for other stuff through the years but ended up staying there through the thick and thin of it. He'd have some stories to tell you, like when he had Bill Clinton in for a Guinness, I think there's a picture here somewhere? You know when he was over trying to drum up support for the Good Friday Agreement?"

Taylor nodded. She'd been ten when the Clintons had made their historic visit to offer support to a fledgeling peace process. She remembered the time; flashbacks of watching the visit on television, the rolling news reports, newspapers full of it, even in school the talk of it. Her abiding memory though was the busy week when her father hadn't come home. Within the year he wouldn't come home at all.

"I bet he dined out on that for a while?" she said.

"He was proud as punch. We slummed it watching them from the upstairs window when they visited the factory that used to be across the road." His pupils dilated as he drifted back in the mist of memory. The old factory was now long replaced by boxy social housing.

"Popular fella, Barry?" said Taylor.

"Aye, I suppose. He was a barman, so plenty knew and liked him."

"No bother lately? Maybe barred someone or a fall-out?"

"Sure, there's always someone getting barred then they're back in the next week. Look, I know the Corners doesn't exactly have the reputation of being your run of the mill local but it's a boozer all the same. They all look after each other so they do."

Taylor nodded. She knew that alright. The fraternal code of silence would be at work. Secrets kept from the spouse, crimes and misdemeanours swept under the rickety wooden boards and not discussed on pain of punishment. It was a Loyalist Paramilitary bar. Foremost it was a symbol, the flags and three-storey murals of masked men declaring No Surrender ensuring everyone knew who marshalled law on the surrounding streets. Second, it would wash the illicit gains that McCutcheon earned from their other businesses. The protection rackets, the lock-in card schools and knock-off booze and other counterfeits that would get sold out of the back room every other night of the week. All at bargain-bin prices, and to most of the people in the room with her now, which explained their unease at her presence. The profits all in aid of one primary goal. Defence of the realm. For God and Ulster.

"Was he paid up?" Taylor's voice dropped. Jim Baxter looked around the room. He edged Taylor and Macpherson a little further from the nearest earshot.

"Na, he wouldn't have got into any of that."

"Never?"

"Look, he worked in a UDA bar. He would know who to go to if he needed anything sorted and likely knew more than he should, but was he was straight up, never joined as far as I know." He nodded, voice more insistent. "No. None of that."

"Okay. Sorry, have to ask." Taylor shrugged and Baxter mimicked the gesture in reply.

"Sure, I know you do."

"We're trying to work out if any of this is connected to past grievances between the teams," said Taylor.

"All that carry on with B Company? Sure it was years ago."

"You don't think there'd have been anybody harbouring a

grudge with your cousin over that still?"

"Barry wasn't part of that," said Jim Baxter with a firm shake of his head.

"He gave a statement and was in the bar the night the Monk was lifted by the boys," said Macpherson.

"So were about a dozen others."

"We're just trying to find out if someone had something specific against Barry," said Taylor in reply to what sounded like a dismissal.

"Like who?"

"That's what we are trying to find out," said Macpherson.

"Na, couldn't be. That was all put to bed when Chopper took over. Have youse heard about him?"

"He was having surgery this morning," said Macpherson, producing a cocktail sausage from a napkin and popping it into his mouth.

"He was a lucky boy,"

"If you can call it that," said Taylor. She tilted her head to the room. "How's it all being taken?"

"The lads are restless. They want to send a message."

"That won't help us find Barry's killer."

"Sure I know." Baxter smiled over at his elderly mother and mimed a top-up for her tea, which she declined with a shake of her tight steel curls.

"Barry had just finished doing his taxi licence, you know? I think it was an excuse to get out of the house. Jean's never here half the time, she stays up at the daughter's most weekends with the grandchildren. He said it'd give him a few quid extra to take them all away in the summer."

Jim Baxter helped himself to another couple of sandwiches as he spoke, Macpherson accepting his offer of more sausage rolls while Taylor politely declined, taking the moment to observe the men surrounding her. Most were in some form of sombre formal dress, shirt and black tie with the rest in jeans and bomber jackets. Each group was moored close to each other, talking in hushed tones with the occasional outpouring of louder banter and laughing. A small hip flask was doing the rounds and topping up the teacups. She met the eye of a familiar face. A half nod in acknowledgement, Taylor mimed a smoke, and he nodded. She held up five fingers, and he turned back to his mates.

The conversation dawdled on, Macpherson asking what Jim Baxter had been up to since his days as a gateman and then the quiet goodbyes and promises to keep in touch with any news. Taylor once again offered her sympathy and wishing him the best for the funeral.

"What do you make of that then?" said Macpherson as they excused themselves through a group huddled under the porch and passing around a lighter, cigarettes clamped between teeth.

Taylor looked back at the house. From the bay window, Baxter waved and his mother's rheumy eyes stared at her.

"What I'd expect," she said.

The two police officers stood at the kerbside under red, white and blue bunting that fluttered from lampposts.

"He couldn't work in there and not be connected. There has to be an angle on what got him killed stemming from that association. We'll see what Erin can get off the CCTV at the bookies and take it from there."

"What now?" said Macpherson, blipping the locks on the car.

Taylor nodded, motioning behind her sergeant to where a man had broken away from the group of smokers at the door and followed them onto the street.

"Alright, officers." He exhaled a stream of smoke from the side of his mouth.

"Grand," said Taylor. "You alright?" The man she had recognised inside walked breezily up to the car. Evidently, the recognition extended to Macpherson.

"Worzel, how's it going, have you no birds to scare today?"

Eddie Faulks was a long-limbed, skinny man. His head was too big for his body and he had a shock of strawlike blond hair and a wine stain birthmark running under his nostrils which covered the scar left from a childhood cleft lip. The overall effect had cruelly dubbed him with the nickname of the walking, talking scarecrow from literature and television.

"Just thought I'd offer my services to the constabulary. Fulfil my civic duties and all. Smoke?" He offered out a packet of Benson and Hedges, which both officers declined.

"None of you lot smoke anymore?" He grinned, showing a haphazard row of nicotine-stained tombstones.

"I just fancied a bit of catch up, Worzel," said Taylor, leaning back against the car. Her eye caught Jim Baxter observing the conversation from the bay window.

"How are you doing, Inspector? Commiserations on the Monster thing. I really thought you'd got the bastard," he said, dragging on the cigarette, a manic grin as he exhaled.

Faulks was an old school D Company reprobate with a jacket as long as his leg of previous form and custodial sentences stretching back to childhood.

"There's always a next time, Worzel. Paying your respects, are you?" she said.

"I knew Barry well, so I did. Fixture up the street, he was."

"Anything you can help us with then?" said Macpherson, his tolerance waning.

The skeletal Faulks tapped the side of his nose.

"On the QT I might."

"Come on, jump in. I'll take you for a coffee," said Taylor, opening the passenger door.

"Aw, come on, Inspector. I've been drinking tea in there for hours. A wee pint might hit the spot. Loosen the old vocal cords." He gave a wink.

Taylor looked across at Macpherson, who glared at the dishevelled Worzel and then the car, his nose wrinkling in anticipation of being confined inside with the malodorous man.

Worzel dragged the last of the cigarette to his fingertips and discarded the butt to the gutter, an equally disgusted frown upon his features.

"Don't be telling me you lot don't drink on duty any more either!"

❖ ❖ ❖

Taylor nursed a soda water and lime while Macpherson had opted for a half of stout. Worzel wiped a hand across his scarred and stained lip, removing the froth from his second pint of Tenants Lager. He smacked his lips and eased back in the booth.

"Cheers, Inspector. I needed that." He raised the glass in appreciation. The first pint had barely touched the sides.

They hadn't driven far. It was a short trip out of the estate to the Laganview. The bar's name was ironic given that it was about half a mile from the river that cut through the city, any view of which was obscured by the rows of terrace streets and shops that surrounded the establishment on the corner site of a main arterial road junction.

The lounge was a long affair with round tables and chairs arranged around a horseshoe bar, and the trio had commandeered one of the two larger booths. The walls were in the grip of redecoration and there remained evidence of the work and the tradesmen. A paint-spotted dust sheet had been balled in a corner next to a cut-in bucket fashioned from an old cordial bottle and a set of tired aluminium step ladders. Every now and again an older gent in paint-splattered dungarees emerged from a stairwell door wedged open with a tin of magnolia emulsion.

The smell of food was in the air and genial banter could be heard above the tinny sound of music as the swinging door to the rear of the lounge and the kitchen swung back and forth.

"You're staying out of bother this long while, Worzel. Prison change you last time?" said Taylor.

"Sure, I'm getting too old for that carry on now."

Taylor didn't believe a word of it. Trouble was tattooed right through the likes of Worzel and his compatriots.

"Well, keep it that way. What have you got to tell us?"

Worzel took a long draught of lager and looked around the bar. There were only a few other patrons.

Two old boys played a game of dominoes near the bar, a three-way repartee of commentary and highlights of the week's news going on between them and the bar steward who was emptying a glasswasher. The front door squealed on a rusted hinge and Worzel nervously squinted into the sunlight streaming in, but the door banged shut again without a patron appearing.

"You hear if the shooting had anything to do with Rab Millar?" he asked.

"We can't tell you that, Worzel. It's an ongoing investigation," said Taylor.

"Is that what you heard?" Macpherson took a sip of stout and studied the man.

"It's what's being said."

"We couldn't say anything, even if it was true," said Taylor.

"It wasn't." Worzel drained another quarter of his pint in a thirsty swig. Settling it back down on the table, he wiped a wet ring of condensation with his hand. "I was only out of the bar when that all kicked off."

"Did you see who it was?" Macpherson leaned in on his elbows. Taylor angled her head to pick up on any cue Worzel wasn't giving away.

"No, I swear. I couldn't tell you for sure."

"But?"

"Who comes sauntering in bold as brass about half an hour before?"

"For God's sake, am I getting three guesses or what? Spit it out?" said Macpherson, a fierce scowl across his features.

"Freaky Jackson."

"You're sure?"

"Absolutely."

"I wouldn't have thought he received a warm welcome, considering," said Taylor.

"He didn't. One of the big lads challenged him; the stupid bugger had no idea who he was. Freaky put him down."

Taylor and Macpherson exchanged looks.

"No," said Worzel, backtracking. "I mean he gave him a thump and then he had a few words with Barry and went up the stairs to see Chopper."

Taylor saw nothing that gave away the veracity of Worzel's revelation.

"What kind of words?"

Worzel shrugged.

"The sort you'd expect. It wasn't exactly Piers Morgan's life stories, you know?"

"You didn't stick around?"

"Are you joking me? I gave him five minutes and then went out to get the boys. Fucking Freaky Jackson. He was getting what was coming to him, sanctioned or not."

Worzel drained the glass, thumping it down hard enough to draw the eye of the domino players, a dangerous fire in his eyes.

"We should've retired him a long time ago and here he comes, swanning in there like it was nothing and then battering big Raymie. Bastard."

"Jackson was Millar's mate. How are you so sure that the

shooting wasn't retaliation?"

"Well, for one, I know we never clipped Rab. True bill, I'd tell youse on the QT if we had. Second, Barry was doing a bit of work for Rab on the side. Don't look at me like that…"

Macpherson rolled his eyes, giving a brief shake of his head.

"Barry Corrigan was doing a bit of work for Rab Millar?" said Taylor, her tone belying her disbelief in Worzel's latest revelation. "Who else knew this?"

"It was an open secret. Did you ever hear of Eastside Chauffeur Drive?"

Taylor shook her head.

"It's a limousine company. Barry was driving for them at night."

"Jim Baxter told us he'd just got a taxi licence," said Macpherson.

"Aye, well. Rab got him squared away with it. Barry was driving Rab's birds about in a big Merc. Wore the hat and all." Worzel chuckled and sipped his beer. "Done the door-to-door service. Home visits, you know what I mean?"

"He told you this?"

"God, aye. He was loving it. Rab had him punting them around, some big faces and all." Worzel tapped his nose. "He never said exactly who, though. Between that and doing the airport runs when Rab needed clients picked up, he was well in."

Taylor considered the information.

"You fancy another?" Macpherson pointed at Worzel's empty glass. Worzel clapped his hands, rubbing his palms together.

"Now you're talking. I'll take a wee chaser and all if you're paying."

"You'll take a pint. Do you think I've an expense account or something?" Macpherson took the glass and went to the bar.

"Get us a wee packet of Tayto crisps instead, then."

Macpherson glared back as the barman approached.

"Did you see the shooting?" said Taylor, sitting back and sipping on her drink.

"The boy on the motorbike must have passed me, but I never paid him any heed. I was ripping at your man showing his face."

"Do you think Freaky was there because of what happened to Millar?"

"Had to be."

"Had there been any grief between Millar and Chopper lately with the Monster being off the scene?"

"No. As far as I know, those two have had no chat since the truce." Worzel took the offered Tenants and raised the glass to his lips. "Thanks, Doc."

Macpherson dropped three packets of crisps on the table.

"Have you ever been in touch with Billy McBride?" said Taylor, watching Worzel as he looked at her over the rim of his glass.

"Now and again on the Facebook. He's in England," he said.

"You sure?"

"I dunno. Suppose."

"Ask about for us, will you?" said Macpherson.

"No bother. You don't think he had Rab clipped?"

"We've a list the length of ourselves. Just ruling some out," said Macpherson, sliding over a packet of cheese and onion and snapping it open.

"Have you looked into the Albanians?" said Worzel, mirroring Macpherson and opening a bag of crisps, his long fingers shovelling a handful into his mouth.

Taylor pulled an unconcerned face and took another drink.

"I heard they were looking at doing some business

together?" she said lightly.

"I didn't hear that, but there's a wee scrote been running about telling everyone Rab's getting it and he has form. You should give him a rattle. His name's Nishani. Bekim Nishani."

"Where would we find him?" said Taylor, her interest piqued at a lead but trying not to show it.

"The Albanians aren't like us." Worzel pulled a face, munching open mouthed. "They like to throw it about the showy bastards." He creased the packet and tipped the remaining crumbs into his mouth, balling the bag when he finished. "They run about like they're the frigging Mafia and knock about one of them swanky spots in the town. You'll know it by the cars parked out the front, that one in Lower Franklin Street?"

"The Thirty-One Club," said Macpherson.

## Chapter 22

Shepard peeled off the tape and teased the cotton pad away from the wound to his ribs. The ointment was doing its job, the dressing coming away clean and although the skin around the deep graze remained pink and angry, it didn't look infected. Testing the limits, he moved his arm and shoulder, finding a decent percentage of mobility with a minimum level of discomfort. Pleased, he slugged some disinfectant onto a fresh pad and cleaned the area, dabbing off the excess and then re-covering the wound with a fingertip of antibiotic ointment and a fresh dressing. He pulled on a black tee shirt as he left the bathroom.

The coffee had brewed, and he poured a mug. Taking a swig of the cooled bitter liquid, he carried the cup into the master bedroom. He had taken a six month let on the apartment, paid in advance with cash, with the option of a year's extension, but he wouldn't be there anywhere near that long.

The property was his base of operations, its corner position on the tenth floor granting him an observation point over the Fearon Estate. It also bought him the cover needed to move freely around the area. Residence there put his face about to allay the suspicion that usually came when strangers roamed in uninvited.

Shepard had set up a routine of sorts. Regular visits to the convenience for essential supplies and a daily appearance at the greasy spoon for a plate of watery scrambled eggs, side of fatty bacon, and a brief gossip on the day's weather with the old cook.

Taking another sip of coffee, Shepard walked to the window where he had trained a tripod and a set of Zeiss binoculars on the dilapidated low-rise maisonettes across the way. Placing his eyes to the lens, it didn't take long to witness another of the regular transactions that took place in the graffiti-sprayed stash house below. He watched and sipped, logging the faces in his memory and studying the access routes the boys were using to ferry their products out and the cash in. If the observed routine was anything to go by, the contents of the house were running low and a resupply and cash collection would be imminent. The youngsters involved were confident, yet complacent enough not to expect trouble, and Shepard was confident an interdiction during the handover would cause a maximum impact on trade and send the flag up that Millar's death and the Corners attack were just opening shots of his war.

Draining the last of his coffee he set the mug beside a police airwave TETRA handset charging on a chest of drawers beside the bed, low mumbling and short blips monitoring the communications traffic of the emergency services in the area. All was quiet.

Kneeling, he hauled the olive holdall he had carried up to the apartment out from below the bed. The rest of the haul was secured in a two by one-metre steel building site container in a rented garage three blocks away. The motorbike he had bought on Gumtree and used to cross on the Holyhead to Dublin Ferry was also left there. Conscious of the area and the need for some security, Shepard had jury-rigged an electrical connection to a nearby streetlight providing rudimentary power to the storage space that allowed him to run three surveillance cameras and a small infrared tripwire system linked to an app on his smartphone.

Reaching inside the holdall, he removed several items, placing them on the bed. The old priest had come good. His prior contacts within the rebel movement and then as a facilitator for disarmament had put him in a unique position to know what arms stashes remained accessible and in good condition, just in case, of course. All manner of weapons had flooded the north during the years of the 'Troubles' and while on the face of it both sides of the conflict had put their weapons beyond use, trust was a scarce commodity and all the protagonists had kept a little back for any potential rainy day that lay ahead. It was just another sweetener to seal a bigger deal, another open secret that no one, from the man on the street to the highest Northern Ireland Office official acknowledged.

The first item, wrapped in a clean dust sheet, was the AK-74 assault rifle he had rattled the bar with. Now it was stripped and cleaned, the smell of gun oil filling his nostrils as he pulled out a second weapon.

He wouldn't need the Beretta M9A1 pistol today either, but it would stay under his pillow for personal protection along with the crowbar beside the toilet cistern and claw hammer on the lintel above the front door. Dropping out the M9's magazine, he drew back the slide and double-checked the weapon before slapping the magazine back home and setting the pistol down beside several boxes of ammunition.

Rooting into a side pocket, he removed a box of Hansson Marine flares and a sealed ziplock bag of old street clothes, then two other final items.

Each small block was dark grey and the size and shape of a pack of playing cards; their water-resistant polycarbonate cases housed a board of electronics and a two-pence sized GPS tracker and 3G multi-roaming SIM.

The back of each tracker case was equipped with a thirty-four-kilogram pull magnet and a rubber suction cup to allow attachment which he could then monitor with the same app interface he was using to monitor the lock-up.

Placing the holdall back under the bed, Shepard stood and checked his watch, returning to the window to observe his target area below.

Looking out over the rooftops he could see a cloud squall moving in from the lough. The hills on the other side of the water were fringed with a slow-moving dark cloud mass, and the grey water was flecked with whitecaps.

As the first spits of rain dotted the window, a car swept into the side road, slowing to come to a halt outside the graffiti-covered maisonette flats. The interior light blinked on as front and rear passenger doors opened and Shepard watched as two familiar faces exited the vehicle.

❖ ❖ ❖

"Is it ringing?"

Taylor nodded as Macpherson gunned the Vauxhall along the winding country roads.

"Jesus!" A white van coming the opposite way strayed across the central white line, and the stubby branches of hedgerow rattled against the nearside wing mirror and up the side of the car as Macpherson took evasive action.

"Prick." He glared in his rear-view but there wasn't even a blink of brake lights as the van careered on along the narrow road.

"Chris?" Taylor spoke into the mobile clamped to her ear.

"Boss? I can hardly hear you?"

"We're on the back road, coming down from Ligoniel. Is that any better?" said Taylor, juggling the phone to her other ear. Macpherson negotiated a hairpin bend, the Vauxhall now descending from the barren, bleak hills outside the city limits into the edges of the capital's suburban sprawl.

"A bit. What are you doing out in the sticks?"

"Following up on something, we were out at a place called Black Hill Farm. It's a known haunt for Maurice Jackson, also goes by 'Freaky'. He'll be in the files as one of Millar and Gordy Beattie's associates. I need to know any other addresses we hold for him."

The trip hadn't taken too long but had proved fruitless. The narrow gravel lane that led to Black Hill Farm ended in large, padlocked gates. A similarly impenetrable wall stretched out into the surrounding bogland and there was no sign of life save for the occasional staccato bark of dogs coming from a concrete and corrugated shed inside. Neither of the two detectives, without a warrant and on naught but the word of a bitter old scarecrow, were willing to risk climbing the gates for closer inspection. When the rain started, it sealed the deal.

"No problem. Anything else?" said Walker.

"Any luck with the van from the bar shooting?"

"I did, aye. White Peugeot Bipper. Registered to a Rhonda Murray in the Fearon Estate. I've an address here. No tax or insurance."

"Any flags?"

"No. No off-road notices or outstanding tickets either," said Walker.

"Okay, head over and check it out and take Erin with you."

"Will do. She's here and wants a word."

Macpherson pulled up at a set of traffic lights as Taylor heard the rustle and murmur of the phone being passed over, Erin Reilly's voice coming on the line.

"Hi, did Carrie get you?" she said.

"No. We've been up the black mountain and coverage is patchy."

"She had a quick look into the property deal on the Springfield Road you asked about."

"Anything?" said Taylor.

"The purchase was through a company called Miltek Refurb. She had a look on Companies House and it's only been set up about eighteen months. The company director is listed as a Robert Sinclair."

"That's one of Millar's aliases," said Taylor, raising a palm as Macpherson glanced across, noting the uptick in her tone.

"The company address is a solicitor's office off Castle Street. They handled and signed off all the paperwork too. Harper, Baxter, Brooke."

"Where is Carrie now?"

"She went out to doorstop the selling agent and see if Miltek had interests in any other properties between then and now."

"Who's the agent?" Taylor could hear Reilly searching the desk for notes.

"Morrow and Burke."

Macpherson, indicating to move into the outer lane around a bread delivery van unloading at the kerb, looked across as Taylor let out a loud nasal exclamation of surprise.

"Something wrong?" said Reilly.

"No, Erin. Thanks, I'll try Carrie here. Did you get Rowdy's paperwork sorted?"

"All in order. He's still in custody are we holding him?"

"We have another few hours before we have to charge so Slippy Reeves can sweat. We have him on the firearm and the drugs and if the arrest and detention paperwork is tight, I'll let the DCI have the last word."

"That'll do. I'm heading to the bookies," said Reilly.

"We had a tip-off that one of Millar's old associates was in the bar before the shooting. It would be good to corroborate it. Chris has the details. See if you can get a positive ID, then head up to the Fearon Estate with him. We'll get a debrief later this afternoon."

The two women exchanged goodbyes and Taylor dropped her phone into the door bin.

"What?" said Macpherson, drumming impatient fingers as another set of lights burned red.

"Millar's property agent for Springfield Road was Morrow and Burke."

"Lightning does strike twice. If you want to head over, I can cut down here?" Macpherson nodded at a side road as the filter light changed to green.

"No, keep going. Let's throw a fox amongst the hounds first and see how they react."

## Chapter 23

A forty-foot long curtain-sided lorry blared its horn and slammed to a jerky stop in a hiss of air brakes and the cry of pained suspension, the driver gesticulating angrily at being cut up by a dirty red van cutting in the gate in front of him.

The forecourt that wrapped around the warehouse had staff and visitor parking at the front and huge roller doors facing the seaward side for delivery and despatch. The red van continued past them all and around the building to the opposite side where it pulled up to a weather-beaten Portakabin squared up to the motorway side of the compound. The squat temporary building sat under a large green and white sign reading 'NORTHERN WHOLESALE HORTICULTURE'. The two men within quickly exited the car, taking the wire-frame steps up and inside.

"Jesus, it'd melt you in here."

"Take that big bloody coat off then, Harry. You look like the Michelin Man."

Gordon Beattie stood to the rear of the cabin with a cup of coffee in hand. He reached out and shook the hand of the other man, who proceeded to strip off a North Face soft-shell jacket.

"What about you, Freaky, any hassle?" Beattie gestured to a coffee urn and half-demolished pack of digestives. Freaky Jackson shook his head.

"No bother. The last of the gear at the farm is heading down to the estate this afternoon and the lads will pick up the cash as usual."

"They're dropping off the cash straight after?" said Beattie.

"Straight after, no bollocking about. I've told them, so I have."

"Okay. The rest of the gear will be coming in over the next couple of days. This needs to go like clockwork because these other boys are coming this week to sign off on the new route." Beattie gave the two men a hard stare. There was no room in his expression for any misinterpretation of how vital his instruction was.

"Have you somewhere safe for it."

"Rab was working with the Albanians on storage," said Beattie, holding up a hand as Jackson began to protest. "They aren't tied to the operation and are offering storage and distribution. I've spoken with Amir, and I'm confident he's on board. He'll do the lift tonight and then take it for cutting, I can't risk the usual channels at the minute."

Freaky sorted through the stained mugs and, choosing one that looked half-clean, poured a cup of coffee. He gave a short nod of acceptance, sitting down on one of the wheeled chairs and skimmed back against the wall.

"Harry, any joy for me?" Beattie remained standing, his tone light but his cobalt eyes still hard as they drew a bead on Harry Carruthers.

"I'm sorry, Mr B. Not yet," said Carruthers with a shrug.

Carruthers wasn't a tall man, but he was imposing, nonetheless. A belly strained under his tight black tee shirt from too many beers, but his shoulders were broad of beam and his forearms were thick threaded ropes of muscle. His flat nose and bovine brow marked him out as a hard case, and it was physicality over his intellect that had granted him a position within Rab Millar's circle. Whether it was doing the door at Risky's or putting the pressure on the clients who thought they could let their tab slip, Carruthers took to the tasks with gusto.

"I've been round the houses and they're all distancing themselves. They have the fear of God up them now after what happened to Chopper and wee Barry."

"What about Gary?"

Carruthers shrugged painfully.

Beattie closed his eyes, licked his lips and put the coffee cup down before the urge to throw it took over.

"I've looked. I've had his squat juked at every couple of hours and I've been driving around the estate myself. When he turns up, I'll know."

"You better," said Beattie.

"I will," said Carruthers defensively.

"What about the girl?"

"She's still in the Royal. I've a wee lad hanging about so when she leaves we'll have a car pick her up."

Beattie nodded his acceptance of the plan.

"Gary will be up the estate today, no doubt," said Freaky, taking a long slurp of the gritty coffee. "The gear's coming in and he'll be there to get his fix." He pointed the mug at Carruthers. "You know the stash, across from Fearon House?"

Carruthers nodded that he did. Freaky, cup in one hand, lifted out his phone with the other and sent a text, Carruthers' own phone bleeped.

"That's his brother's number. He'll be there and make sure he comes in."

"Aye, right. Cheers," said Carruthers, his shoulders relaxing a little. He pulled a pair of cheap spectacles from his jeans pocket and held them to his face, mumbling as he added the number to his contacts.

"Jesus, would you look at the professor." Freaky stamped a foot and laughed.

"Fuck off, will you, I need them for reading. Two quid they were."

Beattie smiled despite the stress that lay ahead.

"Harry, we'll be done here in a minute, wait in the van, will you?"

"Sure thing Mr B. I'll let you know about them two."

"The fewer phone calls I'm getting the better. Ring him, he'll tell me," said Beattie, nodding at Jackson. Carruthers shrugged in understanding and exited.

"What?" Freaky set the cup down and met Beattie's eye.

"Did you have to shoot Barry Corrigan?"

"Fuck off, are you serious, Monster? I'd just watched Chopper get his face shot off and when I came down them stairs, the wee shit had his blood up."

"He went for you?"

"Course he bloody did." Freaky shrugged the scowl off. "What's the odds? He was a dick anyway."

"He was working for us," said Beattie, eyes narrowing in exasperation at Jackson glib.

"Sure, I know that," said Jackson with a nod and a sigh. "He was running Rab's birds about, so what, drivers are ten-a-penny, I'll find you another one."

"That's not the point!" Beattie's tone was razor sharp, and Jackson sat back and put his hands on the table.

"Look, I'm sorry, okay, but flip sake, you're lucky I'm still here. Your man on the bike had the place wrecked."

Beattie cocked his head in acknowledgement of the statement.

"You sure that finger was the Monk's?"

Freaky nodded. "Still had the big ring on it."

"We're in the shite if that bastard has talked, you know." Beattie dragged a wheeled chair from one of the desks, flicking the tails of his three-quarter-length coat to the side as he sat. His left hand rubbing his jaw.

"Sure, who'd know to be talking to him about anything?" said Freaky.

"I don't know, but it's not good, bits of him turning up so soon after what happened to Rab. That's what's keeping me awake."

"I don't think it was Chopper," said Freaky.

"Neither do I."

"What about your man from the Branch?" Freaky lowered his voice as he uttered the last. As though speaking it aloud might invoke an appearance.

"It's complicated," said Beattie. "He's doing what he can, but it's dangerous to dig."

"There's only us that know what really happened then."

Beattie nodded.

"Freaky, I appreciate you falling back in, you know? After all this time."

Jackson waved away the words.

"I'm serious. You, me and Rab. We were some team." Beattie smiled, a memory glazing his expression, then the steel returned to the cobalt eyes.

"You know I had to go it alone, don't you? This thing was getting too big to be skulking around waiting on the peelers to pick a day to knock on the door."

"Monster, seriously, it's no skin off my nose. All that management carry on." Jackson pulled a face. "I couldn't be doing with that and anyway, you can't have too many chiefs can you?"

"Here," Beattie set down a thick brown envelope. Jackson recoiled in his chair.

"No, take it, least I can do for putting your neck on the line there."

Jackson pulled the envelope towards him, thumb teasing the flap and noting the wad of notes. He pocketed it in the lining of his jacket.

"No problem, brother. Sure we're family."

"You're the only one I totally trust at the minute, Freaky. I don't know if there's a tout in the camp or they have a mole in the business, but I know I can depend on you."

Jackson returned the stare, searching Beattie's look to see if there was anything in it that said different. Satisfied he was serious, he nodded.

"What are we doing?"

"This new route," said Beattie. "Rab was helping me grease the wheels when the shutters came down on the bankroll and I need all the cash we can muster. This deal is going ahead, but if I don't stump up the second payment here, it'll be me in the crusher."

"Can you not shift a few quid?"

"Not a mission. Fucking assets and the taxman are up my arse for a shortcut, so every penny in gear that's out there needs to be brought in." He noticed Freaky's eyebrows rise and nodded confirmation. "All of it, and I've told the big players their terms are up and all debts are called in for Friday."

He noted the shift in Jackson's demeanour.

"Aye, I know. Some of them made a bit of noise, but if they don't, you'll have a bit of work to be getting on with." He slapped Jackson on the arm.

"The cash is all going to one of Paul's places. Can you sort our own security to back him up?"

"Aye, I've a few boys that'll do it no bother."

"They're capable?"

"Right as rain."

"Keep them in the dark," said Beattie, waving a warning finger. "They don't need to know what's there."

"Course."

"The boat's coming in tonight. I'll need you to run security on the dock and make sure Amir's boys get the gear away clean. Okay?"

"It'll be sorted," said Freaky with a confident grin.

Beattie pointed over at an old, battered sports bag beside an equally tired set of office drawers.

"That's for the gateman. Shouldn't be any bother; he's

usually stoned by the time you'll be heading away."

Jackson gave a quick nod.

"You're a good lad, Freaky." Beattie slapped him on the shoulder. "Away you go, let me know how Harry gets on. I still want to speak to them other two about what happened to Rab."

Freaky picked up the soft-shell from the back of his chair and as he shrugged his arm into it, he noted Beattie's furrowed brow.

"It's only us were there that night, Monster. Put it out of your head till we get this over us."

Beattie watched his old friend leave and pushed himself back against the wall.

All the years that had passed. All those secrets buried. Was the soil shifting to reveal the bones of the truth?

He reached out and picked up an old Nokia phone atop the stack of invoices on the desk beside him, tapping in a number from memory. There was low music and conversation in the background when the Albanian's voice answered.

"Yes?"

"It's me. That investment I told you about? Well, my friend, your ship has come in." Beattie's tone was light and jovial. "How about we meet for a bite and a glass to celebrate?"

The music faded as the caller moved.

"Usual?"

"Perfect, we can discuss your new terms after. I'll see you there."

## Chapter 24

Lena Borodenko winced painfully as she bumped into the toilet door and then paused in front of the public bathroom mirror to check her reflection.

She would not be winning any beauty contests or having her ego indulged by any fawning declarations of attraction anytime soon.

Peering closely at herself through the swirling pattern of poorly rinsed grime she poked her tongue through the gap of a broken tooth. Beauty had become the beast.

The ward sister had been hesitant at her discharge so soon, but with little threat of serious complications arising, she agreed and took the appeal to the doctor who dutifully scrawled his signature.

Following the discharge, Lena made a call from the corridor payphone to one of her girlfriends begging a favour of some clothes, and a few hours later amid visiting time, here she was, hiding out in a public bathroom.

She nudged the paper stitch on the bridge of her nose with a fingertip. Her facial injuries, although the most prominent, would in all likelihood heal well and heal quickly, and a dentist could have her tooth fixed.

The worst of the pain came from the broken rib, but she could do little other than take rest and allow it time to heal. Time and rest at that minute were the two things furthest from her mind.

A toilet flushed in one cubicle behind her and in a commotion of snapping locks and banging door a woman exited to the sinks, thumping down her handbag and a selection of gaudy gossip magazine.

"Alright, love," she said brightly into the reflection.

"Hi," mumbled Lena, averting her gaze and washing her hands.

"I'm up visiting the old fella. Heart attack. God knows how it happened, he never gets off his arse, the lazy sod."

Lena shook off the water and reached for a paper towel.

The woman followed suit, leaning in close.

"You want my advice, pet. Wait till the bastard's sleeping and then pour the bloody kettle over him." She nodded once, patting Lena softly on the shoulder as she left.

Waiting a few moments to ensure the woman had gone, Lena followed, entering a lobby busy with medical staff, patients stretching their legs, and the public meandering under signs and painted arrows in search of their destination. There was a shop and coffee bar with a queue that extended past a row of vending machines and a car park pay station. Skirting the queue, Lena headed towards a dedicated phone booth for a local taxi firm beside the revolving entrance door, scanning faces in the crowd as she went.

As she reached the phone, her eyes locked with those of a young man in his mid-teens astride a mountain bike outside. He looked away, digging in his puffy gilet and drawing out a mobile phone. He gave her a second brief glance and turned, his lips moving as he spoke into the handset. He hung up, zipped the phone back in a pocket, and then he was off.

Lena picked up the handset. It smelled of stale cigarette smoke and strong perfume. The ring tone trilled as the line connected.

"Taxi?" The operator sounded bright and courteous.

Turning to face into the bulbous acoustic surround of the payphone, the operator spoke again, voice professionally patient at the delay.

"Hello… taxi?"

Lena started as she felt the gentle touch to her elbow.

The receiver dropped from her hand as she turned around.

Her face blanching under the concerned expression of the person beside her, her skin crawling in recognition and at the tender stroke along her arm.

"Magdalena. My dear, look at you. How awful, we've all been so very concerned."

A tinny, distant voice called once more on the hanging receiver, and then the line went dead.

## Chapter 25

A faux wrought-iron portcullis which posed provocatively over the arched entranceway was as resplendent and intimidatory in its coat of shimmering black gloss paint as the commissionaire who barred the way in his contrived militaristic uniform of peak cap, braid and spit-shined boots.

"Sir, may I help you," he said, marching forward to impede any further advance.

Taylor reached inside her jacket and produced her warrant card.

"Police. Might we speak with the manager?"

The commissionaire stood his ground at parade square ease atop the polished sandstone steps and peered briefly at the identification and then turned to Macpherson.

"Can I ask what it's in relation to, sir?"

Macpherson held up his ID.

"Detective Sergeant, son. You'd want to ask the inspector there our business, her being the boss and all." He snapped the ID closed and adopted his own air of retaliatory dominance.

The commissionaire continued to gaze down on the smaller man with an expression of calm professionalism on his swarthy features, his white-gloved hands clasped behind his back.

"Would you have an appointment, Detective Sergeant?"

Taylor looked up at the old stone facade and the lead-lined windows and broad polished sills of the ancient bastion of the old boys' club glared back.

The Thirty-One Club was a private members institution fashioned in the image of those gentrified hangouts of the aristocracy in St James and Pall Mall and had been a staple of

Belfast City since before the Boer War, although its current iteration could only be traced back about twenty years.

The violence of the Troubles, the murder of Lord Mountbatten, and the Brighton bombing had finally put paid to the old guard submitting themselves and their flunkies to the risk of a car bomb or indiscriminate shooting whilst holed up with a gin and high tea. Once the ceasefires began and relative peace resumed, the building quietly returned to its former use whilst still maintaining its air of mystery and exclusivity.

Taylor could make out movement and the shimmer of a chandelier from inside the bay window to her left, which she assumed would be the dining room. The bay to the right at a guess would be the lounge bar and was split from the dining room by the entrance hallway behind the double-height privacy glass of the front door.

"We're making general enquires and it would be helpful if you could show us in. It won't take long," said Taylor.

The commissionaire looked at her, a study from her toes to the top of her head, and then he stood ramrod straight, his eyes darting to the kerb as a luxury car pulled up on the double yellow lines marked along the cobbles. The prospect of a confrontation with a client and the constabulary on the doorstep overrode his obstinance.

"Follow me."

He strode to the door and pulled the brass handle, gesturing the way across the threshold.

"Make yourself known to the reception steward, please."

Taylor nodded and walked ahead. Macpherson loitered.

"That's some motor, son. What is it now? Maybach? You don't see many of those around the town." He positioned himself across the threshold, his hands shoved in his pockets.

The unflappable commissionaire glanced at the luxury saloon as the driver's door opened and a uniformed chauffeur got out and made his way kerbside.

"Sergeant, perhaps you could follow your colleague? The steward will assist…"

The rear door opened, and a conservatively suited elderly man exited the car, the wind catching strands of his hair and whipping them from a balding liver-spotted crown.

"Sergeant?" A tone of concern had crept into the young man's voice.

"Aye. Right enough. I'll go on here, I've seen enough." The sergeant turned toe to toe and looked up into the sharply featured face.

"Bit of advice, son," said Macpherson. "It's not the shine on your boots or the cut of your cloth gets you by in your game. A few manners might take you a long way, though. You should remember it's some of our lot sits on the panel when your licence comes up for renewal." He picked an imaginary fleck of lint from the man's brass-buttoned tunic and tapped the garish badge fastened to the breast.

"There. Fit for the Queen now, you are. You can fall in." Macpherson bid a salute and with a wink followed his inspector inside.

"I can only apologise but we have rules here at the club and…"

Macpherson trundled across the chequerboard floor to where Taylor had found herself barred from further passage by a tall, ruddy-faced man in more immaculate tailoring.

"I appreciate that and as I've said, this isn't a social visit. I'd like to speak to the manager."

The man acknowledged Taylor's request with a nod, then he doubled down on his first refusal.

"It's the club secretary you need," he said. "We have a function on at present in the Wellington Suite and Mr Steinhalter's attention is very much in demand." The steward placed his hands on the green baize of his lectern and offered a practised and apologetic smile.

"Mr?"

"Mark Morgan, ma'am."

"Mr Morgan, we are engaged in following a line of enquiry regarding the death of one of your patrons. Can I ask you to at least inform the secretary we are here?"

Morgan's expression didn't change. The exclusivity and the coveted path to a table at the Thirty-One had ingrained in him a well-polished delivery of polite rebuttal.

At the sound of the main door opening and footsteps, Taylor cast a quick glance to see an older gentleman arrive alone.

Morgan abruptly left his post to greet the newcomer enthusiastically.

"Is it my aftershave?" said Macpherson, dropping his nose to his lapel and giving a sniff. Taylor gave an impatient shake of her head at Morgan's intransigence and scrutinised the exchange.

The steward had engaged the man in a fawning welcome, both men chatting briefly for a moment and then with a slight bow, Morgan led the patron towards the brass-framed double doors of the dining room. The visitor glanced at Taylor and offered a polite smile.

He was a venerable-looking gent with the face of a kindly uncle. Thin as a rake with cheeks showing a flush of broken capillaries, his hair had receded at the crown while the back and sides formed a neatly clipped and silvery grey corona.

His clothing was conservative in function and design, the dark pinstripe suit interrupted with a splash of matching colour in the pocket handkerchief and the old school tie. His black polished Oxfords clicked to a stop as Morgan passed him across to an equally welcoming maître d' who escorted him into the warmth and the clink of crystal and cutlery of the dining room.

He fitted right into the stuffy, ostentatious surroundings.

In contrast, she and Macpherson stood out like balls on a bulldog.

During her brief period of observation and from her limited perspective she had chalked up a professor emeritus of the College of Surgeons and a member of the Health Select Committee leaving the lounge bar in animated conversation. That added to the three QCs, four MPs and a couple of Rt Honourables. There had also been the great and the good of the city's chamber of commerce and at least one captain of industry she had questioned for embezzlement and misappropriation of company finances.

"My apologies for the interruption. Now, have you agreed a time that might suit a return appointment and I can check the secretary's diary?" said Morgan, now returned to his post.

From atop a green leather-bound visitors' book, he palmed a matching jade marble Mont Blanc pen and flipped the pages open, and with the gold-plated nib poised above the pages, he gave an expectant look.

"Son, has the inspector not been clear enough. We're the police…"

"I understand that, sir, however…"

"And we need to speak to your man Steinway about Robert Millar," said Macpherson, ignoring the familiar routine.

The steward closed the book and clipped the cap back on the pen.

"Steinhalter," he corrected. "As I said, he is indisposed and for that, I apologise for the wasted trip."

"Apologies? You're not one bit sorry, fella. If you were sorry, you get on the blower and get him down."

"Mr Morgan." Taylor raised a placating palm to her sergeant.

"May we ask you a few questions?"

"We cherish the discretion of our clientele above all else here, Inspector. I expect there shan't be much I can say without consultation with Mr Steinhalter and the committee."

"Jesus…" Macpherson turned away.

"We are trying to ascertain Robert Millar's movements in the weeks before his death and get an idea of any close associates. We believe he was cultivating a clientele here and it would be helpful to discuss the nature of any of their business arrangements."

"I'm afraid I don't know the name."

"Mr Morgan. I'm just trying to conduct my investigation," said Taylor.

"On whose authority?"

Taylor was taken aback. Macpherson slowly returned his gaze, mouth open.

"I'm sorry?" Taylor managed.

"On whose authority are you conducting your investigation on the grounds of these premises."

Taylor's expression chilled.

"I only ask because I have several members of the Northern Ireland Policing Board and the permanent secretary for the Department of Justice attending the function upstairs. I would expect ultimately it's under their purview. Correct? Perhaps we could interrupt Mr Steinhalter and those gentlemen and you could put your questions to them regarding this…?"

"Robert Millar," she said with a tight smile.

Morgan had played his part well, and she could appreciate it wasn't his fault. He was the sentinel, the keeper of the keys, and there was no real animosity or bitterness in his manner. He'd as likely find himself demoted to the kitchen or out on the street if he started answering her questions or giving her carte blanche around the hallowed walls.

A peal of laughter and a loud tutting pulled her from her

thoughts.

"I must rethink my membership here, Mark. It looks like the committee is scraping the barrel now."

Mark Morgan stepped from behind his lectern to welcome the two newcomers.

"The officers were just leaving," said Morgan, dropping a heavy emphasis on the profession.

Taylor drew herself up and Macpherson rounded low, his centre of gravity lending him the stance of a tiny squat boxer at an angry weigh-in.

The duos now stood toe to toe across the chequerboard floor.

The oil painted faces of long-dead members crowded around the wood-panelled walls, their eyes wide in anticipation of the bout unfolding under their gilded gold leaf frames.

"Veronica, long time no see."

"Monster. Not long enough," said Taylor.

Beattie laughed, the skin around his cobalt eyes wrinkling and his tanned face breaking into a grin of perfect white teeth.

"Aye, right enough. Twenty-five to thirty years would do for you," he said.

Taylor returned the smile. Mark Morgan was hovering on the periphery. An official out of his depth.

"Dead in a ditch might be a preference," mumbled Macpherson.

Beattie nodded a greeting to the man.

"Got the pit bull with you, I see."

The low rumble which began in Macpherson's throat was interrupted by the rasping words of Solomon Reeves.

"Gordon, perhaps we should let Mark see to his duties. I've another appointment at five." Reeves stepped aside and raised a finger to the steward to carry on. He placed his gaze on Taylor and she was pleased to note his clear eyes were a little more red rimmed than normal.

"My office is waiting on notice of Richard Burns' discharge, Inspector," he said. "The clock is ticking." Reeves tapped his leather-strapped Breitling and Taylor ignored the barb, choosing to remain in silent confrontation with her nemesis.

The two stood eye to eye beside their nervous cornermen, who were waiting on the first blows to rain in.

Mark Morgan sniffed loudly, with raised brows and a tight smile, his hands offering an eager gesture towards the exit.

Beattie broke the tense stand-off, a twinkle in his bright eyes.

"Is my usual table ready, Mark?"

"Yes, Mr Beattie."

"Have it set up for company." Beattie stepped up to the lectern and opened the visitors' book. He drew out his own pen and scratched in the names. Snapping the cover closed, he looked back at the two police officers.

"Come on, the pair of you. No point standing here gawping at each other all day when there's taxpayers' work to be done, is there?"

## Chapter 26

"I'm sorry, Constable. She's not available at the moment."

Carrie Cook checked her watch with an embarrassed smile of awkward impatience.

"Really? It's just I was passing and it would be extremely helpful if Ms Morrow could spare just a minute or two?"

The Stepford receptionist returned a blank robotic stare. Her blonde locks were perfectly coiffured and her model looks accentuated by stunning make-up, but her expression was devoid of emotion.

"I'm sorry, Constable. She's not available at the moment."

Cook bit back a reply, glancing around the office, which was arranged into three distinct sections.

A large window cast plenty of light into a long office space painted in pleasant pastels and as it extended towards the rear space, intricately installed hidden lighting panels added a soft ambience.

Arranged along the rear wall were the office staples of copier, filing cabinets, and communal meeting space.

Near where she stood beside the reception desk, a further group of immaculately preened and presented women pecked at keyboards. Each sat at a sleek dark wood and white gloss desk in uniform position on each side of a decorative stairway of floating steps and stainless steel handrails that led up to the mezzanine floor above. Natural light poured in from a lantern ceiling.

Above, Cook could hear the muted conversation of phone calls and conversation, but amidst all this, there was no sign of Daphne Morrow.

"Could I wait?" she said.

The receptionist tapped a console on her desk and

whispered into the sleek headset she wore.

Cook couldn't quite place the language; the Baltic region, perhaps further east. The blonde looked up.

"One moment. You may sit."

Cook smiled in appreciation and again checked her watch in the vain hope someone might notice and get a push on.

A full ten minutes later, as she was on the verge of abandonment, the click-clack of high heels echoed off the steps and yet another statuesque blonde descended, a professional smile of greeting revealing perfect pearly white teeth. She reached out a hand.

"Constable, apologies for your wait."

"Thank you. Although it's me who should apologise for just dropping in like this," said Cook, accepting the offered hand.

"I am Stella Sharp. I'm Ms Morrows general manager. Rita explained you had some questions regarding one of our properties?"

The woman's wrist was adorned with an expensive silver wristwatch and bracelet combination, her tanned arms toned and supple, disappearing into a white, short-sleeve, fitted blouse. A charcoal pinstripe pencil skirt completed the look, and six-inch heels accentuated her long toned legs.

Carrie Cook unconsciously tucked a strand of her own mousy brown hair behind her ear and as she removed her notebook, winced inwardly at the sight of her pale hands and cheap charm bracelet.

Sharp towered over Cook and would have even if it wasn't for the fact she was wearing sensible flat pumps. Her favourite high street navy skirt suit now felt dowdy amidst the cashmere, silk and calf leather that was adorning the house supermodels.

As she took a dry-mouthed glance around the office with the soulless eyes of the receptionist on her, she had the overwhelming memory of being back at school and under the gaze of haughty peers as they picked teams on the sports pitch.

"Yes, a few general enquires," said Cook, forcing a smile.

"Please, this way."

Stella Sharp led her to the rear of the office. Cook in passing observed property brochures, framed endorsements, and real estate annual peer of the year awards then as the office dog-legged, she found herself momentarily disorientated.

The establishment had taken over several others adjacent and knocked them through, offering a space that you couldn't see from the street. The extension allowed a further thirty desks to be installed, with perhaps fifty staff sat back to back behind keyboards and monitors operating the day to day of the busy business.

Stella held open the door to a large glass cubicle positioned as the centrepiece of the extension.

"Tea?"

"I'm fine. Thank you."

Sharp nodded, turning to a young girl nearby. Cook guessed she couldn't have been much more than a teen.

"Rachael, water for the room."

The teenager mumbled in deference and left her chair to fetch the order.

Cook watched her leave in hurried obedience. Her legs were stick thin and her footfalls barely audible on the gleaming wooden floor as she receded towards a seated break-out and kitchen area.

There was a muted atmosphere. Conversations were few, and those that could be heard were directed into headsets. The workforce was entirely female and mostly Asiatic but roughly a third was made up of Middle Eastern and Caucasian faces, all bowed low, gazes directed into computer terminals. The odd sniff and cough, but none of the craic Carrie would associate with such an open-plan and dynamic office. The glam factor that dominated front of house was absent here at the coalface.

Peripheral movement caught her eye, and she turned to see a man she hadn't noticed leave his desk and begin what would become a single circuit between the desks, past each employee and then back to his own chair. It was all eerily reminiscent of an examination hall.

"Shall we?"

Cook broke off her observation and smiled, accepting both the offer of the open doorway and one of the plushly upholstered chairs that framed a long, tempered glass table. Sharp sat down opposite and placed her mobile phone at a right angle to the edge, shuffled her chair back, and crossed her legs, relaxing into the leather upholstery.

"So, please. How may we assist?"

"I'm very impressed, Miss Sharp," Cook cast a look of wonder around the space. "Business must be brisk?"

"We are in the fortunate position of holding a significant number of contracts at present but it requires a great deal of administrative work." She aired a manicured hand at the people outside the box.

"So I see, how many staff have you here? Fifty, sixty?" said Cook brightly.

Stella Sharp smiled, her head weighing an estimation.

"We have enough to be getting on with."

"Even so." Cook raised her eyes in what she hoped passed for admiration. "Is Morrow and Burke the largest agent in the sector at the minute?"

"Are you here to research our company, Constable, or was there something specific you require my help with?" Sharp smiled, her pink tongue darting across straight, white teeth, the disarming grin morphing into a resemblance of something more feral.

A knock on the door interrupted the women. Sharp called for the girl to enter.

Rachael placed a tray holding a long-necked decanter of water and two upturned glasses on small paper doilies.

Carrie Cook smiled in thanks, but the girl didn't meet her eye. As she placed the refreshment down, her sleeves slid back, revealing wicked marks above and below the bony outcrop of her wrist.

"Thank you, Rachael, that will be all."

The girl half bowed, breezing out like a ghost.

"Please, I hope you don't think me rude, it's just we are very busy," said Sharp.

"I understand. Is there any chance Ms Morrow will join us?"

"I'm afraid not. Ms Morrow chairs a monthly meeting with the council and several social housing providers. We offer our professional service and surplus stock to those organisations on an ad hoc basis."

"I see. I didn't realise private management linked into the social sector. Is that something you've always done?"

Sharp upended the two glasses and poured one for Cook as she answered.

"Morrow and Burke offer a wide range of services. Of course, predominantly we are a private equity company with our backbone being rent, property sales, and unit management, but Ms Morrow believes we should leverage our success to advance the quality and availability of accommodation to those in a less fortunate position. Our involvement has been relatively recent. Eighteen months perhaps." Sharp sat back and recrossed her legs.

"That's extremely philanthropic of her," said Cook.

"It has become one of the missions of our company to bring up the standard of available housing. With your

Troubles and what have you there was little appetite for investment." Sharp gave a shrug of resignation.

Cook made a scribbled note and took a drink of the water. It was ice cold, the decanter already condensing, and she carefully placed her glass back on the paper doily.

"It's an investment property I'm enquiring about, actually. You acted as agent for the seller."

"Do you have an address?"

"The Old Mill. It's on the Springfield Road, close to the junction with the Falls Road. It's quite a distinct property." Cook showed the woman an image she had saved on her mobile phone.

"I know the one. What's the query exactly?"

"The property was being sold to Miltek Refurb, but the sale didn't go through?"

"I seem to remember something."

"Do you know what happened?"

"With the sale?"

Cook nodded.

"Off the top of my head I don't but it could be any number of things. The buyer pulled out, the seller changed his mind."

"Is that a regular occurrence?" said Cook.

"More than you might think."

"The Belfast planning office portal shows Miltek Refurb had plans to develop the site into luxury apartments."

"As I say, the details escape me, but that might have been the issue. The area, well it's not one of social deprivation however it is what you might call working class. It wouldn't quite be the up-and-coming location for top-end apartment living."

"Nothing to do with local objection?"

"Constable, I have neither the file to hand nor the powers of recall you require for your chosen profession." Sharp shrugged as elegantly as if she was throwing off a fur wrap.

"I couldn't say."

"Can you get the file?"

"I'm sorry," said Sharp, although her expression was saying the opposite. "Not at the moment. I would need to have someone go through the records department. Perhaps if you leave your contact details I'll have somebody make an appointment for you, say next week when we have a little more time?"

"It's okay. I'm able to wait," said Cook, ignoring the hint and reaching out for another draught of water.

"Unfortunately, demands on my attention today are quite pressing. So…"

Carrie placed the glass beside the doily. Sharp keenly watched the wet ring form at its base.

"When the deal fell through, did Miltek show any interest in similar properties or other potential developments?" pressed Cook.

"I'm not sure if discussing particulars, even with the police, falls quite within the boundaries of our client data protection policy."

"It might be quite important."

"That might be so, Constable, but.."

"We are investigating the death of Miltek Refurbs Managing Director."

Cook noted a minor narrowing of the eyes, almost imperceptible with the extra-length lashes and mascara, but it was there.

"I'm dreadfully sorry to hear that but, how can we possibly…" Another of the elegant shrugs and a toss of her platinum ponytail.

"Routine background. We are trying to establish if his death might be connected to any of his business interests?"

"It wasn't an accident?" said Sharp.

"No, he was murdered."

This time there was a definite reaction. Protest she might, but Cook now knew she had at least heard of, if not had dealings with Rab Millar.

"Constable, I really want to help, but as I'm sure you can appreciate, I have superiors who will need to sign off on any of your requests. The legalities aside, we have a duty to protect our clients and their investments from the potential financial impact something like this might cause."

"I'm sorry. I don't understand?"

"Our business flourishes due to reputation. To be mentioned in the same headline as murder, for example?" Sharp let the implication hang.

"This is a police investigation, Miss Sharp, not the tabloids raking for dirt."

"I appreciate that, I really do but, for the purpose of argument if this company has appropriated our services in a purchase or as managing agent of other properties, how long before we are the subject of those enquires? The final call will have to be by Ms Morrow. Do you have a card?"

Carrie Cook knew when the door was getting shut in her face. She lifted her handbag onto her lap and removed a business card.

"Thanks for your time, Miss Sharp. If there's anything at all regarding Miltek," said Cook, offering the card.

The leggy blonde was already on her feet, chair tucked back, door open. She snapped the card from Cook.

"I'll have someone call you."

"I'd appreciate that. I'm sorry for barging in. Thanks for the water."

Sharp held the cubicle door open and Cook stepped back into the open-plan office, which still hummed with muted voices and the tack, tack of keyboards.

The man was now standing at ease, back against the wall, regarding her as she shook Sharp's hand.

"Actually, all the water. Sorry, would you mind if I used your bathroom?"

Sharp nodded impatiently, directing her back towards the main office and a glass-panelled door.

"Through there. Ladies are at the end. You can find your way out?"

"Yes. Perfect, thanks again. I'll wait for the call."

Sharp breezed away in a click-clack of her designer heels, ponytail swishing back and forth.

Cook pushed through the door and entered a tiled hallway with five other doors off it.

The ladies and gents were obvious from the signs and as she passed another, she noted it was a utility store from the wheeled red mop bucket and detergents.

The next she opened to find a general storage cupboard not much deeper than a wardrobe. It was shelved, with packs of promotional material heavily featuring Ms Morrow, and bundles of property sector monthly publications.

The last door was locked.

Entering the ladies, she wasn't shocked to find it was larger than expected. Everything about Morrow and Burke was in excess.

The walls were a deep charcoal and the floors pristine grey ceramic wood effect tile. On one side were eight cubicles, each closed off with a darker peppercorn door and opposite, an equal number of shining sinks below a framed mirror. Expensive pump bottles of hand wash and moisturiser were arranged to the left of each mixer tap and an enormous bouquet of fresh flowers sat on a free-standing black gloss plinth.

Cook set her handbag on the sink and looked at her reflection, tousling her hair back to something resembling how she'd left the house. She tucked her blouse in and straightened her jacket and skirt, dusting the shoulders and picking a thread from the buttonhole. She huffed a self-conscious sigh at the thought of running the gauntlet of Amazonians on the way out.

Behind, a toilet flushed, and a door clicked open. Cook had a full view in the mirror's reflection.

"Hi. Rachael, isn't it?"

The girl froze in the open doorway. Cook slowly turned, a warm smile on her face.

"Thanks for the water."

The girl's hair fell over her face and she edged away from the door and towards the sink.

"How do you like it here?"

Rachael turned the tap, avoiding eye contact and nodded.

"It's good."

"You just left school?" said Cook.

She ignored the question. The hand washing again revealed the cruel marks on her wrists.

"They look nasty."

Rachael shook off the water and reached for some paper towels to dry her hands. In her haste, they didn't make it to the bin.

Cook stooped and collected them.

"Are you okay, pet?"

Rachael had her hand on the door handle. She pulled it open an inch.

"I overheard you."

Cook didn't say anything for fear of putting the girl off.

"About Miltek. The Mill."

"Yes, Miss Sharp is going to help us look into the gentleman who was interested in buying the property."

The girl gave a brief snort.

"He wasn't a gentleman."

"Rachael…"

But she was gone. Cook made to follow, cursed, returned

to the sink for her handbag and followed.

The door to the office was just drifting shut, so she dashed and pulled it open.

"If I've said it once, I've said it a hundred times. If the reckless little bitch can't do her job properly, then I'll send her back to the…"

Stella Sharp was in heated conversation with Ms Daphne Morrow. The discussion ended abruptly at the sight of the police officer.

"Ms Morrow." Carrie Cook stepped forward. She glanced to the right, but there was no sign of Rachel at her desk.

"Detective Constable Cook. Glad I caught you both. Sorry, Miss Sharp, it completely went out of my head. My inspector had made a request for some CCTV footage from the Speakers Square development. Is that something you could provide?"

The older woman gave her a withering gaze.

"I'm afraid we have discovered an IT issue this morning with several of our remote viewing applications. The hard drives seem to have wiped themselves. Our security company says they will have them replaced in the next twenty-four hours." Morrow gave an impatient snort. "Excuse me. I'm expected on a call. Miss Sharp will see you out."

She turned and stalked away and Cook watched as she passed through the office like a dark cloud, each of the girls burrowing just a little further into their tasks until she had passed.

A scowling Stella Sharp stepped forward. There were no further pleasantries as she bid her towards the exit.

## Chapter 27

"How are you getting on with finding out who clipped Rab?" Beattie unfastened the single button of his suit jacket and sat.

Reeves' breeding overrode his hostility, and he politely pulled out Taylor's seat before taking his own. Macpherson flopped down on his like a petulant teen dragged to a family dinner.

"Might go a bit quicker if you told me what you had him up to?" Taylor sat comfortably, straight-backed, palms folded on the table and held Beattie's stare.

Macpherson perked at the riposte, giving a sharp inch of nod in silent approval.

A starched white tablecloth was the battleground between them now, each place set with the weapons of war: fat-bowled wine goblets, fine-stemmed water glasses, and polished sterling silver service. Macpherson eyed the four forks, a trio of spoons and a pair of knives with suspicion. Each place setting was topped off with a brilliant white linen napkin with both the motif '31' and a buttonhole embroidered in purple thread.

Beattie huffed a laugh, breaking the staring contest as he plucked a proffered wine list from the hand of the sommelier.

Taylor took the opportunity to further observe her surroundings and re-centre as Beattie asked for a moment to choose. Observing the tables and then the wood-panelled room, she blinked away the imbalance of emotion that had arisen as she came face to face with the man she had hunted for so long and the incongruous surroundings of a high-class lunch.

They could be any foursome from any business sector out to seal a deal or celebrate a victory. The only exception to the norm was that Taylor was the only female in the room. Every other patron and member of staff was male. The club did not accept women, not even as guests.

Conversation had wilted, the clink of cutlery abated, and silent stares followed as Mark Morgan had led them to Beattie's table. The Thirty-One was a sanctuary to these men, a domain of masculinity and, of the twenty or so diners, most were over sixty, all were white, and all wore dark suits and old school tie. Each, to a man, held an expression at her appearance, that at best could be described as novel amusement and at the worst wholly hostile.

Beattie's table was not one of the most desirable on offer, but she felt it suited him, tucked away from the door and the bay windows, half hidden in a recess and shadowed by a chimney breast, bathed in light and shadow.

Beattie revelled in the chaos he had created, offering a silent nod or wave, and a relaxed shrug at one acquaintance. Taylor strode nonplussed behind in a tailored charcoal wool blend trouser suit, dove grey turtle neck polo and low suedette loafers with a gold bar detail. Unquestionably and unapologetically feminine.

Macpherson followed her, as always a little dishevelled. Shoes in need of a polish, suit jacket wrinkled and in need of a dry clean, but the force of his stare as he glared at each man he trundled past dampened their verve to comment and left them reaching for their claret.

No women, thought Taylor again cynically. Not in here anyway.

She had noted the purple velvet rope and the stairway beyond. Shielding the route to the inner sanctum; the hidden place beyond the grandfather clocks and cosy fireside armchairs with their chessboards and snoozing players. The drawing rooms and lounges sealed away from sight where Rab Millar would have closed his deals with a Cuban cigar and a peaty single malt and where women like Lena Borodenko eased a gentleman's attention away from the wild honey panna cotta and lemon meringue of supper and on to finer desserts.

"The food a bit better in here than Maghaberry is it?" Macpherson said drawing a grin from Beattie. His stint in the maximum-security prison had been short-lived.

"I wouldn't know, Doc. Solomon here didn't even give me time to get my breakfast before he had me out."

"There's always next time," said Taylor, her attention now firmly back to the present.

"There won't be a next time, Veronica. You had your chance, I'm not going back."

There was a gleam in his eye, and not for the first time she thought he was attractive. He had the look of a leading man, in a sort of old Hollywood way. A James Dean or a Steve McQueen. Handsome with a hard edge, and both ruthless and reckless with it; par for the course for a drug dealing, murdering scumbag.

Beattie called for the sommelier.

"The St Romain Chardonnay."

"Very good, sir."

"We're not drinking," interrupted Taylor. "Can you have some water brought with it?"

The sommelier hesitated and glanced at Beattie for his answer.

He pursed his lips, a grin playing at the edges. He offered the sommelier an open palm to Taylor.

"Still or sparkling… ma'am?" he asked eventually.

"Sparkling. With lime, please."

The sommelier bowed his head and beat a retreat.

"So, are we celebrating an overdue change of career then?" said Taylor.

Solomon Reeves opened his mouth to speak, but Beattie

quieted him with a gesture, offering a resigned smile at Taylor.

"Do you seriously see me turning my back on everything I've worked for?"

"No. I don't suppose I do."

"Why would I? Look at the life I've built."

"One where you constantly look over your shoulder?"

Beattie sat back and opened his arms.

"For you?"

"Not just me." Taylor leaned onto her elbows and smiled sweetly. "There's worse than me looking to put a bullet in your back."

Solomon Reeves' expression was one of confused annoyance.

"Was that a threat?" he said.

"I'm just saying. Rab Millar. Duncan McCutcheon. Barry Corrigan. You're all old pals, aren't you?"

"Inspector Taylor, if you want to question Mr Beattie then…"

"Relax, Solomon," Beattie chided. "We're all friends here, aren't we, Veronica?"

Taylor pursed her lips and cocked her head in thought. Beattie laughed.

"All pals and most of them dead. It's not looking good for McCutcheon if you're interested. I wonder if one day I'll get the call and it'll be you I'm looking down at?"

"With a tear in your eye, no doubt."

"Just offering my observations," said Taylor.

"So what? Anybody that's done good and raised themselves in this town has a target on their back. Are you saying you don't? There's not a dozen other fellas looking for a step up in the ranks and you're blocking the road. They're asking themselves, is it because she's competent or because she's a woman? Maybe you're thinking that too? Must eat at you now I'm sitting here and you're back in the barracks raking over the ruins of failure?"

A black-tied and aproned waiter appeared, fussing over pouring the Chardonnay and the arrangement of the ice bucket. A second man arrived momentarily and placed down the sparkling water.

"Who said anything about failure?" said Taylor.

Beattie raised his glass. Taylor lifted hers in return.

"This looks like freedom to me." He took a sip with a satisfied smack of the lips.

"The life you live is a prison without walls and you know it. Every move, every meeting, every call. When was the last time you felt relaxed? The last time you weren't waiting up for the knock on the door?" said Taylor.

"So? I sell up and hit the Costas. Live out my life watching sunsets and drinking Pina Colada?"

"A bit like Billy McBride?"

Beattie's grin died a little, curling in death to a sour imitation of itself. He masked the worst of the damage with another sip of Chardonnay.

"You might never get another chance at a normal life," said Taylor.

"Your kind of life? Salaried, throwing away your best days chasing men like me and maybe, if you're lucky, you get a watch and paltry pension for your trouble. No thanks," Beattie sneered and took another drink.

"I don't know any other life," said Taylor.

"Neither do I."

"I guess we just keep playing our parts then."

"I guess we do."

Taylor raised her glass. Beattie toasted and took a swig, aiming his glass at her on the downswing.

"If you ever get fed up on that side, I've a place for you."

Taylor gave an amused shake of her head at the

suggestion.

"You've no place for me, Monster. But I've a place for you. It's six by eight with three square meals a day. It's only a matter of time," she said.

"You want a second crack?"

"You think I won't take it?"

"I'd be disappointed if you didn't," said Beattie.

"Next time, it won't be a near miss," promised Taylor.

There was a cool silence around the table. Macpherson hadn't touched his water and Reeves sat quietly, head turning in subtle side glances as the conversation ebbed and flowed, his untouched glass of Chardonnay in hand. Glancing down, he brushed away a droplet of condensation that had fallen onto his lap.

"What then? It'll be a pretty lonely life you're left with?" Beattie leaned forward.

"I'm sure I'll manage."

"No. I don't think so." Beattie locked her in his stare. "I think you'll realise you got what you wished for, but it'll be a bitter disappointment."

"You think?" chuckled Taylor.

"Yes, I think the fire that gets you out of bed every morning will die and you'll be half the woman you are now."

It was Taylor's turn to scowl. Her expression reignited Beattie, his cobalt eyes penetrating the veneer of patient professionalism, and she felt the hate well up. Taylor's breath caught in her throat. She swallowed, knowing he wasn't far from the mark. Put him away and what? Find a man, marry, have kids? Not likely. More chance she'd be checking the prison every week to make sure he was there. Fixated on his incarceration. Haunted by his victims.

"Maybe. Who knows?" she said.

"Who knows?" Beattie agreed. "Maybe you walk out of here and our paths never cross again?"

Taylor took a final sip of her water. She stood and Macpherson followed suit.

"Desmond Neely. Seventy-one." Her voice was crisp and unwavering.

"Am I supposed to know the name?" Beattie's lower lip jutted, a slight shake of the head.

"Two broken knee caps. Right arm fractured in two places. Three broken ribs, a punctured lung, and two cracked vertebrae. His ears were cut off and put in his mouth and you sewed that shut along with his eyes."

Beattie's stare cooled.

Taylor, surprising herself, reached out a hand.

Beattie took it, his palm warm and dry, his grip firm.

"Thanks for the drink. I'll see you around, Monster."

Beattie held her hand as he stood, neither willing to break the connection.

"Not if I see you first, Veronica."

## Chapter 28

John Barrett rose and warmly welcomed his guest from the maître d', who bowed his head and bid the gentlemen a good afternoon.

"Rodger, so glad you made it. I hope you don't mind, I've taken the liberty of ordering something to drink," said Barrett.

Barrett's guest unfastened his dark suit jacket and sat down without preamble.

"Is there a problem, John?"

The accusatory tone surprised Barrett.

Rodger Callahan represented the consortium. He may not have sat at the high table, but he stood firmly on the right hand of it. His current purview over the European and North African operation had brought the two men into orbit, and Callahan was rigorous in administering the agenda set out by the faceless group.

Barrett reached for the bottle of Gevrey-Chambertin burgundy and poured his guest an inch and a half.

"I'm afraid you have me at a disadvantage? I'm not aware of any problems?" Barrett replaced the bottle where it had stood and refrained from taking a sip of the wine, meeting the steely gaze of the older man. Callahan searched the face, then pursed his lips and glanced slowly back at the lobby.

"The constabulary are in the lobby."

"I see," said Barrett, momentarily relieved. "I expect it's nothing. There is a function today. I was chatting to a colleague from the Justice Department in the lounge a little earlier."

"Detective Inspector Taylor is in the lobby," said Callahan with a withering look.

"Oh," said Barrett, his mind recalculating potentialities.

He had assumed the older man had observed the occasional uniform or plain-clothed protection officer that could be found loitering in anticipation of their charge's exit. Taylor was a different matter. Taylor shouldn't have been able to bless the threshold, never mind pass across it.

"If it amounted to anything, I would have heard."

"Yes?"

"Absolutely. Chin, chin." Barrett picked up his glass and his guest relaxed a little, air chinked in toast, and took a sip.

"I leave again this evening. Just a flying visit."

"Productive?"

The grey-haired man nodded. No words of thanks or acknowledgement as the waiter returned with two bound menus.

"I was in Dublin this morning. We have another avenue of distribution there which seems acceptable."

"Very good," said Barrett, nodding in thanks to the waiter and opening the cover of his menu.

"Our timeline?" said Callahan.

"On schedule. The MV Madeline is scheduled to dock tonight and our South American guests shall be with us as planned."

Callahan took a sip of wine, swirling the liquid around the large glass bowl.

"What about our other dignitary?" he said.

"The general leaves Kinshasa this evening," said Barrett.

"Splendid, if not a little unorthodox."

"He wishes to inspect and approve his order," Barrett shrugged. "It's a formality. He wishes to press the flesh, so to speak."

Callahan chuckled.

"His manifest is in order?"

Barrett took his attention away from the wild roasted

guinea fowl and braised garlic potatoes.

"The export is being prepared for transportation. Both parties will be pleased with the merchandise we are offering."

"Perfect. Well, as ever, you have things under control. Well done, John."

Barrett basked in the warm glow of praise, the light of it dying suddenly as the door to the dining room opened and he laid eyes on the group who entered.

As the rage welled up, Barrett was inwardly conflicted at the sheer audacity of Beattie who, bold as brass, peacocked through the dining room, the thorn in their side at heel behind.

Barrett knew Beattie better than to believe he was unaware of his presence, but as he meandered his way through the tables, he made no acknowledgement.

The silence that followed in the wake of the young inspector was stark. She marched through the ranks of the curmudgeonly old members, strident and stern. Her own subordinate trailed in her wake throwing daggers at those who thought to comment.

Barrett's anger tempered into respect for Beattie. This was a new level to keeping your enemies close, the man had balls to both thumb his nose at tradition and invite the viper to his breast.

Of course, it would also put forth another narrative and perhaps polish the tarnish of late amongst those in the club who had sought to distance themselves. The presence of the lawyer Reeves would likely aid matters and Barrett's own repartee with the justice minister's aide had revealed the ACC wanted Beattie on side to deal with the fallout from his old partner's murder.

If it didn't blow up in his face, then such a public burying of the hatchet, if that's what this was, may be the very thing they needed to put Gordon Beattie and Finntek back in the headlines for the right reasons and leave their other business in the shadows where it belonged.

## Chapter 29

The rain had started again as Chris Walker eased the pool car out of the country-bound traffic and onto the M2 off-slip, indicating across lanes and negotiating the sweeping descent to the main A2 that fed into the northern fringes of the city.

Headlights from the ribbon of traffic coming in the opposite direction flared on the dirty windscreen. He jabbed the washers only to receive the pitiful dregs of the tank.

"Ack, if it's not fuel, it's water. I swear every time I take a car out there's something."

He flicked the wiper stem to double speed, which only aided in smearing the windscreen further.

"There's a garage round the corner; we can top it up there on the way back. Estate's just across the road, look, that's the block there."

Erin Reilly took her eye off her phone and pointed out of the passenger window at the high-rise looming above the slate roofs.

"I see it. Have you had any luck getting that to send?" said Walker as Reilly once again stabbed at the phone screen.

"Nope, I think the file's too big. It'll have to wait till we're back to the nick and I'll get it from the cloud."

Their trip past the bookies had struck paydirt. A liveried Land Rover had been back at the end of the road and the chalked circles in the street and the boarded-up windows and battle-scarred walls of the Corners Bar all remained as stark evidence of the shooting.

There were half a dozen customers in the bookies and after a short explanation and a moments wait for the acting-manageress, Carly, they were let through the heavy-duty Plexiglas security screen. The cashiers' area was hot, a blow heater was hammering away under the desk, and after she had settled with a punter, Carly led them into an equally stifling and claustrophobic office.

Pine-scented detergent from the adjacent toilet filled the room. A laptop PC and monitor sat on a badly erected shelf and reams of CDs had toppled onto the floor where a double stack of dockets made up for the lack of a chair.

Carly fished a child's school jotter from under the monitor and two-finger tapped the password in. Ten minutes later they had some footage. It wasn't great, but there was at least one frame of a profile of a man passing the camera nearest the Corners. Black jacket, jeans. Head down until he'd turned to watch a police Land Rover pass.

Several failed attempts to put the watermarked two-and-a-half minutes onto disk left Reilly using a USB lead to download it directly to her phone and so far the entire trip to the Fearon Estate had been a failure in getting it sent back to base.

"This us?"

"Looks like it," said Reilly, scrubbing a porthole in the passenger window. "Twenty-seven B. Downstairs flat."

Walker hauled on the handbrake and killed the ignition. As he unclipped his seat belt, the door to the flat opened, and a man exited, the door slamming shut behind, the knocker flapping loudly. As he reached the end of the overgrown garden path, he hauled at his crotch and rearranged his loose shirt tails.

"This Rhonda Murray's place?" Reilly asked, pushing the passenger door closed as Walker also stepped out.

The man froze like a deer in the headlights; took a frantic glance left and right. He was mid-thirties, mid-height, a joe average but not stupid enough to miss they were police.

"Rhonda Murray?" she said again.

He nodded quickly, his eyes not meeting hers. Walker

approached him, and he sidestepped, clearing the weedy footpath to the rusted iron gate.

"Can I go?" he mumbled.

"Sure." Walker jerked his head, and the man hastened away, turning his collar up against the rain. Approaching the corner to a narrow alleyway at the end of the block, he shot a quick glance back.

The space at the end of the row was marked out for cars, but only one rust bucket sat on flat tyres and dented rims. There was no sign of any van.

The maisonette flats themselves looked tired; the render scored and patchy, paint bubbling on window frames, and the glass darkened and matt with grime was now streaked with raindrops. A gate to the garden had fallen an inch and scratched across the concrete path which itself was a death trap of cracks and potholes, the small patch of greenery either side more dandelion and jaggy nettle than anything else.

Reilly rapped the knocker.

Walker double-checked the painted house number pinned beside the door and braved a step into the weeds. The inside was obscured by a once-white net curtain. He took a step back and found the same arrangement in the upper windows.

Reilly put a bit more force behind the knocker a second time, prompting the dull tones of a voice. The words became louder and more aggrieved as they approached the door.

"You couldn't be back already? Did you forget your kecks or what?"

The rasp of keys sounded across wood and then the rapid unfastening of Yale lock. The door jerked open, revealing shock written across the face behind it.

"Mrs Murray."

The door closed again, and Reilly rushed to put a hand against the frame.

"Mrs Murray, we just need a quick word."

"I told them other two yesterday. Now away on."

"I'm sorry, the other two?" said Reilly, brow creased in confusion.

"Aye, the other two. I've no money to give you. If you want to take the bloody dryer, go ahead. It's not working anyway."

Walker gaped at the exchange. Rhonda Murray scowled at the hand holding the door open.

"I said away on. Shift, you're letting the rain in."

Reilly found it hard to determine her age, the paperwork said late thirties, but she looked twenty years older. Her skin was stretched over too much face and the thick black brows looked to have been whacked on with a marker. Mascara clotted the lashes of eyes sucked into chubby cheeks and her hair was dyed, blonde but dark at the roots, and stuck to her head in sweaty curls behind her ears, each pierced at least three times. Large hoops hung as low as the fuchsia pink flannel robe that was failing to maintain her modesty.

It gaped at the stomach, flimsy belt barely holding her in, and milk bottle white legs peeked out from the hem ending in tiny fat feet with scarlet painted toes.

"I think there's been a mistake," said Walker.

"Too right," she agreed, her smoker's pout wrinkled and a nicotine-stained finger jabbed at him.

"Cowboys, you lot; sold me a pup. I told you it doesn't work, so stop hassling me to pay for it. Go on before I call the police."

Reilly stepped back from the door and showed her warrant card.

"We are the police, Mrs Murray. Detective Constable Reilly."

Beady blackened eyes peered at the identification.

"Who phoned you? I never phoned you? I told them, it's broke."

"We're not here about a dryer," said Walker, his own ID extended.

"You're registered as having a white Peugeot van."

"I don't have a van."

"Really? The DVLA have you as the registered owner of a white Peugeot Bipper. DGZ…" Reilly began.

"I've no van. I don't even drive."

"Can we come in for a minute, Mrs Murray? Get out of this rain," said Reilly, offering a shrug at the elements and an apologetic smile.

Murray hesitated and then peered around the overlooking windows, tutting.

"Aye, get in. Better than being the talk of the close with you lot on the doorstep poking your nose into people's business."

She loosed her grip on the door and turned to saunter back up the narrow hallway, her hand digging between her buttocks through the flimsy material as she went.

The welcome was even less inviting on the inside; bare boards streaked with grime, a handful of crushed cigarette butts in a cup and a can of Special Brew on top of a doorless electric box. The hallway smelled of damp and fried food, but the living area made it look like the Ritz by comparison.

The space was open plan, the lounge opening into a kitchenette where every square inch of worktop space was buried under mouldy dishes and old takeaway cartons.

A futon bed dominated the space. Its filthy sheets might once have been red but were now washed out and stained, the tangle strewn half on, half off an equally dilapidated mattress. The scent of sweat and sex was intolerable. It didn't take a stretch of imagination to understand why her visitor had been in a rush to get himself away.

"Sit yourselves down." Murray collapsed on the bed in a wobble of fuchsia robe and barely concealed flesh. She gestured at a sofa under the window. "Just throw that stuff on the floor. I'll lift it later."

Walker looked around, thinking he'd been at tidier crime scenes. The stuff was more food wrappings and some clothes. What qualified as later was anybody's guess considering the similar mountain piled alongside.

"It's okay, Mrs Murray. We'll not keep you," said Reilly, digging in her biker jacket for her notebook. "Peugeot Bipper. White. DGZ Eighteen, sixty-seven. You sure it doesn't ring any bells?"

Murray had preoccupied herself with searching the carnage around the futon, eventually finding a bottle with a couple of inches of cola in the bottom. She swigged it down and tossed it aside where it rolled beside some empty bottles of supermarket brand vodka.

"Van? Maybe it's our Bobby's."

"Bobby, is he your…?" Reilly glanced around the devastation for a clue, caught on what to guess.

"Bobby's dead," said Murray.

Reilly swore to herself and took a composed breath.

"Bobby's dead," she said, receiving a nod of confirmation from Murray.

"Aye, but he had a van," said Murray, miming turning a steering wheel. The movement splayed the dressing gown open further.

Walker tried to keep the horror from his face as she rearranged the gown, too late in focusing on a spot of damp behind her shoulder as she tucked in a breast and recrossed her legs, exposing herself in the process.

"My Barney uses it now. Is that the one? I don't drive, you see."

"Is Barney your son?" he said, maintaining his focus and trying not to smell and speak at the same time.

"Aye, did I not say that?" said Murray, looking at him

quizzically.

"Do you know where we'd find him? We just need to ask a few questions about the van," he said.

"Is he in trouble?" Murray drew up sharply. "I'll kill him if the wee bastard is in trouble again. I've told him…"

"He's not in any trouble. We just want a word," said Reilly, figuring it was pointless giving her the tax and insurance speech.

"I bet you it's them ones he runs about with. That wee shit Billy is up to all sorts. My Barney's too soft for his own good."

"Billy?" said Reilly.

"Aye, Billy Webster. They knock about them old flats. Those over yonder, below the tower."

Reilly and Walker turned in unison, following her gesture. Fearon House loomed through the darkening afternoon gloom and the grime of the front windows.

The flash washed over the rooftops an instant before the thunder. The bloom of black smoke and orange flame coming a second later.

## Chapter 30

Billy Webster put the phone back in his pocket and looked out at the falling rain. The distant hum of traffic from the motorway and main road was dulled by the gurgle of rainwater being greedily swallowed by a gap-toothed drain cover. His concentration lapsed as he watched a drip pitter-patter from the broken guttering onto the carcass of the flat's old gas box in a metronomic rhythm.

Webster's position afforded him an unrestricted view across a waste ground of rubble and weed that led to the roadside. Only an occasional car, tyres hissing on the wet tarmac, or umbrella carrying pedestrian passed, the latter careful to cross over to the opposite side of the street to avoid the skeletal remains of the flats.

From the doorway of the centre flat, which formed the elbow of the three derelict structures, Webster watched two youngsters dip in and out of their respective plots as customers approached. There were two distinct sales funnels, one leading from the low block of shops and the lay-by near the entrance to the estate and the other a track of graffiti and needle-strewn alleyways that fed between the maisonettes and the terraced housing of the estate. The transaction was practised to a fine art, whichever route the customer chose, each swift transfer of cash mirrored in the palm-to-palm handover of merchandise.

The two youngsters occupied in the deals were barely into their teens. The kid to his left, in oversized cap, jeans and jacket ambled out in confident strides to intercept the quick steps of a twenty-something man, easily marked as a blow-in. He'd the look of a city party boy, slick and out of place, his car parked up by the shops and his head on a swivel as he trotted up to the boxy flat to score crack and benzos, one for the lift and one for the dip.

The punter's head jerked as he pulled a fistful of notes from his pocket and headlights illuminated the pair; a van slowing as it cruised past.

A harsh word and a nudge from the youngster and then he was on his way, quickstepping back to the lay-by where he shot a nervous look over his shoulder as he climbed into the luxury interior of a Lexus.

The red van flashed its lights and Webster raised his hand and pointed a finger over his shoulder. The driver acknowledged with a wave and turned up the side of the flats without signal.

Webster looked down at his phone and then once more back into the street.

There was still no sign of Gary, just a couple of shambling regulars emerging from the alleys wearing his and hers padded check shirt jackets, the tops torn and grotty and not a knee in either of their jeans. The man carried a throwaway carrier bag of Special Brew and the woman carried him.

As the kid in the cap jogged back to deposit his cash, the second teen made his approach to the pair. The two customers handed over their dues, the kid pocketed it, then led them to the door of the doss house where he handed them over to a third youngster who would dole out the cocktail of fentanyl-laced heroin to the duo of docile junkies.

The three disappeared through the broken and blackened door to where they would find a corner in one of the mildewed rooms and shoot up on a filthy mattress. The kid remained inside as insurance to see they didn't die and need to be dumped or worse, have to burn the place down and force the business to find new premises.

Webster spat into the torrent of glugging water and then turned back inside to meet his visitor.

❖ ❖ ❖

Shepard didn't recognise the van, but he knew the man behind the wheel, Harry Carruthers.

Carruthers abandoned the van on the patch of waste ground behind the flats and stepped out. A black beanie hat the only addition to his regulation ensemble of padded coat, black jeans and work boots. Uttering a low curse, he stepped over a dog turd and kicked a faded beer car on his way to the rear of the flats.

Shepard watched for any other movement as Carruthers approached the centre flat but there was none. Neither of the first-floor bedrooms nor the cracked and frosted bathroom windows held light or movement.

His close observation point in the undercroft of the stairs meant he was invisible to anyone looking in. He shifted against the concrete wall of the stairway, focusing in on the buildings outside.

The right-hand maisonette had flickering light and the occasional shadow puppet show of movement at the windows to the kitchen and the upper floor. He knew that to be the flophouse where anything from half a dozen to ten regulars could be found comatose with needles in their arms or crack pipes scattered around them and a couple of minders cooking up the tar and watching over business.

Shepard had identified Carruthers early during similar surveillance on Risky's. A regular on the club's door, he was Rab Millar's occasional driver and had been absent during Shepard's surgical hit on the club. This was the first time he had been sniffing around the estate, though. The coincidence of it didn't bother Shepard. While Carruthers was a step above the minor underlings he had been observing for the past week, he didn't pose such a significant threat to warrant an abort, just another on-the-fly calculation and adaptation to the plan. It was one additional hostile, not a company of armoured Russian troops or khat-hyped local militia to contend with.

Carruthers pushed aside the rotten planks that formed a back gate and disappeared from view. Shepard settled back and waited on the two vehicles that wouldn't be far away.

❖ ❖ ❖

"No sign of him?"

"He'll be here." Webster held the back door open with his foot and motioned for Carruthers to enter.

"I've been round the squat and he hasn't been there," said Carruthers.

"I said he'll be here. I've texted him so I have."

"You sure he hasn't sold the bloody phone?"

"Harry, relax. He'll be here," said Webster, with finality.

Carruthers reached into the carcass of a cupboard for a beer.

"Is it not a bit weird scoring your brother gear?"

Webster shrugged.

"If he's going to do it, he's going to do it," he said.

Harry nodded as he pulled the ring tab.

"You think I'd rather he got it from some other scumbag? At least I know what he's taking. Have you seen some of the shite out there at the minute?" said Webster. "What about them three up the west? They lay for a fortnight until the neighbours reported the smell. The dog had been at them and all." Webster's expression was one of disgust.

"I just think it's a bit fucked up, that's all," admitted Carruthers.

"Well, it is what it is," said Webster.

Carruthers swigged back his beer and walked into what had been the main lounge. Cursing, he jerked at the zip of his jacket. Two Calor Gas three-bar heaters were on full pelt and had raised the temperature in the small room to something resembling the tropics.

"Are youse serious?" he said, dumping the jacket on the back of a chair.

"If we don't have these going the place is Baltic, and it keeps the damp down. Come back once it's been lying empty for a couple of days and you'll change your tune," said Webster.

"Are they all like this?"

"Aye, we rigged up a couple of patio heaters down the end after some fucker froze to death over the winter. We get the bottles off your man down the end of the road and then square him up with a couple of grams every week or so for the bother."

Carruthers shook his head in disbelief.

"Would it not be easier to just find somewhere with the gas turned on?"

Webster clicked the heaters down to a bare minimum.

"We had some of them plug-in blow heaters but they weren't worth a crack. We've the free electric running off the BT box out the back for light and stuff but can't get heat any other way."

They had painted the front window opaque with swirls of emulsion paint to deter anybody stupid enough to be nosey, the tin dumped carelessly in the corner. Its remaining contents were now pooled on the floor, discoloured and rock hard.

The carpet that had once been someone's pride and joy, was threadbare and burnt. Discarded cigarette butts and homemade bongs of plastic bottles littered the space. Plastic sporks and takeaway cartons had been kicked to the corner and the crust of a mouldy pizza lay in the middle of the floor.

Facing the door to the hallway, two dozen house bricks formed the legs of a table, a door unscrewed from somewhere else in the house now the surface, and arranged on that like a tabletop war-game, were packages of pills, bars of weed and wraps of powder.

Beside the table a section of floorboard was propped against the wall and, crouched over the space like a Parisian gargoyle, a bug-eyed tweenager wrapped five-pound notes in elastic bands, stacks of other denominations formed into bricks by his knees.

Carruthers flopped down on an old sofa, resting his beer on the one broken arm, and flicking off a butt that had melted a black burn in the upholstery.

"What time are they due?"

"Should be anytime," said Webster, sitting astride an old dining chair and pulling out his phone.

"Anything?"

"Harry, get a smoke down you. Gary'll turn up."

Carruthers took a final swig from the can and jettisoned it towards the empty fireplace.

Gary better turn up, he thought. His guts twisted as the gassy lager hit his stomach.

The girl was in the wind, snatched from under his nose. He'd taken the call from his snitch at the Royal, only to be told she'd been collected by somebody. Picked up and driven away in the back of a dark blue Beemer. He didn't even get the whole plate.

Carruthers looked at his watch and then got up to grab another beer.

Webster's brother was beyond doubt the consolation prize, but leaving here without him? Harry Carruthers knew that would only leave him facing the Monster's wrath.

❖ ❖ ❖

Shepard heard the throaty growl of exhaust and the whine of turbo before he saw the headlights swing into the end of the road.

He took a quick glance at his watch, the luminous index and numbers confirming what he knew.

Amateurs.

He had to hand it to them for consistency, though. Every hustle had been within a ten-minute time frame.

This was no exception and should it play out as normal the second car should be along in the next minute or two.

Both vehicles would bump up on the kerb next to the centre flat. The drugs would be unloaded from the first and taken inside, the cash would be brought out and transferred into the second. It would be all over inside fifteen minutes unless they took the opportunity for a quick toke.

He'd seen that happen twice, confirming either total confidence in their operation or stupidity in taking the risk of a routine traffic stop and having to explain where the boot full of used notes had come from.

Either way, he didn't particularly care. The vehicles would sit abandoned for about seven minutes while the work took place.

Seven minutes was plenty of time to attach a tracker to each.

Seven minutes to trace the drugs to their source and track the cash to the stash.

Stage three was then to put the shithole den opposite out of action. Permanently.

*Chapter 31*

"Billy. Lads." The newcomer gave a nod in greeting.

Webster, filling the table from a holdall at his feet, mirrored the gesture as each hand pulled out cellophane-wrapped bags of pills and power. The courier, a broad-bellied lad, was doing the same from a second bag. His track bottoms riding low on his hips and the crack of his backside on display. Every third deposit, he paused to haul them up.

A second face appeared through the open door to the kitchen and dropped two more Adidas sports bags next to the youngster and his Lego blocks of banknotes.

"Fill her up, skinny," he said, eager to fulfil his duty of collecting and depositing the ill-gotten gains. "Alright, Billy?"

The youngster pulled a face but set about the work as instructed.

"You see my brother on the way in?" said Webster.

"Na. Sure, is he not usually here waiting for a jag?" said the newcomer, then frowning added. "Where's your Siamese twin?"

"Barney? He's over minding the junkies. His dog died."

"Joking me. Shit one."

"Aye. This is Harry." Webster jerked his chin towards the sofa.

Carruthers grunted at the cash collection boys and paced to the front window, peering through the smeared glass. The world was now a dreamy orange blur as sodium streetlights battled the gloom and reflected on the puddles.

"Is that the lot?" The second collector booted the first holdall which was now full. The kid was already well into packing the second.

"That's it," confirmed Webster, then pointed at the

makeshift table, addressing the big lad whose job it was to resupply the stash house. "Is that the last of the gear?"

Hauling up his track bottoms, he confirmed with a nod.

"You much more to do?" said Webster to the cash collectors.

"Three after you," said the first man. "The card school. Your man's gym and the ice cream place."

"You seen Freaky?" asked Webster.

"No, but I heard about the Corners."

Webster set the last house-brick wrap of cannabis on the makeshift tabletop.

"I was there," he said.

"Dead on." Courier and collectors looked at him sceptically.

"I'm telling you. Ask Barney next time you see him, the tit pissed himself." Webster laughed, shaking his head. "Mental, it was."

"Them bastards deserved it if they did that to Rab," said the first man. "You hear anything about us going after more of them?"

"Nope. Just been told to get this gear shifted and that cash out of here. Did you have any bother coming across?" said Webster.

"Sure when's there ever. Piece of piss," said the second.

"Piece of piss," agreed Webster.

Carruthers grunted from his position at the window, Webster ignored the impatient grump of the older man.

"Smoke?" he said.

The drugs courier hauled up his pants again and gave a vigorous nod, agreement following from the cash collectors.

"Now you're talking. Get her spliffed up."

❖ ❖ ❖

Shepard felt the magnets pull and heard the dull metallic thud of connection. The Toyota had been straightforward, but the Subaru skimming the ground on fat, low-profile alloys had left him fiddling to make sure the tracker wasn't bashed off by the first speed hump it hit.

"What are you doing?"

Shepard's head cracked off the bumper in surprise. He pushed his weight off the wet street and slowly brought his head around.

The first thing he saw was dirty trainers, laces untied and trailing in the wet like dirty grey worms. Then a pair of pipe cleaner legs in filthy skinny jeans and a pale face looming out of a black hoody. Acne scars were visible under a week's worth of bumfluff beard. The saucer eyes stared in unblinking incomprehension at why a man was lying in a puddle under a car as the rain lashed down.

Shepard moved to one knee and then using the car for balance stood. Feigning unsteadiness, he reached out a hand and offered across a selection of old crushed cigarette butts and a bent needle.

Shepard's hair was soaked and stuck to his head, water dripping from his eyes and beard onto a filthy donkey jacket. He wore a pair of workman's cargo pants, the pockets torn and seat ripped. The wind and the rain exacerbated the stench of piss and body odour rising from the old clothes.

"Fuck's sake. No thanks. Away on, don't be hanging round here, alright?" said the boy.

Shepard shrugged, slumping against the car and jamming a butt between his lips. Patting himself down, he produced a lighter from a pocket. He thumbed the wheel, the flint sparked but failed to light. He put it back in his pocket and shuffled away.

"I mean it," said the boy. "Don't be hanging round here, it's bad news." His words were snatched at by the wind.

Shepard ambled on, stooped over and eyes searching the ground, resisting the urge to glance back. The kid was perhaps early twenties with translucent skin and a malnourished frame. The last time he'd seen him he was leaving Risky's with a spring in his step and the look of somebody who'd done the double at the derby.

He put the near miss to the back of his mind, a slow breath in through his nose ratcheting back his heart rate. Discomfort in the wound to his side but a nod to fate it hadn't been the courier boys come back early or one of the BMX bandits that sometimes kept dick over the flats, circling like two-wheeled vultures waiting on carrion to draw a last breath.

Pushing self-criticism for missing the kid's approach away, Shepard shoved open the door to his lay-up point and drew out his phone as he again squeezed into position by the stairs.

The LCD screen, already set to night shift and dark mode, produced very little light as he fired up the app and confirmed the trackers were paired and displaying. Two blue dots and two little rows of coordinates pulsed on the map screen. Shepard left the app running and returned the phone to his jacket.

Movement across the waste ground caught his attention. The back gate of the centre flat opened and the four figures he'd observed entering twenty-five minutes earlier emerged. A flare of a cigarette came from the second in the group and then a shower of sparks as it was flicked away.

Moments later brake lights bloomed, and then the throaty rumble of an engine followed. Bulky holdalls were jettisoned into the boot of the Subaru, and then two cars rolled off in opposite directions.

Exiting through the rear stairwell door, Shepard began the circuitous route to his next objective.

❖ ❖ ❖

Gary Webster was clucking.

He had the shivers and the sweats and although the soaking he'd taken on the walk from the bus stop had not helped, it wasn't the reason for his misery.

His biology was craving a top-up and his physiology was in full rebellion, reminding him it was no longer a recreational choice but one as essential as air. As he trudged through the puddles, all he could think of was the baggie and the blast of gravy that would make him better. A hit to kill the crushing super-flu and melt him back into warm oblivion. He pushed open the gate and entered through the back door, his feet crunching over broken glass and tiles as he walked through the galley kitchen and into the lounge.

"Where the fuck have you been?" said Carruthers.

"Harry? What are you doing here?" Gary Webster's foggy brain struggled to comprehend the man's presence.

"Never mind that, come on. You're coming with me." Carruthers had to swing forward twice to get enough momentum going to lift himself from the low sofa.

Gary Webster stopped in a jerky mid-step as though hit by lightning, darting a startled glance at the two faces in the room, his hand wiping perspiration and rain from his face.

"Gary, chill out. Here, this'll take the edge off. It's alright, Harry will drop you back to me after," said Billy Webster, offering a cling-wrapped speedball to his brother.

"Don't be giving him anything, for God's sake." Carruthers made to reach for the cocaine, benzodiazepine mix, but Webster deftly swapped hands.

"Harry, if you're taking him to see the boss and he's knocking you're the one who's going to look like a twat," snapped Webster. "Come here, Gary. Get that down you. You look like shite, where have you been?"

Gary Webster shuffled forward and snatched the drugs from his brother's hand like a starved dog.

"Around," he mumbled, flopping in the space abandoned by Carruthers.

"I've been trying to find you for days." Carruthers shifted

impatiently.

"It's roasting in here," said the younger Webster, carefully pouring out two lines of the combined drugs on the arm of the chair, aligning them a notch straighter with his little finger. A quick lick and then he hoovered up both in two well-practised motions, throwing his head back and pinching his nose, his eyes screwed shut.

"Nobody has seen you since Risky's on Sunday," said Billy Webster.

"So?"

"So the big man wants to know what you were doing and what you saw before Rab got clipped. You told me you saw the fucker?" Carruthers wasn't averse to a line or two of coke but his mouth twisted in distaste as he watched the younger man drool onto his vomit stained hoody.

Gary Webster, preoccupied with dishing out another line, was oblivious to the look and ignored the question.

"Gary?" said Billy patiently.

"What?"

"Risky's, what were you doing?"

Gary snorted up the latest line and sank back into the worn chair. His eyes glazed as he stared at the ceiling then back down at his hands, nails bitten to the quick, his knuckles split and bruised from beating on the girl.

He looked up at his brother and Harry Carruthers.

Both stared at him, their expressions, he imagined, akin to those a zoo animal would be familiar with, then a vague notion in the back of his throat.

A smell that was sweet and a bit rotten. He glanced down and for the first time noticed the state of himself. He choked out a snorting cough, a trail of mucus peppering the leg of his jeans. The odour was more intense now.

"What's that smell?"

❖ ❖ ❖

Shepard pushed open the back door with only a gaping round hole where the barrel of the old Yale lock had been it took nothing more than a few ounces of force to send it moving inwards.

The mouth of the teenager who stood opposite him formed an O of utter surprise at the intrusion.

One fist gripped a baggie of heroin, the other falling from the head of the woman knelt before him to drag his track bottoms up from around his knees. A strangled gasp of surprise died in his throat as Shepard took three quick steps forward and lanced a straight-fingered jab into the soft flesh under his Adam's apple.

The lank-haired woman scrambled backwards, sticky drool smeared her chin and her bloodshot eyes tracked the boy's body as it fell limply to the dirty linoleum. He lay still, curled foetal with his bare arse pressed against the counter he'd been leaning on, his erection fading fast. The precious contents of his fist fell to the floor and as her hand snaked out, Shepard's boot trapped it.

The woman hissed, and he looked down into the desperate face. Her thin arm showed track marks under the rolled-up sleeve of her padded check shirt, and she smelled worse than he did. Dark staining on her jeans suggested she'd either shit herself or lain in someone else's since they had last seen a wash. The dead look in her eyes told him all he needed to know. That she didn't care, she'd do anything for the bag of brown.

Shepard released his boot and picked up the drugs, waving the baggie like a hypnotist.

"How many?" he asked.

She licked her lips, yellowed stumps poking from badly receded gums, eyes narrowing in suspicion.

"Well?"

"Him," she cocked her head, first at the unconscious body then towards the body of the flat. "And another two."

"Where?"

"Wee Barney'll be in the house somewhere. The other will be out the front," she mumbled, wiping her chin.

"Watching for more of your lot?"

She nodded.

"Is there more like you in there too?"

She nodded again.

"Stay here and when I come back, you can have this and whatever else I find. Just sit right there and keep your mouth shut."

She didn't respond, just maintained her rigid focus on the bag. Shepard pitied her but resigned himself to the fact he'd put her out of her misery if she posed a threat or raised an alarm.

But she didn't move, her eyes slavishly on only one desire. He waved the baggie at her once more and turned his back, exiting the kitchen.

❖ ❖ ❖

Barney Murray watched his stream of piss hit the blackened U-bend and wrinkled his nose at the stench that rose from the waste pipe. Then he remembered his dog and spat an angry gob of phlegm against the graffiti-covered wall. It dribbled slowly towards the cistern as he shook off and backed through the open toilet doorway.

Other than the entrances there were no doors in the flophouse, to do so posed the risk that some tired old junkie might decide to throw up a belt in the depths of a downer and bring an end to their craving, and that was hassle no one needed.

Barney walked into the lounge and looked at the faded floral curtains.

"Bastards." He reached down and picked up the joint he'd

left in the bottom of a sliced up beer can. The staccato replay of Freaky killing his poor dog flashed in his head as he sparked a lighter to get the reefer going again.

The floorboards creaked above, an avalanche of dust falling through one of the holes in the ceiling plaster, the sound of someone rolling over and the hiss of the patio heater thankfully the only noise now Kevin's groans and goading encouragement had stopped in the kitchen.

"Dirty bastard," mumbled Barney, pacing the floor.

Satiated, the prick would be skinning up while the old slapper, Maggie, would be shooting her reward into her arm, her old fella comatose upstairs an absent memory.

Barney continued his orbit of the room. A sports bag of cash liberated from the week's punters lay unzipped in the corner, Barney had been stacking and wrapping the notes with elastic bands but the pattern of the curtains kept distracting his count, the material too much in keeping with the floral quilt he'd buried the dog in the night before, reminding him of the animal's weight in his arms and then the sudden release as he pitched her into the hole at Black Hill Farm.

Tears sprang hot on his cheeks and in a rage, he grabbed the curtains' hem and dragged them down. The whole rotten curtain pole followed, hitting the edge of the table and upending it, scattering bags of heroin all over the floor. Barney cursed, leaving the drugs where they fell, and stalked out towards the kitchen.

*Fuck Kevin*, he thought. *I'm not sitting around watching the place while the dirty wee bastard gets his jollies. He can clean the shit up.*

Barney stamped across the floor. He was going home, but as he traversed the small link hallway, his steps faltered.

A body lay on the floor.

"Billy?" Barney squinted into the gloom at the kid who

wheeled in the punters. The boy was flat on his back, arms askew, feet tucked under his knees. The hair on Barney Murray's neck rose in fright as he felt a hand touch the side of his head. Mercifully, it was the last sensation he felt as his head was smashed into the wall and consciousness dropped away from under him.

Shepard reached down and roughly turned the kid's head to inspect the damage. He'd have a bump the size of an orange, but he'd live.

Grabbing the two by the scruff of their collars, he negotiated the tight space, dragging them into the kitchen and dumping them beside the still unconscious lothario.

"Time to earn your medicine." Shepard held out a hand and beckoned the woman up. She tentatively stood.

"Let's get your mates out of here," he said.

Shepard led the woman through the squalid flat and ushered her into the hall. She looked up the gloomy stairs.

"Up you go. You have two minutes. Here, tell them there's more where that came from." He pushed the heroin into her hand.

For a second she looked as though she'd refuse, her glazed eyes absorbing the graffiti tags on the wall. She glanced back to the kitchen where a shoe from one boy had fallen off and lay against a scuffed skirting. As addiction overcame fear of consequence, she snatched the bag and ran up the hall and out the open front door.

"Fuck," spat Shepard.

He turned back into the lounge, where a wash of heat from the patio heater hit him and he followed the orange hose around the room to where it passed into the kitchen through a hole left by a bashed-out brick. A thought struck him.

He dragged an old armchair into the centre of the room, dumped on a set of curtains and the remnants of a table which lay upended on the floor. Grabbing a handful of scattered heroin bags, he left the lounge again and took the stairs two at a time.

The first room on the landing was empty, so he moved to the next where three bleary addicts lay slumped on a mattress. A candle burned low, the paraphernalia of their addiction strewn around them.

Shepard pitched one of the heroin bags onto the floor, held up another and tossed it out onto the landing, slapping the wall hard.

"Go on, out. There's more down the stairs. Hurry up. Go!"

There was a wild scramble as three sets of greedy hands reached for the package.

Shepard stepped aside and tossed another two bags over the bannister as though he was throwing chump to starving sharks. He barged into the next room and physically tipped a slumbering man off the thin mattress he was sleeping on, a few kicks momentarily bringing him to the surface of consciousness.

Shepard left him to struggle upright and looked over the handrail at the junkies now exiting the flophouse into the street. They shambled away, all huddled together with their prizes clutched to skeletal breasts.

He scouted the last rooms, the first a small airing cupboard that smelled of dust and then a grotty bathroom. An inch of putrid black water and an unidentifiable sludge filled the bath. The toilet seat was broken and stood against the wall, the cistern smashed but still attached by rusted bolts. The floor was a carpet of foil, burned plastic spoons, and spent syringes.

Confident there were no more punters, he returned to the second room and slapped the still slumped man hard on the cheek.

"Out. Go on. Move!" he yelled.

The man gave a grunt, eyes failing to focus and rolling

back in the head. Clarity losing the battle against chemistry.

Shepard hauled him up and manhandled the dead weight to the top of the stairs, tipping him off the top step with a shove of his boot.

The bone juddering slip-slide had the desired effect. Fight or flight kicked in as the body ricocheted off the bottom step and hit the hall wall. Scrambling onto his knees, the man was breathing heavily, disorientated by the sudden awakening.

Shepard started down the steps, receiving a fearful bloodshot glare as the man crawled away, rising unsteadily to his feet and running into the rain and the passing headlights of a car.

For a handful of heartbeats, Shepard watched, letting him get clear before entering the lounge again. He gathered the remaining drugs and tipped them on the hastily stacked pyre. It might not be the eleventh night, but the estate was going to get a bonfire. Any other flammable material followed: old food cartons, cushions from the threadbare seats; he snatched up a grey sports bag and threw it on top. A cascade of stacked banknotes tumbled out. Shepard paused, collecting one stack and riffing the edge. The deck was an inch thick and had to run to about a grand and the bag was stuffed with the same.

The scene in the kitchen hadn't changed when he entered, and it took a few minutes for him to drag the three bodies clear and dump them kerbside. Close enough to be front row, but far enough that they'd get away with a minor singeing.

The collection of gas bottles hadn't been secured, so he turned them all off, then removed a squat grey ten-kilo bottle and carried it inside. The second drawer he checked held some old cutlery, from which he selected a serrated steak knife. Back in the lounge, Shepard propped the bottle beside the pile of fixtures and furnishings, opening the valve to allow the contents to dissipate, then he slashed the pipe feeding the heaters.

Retrieving the bag of cash he moved back to the yard and flipped the valves of the gas bottles back on.

With his back to the three bodies and the decrepit den in front, Shepard pulled one of the Hansson Marine flares from his jacket and waited until the smell of the built-up propane reached him.

He unscrewed the flare's red cap and threw it towards the open back door. Gripping the firing pin, he ignited the flare in a hissing shower of sparks.

Fifteen thousand candlepower of red light bathed the waste ground around him and threw a hellish flickering shadow up the facade of the old building.

With the flare extended out in his right hand, Shepard let it race, in just a few seconds, from two hundred to two thousand degrees and then tossed it inside.

❖ ❖ ❖

"Gas," said Billy Webster.

A tremble and a sudden rush of hot air preceded the violent explosion from behind the flats. A harsh tear of metal and then a pressure wave rocked the room, the back gate slamming against its moorings and the kitchen window crashing in, sending a shower of tinkling glass across the worktop and floor.

Billy Webster stumbled in surprise, ducking against the table of drugs. Carruthers pitched forward and found himself entwined with the younger Webster. Gary, fighting Carruthers off, dug in the chair's crevasse for the baggie of spilt speedball, motes of dust and wads of plaster falling from the ceiling around them.

"Jesus. What the hell was…"

"Up!" yelled Carruthers, manhandling Gary from the sofa and pulling Billy Webster to his feet.

"Move! Get out now," he reiterated.

"The gear!" shouted Webster.

"Fucking leave it!" Caruthers forcibly shoved the two boys out of the lounge and into the kitchen.

The area behind the flats was aglow from two separate fires.

A tower of burning black smoke roiled from the end flat and twisted to join the column that was rising from Carruther's van.

The three men ducked involuntarily, shocked as a secondary explosion from the vehicle blew sparks and flame thirty feet into the sky.

Somewhere in the distance, they could hear sirens.

## Chapter 32

DSIO Phillip MacDonald rested his plastic cup of water on top of the dispenser and turned to look at the board which now ran to two, possibly three murders and half a dozen connected and active investigations.

"Maurice 'Freaky' Jackson." He pointed at the latest addition to the board.

"Inspector Taylor's team has identified Jackson as being in proximity to the Corners Bar at the time of the shooting. Well done to each of you."

Taylor nodded her gratitude for the generous statement.

"Partial CCTV and a confidential informant would seem to confirm this." He took a pointed glance back at Taylor and Macpherson before continuing. "You'll find in the briefing notes a retrospective report from Sergeant Pietersen. Jackson was involved in an altercation at 'No Alibi' a nightclub managed by Rab Millar, deceased." He taped the picture at the centre of the board. "DS Macpherson has included in the brief an overview of Messrs Millar's and Jackson's history."

MacDonald invited a tall, uniformed officer at the back of proceedings to move forward.

"Inspector Connor?"

"Sir, I've informed Section Four to be on the lookout for the person of interest." Connor was a tall, thin man with a shock of sandy hair and a handsome face. He gave a tight smile as he addressed Taylor.

"Ma'am, we have a car at Black Hill Farm and should anyone surface it will be reported back in for action. Patrols are also in attendance on the Fearon Estate following this evening's gas leak. We got notice from your DC of an associated address for Jackson on the estate, but it's abandoned. Derelict," he added for clarity.

"Thank you, Inspector," said Taylor.

"It would seem Mr Jackson has tangled himself up in this mess somewhere, so we're keen to speak with him and see what he has to say for himself. As you'll see from Doc's report, he is to be considered dangerous so approach with caution," concluded MacDonald.

A sea of nods from those assembled granted the DSIO the opportunity for a sip of water.

"What's happening with Rowdy Burns?" said Taylor.

"The DCI is keen to press on. The charges are being considered by the PPS to see if they meet the test for prosecution."

Macpherson smacked his lips and put a tepid tea on the floor by his chair.

"Prints. Confession to possession of firearm and drugs. Ding, ding, ding. We have a winner," he said, raising a fist into the air.

"I'd think so, yes. We'll see if he decides to cooperate a little more once he's facing a stint," agreed MacDonald. "Unless there's anything else? No, okay. Break into your teams and familiarise yourselves with assignments and developments so far. We reconvene here at nine am."

A murmur and the shuffle of chairs swept through the crowded briefing room as the shift rose to their feet.

"Veronica, Doc. Do you have a minute first?" said MacDonald.

"Sure," said Taylor.

Macpherson drained the dregs of his tea and ditched the container in the bin beside the water cooler.

MacDonald stooped and plucked it out.

"Different recycling," he said, passing it back and pointing at a black bin beside a photocopier.

"Really?" Macpherson rolled his eyes as he turned away

from the DSIO, Taylor reading the silent curse on his lips.

"What do you need?" she asked MacDonald.

"That was good work identifying Jackson."

Taylor batted away the compliment.

"He wasn't hiding. It would have come to light."

"It should have come to light sooner considering the number of witnesses but fair play to the pair of you."

"You're very welcome," said Macpherson, a broad smile on his face.

"Given what you say about him, Doc, how worried should I be actioning a couple of uniforms to pick him up?"

Macpherson blew out a breath.

"I'd send nothing less than an ARU. He's form for violence and resisting. If you get him at the farm, there are the dogs and I won't lie, there's a better-than-average chance he'll be armed."

"That's what I thought you'd say. Now, to add a twist. We had forensics return a positive ID on the finger. It was Billy MacBride's."

"I told you it was." Macpherson clapped his hands.

"What are the chances this is all Jackson?" said MacDonald.

He read Taylor's scepticism and raised a defensive hand.

"By your own words. He has the means. A violent offender with access to firearms. Motive? Recent altercation with Millar. No love lost with the D Company boys. Opportunity? You've identified him at the scene." MacDonald tapped the quarter profile CCTV still.

"He didn't kill Rab Millar," said Taylor.

"Really?"

"We have a lead Millar was snapping up properties across the city and, depending on his tactics, he might have stepped on a few toes. I've an information request into Land and Property Services on the purchases and I'll have one of my

DCs hunt Companies House for more detail."

The DSIO turned to face the briefing wall, as though a wide-angle view would suddenly throw light on how each of the individual players were tied together.

"For Christ's sake, give me something."

"Jackson's involved," assured Taylor. "He was at the Corners, no doubt there. But if he knew the hit was coming, it was pretty stupid to be inside when it went down?"

MacDonald winced and then nodded.

"You mentioned Pearson's report?" he said.

Taylor moved up to the briefing table and searched through a ream of paperwork. Selecting the render she had received that morning, she stuck it to the board with a couple of clear pins along with a social media screengrab of Jackson posing with a Czech nine millimetre handgun.

"SOCO assess this as the position of the shooter and eyewitnesses confirm. At some point, he changes target." Taylor tapped the print. "A dozen high calibre rounds hit here and then over here, more casings. Different calibre, nine millimetre." She traced a route from the alleyway to a spot across the street and laid out her hypothesis of Jackson having a back-up.

MacDonald ran the scenario through in his head as Taylor continued.

"There was no love lost between the punters in that bar and Freaky Jackson, so why was he in there? We'll have to ask him, but I'd be surprised if it wasn't to put pressure on McCutcheon over Millar's death or to find out what he knew. Now," Taylor pulled out another picture from the stack. The hairy digit with the sovereign ring. "Did he bring this? Was he confronted with it? Where does McBride fit in the overall picture?" she said. The thread was there, but elusive. Nagging in the background and she couldn't place it yet.

"Did anything come in from Southampton yet?" said

Macpherson.

MacDonald shook his head. With no sign of hide nor hair of McBride, it wasn't looking good for him.

"I'd be fairly confident, because of the bad blood between the firms, Freaky Jackson murdered Barry Corrigan." Taylor tapped the print of the thug with the gun. "Means and opportunity."

"Motive?"

"Hated each other," she said.

"Even though we've just established Corrigan was a driver for Millar? Does that not place them on the same side?" said MacDonald.

"Did he want to shoot Corrigan or did he have to shoot Corrigan? Probably the second. I don't see any other way he was getting out in one piece. Truce or not, Corrigan was McCutcheon's man through and through, and they were under attack. Jackson was in the wrong place at the wrong time. Our informant has already said the word was out Jackson was in the bar and the sharks were homing in."

"So who is our friend on the motorbike and how does he fit?"

Taylor now moved to stand beside her DSIO. The entire investigation spread out across one wall. Disparate pieces of different puzzles all muddled through each other.

"That's the million-dollar question but I'll tell you something for nothing."

Phillip MacDonald glanced at her out of the corner of his eye as she spoke.

"I've just looked Monster Beattie in the eye and he knows more about what's behind all this than he's letting on."

## Chapter 33

Taylor pulled her mobile out and opened the text message, admonishing herself as she saw the reminder from Jack Collins at Section Eight.

*Ronnie, need that report from Sunday night. Happy is getting pissed. Do us a favour and fire it across, J.*

She dropped the phone onto her desk. Leonard Gilmore was Section Eight's inspector and his nickname had been granted in ironic acknowledgement of his predisposition for being in a foul mood ninety per cent of the time and his hangdog expression. That being said, he was solid and fair and she knew she had dropped the ball by getting swept up in Millar's killing and not fulfilling her obligation to process her report through Jack Collins.

Her bed and a bath to wash the stink of Gordon Beattie off would have to wait. She flexed her hands and felt her skin crawl as remembered the touch of his warm palm and the cool look in his eyes. She pushed the thoughts aside and wheeled her chair across to the team conference table.

There was a distinct smell of acrid smoke reminiscent of the morning after the eleventh night bonfires. Heads turned and noses twitched when anyone passed the CID cubicles, the scent of incinerated wood, metal, and plastic particles lingered, clinging to every fibre and follicle on the two DC's persons.

"You okay?"

Erin Reilly and Chris Walker nodded in unison.

"They're saying gas bottles?" said Taylor. Reilly nodded, sniffing at her sleeve.

"Yes. We saw it go up. It was a set of derelict maisonettes across from Fearon House," said Walker.

"Kids?"

"Dunno. I spoke to a youth councillor who was there, and he said they were notorious for drugs. Reckoned a significant portion of the estate's pill problem was dealt from there and one property was a doss house for heroin abusers."

"Can we corroborate?"

"I asked the crews in attendance and they said it wasn't the first time someone had called them to reports of antisocial behaviour. There was a red van burnt out too and the initial hypothesis is it was dumped and set alight igniting the gas, but NIFRS are dismissing that," said Reilly.

"Casualties?"

Reilly shrugged.

"We don't think so. NIFRS are waiting on the end structure to be deemed sound before they go in there. The watch commander told me he saw nothing to suggest any on the walk-through of the linking properties, although they were all gutted by the fire."

"This van? Was it the one you were looking for?"

"No. But we did manage to speak with the registered keeper."

"Any reason they were doing loops of the Corners?"

Reilly and Walker shared an amused look.

"She doesn't drive, and it's her son's runabout. Dead end. He wasn't about."

"Shit," said Taylor.

"Hang on," said Reilly with a twinkle in her eye. "The kid is called Barney Murray, the mother told us he knocked about those maisonettes with a mate called Billy Webster."

"Why does that name seem familiar?" said Taylor.

"Webster was one of Graham Bell's crew. FCB. The Fearon Charlie Boys. They terrorised the estate until we put Bell away for an eight stretch last year."

Taylor could picture the gang tag and the picture of the ragtag crew in their snapback caps and the kit of the prestigious Spanish football club from which they adopted their initials.

"It's not that, but go on."

"Murray and Webster were never away from the flats. The suggestion we got from the youth councillor is they were fronting the place for one of the local players and using youngsters as mules and cut-outs. A few of the kids operating there were very young, pre-teens, and he had been trying to intervene to get them away from the scene, but he wasn't having much success. We reckoned the older two would have form, so we just started a dig through the archives and Chris pulled this."

Reilly removed a printout from under her laptop.

"This is Webster's jacket from youth justice. See anything?" she said, handing it across.

Taylor took the print and scanned the copy.

Billy Webster hadn't stood a chance in life. In and out of school and removed from parental care on at least three occasions. His mother, Irene Webster, had her own short but chequered history. Several brushes with law enforcement and social services, a running tally of domestic violence interventions and then her life was cut short at the ripe old age of twenty-eight, leaving behind two boys. Ages nine and twelve. William Neil Webster and…

"Gary Webster."

Reilly and Walker nodded in sync.

"Gary Webster. The witness we've been searching for from Risky's." Walker looked pleased.

"Now his brother is linked with the Murray kid. Small world," said Taylor.

"It gets smaller." Reilly spun her finger, gesturing for a

further read. Taylor obliged and half rose to her feet when she saw it.

"They're Freaky Jackson's nephews!"

"Bingo."

"This is great work, the pair of you."

"Cheers, boss," said Walker, beaming at Reilly.

"See if you can dig up anything that will put us onto these two. Addresses, known hangouts or other associates. We need to find them. They might be our fastest route to finding Jackson and getting a handle on what is driving all this."

"Will do," said Reilly standing from the table with a satisfied grin.

"Good job, Chris." Taylor patted Walker on the arm as he rose too. "Look, it's late. Give it another hour and if you find anything before then bring it to me. If not, then clear out. We can pick it up in the morning." The constables nodded.

"Do me a favour though and if Sergeant Harris is about ask him what are the odds of an early doors knock-up in the next day or so," said Taylor.

"We'll ask now, guv," said Reilly, her elfin face brightening at the thought of booting down doors with the TSG troops.

She motioned for Walker to take the lead and they moved off, exchanging greetings with a uniformed WPC in hi-vis vest who rapped the edge of the desk as she got closer. Taylor looked up.

"Ma'am. Leigh-Anne Arnold, I was asked to run this across to the Royal."

"Hi, Leigh-Anne. Problem?" Taylor noted the pink and black holdall in her hand.

"Not sure. The patient had discharged herself."

"Okay," Taylor frowned. "Did she get accepted by Sanctuary then?"

"That's the thing. She'd gone by the time they agreed to send someone across to get her."

"Hi, Leigh-Anne." Carrie Cook appeared over the police constable's shoulder. Arnold reciprocated the greeting and continued.

"The ward sister was pulling a double, so she could narrow it down to her leaving between twelve thirty and one o'clock"

Arnold pulled out her notebook.

"Miss Borodenko had requested discharge. The doctor gave her the once over and agreed she could go. The sister said she used the ward phone and one of the porters dropped in some clothes about an hour later."

"Do we know who she called?"

"Actually, I do, because the sister had to place the call for her. She'd written the number down so I googled it and it's a private members' club over in the east. Corner of Chatswood and Thornworth Street. Ruby Stone's. I've never heard of it."

Cook shook her head too.

"Thanks, Leigh-Ann. Is it a stretch she got a name?"

Arnold nodded.

"Sapphire." She arched her brows as Cook huffed a giggle. "Seriously, who calls their kid, Sapphire," said Arnold, offering a professional nod at Macpherson, who was approaching the table.

"Jesus, are you here on work experience?" he said.

"Ignore him," said Cook as Taylor pulled a chair out for her sergeant. He flopped down beside the still standing police constable and looked up at her studiously.

"I swear you lot are getting younger. I thought Erin was a pup, but what age are you? No offence, like," he said with a wave of apology.

"None taken, I'm sure," said Arnold.

He peered like a meerkat at the WPC's notes.

"Tidy writing that, though. Handy for court, keep that up and you'll go far."

"Thanks, Sarge." Arnold's expression was one of bemusement as the distracted DS rummaged through his pockets for a snack.

"And you needn't head into Ruby's dressed like that by the way or they'll think you're an act," he said.

The three women look at him in confusion.

"Ruby Stone's is a skin joint." With an expression of triumph, he pulled another chocolate bar from his jacket pocket, then looking at the three open mouths, he shrugged.

"You know, a strip club?"

## Chapter 34

"A strip club."

"Aye, and it's not exactly Spearmint Rhino either," Macpherson confirmed, splitting apart a four-finger KitKat and offering it out.

"You're a dark horse. What's Moira have to say about this pastime?"

"Away on, you cheeky witch." Macpherson waved what remained of his chocolate finger at Cook. "I've been coppering this town since you pair were in nappies. You get to know, alright."

"As you're obviously the expert, what's the chances it's the bar Lena told us about? The one she left Sanctuary for?" said Taylor with a smirk.

"If I was a betting man, I'd say it was fair to certain."

"You are a betting man," said Cook, ignoring the faux stunned look on her sergeant's face.

"Character assassination, that's what's going on here. I preferred it when they didn't have women in CID." He winked, his beard broken in a grin.

"It's an attitude like that has kept you a DS your entire adult life," said Taylor, only half joking. She loved the man, but he was an old-school copper. In Macpherson's eyes results came from a lifetime's experience gained on the job in the most challenging of times, and while he would be the first to embrace new principles of policing, it was only to see how quick he could send them off to the scrap heap.

The DS blew out a scoff.

"It takes boots on the ground, not backsides behind desks to take these bastards off the streets, girls, and don't you forget it." He gave them a stern but well-meaning look. "I'm not cut out for bloody spreadsheets and policy meetings," he added with a shudder.

"Can you imagine?" said Cook. Taylor rolled her eyes in mock exasperation.

"Why didn't she take the offer of help? It's not like she didn't know what to expect with the charity." She closed her notebook and placed her pen on top.

"I think that's the problem," said Macpherson, balling the chocolate wrapper and launching it at the wastepaper bin.

Both Taylor and Cook waited for him to elaborate.

"It was you who brought up Sanctuary at the hospital. Not the girl." Macpherson pointed a finger.

"Yeah, she was resident before she went to the wind and ended up in Millar's stable. I think the fact that ended with her in a hospital bed proves it wasn't her best judgement call."

"Aye. Fair enough, but she didn't look too happy with the thought of traipsing back to them. Her lips might've been saying yes, but there was something about her that was saying no chance."

"The pregnancy?" suggested Cook.

"It's not like they'd object. They set the place up for women and families fleeing domestic abuse," said Macpherson, flicking crumbs from the desk.

"We only have her own word for it she left of her own volition. Carrie, try to set up a meeting with them tomorrow. Score a look through what we have on Lena, who her caseworker was and when and where she stayed exactly. There has to be something that gave her pause to go back."

"What are we doing?" said Macpherson, already knowing the answer.

"You, my salty old sea dog, are going to take me to a strip club."

"You're a glutton for punishment, guv," groaned Cook,

shaking her head in disbelief.

Macpherson put both elbows on the table, hands two feet apart.

"Wednesday night for that, Carrie. That's the night the kinky one's come out in Ruby's. Big Brenda." Macpherson puffed out his cheeks. "She puts this wee skinny twig of a boy through his paces like she's breaking in a…"

"Okay. Okay. We're scarred with the mental image, Doc, thanks," said Taylor, slapping his elbow from the desk.

Macpherson just shrugged.

"Carrie. Do you want to fill us in on Morrow and Burke?"

Carrie Cook opened her notebook and took a second to organise her thoughts.

"It might be something, it might be nothing," she said at length.

Macpherson slipped his elbows back on the table.

"You've us hooked now, Carrie. Crack on and spill the beans," he said.

Taylor could see her DC was nervous.

"Morrow and Burke. Premises off Chichester and Donegall Square East. A top-end realtor and management agency, the place reeks of having a fortune dropped on it."

"I'd say so if they're representing the likes of the Speakers Square development. Malcolm Howard said they look after most of the top tier accommodation in the city," said Taylor, agreeing with the assessment.

"I had a meeting with the general manager, Stella Sharp. She confirmed as much, but they also offer resources to a wide section at the opposite end of the market. I only caught Daphne Morrow for two seconds as I was leaving. I asked about the Speakers Square CCTV and she says they have lost all the footage." She pursed her lips as Macpherson's brows rose. "She said it was a technical error. She wasn't the most pleasant person I've ever met."

"Did this Sharp woman say why she swerved the meeting?"

"She was participating in another with the council and social housing contractors. Morrow and Burke contract out several developments and empty dwellings to cater for social use."

Taylor considered this.

"Did they mention if Sanctuary was one of these?" she said.

"Sharp didn't say. That's the something and nothing," said Cook.

"Go on?"

"She avoided all of my questions. I put it down to her being caught on the hop. I doorstepped them right enough, but it wasn't as though I expected it to be…" Cook thought back to the meeting. "Hostile?" she said with a frown.

"You think she was being evasive?"

"I don't know. In a roundabout way, she confirmed dealings with Miltek and offered to dig up the background on the Old Mill deal, but she wouldn't say why it fell through or if they had other deals on the go. She played the data protection card."

"You didn't give the solicitors that represented Miltek a nudge?"

"Harper, Baxter, Brooke? No, I thought given our current standing with our cousins in the legal profession I'd get short shrift asking about Millar," said Cook. Taylor bit her lip and then gave a conciliatory shrug.

"Yeah, you're probably right. I don't think you'd have got through the door with them. Give this Sharp woman a few days and then chase it up. Maybe the unscheduled visit blindsided her."

"I don't know. I've a gut feeling she knew Miltek was tied to Millar and the type of business he was in. Finding out he was dead got a reaction, that's when she shut me down."

Both Taylor and Macpherson absorbed the report. Cook skimmed back and forward through her notes.

Taylor tried to thread this additional information into the loose tapestry of the investigation. Rab Millar was a pusher and a pimp, so it made sense that he would need somewhere to establish or expand business, and a way to legitimise his ill-gotten gains. Would property be it? Miltek wasn't a convoluted scheme of shell companies, it had been straightforward to tie directorship to him.

The image of the battered and bruised Lena Borodenko came to her mind and the lavish setup of the boudoir and her pregnancy. The reason she had ghosted from hospital was a question mark.

Taylor let the pieces shift in her mind. Morrow and Burke managed Speakers Square. Millar was a client of Morrow and Burke. Morrow and Burke were offering properties to social care organisations. Possibly Sanctuary, which brought her back to Lena Borodenko's flit.

She heard Cook's words rattle around in her head. Something and nothing.

"Dig into Miltek, Carrie. Financials, holdings, any other partner organisations. Start with the basics and build up. Let's see if Millar was buying in the wrong backyard or if it's something more."

"There's something else not sitting right with me," said Cook.

Taylor broke from her thoughts of trying to thread the needle and nodded for the DC to continue.

"When you walk into the offices, it's like…"

Cook took a breath, searching for a way to explain the duality of her trip to the agency.

"The whole front office is window dressing. It's like you've stumbled into the Stepfords. It's like a model agency. The women are glammed to the nines and I felt, I don't know? Intimidated."

"Maybe it's just the image they are pushing?" said Macpherson. "Sounds like those TV shows Moira watches, you know? LA pads. High-Class Homes of Hollywood. That sort of thing. All bleached blonde bimbos, Louboutins and fat commissions."

"Louboutins, seriously?" said Taylor.

"I know my wardrobe doesn't exactly scream Belfast Fashion Week, but I don't live under a rock, Ronnie." Macpherson smoothed his rumpled jacket with a frown.

"That's exactly what it reminded me of," agreed Cook with a laugh.

"What you see from the outside is the tip of the iceberg. They must have knocked into about three other units. There's an administrative area, but it's nothing near as slick. To be frank, it felt like a sweatshop."

"A sweatshop?"

"Yes. No craic. Noses to the grindstone. An undercurrent of something, fear is maybe a stretch but…" Cook shrugged. "There was a supervisor type sat at the front and doing laps checking over shoulders. Most of the staff were Asian, but I'd take a punt a fair lot of the rest were European and former Soviet bloc."

"Cheap foreign labour," said Macpherson, "Wouldn't be the first company to try it."

"I thought the same, but there was a girl. Young. Teens. She had restraint marks on her wrists." Cook explained the brief interaction with Rachael.

"She mentioned Millar. By name?" said Taylor, perking up.

"Sort of. She knew of Miltek, and she seemed to know what type of gangster Millar was."

"Any chance you could get to speak to her again?"

"I'll try," said Cook. "By the time I got back into the office,

Sharp was getting the rough edge of Daphne Morrow's tongue about something and I got the impression it was to do with the girl. I got the evils, the bad news about the CCTV, and then shown the door."

"You were right to trust your gut, Carrie, this crowd stink," said Macpherson. He glanced to Taylor. "That Howard character gives me the creeps and all."

"The DCI will want more than gut feeling, Doc," said Cook.

"We get at this wee girl then? She knows something."

"I'm sorry, guv. I knew they were freezing me out, but I figured a tactical withdrawal was best."

"You did the right thing, Carrie. We have to just go easy. Give it a day or so and touch base again. Maybe try to instigate a bump into this Rachel, or at least run a description through the database. Check her against missing persons too."

"Yes, guv."

"It was a good job digging up Miltek." She gave the DC a smile of praise. "You head on and see if you can set us up with Sanctuary tomorrow and we'll see you in the morning."

"Will do. Night."

Goodbyes said, Macpherson stretched out his back, vertebrae popping as he arched.

"Will we try Ruby's then?" he said with a yawn that nearly swallowed his head.

"You want to skip the spare bed tonight and get a proper sleep, Doc," said Taylor.

"It's not the months on the calendar, it's the miles on the clock, miss."

"Whatever you say."

"So Ruby's or what? Shout you a Maharaja on the way home?" said Macpherson.

"Do you think she'll be there?"

"Doubt it but this Sapphire probably will be and if she's not, then we'll find out where she lives and probably find the pair of them."

"What time does it wrap up?"

"Late." He glanced at his watch. "There's plenty of time. It'll just be warming up."

"I want to head up to operations and see if the intel branch has any skinny on this Albanian, Nishani, now Lena, Rowdy and Worzel have all mentioned they were hand in glove with Rab."

"Want me to come?"

"It's okay. I want you to look at something else for me."

"Oh?"

"I want you to dig through the archives and see what exactly might link Billy McBride and Rab Millar besides the obvious. I know McBride's not confirmed dead, but presuming he is? There's no way those two dying over the course of a couple of days is a coincidence."

"That's ancient history, Ronnie. The files have probably ended up in the incinerator after this length of time."

"I know, but humour me."

"Am I looking for a flashing arrow pointing to the Monster?"

Taylor gathered up her notebook and tidied the desk.

"Millar. McBride. The attack on the Corners. Corrigan. Now this gas explosion in Jackson's backyard. They might not be connected, but I can't shake the notion somebody is doing their level best to poke the bear. There's a motive right under our noses that we can't see yet."

## Chapter 35

Criminal Operations Branch–Intelligence Division, was a section of blue baize cubicles similar to those in CID, however, they had a much tidier kitchen and did a line of fancy coffee. Taylor accepted the recommended Firenze Arpeggio, which came in a double-walled glass cup while Juliet Sommers ruined her own Venezia with three sachets of sugar.

The place was spotless and Taylor, sipping the intense, creamy brew couldn't help but be envious.

"Do you have a spelling?" asked Sommers as they sat down at her workstation. She slid across a bright New York City coaster onto which Taylor deposited her cup.

"I can guess," said Taylor.

"It's okay. N-I-S-H-A-N-I." Sommers rattled the spelling across the keys and hit a search, waiting while the program did the work.

"How you keeping?"

"Back in the saddle," said Taylor.

"I heard. With a double murder too. No rest for the wicked."

Taylor took a sip and a look around the workspace. A stack of folders sat on one side of her desk, with Post-it notes and a to-do list pinned on the cubicle wall.

"What about up here? Flat out?"

"Always." Sommers placed her attention back on the PC and her fingers flew across the keys again, followed by half a dozen mouse clicks.

"Bekim Nishani. Twenty-five. Originally Kombinat. Tirana. Albania. Widowed father and child moved to Ireland in ninety-seven, following civil unrest in the country. Mother stayed behind with elderly parents. No record of her following." Sommers shook her head. "Imagine fleeing a civil war to come here? Home from home, huh?"

"No flags on any involvement with the violence?" said Taylor.

"Kid was only two. The father had been picked up in a sweep on groups trying to overthrow local government in the aftermath but was released. No charges."

"Where did they originally settle?"

"East Antrim. In the Mossley area of Newtownabbey, Mr Nishani, senior, gained employment in one of the textile factories in the area."

"No bother since?"

"Once for DUI. Fined and received a suspended sentence. Nothing since."

"Anything to suggest he got tangled up with the local hoods?"

"Nope. Father was a model of successful integration. You looking for specifics?"

"Links to organised crime."

"Hmmm," said Sommers, brightening. "That's something I can probably help with. What got you on the scent?"

"Bekim Nishani was named by a CI as a person of interest. I've also had generic foreign and specific Albanian pointed out to me in the course of the Millar investigation. I guess what I'm asking is do we have an active criminal element of Albanian gangs in the province. I've seen the intelligence on the wider UK rise but I thought our lot kept the weeds down so to speak."

Sommers chuckled as she drew up more information.

"They do that alright. There is a rise in organisation and proliferation across the border but 'our lot' as you say keep the opportunists in check. There's less than a handful of players here. You would class them as small-time criminal enterprises. Well, more a franchise if you like."

"Operating under the larger umbrella?"

"Yes. They pay their dues and stay within set rules. They usually stick to protection rackets, people trafficking, prostitution. Usually, they move on from that to drugs. Higher return on investment and a ready supply from their sponsor."

"Okay. Does Nishani have any connection to our players?"

"Let's see." Sommers minimised a window and launched another, connecting through the local intranet to the larger intelligence database.

"Bekim Nishani. No juvenile record." She skimmed the report, lips moving but silent as she read. "Ah, now we're talking. He was charged with assault and demanding money with menaces from a shop owner in Mallusk. His sentence was suspended, then later activated following a fight outside a city centre club. Nishani attacked the same man again, he pleaded guilty to unlawful and malicious wounding and did nine months of a two-year stretch."

"Sounds promising."

"He had another run-in for possession of Class B, but it wasn't pursued. A further court appearance for unpaid parking fines and he has nine points on his licence, the most recent for speeding."

"So, he's kept his head down?" said Taylor with a sniff.

"So it would seem. This is where it gets interesting, though. All the parking fines fell within a half-mile radius and two of the speeding were by the same static camera in the Belfast docklands. Van registration HGZ eighty-two, forty. The van and Nishani are on the books of Sulejman Meats."

"What are they? A butcher?"

"It's a meatpacking plant. Their premises are on an industrial estate in Newtownabbey near to where Nishani is residing. They specialise in the preparation of beef, lamb and pork products. We also believe it's a front for this guy."

Sommers double-clicked a file to reveal a surveillance photograph.

"Amir Kazazi," she said.

The shot showed a dark-haired and clean-shaven male, late thirties with a cigarette poised beside lips.

"Who is he?" said Taylor.

"One of the handful I mentioned. On the up and up this last several months. There are about three ongoing investigations into his operations. Officially, he is the managing director of Sulejman but, once the forensic accountants began rooting through his books they found a web of shell companies and offshore holdings all going back to the old country. He's also linked to half a dozen cafes, bars and snooker halls in Tirana."

"Anything on him snapping up property over here? Business or otherwise?" said Taylor.

"The team's still digging. Nothing on here though."

"Keep an eye on it for me, will you?"

Sommers nodded and typed a note.

"What's he fronting?" asked Taylor.

"Narcotics recruited an informant inside Kazazi's gang who are all pretty tight, I have to say. He was in trouble himself, so cut a deal. He gave up a decent shipment of pills to show his commitment and promised a lead into a much bigger pipeline but he didn't follow through."

"How come."

"It went cold, probably the informant's paranoia kicking in. Narcs chose to let him fly with a view to trying when he found his balls again."

"Murat Hassan." Taylor speed read the details on the informant as Sommers put them up.

"I can put you in touch with the handler if you like?"

"Yea, send me the details. What else have we got on

Kazazi?"

"Sulejman transports their products across the North and South to distributors, mostly vacuum-packed joints and cuts for the catering and hospitality markets. They also have lorries crossing to the mainland routinely and we are fairly sure a number of those crossings are smuggling contraband, likely tobacco and drugs, probably people. The Albanian gangs have cornered the market in the modern day slave trade. Prostitution we mentioned but then there's construction, domestic staff, fruit pickers, shell fishing, maybe Sulejman's meat-packers. This is before we touch on weed farms and the hidden stuff."

"This is great, Juliet. Any chance you could do me a pack up and send it across?"

"Sure. Tomorrow okay?"

"Absolutely. Look, I really appreciate it. Thanks for the coffee!"

"No problem. Just don't tell Doc. If he gets wind, we'll never be rid of him."

❖ ❖ ❖

Macpherson stabbed out the passcode with a stubby finger and a series of beeps emitted from the code lock. An acknowledgement light turned green, and he twisted the awkward mortice lock to gain entry.

They called the old space the land that time forgot. Once a secretarial office and then an overflow of administrative space for Section Seven before they got their airy new floor space on the fourth floor, it had finally and brutally been repurposed as an overflowing and abandoned storage space.

It also stank to high heaven. There was an underlying reek of sewage and dirty water, although over the years no one had quite put their finger on the source.

The room was racked out, floor to ceiling and wall to wall in rows of angled steel and hardwood shelving, the anchor screws drilled straight into carpeted floor tiles and old socket boxes and light switches were trapped where they lay.

The only light in the room came from three linear fluorescent strip lights which had survived the repurposing and had been missed in the energy efficiency purge. They sounded a tick, tack, tack as they fought for life and then their dull hum and harsh light battled the shadows thrown by the shelves, one lamp sporadically flickering off and on as though in protest at the struggle on past retirement.

Macpherson whistled happily as he nudged the door shut with his heel. Smell aside, it wasn't the worst place. It offered peace and quiet, that was for sure, and back in the day he'd have happily taken the fight to the thick smell with the fragrant aroma of a cigar, but those days were long gone.

A lonely desk sat in a corner, the single lamp on top might have been there since the eighties. Beside the desk stood an office chair, the stuffing spilling from a torn seat but comfort restored by a cushion someone must have stolen from their granny's house.

Macpherson sat and flicked on the lamp, taking a moment to survey the place. A touch of melancholy to be among the ghosts of a career enveloped him, alongside a warm glow that he'd taken a fair chunk of the hooligans off the streets; for a while, anyway, most just slipping back into their sordid ways when they were released. Those who broke free usually moved on. To Scotland mainly, the shared affinity and welcome of the Celts more embracing than the fear and intimidation that lurked around every corner at home. The gangs were never really ready to release you from the grip of the brotherhood.

Which brought his mind back to the task at hand. Billy McBride.

Standing, Macpherson worked his way along the shelves, tracing a finger across the identification tabs taped to the lip of the shelving. With each passing footfall, he stepped back in time, occasionally pausing as he recognised a case. Finally finding what was needed, he used a small footstool to access the upper tier, reaching to pull out the box of material relating to McBride's exile from Belfast.

Returning to the desk, he set the box down, angled the lamp, and dropped the lid on the floor, the stale and dusty motes rising from the box catching his throat.

The reports concerning Billy McBride were contained within a larger set of files relating to the unsolved murder of Martin Coleman. Macpherson drew out each of the faded blue and magnolia dossiers and spread them out. Inside each was a bundle of photographs, the first monochrome eight by five showed McBride grinning. Taken with a telephoto lens it captured McBride stood beside a grave, surrounded by similar roughnecks, all wearing nylon bombers or leather jackets over white shirts and black ties. Another shot had him framed with Coleman, compatriot and rival caught in a grudging handshake. Just in shot behind, Macpherson could make out a youthful Gordon Beattie.

The DS felt an involuntary chill as his eyes were drawn to McBride's finger and the signature sovereign ring. An unlikely item that put him inside for a time when forensic officers tied the imprint to the facial injury pattern on one of his victims. The volatile McBride, known for his temper, admitted beating the man to a pulp although he couldn't remember why.

It was his unpredictability that became his downfall. Prone to rages and blood lust, McBride and his gang were suspected of upwards of twenty-six murders. Mostly innocent Catholics including two teenage boys who were said to have been stupid enough to slight him over rumours of his sexuality, a shadow that followed him given his penchant for having younger foot soldiers carry out his commands and the drug and booze-fuelled party binges that followed.

The murders of fellow Loyalists Lofty Price and Edgar Hollie, unclaimed but purported to have been sanctioned by McBride after the men had picked a fight with one of his favourite fledgelings, would have sealed his fate if it hadn't been for the murder of Martin Coleman.

Coleman had been the charismatic and ruthless gang leader of the Eastside True Blues. Quietly progressing into the UDA before taking a more militant role with the Ulster Freedom Fighters, Coleman's direct action against known nationalist figures and those he deemed sympathetic to the notion of reunification was often swift and always brutal, and widely well-received by the parent organisation.

Macpherson flicked through the old pages, re-reading the tale of the growing feud which boiled down to a difference in direction.

Senior leadership within the city's largest Loyalist groups, one of them being Coleman's, had decided McBride's rising volatility and growing pursuit of narcotics and harsh intimidation of his own community was impacting on the movement's main agenda and threatened to embroil the fraternal brotherhood in a bloody civil war. It was a war that was to be averted when Coleman was found dead in a ditch.

Macpherson slid the crime scene report out. Remarkably there were only four foolscap pages and several glossy images.

Twelve yellow number flags were dotted around his prone body. Blood pooled underneath. A whole clip emptied into Coleman's back on a cold country lane near Portmuck. Macpherson pictured the little hidden harbour on the Antrim Coast; sheer cliffs and rough pebble beach served by narrow winding lanes at the mercy of the Irish Sea.

The authorities, notified by an anonymous caller, had been delayed in reaching the scene by a road traffic accident that impeded the one road in. On passing the blockage, the first responders found Coleman dead at the scene. Macpherson noted William Law's name on the report, although he was but a humble inspector then.

The report went on to include Superintendent Wallace, seniority of rank wheeled in to shore up the narrative when the RTA was determined to include fatalities and police actions to secure the Coleman crime scene came under scrutiny in the event those unfortunate deaths may have been averted had it not been for the haste to get to Coleman. The conclusion, signed off by Wallace and his superiors at the time, was that they wouldn't have.

Each of the files had more recent tags: the small apostrophe logo of the Historical Enquiries Team (HET) prevalent alongside the officious labels of the Police Ombudsman's Office.

Macpherson sighed and slid the paperwork away, looking around at the ghosts on the shelves, his melancholy rising.

Neither the original investigation nor the HET had made any headway into the killing. The caller was never identified and there were no witnesses to the accident who may have seen the killers leaving.

Given the animosity between the men and the immediate threat to his life, Billy McBride was prime suspect, however, he had been recognised by multiple witnesses in a city centre pub; a reliable informant confirming his presence had cemented his alibi.

With suspicion moving away from McBride, Beattie and his crew fell into the frame. Rab Millar was known to be dabbling in the same burgeoning drugs trade as McBride and the mystery of how Coleman had either been lured to or taken to the murder site was unknown, but as he and Beattie were never far apart, the questions were raised. Beattie's alibi for events though was as ironclad as McBride's, he and his crew having been stopped and held at a joint security force checkpoint twenty miles away.

Such as it was and such as it is, thought Macpherson. One more dead gangster who lived by the sword and died by it. Whether the investigation had the impetus to find the killers or not didn't really matter. The consensus was that justice had found Coleman in the end.

Macpherson smoothed down the edge of an HET label. The group created to undertake the review and to thoroughly investigate the thousands of unsolveds was now as cold and dead as the cases themselves. Macpherson gathered up the files and began to slowly repack them.

Whatever Ronnie Taylor had hoped to find in the file that would link McBride and Beattie might have been there at some point, but now, after so many fingers and such a passage of time, there wasn't a damn thing. The details were either deliberately vague or just plain obfuscated and like most of the cold cases on the shelves, he had the impression this one too would never see that critical breakthrough. Macpherson put the box back on the shelf and left. As he flicked off the lights and closed the door, he could feel the thousand voices locked in their boxes silently mocking him.

## Chapter 36

The rhythmic tone of the reversing sensor steadily increased in pitch as the first Ford Transit van backed up.

"That's us now."

A hand raised in acknowledgement from the cab, then the squeak of brakes sounded and a pneumonic rattle as the engine shut down and the driver hopped out.

As Freaky Jackson watched the driver trade small talk with the banksman, his walkie-talkie buzzed to life with a harsh crackle. He turned the earpiece volume down as the distorted voice came through.

"That's number two through. He's clean."

Jackson whistled and motioned the banksman to direct in the second vehicle.

"Got him. Hold the next ones until these two are away," said Jackson.

"Aye. No bother." The confirmation came in a gravelly buzz of static.

Jackson and his three-man crew had arrived later than scheduled. If the gateman held any tension over the fact things were running behind schedule, he didn't show it. He accepted his payment with a soundless nod and lifted the barriers to the compound for the group to enter, Jackson as a precaution leaving one of his crew in the Portakabin to sip milky tea and keep an eye out for the Albanians' transport to arrive and to ensure their man on the gate didn't get any ideas to abandon his post. While the suspected tout of a previous seizure was now buried under tons of fast-set ready mix, that wasn't to say the sneaky bastard cops didn't have another snitch in the wings.

Jackson walked across the strip of tarmac road which cut

through the yard of stacked intermodal shipping containers. The port's urban freight distribution system was a twenty-four-hour and multimillion-pound operation and away to his left on the seaward side, he could make out the silhouette and rumblings of a large container vessel as it docked under a gantry of cranes.

A cigarette tip flared away to his right. The smoker lurked in the cab of a forklift, parked in the lee of a mammoth stack of red P&O sea cans.

"Is this us?" said Jackson as he approached.

He'd never set eyes on the man before that night, but the fella had been waiting where arranged and guided them through the maze as promised and so far, all had chimed like clockwork.

"Aye." He jumped down from the forklift and tapped the ISO data plate on the right door. The Customs Seal remained intact on the left. "Are you right?"

Jackson gave his approval with a slap on the shoulder.

The man's practised hands unfastened the lockbox attached to the right-hand door and then released the padlock. Years of abuse and the harsh conditions at sea had weathered and warped the forty-foot container. The yard worker pinched out his cigarette and took a waiting club hammer and long steel pole from the rear of his forklift truck, moving back to the right-hand door. A few blows released the handles from their latched position. He grunted with effort as he applied the bar to prise open and swivel the handles, releasing the locking cams. The door screeched open, and he stepped aside quickly as Jackson moved in to inspect the contents.

Inside the container and stacked three high, each pallet of concrete products was wrapped in cardboard and heavy-duty nylon coverings.

Jackson clicked on a Maglite torch, sweeping the beam

through the narrow niches between the pallets. Not that there was much to see. He clicked the light off and turned back to the forklift driver.

"We're good. Get them loaded."

## Chapter 37

"You can't be serious?"

"I told you. Benidorm meets backstreet Belfast. Sure, you couldn't beat it." A huge grin of amusement split Macpherson's face as he looked at Taylor's shocked expression.

The focal point of the main function room was a raised dais that even those of the most optimistic persuasion among the bellowing audience would be hard pushed to call a stage.

The backdrop was swathed in crimson curtains that had long since seen their best days and the planks of the floor, although painted matt black, were so badly scuffed in places the natural wood shone through.

The object of the whooping crowd's attention was a dwarf in oxblood DM boots, a glittery red G-string, and matching bow tie gyrating enthusiastically to the thumping dance beat of a Major Lazer track. The deep bass punctuated his moves and a rainbow of strobing lights crisscrossed his stage and the function room floor.

Banquette seating in heavy red vinyl ran around the walls to join the bar, which was opposite the raised dais with a handful of standing tables filling the space between and, although not packed, there were more people than Taylor had expected for a mid-week night.

Several scantily clad girls collected the drinks from a service area and distributed them around the patrons, a round of shots and pints to one group of lads and a couple of iced buckets of alcopops and cheap cava to another table of mixed company. One of the women dancing on her chair was encouraged down by the waitress as she placed the drinks on the table.

"Do you see your man?"

"Nope." Macpherson swept a glance around the room and then clocked the barman looking over. He nudged Taylor to follow.

"Alright, darlin', brought your da out for the night? What can I get youse?"

"How about you get me Tommy, and less of the cheek or you'll get my boot up your arse, son," said Macpherson, opening his warrant card. "Soda water and lime for the lady and I'll have a pint of blackcurrant cordial while you're at it."

The barman muttered a curse under his breath and moved aside a curtain at the edge of the bar. His words were inaudible but Taylor lip-read 'fuckin' peelers' followed by a flurry of gestures as he juked his head into the space beyond. Dropping the material back into place and with a face like a wet weekend, he went about obtaining Macpherson's order.

The curtain shifted and a man of medium build in a much too shiny jacket and tight jeans emerged. He had a hooked nose and his slicked-back hair formed a sharp widow's peak. A gold hoop and a single diamond studded one ear.

"It's yourself," he said.

"Tommy." Macpherson took the man's offered hand.

"Tommy, this is Ronnie," Macpherson shouted over the music. Taylor smiled politely as the man looked her up and down.

"Jesus, Doc. She's too good for the likes of you."

"Watch your mouth, Tommy boy. This is my boss."

"Ah, pleased to meet you. I'd say you've your work cut out with this one. Aye?"

"Oh, I don't know, he has his uses. Nice place," lied Taylor.

Tommy Rice laughed, not in the least fooled.

"What's this then, business or pleasure?" He rubbed his palms together and then held them up in surrender. "You don't need to say. It's always business with you lot. Come on through, I can see wee Charlie is distracting the pair of you."

Macpherson chuckled. Taylor looked back as a roar went up from the assembled patrons, just in time to see wee Charlie's red G-string arc into the air towards her.

❖ ❖ ❖

They had left their drinks untouched once Tommy Rice had confirmed Sapphire, who was, in fact, Hannah Swift, was upstairs preparing for her shift under the spotlights.

With the reassurance they weren't about to cart her off in cuffs leaving him in the lurch, the stage without a star, and more importantly the punters without an act to accompany their raucous drinking, he directed them down a dingy hallway and up a set of uncarpeted stairs to what he grandiosely described as the dressing rooms.

"Christ's sake, Tommy, I told you I was getting ready!" The girl swivelled around with an angry expression. "Who the hell are you?" She drew a make-up stained towel up around her bare breasts.

"Police, Hannah," said Taylor, showing the girl her warrant card.

"I'm on in twenty minutes. Do you mind…" Hannah rolled her head, indicating the table full of war paint, hairbrushes and tongs.

"We don't mind. You carry on, we just have a few questions," said Taylor.

The girl shrugged and turned to face the mirror. Macpherson surveyed the room.

Hannah Swift sat cross-legged on a stool, naked but for a pair of black lace panties and fishnet stockings. A pair of strappy six-inch platform stage shoes sat beside the stool alongside a set of black feathered wings.

"You want to watch the stairs in those? You'll break your bloody neck," offered Macpherson with a nod.

The girl smiled into the mirror, sponging contour on her

jawbone. The dainty foot she waggled out from below the desk was shoved incongruously in a novelty unicorn slipper.

"Learned that lesson. Turned my bloody ankle and couldn't work for a week, but did your man there pay me?"

"You should have stuck in a claim," said Macpherson. He picked up a photo frame and studied the picture. Taylor looked over the girl's shoulder, speaking to her via the mirror.

"We need to ask you about Lena."

Taylor half expected her to deny it. To ask who and close the conversation down.

"I thought you might," said Hannah, swapping the sponge for a brush.

"She phoned you today?"

"She did." The brush strokes were short and sharp as she blended her make-up, avoiding Taylor's eye and instead concentrating on her own face.

"Do you know where she is?" said Taylor.

"I dropped her some stuff to the hospital. She told me on the phone she had a few other things to do but would come to mine after. She didn't."

"She was a no show?" said Macpherson, surprised.

"Yes, and I waited like an idiot, and now I'm late. You know he'll dock my pay if I miss my start?" She aimed the beauty blender at the curtained door to the stairs.

"Any idea why she'd not show up?" said Taylor.

"No. I don't. She probably got a better offer." Hannah pouted, raising her eyebrows as she frowned at her reflection.

"Is this the two of you?" Macpherson pointed to the picture in his hand.

"Yep. She worked here too for a bit."

"You got her the gig?"

Hannah cocked her head and looked Taylor's reflection in the eye.

"She told us she worked in a bar dancing," said Taylor.

"Yeah, well. This was the place." Hannah extended her hands in a show of the cramped space.

"You've no idea why she'd stand you up?" said Macpherson, placing the picture back down.

"I already said so."

"What about why she wouldn't take a spot at Sanctuary?" said Taylor.

Hannah turned in her seat and gave the inspector a stern glare. She had a face that was both soft and hard at the same time. She was pretty with good skin tone and had the same look in her eye as Lena, one that showed the scars of old battles.

"Go back there? She'd have to be desperate."

The venom in the girl's voice caught Taylor unawares.

"I would have thought it would be the perfect place to reflect and get her back on her feet considering what she went through."

"Oh, aye?" The girl scoffed and turned back to the mirror. "You've no idea, lady."

"You were there too?" said Taylor.

"I was. Did about a year until I jacked it in."

"Why, what was so bad you left?"

The girl paused in her regime and turned to face the officers.

"You sound shocked? But then you probably see the press releases and hear all the stories pushed out by the marketing campaigns. Most people can't help but buy into the bullshit."

"I have to be honest," said Taylor with a shake of her head. "I don't know that much but what I've read about their investment and the services they offer, it looks like a decent opportunity for people caught in a trap and needing a way out."

"Did she tell you why she left?"

"She was vague," said Taylor.

"She didn't want to come out and say it, eh?"

Swift took a hairbrush and began sweeping it through her long dark locks.

"Well, I'll tell you why. First, they break you down even though you're at the bottom to be there in the first place. Then they farm you out around their wee network." Hannah raised an angry finger. "You can cut it whatever way you want, but it's slave labour. Okay, maybe one week it's the church or a Women's Aid group if you're lucky. If not they rent you out to the suburbs where you wash, clean, iron, and suffer whatever abuse the lady of the house and her friends say behind your back but just loud enough for you to hear. 'Junkie'. 'Slut'. 'Any wonder they took her children?'. All while they all sit getting pissed in the middle of the day, the bloody hypocrites. And that's before the over-friendly shite of a hubby comes home."

"Hannah, you make them out to be some kind of cult."

"I'm just telling you how it is. I complained and life became unbearable. When I left, history repeated itself with Lena."

Taylor considered the girl's revelation. Macpherson's brow furrowed in thought and he took a rest on the edge of an adjacent dressing table.

"When she left here? Do you know who she went to work for?" said Taylor.

The girl nodded.

"Did you keep in touch?"

"On and off. We cooled off after I knocked her back in coming to join her." She saw Taylor's expression. "Look, I work here to put myself through my degree. I've no intention of giving up the last five years to become some dirty old man's humping post," she said with a shudder.

"What are you studying?"

"I'm doing an MSc in Pharmaceutical Analysis."

"Fair play to you. I could barely spell it," huffed Macpherson with a half shake of his head. He gestured at the photo again.

"Did she have any boyfriends you know of?"

"Why?" said Hannah.

"If she's stood you up and you think she got a better offer, maybe there's a fella?" he said.

Hannah looked uncomfortable.

"You knew she was pregnant, didn't you?" said Taylor.

"I…" she closed her eyes for a second. "She told me."

"Did she tell you who the father was?"

A shake of the head.

"We had a massive argument. One of her clients is all I know. Silly cow, of all the stupid things to let happen."

"Still, she must have trusted you. Reaching out today?" said Taylor.

"Knows I'm a soft touch more like. I put fifty quid in that bag, I don't suppose I'll see that again, and it's not like I can afford it either."

There was a rap on the stairs.

"Five minutes, Sapphire. Get a wriggle on, love."

Taylor produced a business card and placed it among the tubes of make-up and pots of varnish.

"If she shows up, let us know, will you?"

"What's she done?"

"Went and got herself beat-up and witnessed a murder," said Macpherson.

"Christ, she never said," Hannah clutched the slipping towel. "She just asked me to loan her some stuff and for a place to crash for a few days."

"Did she mention if this client was someone she was seeing outside the course of her job?"

"Honestly, I don't know. I told her I didn't want to know and, God forgive me, I said it would be better if she got rid of it." Hannah sighed. "She's not naïve, but she's impulsive you know? Maybe she thinks I'll have another go about the pregnancy or give her a hard time over the work?" She picked up the card and read it. "If she shows up at mine, I'll call. Okay?"

Taylor thanked the girl.

Hannah Swift gave a tight smile and set about fastening the eyelets of a cupless lace basque she had wrapped around herself.

She spoke over her shoulder as Taylor swept the curtain aside.

"If you find her. Tell her not to worry about the money and I'm sorry. Tell her I'm sorry for what I said."

## Chapter 38

"Why the fuck did you not answer your phone?"

Freaky Jackson was a head taller than Carruthers, and he used every inch as he faced down the angry man.

"Because I was on a job and unlike you, I'm not bloody stupid enough to get myself nicked by having my mobile data picked up when the filth does a cell tower search," snarled Jackson.

Carruthers shook his head as he circled a few paces away, tension high and the cortisol comedown flushing the stress through his system.

"Calm down and tell me what happened," said Jackson, leaning back against the nondescript Ford Mondeo.

The underground parking lot was quiet. A handful of cars were lined up in the bays, and Carruthers nervously snatched a glance up at the ramps every time he heard the squeal of tyres somewhere above them.

"We don't know. There was an explosion at the crack house."

"Like a pipe bomb?" Jackson felt a twinge in his gut. The attack on the Corners and the image of Chopper's face catching a bullet flashed in his mind.

"No. The gas bottles went up. It gutted the whole place and wrecked my bloody van."

"The money?"

"Away, but we had to abandon the stash."

Jackson shook his head in annoyance. That wasn't going to go down well, although cash was king at the minute, so Carruthers may well be able to breathe easy. For the time being.

"He'll want to know everything. Did you get the wee lad?"

"He turned up," said Carruthers, jerking his head back to indicate a beat-up Berlingo. "He's in the van."

A decal reading 'Plumb and Heating Services' split the side panel door.

Both men turned at the sound of a heavy door opening and the hubbub of a restaurant kitchen spilling out; distinguished by the sounds of pots and pans clanking, indecipherable shouts from the pass, and the hiss of steam and jetting water.

Jackson recognised the suited figure who looked into the garage and then turned back into the kitchen melee and spoke, standing aside to let a second man past.

Gordon Beattie strode out, wiping his hands on a cotton napkin.

"This better be good, gents. You're ruining a very expensive Wagyu rib-eye."

Both men greeted their boss with an apologetic nod.

"Well..." said Beattie.

"One of the houses on the estate is offline. Gas explosion," said Jackson.

"Another hit?"

Jackson shrugged. Carruthers looked on uncomfortably.

"The cash got lifted, but they lost the stash in the fire," said Jackson.

Beattie pulled a face.

"That other thing go okay?"

Jackson nodded.

"How much was lost?" said Beattie.

"How much?" prompted Jackson.

"I... I don't... I was there to lift the wee lad," said Carruthers, stumbling over his words.

The three men looked up sharply at the sudden rattle of the nearby van door opening. Beattie raised a hand quickly and the suit on the kitchen entrance returned his hand to his side.

"Forty-five grand's worth, Mr Beattie."

"Forty-five." Beattie whistled.

"Give or take." Billy Webster stopped a few feet away from the men.

"You got that kind of money lying about you, kid? Are you able to replace my money?"

Webster shook his head.

"No, you fucking don't, do you? But it's your job to see it's kept safe, so I'm in a predicament now, aren't I?" Beattie tucked the napkin in his pocket and stood at ease, his hands folded behind his back.

"Who's this, Freaky?"

"Billy Webster, boss."

"Billy. Billy. Billy." Beattie shook his head. "Forty-five grand?"

Webster sniffed, looking at the ground and then at Jackson. Finally, he turned to Beattie.

"If I can give you the fella set the place on fire, can I work for you?"

There was a stunned silence before Beattie's laugh resounded around the space.

"Fuck sake, Freaky, where d'you get this one."

"I mean it, Mr Beattie. Work for you. Like these two. I don't want to be babysitting crackheads or doing the shit jobs that Matty or Lenny Butler or any of them other ones can't be arsed doing."

Beattie shook his head, more intrigued than amused.

Webster looked over at the van, gesturing at the passengers nervously waiting inside.

Two timid faces alighted. One whose eyes were wired to the moon and the other sporting a growing black eye and a long laceration on his cheek. The lot of them smelled like damp, burnt wood.

"Tell them. Tell them what you just told me in the van."

Webster reached out and pulled the smaller boy forward.

Barney Murray cleared his throat, the first words lost in a croak. He tried again.

"I think I saw the fella done it. I mean, I did. When I was on the ground outside and he lit the place up." Murray looked about, the abject fear of telling and what would happen if he didn't, eating him alive. It wasn't helping that Beattie didn't seem convinced, and Freaky Jackson looked like he would take pleasure in smashing his bones and sucking out the marrow.

"We've seen him before," stammered Barney. "On the estate. With a girl we know. She can tell us who he is."

## Chapter 39

Taylor was first into the office and felt great considering.

On leaving Ruby Stone's they had driven by Hannah Swift's address. With the house looking silent and empty, Macpherson had poked a hand through the letterbox and peeped into the dark hall which led to a flight of stairs. He returned confirming it was as quiet as the grave.

At that point, ready to go home, Taylor had allowed herself to be cajoled into a visit to the Maharaja for a delicious vegetarian dopiaza and two Cobra beers. Macpherson regaled her between mouthfuls with tales of Ruby's in bygone days, first when it was the Crooked Harp and then when it became Willie Wylie's. The details and stories flowed as he demolished samosas, a plate of tandoori chicken and a naan bread the size of a dinner plate.

Taylor now sat at her desk and, feeling better than she should, opened her PC word processor and booted up the template to begin writing her report. The clouds had been dispersed by early morning sun, and the ancient sandstone building opposite glowed as the strong rays illuminated it. Belfast, it seemed, had decided for the first time that week to show a brighter face.

The background hustle of office cleaners and then staff arriving was just building as she wrapped up her report, launched the internal mail app, and then sent it on. Leaving her desk and heading out of CID, she took the long corridor and stairs up to the canteen.

As she hit the landing, she caught a warm kiss of air and the smell of baked goods and fried food and on entering, although receiving several nods and a couple of muted good mornings, she didn't see the face she was in search of so instead helped herself to a cappuccino. As she fished in her pocket for change to pay the chirpy cashier, a voice close behind jolted her.

"If I didn't know any better, Detective Inspector, I'd say you've been ignoring me!"

"Jesus, Jack, you near gave me a heart attack!"

"Guilty conscience, that."

Detective Sergeant Jack Collins smiled, revealing a row of straight white teeth that stood at odds with a nose that had seen one too many breaks and a set of cauliflower ears. His hair, still damp from the shower, flopped across his forehead and needed a cut.

"Here, give me that. Take for this too will you please, Cath," said Taylor.

Collins protested, but Taylor paid for his drink anyway.

"Sorry, Jack. I swear I was in here looking for you. The report should be in your inbox."

Collins nodded his thanks.

"Keeps Happy off my back. You want to grab a seat?"

Taylor nodded, and they grabbed a free table near a window where they could watch the rush hour traffic cross the Queen Elizabeth Bridge and the dark waters of the river churn through the Lagan Weir and out to the lough beyond.

"How is he?"

"Happy? How's he ever? Ack, he's not the worst. That business on Sunday has him up the high doh, though."

"I thought it went okay?"

"Aye, it did," said Collins, dumping a couple of sugars in his tea. "We searched the house after and there were signs of a struggle. It took a bit to get the woman to open up, but she's singing like a bird now."

"So what's the problem?"

"Your man is a partner in some swanky solicitors. Happy's getting it in the neck from the brass. They're going ballistic because it all got a bit dynamic."

"He took his wife and baby on a joyride through the town while they were all doused in petrol. It wasn't our fault it went that way. You'd think they'd be content no one got hurt."

"Aye, the wife is saying that he was trying to get rid of her and the baby. He's saying she doused herself and that she suffers from post-natal depression and he was trying to get her to hospital."

"Bollocks, she was covered in defence wounds?"

"You don't need to tell me, Ronnie. When I tackled him, he had a bloody big kitchen knife."

"What's Happy going to do?"

Collins shrugged.

"Try to get him to plead down and hope it goes away. The press are on it though, and he's tortured with requests for statements."

"Bradford, Bexley? I heard his name on the news."

"Baxter. Bryce Baxter of Harper, Baxter, Brooke. His old fella's the one with his name on the door. Charles Baxter, but Baxter Junior is fairly well known in his own right."

Taylor took a sip of her coffee. Her conversation with Carrie Cook the previous evening and the connotations of this revelation swirled around in her head as she swallowed.

"What's the chances I could get a word with him?"

Collins, sipping his tea, narrowed his eyes.

"Why?"

"Cards on the table?"

"Yes." Collins put his tea down and crossed his arms, the sensation he wouldn't like where this might go crawling up his back.

"The firm came up in connection with something I'm working on."

"Rab Millar?"

Taylor winced, knowing the position this was putting Collins in. She shrugged a silent apology.

"Christ, Ronnie, you want me to ask Happy if you can interview Baxter in relation to the Millar case, are you mad?"

"I can ask him myself. I was just asking what were the chances," said Taylor a little more sharply than she meant to. Collins shook his head as he replied.

"A snowball in hell's chance."

He took a long swig of the tea, then looked in the cup as though wishing it was something stronger and sighed.

"Tell me what you've got."

❖ ❖ ❖

An hour later, Taylor had finished the brief with her team.

Walker and Reilly had confirmed that Sergeant Harris could arrange the TSG team as long they could supply a target address and the operation got signed off by the SIO, while Cook had managed to track down Lena Borodenko's case officer who was also available for a meeting.

Macpherson, arriving in on time but bleary-eyed and clutching a greasy bag of sausage rolls, had happily agreed to spend the morning drinking tea and going through the case database and following up on leads and forensics before helping Walker and Reilly in the search for Jackson's bolthole.

With the team heads-down, Taylor dotted the I's and crossed the T's on the Rowdy Burns' arrest and issued them to a uniform constable to pass on to the custody suite where DCI Reed had confirmed the PPS was confident the threshold for prosecution had been met.

"Doc?" she said as the PC left.

Macpherson dusted crumbs from his shirt front and mumbled through a mouthful of sausage meat and pastry.

"I'm calling it a possible misper." Using her keys to unlock the bottom drawer of her filing cabinet, she removed the evidence bag containing Lena Borodenko's laptop. "Can you get this down to tech and see if they can get us in? We need emails, financials anything that points to where she's gone or why Millar had her brought in."

"You forgetting something?" said Macpherson, brushing his palms together over a wastepaper bin. Taylor sighed.

"Look, here's the chit. I've signed it," she said, holding up the appropriate piece of paperwork. "As far as anyone else is concerned, we had it at her request along with the other personal items to be delivered to the hospital." She tapped the filing cabinet, which still contained the sports bag.

"Aye, okay," said Macpherson, a smile creasing his face. "I blame myself, you know. You've picked up all sorts of filthy habits."

Taylor shook the evidence pouch at him as the last of the savoury roll disappeared into his mouth.

As Macpherson made good on his promise to get the machine looked at, she called Carrie Cook and prepared to make the trip to Sanctuary to meet Lena's counsellor.

Ten minutes later, Taylor weaved the pool car through traffic. There was still a vague smell of smoke from the events of Sunday night which took her thoughts back to her canteen meeting with Jack Collins. He had reluctantly listened to her as she laid out Millar's connection to Miltek and thereby Harper, Baxter, Brooke, and although it was tenuous, he had agreed to take it to Leonard Gilmore, but he didn't make any promises something would come of the request.

The tail end of rush hour was petering out, but as a precaution, Taylor took the city route rather than face the bumper to bumper of the Westlink. As they passed the rear entrance to City Hall and then cut across Bedford Street, Taylor noted a concierge from the Grand Central Hotel having a crafty cigarette beside a builder's skip. Across the street, construction workers in yellow vests queued at a turnstile to enter the site, netting and billboards covering the high-rise scaffolding, which she also noted with a frown held the logo of Finnrock.

"How was your night out?" asked Cook with a grin.

"You wouldn't believe it if I told you?"

"Really?"

"Apart from nearly having my eye put out by a stripper's G-string, it was a dead end. We spoke to the girl, but Lena had stood her up. She seemed genuine enough," said Taylor.

The traffic opened up as they hit the Golden Mile and then the Lisburn Road, managing green lights until they got caught at the Balmoral flyover, from where it was a short drive to Sanctuary's new headquarters.

A resplendent facade welcomed them and Taylor negotiated a driveway bordered on each side by grass, newly planted shrubbery, and decorative landscaping before reverse parking into a marked visitors' bay. Both detectives showed their identification at the oval reception desk and were pleasantly asked to wait. It didn't take long before they were greeted.

"Detective Constable Cook?"

"That's me."

"Pleased to meet you, I'm Deborah Sall."

Sall had a warm welcoming smile and wore a black dress with a bright pink lily print. Cook introduced her superior and the two women followed Sall out of reception and up a wide staircase. As they passed the inauguration stone, Taylor's eye was once again caught by the mention of Finnrock and she paused to read the plaque.

"We were lucky there happened to be a visit to the province that day," said Sall. "It was quite last minute, but she was generous enough to mark the opening and to spend a bit of time here. Lovely girl. She was very warm."

Sall had paused as she waited for Taylor to finish, offering the royal anecdote as much to Cook as the interested inspector. Taylor's eyes moved from what she had actually been reading to note the name of Her Royal Highness and the details of the ribbon cutting.

"I'd heard that. Sorry, carry on," said Taylor.

Sall led them onto a balcony overlooking the lobby before badging through a double door. A short walk through an open-plan office space led them to a plush but informal meeting room where she offered them seats. With small talk and an offer of drinks over, they faced each other across a coffee table. A few business periodicals lay on the surface. Cook reached out and turned one slightly, easing it back as Sall placed a selection of treats on the table.

"Thanks for agreeing to see us," said Taylor, declining the offer of a shortbread biscuit.

"Not at all. I've often thought of Lena. The poor girl didn't arrive here in the best of circumstances, and I had great hopes we could see her through her challenges. I was surprised when I heard she was coming back, but now I believe that has been shelved. Has something happened to her?"

"Miss Borodenko was the victim of an assault. She was hospitalised but subsequently discharged herself. At the minute we aren't sure of her whereabouts and are trying to locate her. It would be helpful if we could piece together some of her history," said Taylor.

"Ah, I see. Well, fire away." Sall nibbled at a petticoat tail biscuit.

"Can you tell us how you came to be assigned as Miss Borodenko's caseworker?"

"Pot luck? Well, that's not totally true. Of the councillors and caseworkers here there are several of us with specific backgrounds: substance abuse, domestic violence, mental health, that sort of thing. It just so happened that Lena's referral to me came as part of her community service for a drugs offence."

"You being an expert?"

"Me having experience with both offenders and substance abuse, yes."

"How was she?" said Taylor.

"Perfectly pleasant, if a little withdrawn. She had recently lost her father and I think she felt a little alone in the world."

Taylor set her coffee cup down on the saucer.

"No other family here?"

"None. She hails from Macedonia. She spoke of brothers, but as far as we determined, she was here on her own. Certainly, she had no external visitors."

"Where was she living? It wasn't here?"

"No. No. We do now have the ability to accommodate about fifty. That's a selection of single dwellings and about a dozen larger accommodations for family units. Lena was placed within the community. We are lucky to work closely with social housing and other providers and in her case, it was a small secure, apartment development in the Annandale area."

"How does that work exactly?" said Cook.

"In what respect?"

"You mentioned it was secure, but it's on a private development. We are assuming these girls aren't under lock and key?" said Taylor.

Sall winced and then made a half shrug.

"You're quite correct. In this particular instance, it is supported living so we have a team who take shifts on site. The block maintains security by electronic access and the residents sign in and out. Visitors are by appointment."

"It's not by any chance a Morrow and Burke property?" said Cook, indicating one of the recent periodicals which featured the agent's logo prominently.

"Actually, yes. It is. They are extremely generous in their

commitment to our charity."

Taylor nodded in the general direction of the entrance.

"I noted at the plaque you have quite a number of local sponsors," she said.

"We are very fortunate," said Sall with a warm smile.

"What is Harper, Baxter, Brooke's involvement?"

"They would handle any legal assistance our patrons might require. In Lena's case, they represented her in her hearing and also assisted in some issues she had with replacing a missing passport. It's quite common to avail of their service. It's not all criminal cases either. Predominantly we are talking about people suffering upheaval because of family circumstance and who find themselves in need of protection orders, issues regarding child access, dissolution of marriage or property. It's a vital service for us." Sall set her cup down, adjusting the hemline of her dress.

"Who oversaw Lena's community service?" said Taylor.

"That would be me. It was arranged through the scheme and I signed off the reports which were duly submitted via Harper, Baxter, Brooke to the courts service."

"Would we be able to have access?" said Cook.

"I could check. I don't see why not."

"What exactly did the court impose?" said Taylor.

"She had to enrol in our substance abuse programme which she completed but to be honest, Inspector, she didn't strike me as a habitual user. Off the record, I think she was unlucky. She just found herself in a difficult position, far from home, and was trying to self-medicate." Sall gave a shrug and empathetic smile. "Typically the programme also imposes an element of work for the benefit of the community and Lena was involved in a few of those too."

"This is the community outreach work?" said Taylor.

"Yes. We have a number of charitable foundations, religious organisations, and other service providers who are kind enough to allow our patrons to assist them. It's mutually beneficial. We find that in a lot of cases these men and women have either been out of work or have never worked, and we see them grow in confidence and address the imbalance in their lives as they find avenues in which to apply themselves."

"What about private individuals, Ms Sall? Where do they fit in?"

"They simply make an enquiry and donate to us here at Sanctuary, or come recommended through one of our partners or schemes. They are vetted beforehand, of course," Sall added.

Taylor nodded, Cook continuing to write shorthand bullet points in her notebook.

From her seated position Taylor could see out into the large open-plan office where a junior staffer traded words with some colleagues, showing off a beautiful bouquet of hand-tied flowers. Deep red Naomi roses complemented by purple tulips and coppery Italian Ruscus. She entered one of the far offices before exiting again a moment later with a beaming smile, but minus the flowers.

"Lena Borodenko took part in several of these arrangements, didn't she?" said Taylor.

"She did." Sall may have been prepared for the direction of the conversation, but she was evidently a woman more at ease extolling the virtues of her work than some of the more indecorous occasions that required dealing with.

"How was she assigned? Is there a rota system or is it by recommendation?"

"A little of both. We try to pair patrons and clients as best suits their needs. Lena was popular, and she had some experience in the domestic and commercial cleaning industry, so we used that to her advantage. I believe towards the end of her time with us she had shown interest in using the contacts she had made to go self-employed with the aim of building a modest business of her own."

"Ms Sall, when I spoke with Lena she mentioned she had been having some difficulties? Is that something you're aware of?"

Sall sat up a little straighter. She made to talk and stopped, then sniffed, taking a moment to choose her words.

"Inspector, there was an incident towards the end of her tenure, however, nothing was proven and Lena dropped the complaint," she said.

"What was the nature of the complaint?"

"It was a bit tit for tat." Sall steepled her fingers in front of her heart. "There were accusations made."

"By Lena?" said Taylor.

"Initially by the client. She was quite effusive in her apologies at coming forward, but it seemed there were valuables disappearing from the house. A little cash here and there, some jewellery and bizarrely some underwear. She felt as Lena had access, it must be her."

"Did she offer any proof this was the case?"

Sall put her hands on her thigh and smoothed the material of her dress.

"No, and Lena denied it, obviously. Her retaliation was to suggest the client had been taking her to friends' houses and accepting payment while Lena sat their children or carried out other menial tasks while they lunched. When she complained about it, there was allegedly some intimidation and she was coerced into silence with some money."

"Could she…"

"No," Sall interrupted. "She had no proof either. "

"This client?"

Sall shook her head.

"No longer part of the scheme. Up until that point, they had an exemplary record in aiding us with placement and support to help our patrons. Both allegations were fully investigated internally, and no grounds found to escalate it further. Lena left their employ and our scheme shortly after."

"Do you not follow up or are there no procedures when your patrons leave your care?"

"Yes. Of course. I tried personally as her counsellor, and I know colleagues tried to follow up after that, but she just cut contact. Unfortunately, we are not obliged to force people to stay nor pressure them to return no matter our opinion on their choices."

"You're aware of the direction she took?"

"I just heard the speculation, Inspector. It's sad, I had great hopes." Sall sighed. "She's not the first, nor the last, I'm sure. We have people reunite with violent partners or fall back into old habits more often than we would like to admit."

Taylor's eye caught a woman leaving the office on the other side of the floor. She had a glow about her face, freshly applied gloss on her lips and a purpose to her stride. Her pleated skirt, which fell to her shapely calves, swayed as she walked. She was in her late forties, her dirty blonde hair twisted into a tight French plait and a fringe hung across her forehead. A simple string of pearls around her throat matched the one on her wrist.

"She was acquainted with another patron of yours, Hannah Swift," said Taylor as the woman moved from sight.

"They were resident on the same scheme. Not for long," said Sall. "A month to six weeks. I'm afraid Hannah was trouble. She was asked to leave for breaking curfews and infractions on our drugs and alcohol policy."

"But they kept in touch?"

"Again, we can't impose our will. Maybe softly discourage but ultimately…" Sall shrugged.

"If it's any consolation, Miss Swift seems to be trying to turn it around," said Taylor.

"I wouldn't know, Inspector, but yes, she was an intelligent girl who made poor choices."

"Did Lena have any other friends within the scheme? Someone she could turn to now? We would like to find her as soon as possible."

"There would have been several that she shared with. There is a communal area and a small garden they would have used as a social space. I'll make their names available."

Taylor thanked her and after several more minutes of confirming the address of the scheme at which Lena Borodenko had stayed and providing Sall with both her own and Cook's contact details, the women left and returned to the lobby.

As she descended the final few steps past the inauguration plaque, Taylor spotted a familiar face.

An enthusiastic handshake turned into a peck on the cheek, the blonde woman clutching the pearls at her throat as the gentleman spoke a few words that caused her to laugh. As she turned towards the police officers she was flushed, a friendly smile on her face.

"Councillor Howard. Good to see you again," said Taylor.

Howard's hand dropped to his abandoned briefcase, and he stepped back with a brief frown, and then his professional demeanour kicked in.

"Inspector, a pleasant surprise. How's your investigation proceeding?"

"Steady. We're following several positive lines at the minute, although we had a setback regarding the security at Speakers Square. Your wife wasn't able to retrieve the CCTV for us."

"A shame. Technology is great when it works. I saw on the news you were at that ghastly shooting. Getting anywhere?"

Sall stepped in before Taylor could reply, offering a palm towards the woman.

"This is Director Jane Richards, she's head of services here at Sanctuary."

"Director," Taylor offered a hand in greeting. "Ms Sall has been helping us with a few enquires. I apologise for keeping her from her work."

Richards' warm and open expression had curdled and her handshake was limp.

"We are glad to be of help, Inspector. If there is anything else Deborah or any of us here at Sanctuary can help with, let us know." She turned her face up to Malcolm Howard. "Shall we? Apologies, Inspector, we have a meeting with the finance committee over additional funding grants. Good to meet you."

Taylor agreed likewise and nodded to Howard as he followed Richards up the sweeping staircase.

As the automatic doors slid open and the cool air gusted from the car park into the lobby, she looked back and caught Howard's stony stare.

## Chapter 40

The driver hit the locking bar twice with a heavily padded gloved hand and then twisted the mechanism to release the van's rear door. Pulling it aside, he looked in at his passenger, giving a nod and gesture that it was safe to exit.

Gordon Beattie stepped down from the tailgate and looked around the warehouse, his senses immediately assaulted. The noise of industrial cutting equipment was deafening.

The sound of Stihl petrol disc cutters ripping through concrete vibrated in his chest and the stink of their fuel fumes was heady in the air. Men breaking down larger sectional items with demolition hammers accompanied the cacophony of the cutters, the rat-a-tat of the pneumatics like gunfire. He watched as one man raised a hand, his partner halting the drill's motion. From the wreckage, the first man hauled a battered steel box, dragging the item to a stack of similar boxes where the two hefted it onto the growing pile. As he pulled down the mask to hawk a gob of spittle, Beattie noted it was Bekim Nishani, red defenders covered his ears, nose and lips stitched and covered by broad plasters. Nishani replaced his mask and returned to work on a new section of concrete slabbing.

Positioned inside the warehouse was a double-height shipping container converted to an office structure. It stood next to the large roller shutter door that his transport now drove back through. On the balcony, the figure of Amir Kazazi waved down, a set of bright yellow defenders covering his ears.

Beattie waited as a small bobcat digger slewed past, shovel aimed at a pile of discarded rubble. As the driver put the shovel to work moving the spoil from the ground into the belly of a large skip, Beattie quickly crossed the space and took the steps up.

Kazazi grinned, ushering him inside through the thick steel door, dropping the ear defenders on the desk as soon as the door closed.

"It'd deafen you out there and those bloody things sweat you," he said, pointing at the offending ear protection. "It looks good down there, Monster, yes?" His hair was damp, and he wiped sweat from his sideburns. From the window, Beattie appraised the operation below. A little rough around the edges, but the Albanians were in full swing.

"Christ, Amir, I might sub-contract you out," said Beattie with a grin of his own. "What do you normally use this place for?"

"I don't. Mostly it's a place to park up wagons and keep them out of the way, sometimes it's a cargo transfer station. Once the wagons leave the port at Larne, we sanitise them here before they head into the city. Whatever's coming in goes out in another transport. It's low key. Don't worry."

"I wasn't." Beattie slapped the man on the shoulder and turned to a battered table. A film of dust covered a scarred surface of illegible engravings and tea rings. At its centre lay one of the steel boxes. Kazazi lifted a claw hammer, a cold chisel and a set of short-handled bolt cutters from the corner of the room.

"Let's get a juke then, Amir," said Beattie.

A heavy padlock secured the box. Kazazi fitted the blades of the cutter around the shackle and cut it, discarding the lock onto the floor. The hasp still bore traces of concrete, which he freed with little effort using hammer and chisel. Now separated from the staple, he tapped the sliding lid free, before pushing it open to reveal eight packaged blocks, each heavily wrapped in parcel tape. The lid followed the lock to the floor and Kazazi removed one block and offered it across.

"How many so far?" said Beattie.

"Twenty-five."

"A bit over halfway." Beattie nodded approvingly. "You know what you're doing with it once it leaves here?"

"Yes, same facility that I use myself. Food processing with a sterile setup. I brought in ten of the people on your list to do the cut, and my drivers will deliver to your distributors. It won't be a problem."

Beattie slid a small penknife from his inner jacket pocket and slit the external wrap. Inside, the block of cocaine was further wrapped in tightly wound clingfilm. Each block had a label depicting a double-headed snake.

He considered the economics. There were thirty-eight boxes in the consignment. If as expected they had all survived the process, that was just over three hundred kilos. The slightly inflated cost of purchase at El Jadida and then the manufacturing and shipping put his overheads at nearly three million pounds. The shipment would return four times that retail, and combined with the debts he had called in and with the earnings of the previous shipment, he'd take away more than enough to satisfy the deal with the South Americans.

"Amir, I'd my doubts you'd pull this off, but this isn't too bad for a first crack." He slapped his hands together and again looked out at the feverish labour of Kazazi's crew.

"Does that mean you'll give me a couple more days to get your cash together?"

Beattie turned back and smiled without warmth.

"No, it doesn't but I'll tell you what, once this is all over, you can keep your sixty days. I'm going to have so much of this coming in direct that if you support me and partner up now with the storage and distribution, you'll be able to use the profits to offset the forty per cent."

Kazazi looked at the box of narcotics. Beattie read what the man was thinking.

"Thirty-eight boxes, Amir. We're talking four times that every four to six weeks and you get a cut from the bottom line."

"No risk?"

"There's always a risk. But I've custody of the gear from the minute it hits the dock in Venezuela. It's my shipping company and I receive and process it from El Jadida on. You get a percentage minus cost for every gram you take off me. Sure, you couldn't beat it."

Kazazi reached out a hand.

"Deal," he said.

"Deal," agreed Beattie. The two men shook and slapped each other on the shoulder.

"How's Bekim?"

"He will be fine. He has a bruised ego, but he's a good man. This is now water under the bridge."

"Good. I need to make a call here. Away down and see how the lads are getting on, and tell them I'll give them a cut of what the spoil will make from the aggregate top line. They're doing a good job. Make sure Bekim knows he'll get a double share for the inconvenience he's suffered."

Once the Albanian had left, Beattie pulled a cheap Nokia from his pocket and hit the single stored number.

"It's me," he said when the call was answered. "That contingency is all going to be in order. You can let them know it's on as agreed. No change to location or timeline. I'll have the finances in place for the buy-in."

He quit the call, unclipped the rear of the phone and removed the SIM, cracking it in half. Then he dropped the Nokia to the floor, picked up the claw hammer and put it through the screen.

## Chapter 41

There was a quiet buzz of energy in the CID suite as Taylor and Cook returned, and Walker, upon seeing his inspector, nudged Reilly before standing to intercept her on the way to her desk.

"Guv, we got a hit back on the van from Risky's," he said as she closed. "We had a phone call on the switchboard. The call came from a business owner who remembered a van driving around near Greencastle. He had a few orders to get out for Monday morning and the rest of the business complex was closed. It went out of his head until he saw the information appeal on the news."

"When was this?" said Taylor.

"Same night as the Millar shooting."

"Where?"

"Mountainview Crescent, it's a small industrial estate off the Upper Road. It's only about a mile from where I lost it at TICC."

"Get it up on the maps for me. I'll be over in a sec." She checked her desk for messages and had a quick scan through her emails, but there was nothing yet from Collins.

Macpherson appeared from the kitchen with a cup of tea and half a sandwich.

"Are you still eating?"

"You can't fatten a thoroughbred, Ronnie." He washed down a mouthful of bread with a swig of the tea.

"Did you get the laptop away," said Taylor.

"Yes, they're swamped. But I asked nicely," he added, seeing her expression, then he shrugged. "Don't hold your breath. How did you get on?"

"Nothing we didn't know. The woman we met was helpful

enough, a bit cagey on the circumstances of why Lena left, but she agreed to give us the names of other friends that she might have met there. We confirmed that Morrow and Burke are one of Sanctuary's partners. So are the solicitors that carried out Millar's property deals."

"So?" said Macpherson, taking another chug of his tea.

"I don't know yet. Was Millar recruiting vulnerable women from Sanctuary?" Taylor's unfocused gaze drifted across the office, the question as much to herself as to Macpherson.

"It's possible. It wouldn't be the first time somebody targeted an organisation like that. Remember the team recruiting troubled teens from a support unit up the west. They lured them in with rave parties and speed and the next thing they were muling drugs in from Ibiza."

"It's becoming a bit incestuous for my liking," said Taylor. "I saw Malcolm Howard lurking about with the director of services too."

"Oh, aye. What was he like?"

"She. Jane Richards. She didn't say much other than hello."

Macpherson wrinkled his nose as he chewed.

"I'm going to get Carrie to engineer another meeting with the girl from Morrow and Burke's office. We need to find out how well she knew Millar and see if he had influence other than as a client," said Taylor.

"Do you want me to go with her?" said Macpherson.

"She might open up if it's just Carrie. No offence, but you don't come over as Captain Sensitive."

Macpherson recoiled in mock horror.

"What about that time I was Santa Claus for the Children's Trust Christmas party? You weren't saying that then."

"You were hungover as I remember," said Taylor, chuckling at the memory. She nodded across the office. "Chris and Erin caught a break on the van. You coming?"

She was just making her way towards Walker's cubicle

when she heard her name called.

"DI Taylor. Two minutes?"

Gillian Reed stood in the open doorway and beckoned her across.

"Ma'am?"

"You all look busy?"

"Getting there. We've a few lines we're getting our teeth into. A tip came in on the van following the press briefing," said Taylor.

"Keep me in the loop." Gillian Reed steered Taylor to a quieter corner and faced her. "I've just been speaking to Inspector Gilmore over at Eight. He wants to know what his suspect has to do with Rab Millar's death."

"In theory nothing, but the gentleman in custody is part of a solicitor's firm we have tied to Millar and, just now, to Sanctuary. I think our queries will stonewall if we go to them direct, so, I'm hoping because of his predicament, Inspector Gilmore's suspect may have an incentive to answer a few questions about what Millar was up to before his death."

Reed considered it.

"It sounds like a two hundred and fifty to one at the National, Veronica?"

"At the minute I might take those odds."

"Well, seeing as you were instrumental in the arrest, Gilmore is giving you a crack but be careful it doesn't blow up in your face. The Baxter crowd isn't taking any prisoners. Get it over with as soon as you can. Lenny Gilmore wants it off his plate, and he's getting to the point where he's going to have to charge or release."

"Ma'am."

Reed took her leave and Taylor returned to Walker's desk. He had pulled up a plan view on Google maps and opened a second search window.

"Give me the overview again," said Taylor.

Walker tapped his ballpoint pen against the screen.

"Caller's unit is here. He spotted the van after six and thought the driver might be lost until he saw they were still driving about forty-five minutes later."

"He's sure it was our van?" said Macpherson from his seat on Walker's left.

"Wrote the reg down."

"Get up what you can on that estate? Let's have a look at the units," said Taylor, her mind turning to the geography of the area.

"Guv?"

"Carrie?"

Carrie Cook had her mobile pressed to her ear. She took it away and pressed it against her chest.

"Fire Investigation Team," she said with a nod to the handset. "The van fire started in the front passenger seat. They have traces of accelerant on fragments of the fabric seam that was protected by the metalwork and evidence of pooling under the seat. There was also secondary evidence in the area around the vehicle. The suggestion is something crude, a petrol bomb most likely. The team took a crowbar and a crate of empty bottles from the yard to give them the once over, but the big score is that they are confident the van was carrying a significant quantity of narcotics. There wasn't much left, but they've analysed the ash and got some primary evidence from inside the rear framing. The lead investigator is putting his money on cocaine, and a lot of it."

Taylor mouthed her thanks.

"I just sent you an update email on Miltek." said Cook.

"I'll check for it here in a minute."

Cook nodded, putting the call back to her ear and heading towards her own desk, just avoiding a collision with Reilly who was pacing the perimeter of the cubicles, her phone clamped to her ear.

"There's your list," said Walker, dragging and dropping a web page for Mountainview Crescent Industrial Estate onto his second monitor. "Usual stuff. Print workshop, paint and panel repair. Dog groomer." Walker mumbled as he scrolled the list. "Wave-Pro Blinds, Fireplace Factory. Welder. Homes and Interiors…"

"What's that?" said Taylor, jabbing a fingertip at the screen. "Signal Foods?"

"Yes. Does this carry information?" The red crest of the logo had a recent familiarity about it.

"There's a hyper-link," said Walker, clicking. A fresh window opened taking them to a web address for Signal Foods, frozen food supplier to trade and event catering. Walker continued to click through the website, Taylor stopping him at the contact us page.

"That's it," she said.

"What?" asked Macpherson. He looked over Walker's other shoulder, mouth falling open. "Jesus, do you see that T-bone." His eyes were now on stalks at the glossy hi-def promo picture of a juicy steak.

"Head office," said Taylor, pointing at the small section to the bottom of the page. "They're a subsidiary company of Sulejman Meats. Intel have it as a front for an Albanian gang."

"Bekim Nishani? " said Macpherson perking up.

"He works for Sulejman."

"I've an address on Webster!" Reilly's face was flushed, and her voice an octave higher than usual. "The youth councillor phoned it in. Flat 1A Leeland Court. It's on the Fearon Estate. Other side of the towers."

"How probable?" asked Taylor.

"He's confident. One of the youngsters on the periphery of the gang gave him the location."

"We're flying here," said Taylor, her heart rate beginning a familiar upbeat march as the prospect of action over investigation took hold.

"Warrants?" asked Walker.

"Not for Signal," said Taylor, nodding to the screen. "I want to give them a chance to tell their story and maybe trip them up, but for Webster, absolutely. Erin see if you can get Sergeant Harris to make a team available for dynamic search asap, and tell him that the subject is likely to resist. Chris, prepare what you have for a section eighteen warrant application and pass it on to DCI Reed. Put together a brief and standby. You two made the connections, so it's your show. Are you both happy to take this?"

The two junior officers nodded.

"Good. Right, we want them in for questioning over being in the vicinity of the Corners attack and driving an unregistered vehicle, and we want that van and a weapon. If Jackson is there, it's suspicion of the murder of Barry Corrigan. Okay?"

"Guv."

Taylor straightened, the rush of adrenaline surging up from her toes.

"Doc, grab your jacket and I'll buy you a steak."

## Chapter 42

Shepard rolled the motorcycle to a stop. He had parked on an escarpment overlooking a small industrial estate; the lane he had followed to get there, ran through a small wood and recreational park and was rutted and muddy.

An arterial road bisected the business units and buildings below and beyond them, a low-rise housing estate infringed on the edges of the green belt. Far off to the left, sunlight reflected off the rows of headstones in another of the city cemeteries, the squares of shiny granite interspersed with patches of green, all laid out in neat squares around a central roundabout.

Kicking down the stand, Shepard seated himself, removed his helmet, and pulled out his phone. Launching the tracking app, he confirmed that somewhere in the compound below, the Toyota was parked up and, pinching the screen, he zoomed in. The car was positioned inside one of the concrete and corrugated steel structures which looked to be part of the production plant. Large, caged vats of what could be colouring or preservative were stacked up along the gable wall of the building, and a forklift truck weaved into view between structures.

The setup was a standard affair with the entire compound surrounded by a chain-link fence topped with razor wire, deterring unwanted visitors. Along the bottom of the slope, trees overgrew the fence, the foot of which was thick with abandoned polystyrene containers, crisp packets, leaves and discarded beer cans. Beyond the wooded slope, it was twenty metres to the nearest building.

A two-storey admin structure faced out to the main road and the car park only had a few cars. Behind admin, were five other units. Each building, he decided, was dedicated to production or distribution based on the vehicle bay doors or the massive extraction vents set into the side panelling.

A CCTV camera was visible on a pole towering over the red and white vehicle barrier in the front car park, the system doing away with the need for a manned gatehouse and as Shepard watched, the barrier rose, triggered from somewhere inside the complex to admit a Signal Foods' van. The barrier remained upright and another two vans sped in close behind the first, skirting the admin building and making directly for the last of the three distribution units, the same unit as the Toyota was hidden in.

He put the phone back in his pocket and pulled out a small pair of field glasses, training the magnifying lenses on the vans as they rolled in convoy up to the doors. The clunk and rattle of the roller door opening was just about audible from his position on the buff.

Each vehicle had two men. Driver and passenger. As the door reached its limit, the vans entered. Shepard watched as a swarthy figure exited and surveyed the immediate area outside. He was mid-thirties and by the look of it had been in the wars, a shade of bruising had formed around his right eye and a broad strip of adhesive plaster covered his lower lip and nose and matched a wad of padding covering one ear. The man puffed the last gasps of a cigarette, then tossed the butt away before returning inside to lower the door. Slung across his back on a webbing strap was an Ingram MAC-10 submachine pistol.

Shepard felt the cool tension of anticipation slip around him. He had thought that tracking the vehicles may require more effort on his part, first to collate where they had been and then surveil and assess each location for its potential to be the point of origin for the drug deliveries or the destination for the cash, but it turned out that the firework display in the estate had driven both to ground and they hadn't moved since. Good news for him. Bad news for them.

He didn't plan on the kid-glove treatment this time either. He filed the appearance of the MAC-10 away. The weapon was ideal for close quarters when pray and spray was the name of the game, and while he doubted every man in the building was armed, he wasn't planning on taking any chances.

The men who had his attention wouldn't want the focus of the police and security services on their business activities and while the attack on the Corners Bar and the burning down of the drug den had been minor actions designed to be an inconvenience, the next stage was to drive the message home. To disrupt the supply chain and destroy their profit. Another tactic in the war he was bringing to their door.

Shepard felt a moment's regret as he looked out across the compound. But not because he knew people would die today; he'd spent the best part of his adult life doing the worst of things to the worst of people and he had made peace with that.

The feeling stemmed from his inability to protect those closest to him. To have been a world away protecting the faceless when he could have been at home protecting his own flesh and blood. It was a regret for the life he would never have.

The men who had left his wife and child to die lived a privileged existence. They ruled through fear and they were untouchable, but they weren't alone in their crimes. They had been enabled, supported and protected, and those who had contributed would pay the price too. Their secrets, their wealth, and their liberty may be beyond the reach of the law, but Shepard knew they would not be beyond his.

## Chapter 43

"Sierra One, Control. Comms check."

"Sierra One, Actual, confirm loud and clear."

"Roger, One. Standby."

Control repeated the checks across the rest of the Sierra and Tango teams. The battered black van that housed control sat in the relative cover afforded by a raised bank of thornbushes and the barbed wire-topped walls of an electricity substation. The target premises lay eight hundred metres away.

Flat 1A Leeland Court was wedged between a row of neat garden fronted terraces and a derelict shop unit in the end stage of demolition.

Much closer, inside their unmarked Volvo, Chris Walker and Erin Reilly remained a safe but actionable distance from the target building, monitoring comms and waiting to receive the go from the tactical commander.

Ahead of them at the other end of the street in the back of a transit van, a compliment of Tactical Support Group operators designated Tango One made ready for the breach. Parked close behind them was Tango Two, a Volkswagen Caddy carrying the dog handler and his toothy charge.

The team remained in observation and surveillance on the premises identified as the current known location for Billy Webster, in anticipation of the moment Control confirmed that the operation was live.

"One, Control. Confirm eyes on Box?"

"One, Actual. Eyes on. No contact," said Reilly.

"Roger One, standby. Vehicle moving towards your position. Wait. Out."

A blue Renault Clio drifted past the observation post.

Vehicle traffic had been almost non-existent and other than an old lady out pruning a blooming rosebush, the terrace was quiet. Several blips came across the bandwidth, followed by the tactical commander's voice.

"All units. Status is green. Say again, status green, proceed to target. Tango One, make ready for breach."

The three units exited their vehicles, the dog handler a little behind as he clipped on his partner's harness and led him to their designated position behind the two detectives and the four-man TSG unit.

There was no obstruction into the small front garden of the flat. The gate had been long removed and the council's recently mowed patch of grass on either side of the path held little in the way of trip hazards.

Reilly thumped a tattoo against the door. In her other hand, she held a copy of the warrant.

"Police. Open up, please."

Behind to her left stood Walker, thumbs hooked into his body armour. To her right, along the frontage, the Tactical Support brick stacked up.

Reilly gave the door another thump, garnering no response. She stood back and nodded to the sergeant. He motioned the next two men in the stack up.

The TSG officers wore dark rifle-green flame-retardant coveralls and ballistic helmets, their sidearms securely holstered. Carrying a scuffed Enforcer entry ram parallel to his chest, the lead officer stepped into position. His teammate, standing out of the range of the backswing, held a similarly well-used three-foot-long iron crowbar.

The sergeant nodded, and the ram arced into the door lock with over three tonnes of applied force, shattering the lock on the single swing and sending the door careering back against the plastered wall behind.

❖ ❖ ❖

Shepard breached the fence line with the aid of side cutters and rushed across the tarmac in a crouch until he was beside the building housing the vehicles.

He had donned a ski mask and webbing, the pouches of which carried spare magazines for the Beretta, strapped in a drop holster on his right thigh, and for the AK-74 which was slung on a tactical strap, stock collapsed and barrel aimed low as he manoeuvred away from the main roller doors to a side entrance he had noticed from his previous vantage point.

A rickety lean-to of two by four and plywood offered inadequate shelter for those needing a smoke break, but the half brick wedging the door open three inches was more than generous for Shepard's infiltration.

Backing up to the side of the door he listened, and placing fingertips on the handle, he gently swung it away, then in a smooth motion he rolled around the edge, weapon raised, sidestepping as he entered so as not to be back-lit by the doorway.

He found himself in a stairwell lobby; flickering lightbulbs were trapped in metal cages and painted iron stairs to his right rose to the first floor. A set of heavy rubber swing doors with clear viewing panels were directly in front.

Shepard moved to clear the stairwell and then peered through the observation panels to the corridor beyond. Coast clear, he eased through, weapon first. The rumble of engines and the muted shouts of conversation sounded from deeper inside the warehouse, and the combined smell of disinfectant and spices mingled in the air. As he moved along the corridor they were joined by the acrid smell of exhaust fumes and a rhythmic metallic tapping.

The corridor teed off. To the right, it ended in another set of rubber crash doors and to the left was a longer corridor with doors off and safety glass observation windows, from the other side of which came the sound of immediate and lively activity. He approached and glanced in.

The area beyond was large, dominated by stainless steel tables, refrigeration units and stacks of packaging material. Threaded through all, was a meandering but unmoving conveyor belt. The walls and ceiling were sheeted in white PVC cladding and the entire space was illuminated by ceiling-mounted arc lights.

Half a dozen men, all wearing builders twin-filter dust masks stood around the stainless tables with mounds of white powder stacked in front of them, their hands busy cutting the product with creatine and dextrose being heaped on by two colleagues from labelled ten-kilo drums. As the group worked, another man entered, accompanied by the armed guard with the cut face, and together they hefted a steel container onto an adjoining table. Shepard noted it was one of several. The guard, a cigarette tucked behind his good ear and the MAC-10 slung carelessly under his arm, spoke, the words lost to Shepard but eliciting a laugh from the men.

Shepard ducked back to cover and stilled himself for the assault, checking over his weapon. The door ahead would offer access, and then it would be a dynamic entry. Fast and brutal. First the gunman, then the cut team and a mobile reload into the warehouse where he would disable the rest of the men and vehicles and then destroy the drugs.

Shepard dropped to a crouch at the sound of a slamming door and a scream. From somewhere close by came raised voices and the distinct crash and slap as rubber doors were aggressively heaved aside, then another scream was cut short by the sound of an open palm striking flesh followed by footfalls on metal. The cut crew inside, insulated by the wall and distracted by their conversations, continued their work. Shepard listened as the aggressive voices and footsteps moved upstairs. If there were hostiles above, he had to identify and amend his plan accordingly.

Staying low under the sill, he moved to the end of the corridor, pausing momentarily at each door before exiting at the end into another stairwell. The commotion he had heard continued with no abatement above. Rifle raised, he started up.

The first floor comprised a corridor with a set of double doors opening into a mezzanine storage area above the ground-floor warehouse bay. The smell of diesel fumes was stronger above and the space was racked out with shelving and cardboard packing crates.

Shepard manoeuvred quietly into the space; cover afforded by the shelving and its shadow dulled what pale light filtered in from obstructed skylights. A small, gated elevator was in place at the lip edge of the mezzanine, and footsteps clanked down a set of stairs towards the ground level. Shepard eased around a covered H-beam to observe a second guard, similarly armed with a submachine pistol disappearing from view as muted conversation rose from the warehouse followed by raucous laughter.

The far end of the mezzanine was sectioned off with a structure of wooden baton and hardboard two metres high and twice as wide. Set into the front face was a door with a closed hatch and a heavy locking bar. Shepard approached, expecting a secure storage area, but was stunned when the smell of sewage and sweat washed over him.

It was a world away from the complex caverns of the Tora Bora Mountains, but he knew the smell of confined, communal living. With his back to the wall, peripheral attention remaining on the stairs, he slid open the viewing hatch.

Shepard jerked back as two wild eyes stared at him. Black hair hanging over the face flicked away and then he was assaulted by snarling teeth and wild screams. He snapped the hatch closed, heart rate ramping at the shock. Beyond the face, there were another twenty women and girls packed into the area, each competing for whatever room there was on the floor while avoiding the overflowing buckets in the corner that gave rise to the stink of ammonia.

Shepard didn't understand the sudden guttural shout behind him but knew the words to be excited, panicked and carrying the tone of a universal challenge.

Turning he saw a swarthy male, mid-thirties and wearing sweatpants and an AC/DC crew neck tee; his right hand waved a pistol.

Shepard snapped up his rifle and squeezed the trigger.

❖ ❖ ❖

Taylor dropped her sun visor as they rounded a long sweeping bend. The traffic was light as she crossed the M2 flyover and then, signalling right, she took the filter light and followed the B51 until it crested onto Upper Road. The satnav announced that her destination was five hundred metres on the right.

"What's the plan?" said Macpherson.

"We're notifying them of suspicious activity in the area, ask if they have any recent vandalism or break-ins to report. Mention the sighting of the vehicle and politely request a look at their CCTV if they have any, and ask to speak with Nishani about his speeding fines." Taylor peered out the windscreen at the passing businesses.

"There you go, might be onto a winner," said Macpherson, pointing out a CCTV camera angled down to cover the front entrance to Signal Foods.

Taylor pulled up to the vehicle barrier and slid her window down. She reached out and pressed the intercom button which warbled back at her, a red light blinking beside the small integrated camera.

After several seconds she received a flat electronic tone. Reaching out she pressed again, this time after several seconds there was a rattle followed by a squeal of high-pitched static.

"Hello?" Taylor held her warrant card up to the camera, the howl of static persistent and disrupting whoever was on the other end of the intercom.

"Police, could we... Jesus!"

Amplified by the intercom but audible through the open car window, the sound of automatic gunfire erupted from inside Signal Foods.

## Chapter 44

"Sierra One. Negative, there's no one here. Control, be advised we have a potential crime scene. Can we request SOCO to our location?"

Erin Reilly released the transmit button and stepped aside to let the dog handler past, the warbled beep and confirmation that scene of crime officers had been requested, received in her ear.

The street was now more crowded as onlookers stepped onto their doorsteps to see what the commotion was about. Flat 1A had a cordon of red and white exclusion tape wrapped around the gatepost and stretching to the next nearest lamppost, and a second police Land Rover was also in attendance. Uniformed officers were holding position along the cordon to deter entry past the flimsy, fluttering barrier.

Reilly turned and re-entered, meeting Chris Walker in the lounge as he snapped images on his mobile phone.

"Did you see the size of that TV? It must be sixty inches."

"Geek, are you jealous?" said Reilly, teasing.

"They say crime doesn't pay." Walker winced and pointed at a blood-stained chair. "Did you call that in?"

"Yeah."

"Detective?"

Reilly turned as the TSG team leader looked into the lounge.

"The flat is empty. There's a small shed out the back and we had a quick look, but it's just junk," he reported.

"Thanks. Advise your team to clear out and have someone start a scene log," said Reilly with a nod of thanks. The officer backed out.

"Actually, can you get the dog to look at the shed as well?

They can't do much more in here until forensics clear it," said Reilly. The team leader nodded an affirmative, and Reilly took another look around the room.

There was no doubt Webster had been there. A copy of the Belfast Newsletter was spread out on a table and opened at the sports section and beside it was a plastic carrier bag with a receipt still taped to the side from two days ago, the order: one crispy duck and pancakes, special fried rice and chicken curry and chips. The empty cardboard and foil containers shoved back inside were starting to smell. A smattering of crushed prawn crackers lay under the scuffed coffee table, its surface scored and bearing the remnants of a joint. The stubbed end lay alongside sprinkles of tobacco, Rizla papers and tiny burnt crumbs of the drug.

"Erin?" said Chris Walker, crouched down and holding the broken door of an old well-chewed sideboard. "There's a hoard in here."

Reilly peeked past his gloved hand to see a stack of pre-pay mobile phones and over-the-counter SIM cards. She opened a drawer to find more of the tiny cards, several snapped in two.

"Bingo," she said. "We might get something from these. Come on, we can bag and tag once the SOCO confirms if this is another murder scene."

Walker opened his mouth to speak when they both received the update on their earpieces.

"Control, All units be advised. Code Zero. Repeat Code Zero. Any available units near Upper Road and the Mountainview Industrial Estate please respond. Officers under fire."

❖ ❖ ❖

Macpherson stood in the middle of the road, arms raised to stop the traffic that made to swerve around the abandoned

Vauxhall, now beached on a small traffic island.

"Move it. Go on. Get back down there! Police, move." He swore as he raised his warrant card, ducking involuntarily as another extended barrage of gunfire rang out.

"Doc?"

He turned to see Taylor was halfway into her body armour and speaking rapidly into the throat mic of her TETRA radio. The front and rear driver and passenger doors were open, and she sheltered behind the car, darting occasional glimpses towards the Signal Foods buildings.

"A steak, you said! Not become a bloody sitting duck!" He ducked in beside her, one arm on the boot lid, the other gesturing at a car, vainly going through the motions of executing a three-point turn. "I'm too old for this caper," he muttered, waving thankfully as the driver sped away.

"You okay?" said Taylor.

"I'm fine. Jesus, you hit that bollard at some speed."

The plastic traffic bollard had been torn from its mooring and what remained was jettisoned against the kerb on the other side of the road.

As they looked through the car windows to the building beyond, the front door to the admin block opened and panicked workers fled across the forecourt towards the barrier. One woman, losing a shoe, tumbled headlong into the ground. Her colleagues swarmed past, spurred on by another burst of gunfire.

"For Christ's sake," hissed Taylor. She unholstered her Glock and gave the magazine a slap, racking the slide to chamber the first round. Leaving the cover of the car, she ran towards the gate of Signal Foods, waving one arm in the air for attention.

"Police. That way. Make your way beyond the car. Quickly. Police," she shouted.

Threading her way through the crowd of panicked faces,

she approached the fallen woman, now struggling up on her hands and knees, her tights torn and blood blooming from a cut knee.

"Up you get. Can you walk?" said Taylor, helping the woman to her feet. Her mascara was smeared and teary eyes stared back blankly. As another burst of gunfire rang out, she screamed in terror.

Taylor half walked, half pushed her to the gate where Macpherson was directing people beyond the police car and back down the hill towards another section of the industrial estate. The staff of several other business units had come out to witness the commotion, some walking to the fringes of their own fence line with mobile phones raised to film the mayhem. He reached out to take the woman.

"Ronnie!"

Taylor spun around in time to see a man armed with a short submachine gun exit one structure and be cut down. Three well-executed shots taking his thigh, side and chest. He crashed to one knee and then flopped prone. Unmoving.

Another terrified wail went up from inside the admin building. Both officers could see the silhouettes of the people trapped inside who had also witnessed the killing.

"Get her back behind the car. I'm going in."

"Wait for bloody back-up," said Macpherson.

"If I wait for back-up, it could be more than your man they're bagging up later. I'll be in and out." She tapped the earpiece. "I'm on comms once the cavalry arrives."

Macpherson swore under his breath as Taylor turned and rushed towards the open front door of the offices. He watched as she paused on the threshold to shout a warning and then, weapon raised, she entered Signal Foods and disappeared from view.

❖ ❖ ❖

The first bullet struck the man in the heart, the second just above his clavicle and he flopped against a section of racking before slumping to the ground dead.

A wail and furore rose from the boxed-off section housing the women, just before surprised shouts erupted from the warehouse below, and then a second later, the metallic clang, clang, clang as ricocheting bullets started pinging off the steel H-beam supports of the mezzanine and the roof struts above. Bright sparks flashed as the rounds impacted the oxidised metalwork.

The vibration of footfalls rushing up the stairs caught Shepard's attention faster than the sound of the heavy steps.

He dropped to a crouch and aimed his Kalashnikov at the head of the stairs and as soon as the head and chest appeared over the top he squeezed the trigger, the weapon's muzzle flash illuminating the darkened space. The rushing figure tumbled backwards as the bullets struck, coming to a slump on the bottom steps.

Badly aimed gunfire returned from below, the rounds thudding into the wooden structure holding the women. Shepard sprang forward, unleashing a barrage in return, rewarded with a panicked shout of pain, his shots winging a second shooter.

Moving, Shepard slipped between the storage racks, ignoring the shouts, screams and thudding from the confined women.

Below was chaos. Two men dragged a bleeding third behind the front wheel of a Mercedes Sprinter van. Panicked shouts in two different languages blended into one garble and then the MAC-10 wielding gunman appeared from the production room and took control with several short sharp statements, shoving one of his compatriots aside.

The group now comprised eight armed men, spread out in the loose cover afforded by the vehicles and the equipment in the bay. One spooked figure crouching beside a van unleashed rounds into the upper section away to Shepard's right, his actions quickly brought under control by the barking of the figure who was now the acting leader. While he couldn't understand the language, Shepard had been in enough situations to know the man was organising a counter-attack, and he had to press his advantage or be overrun.

Raising the rifle, Shepard unleashed two three-round bursts into the side of the Sprinter, the first salvo punching holes into the driver's door and the second into the fuel cap. He risked a glance but didn't see the effect he wanted. He dashed to a second firing position as the group below unleashed a fusillade into the place where he had been a few seconds earlier.

Shepard aimed and fired again, this time rewarded with the sight of fluid pooling onto the polished concrete below the van. As he moved back to the first firing port, the men below returned fire at the empty space above.

Shepard thumbed his rifle's selector to auto and took aim, emptying the remains of the clip into the floor and up the side support pillar of the van. Sparks flashed with each impact.

Just as the clip clacked empty and Shepard dropped it for a reload, he felt a blast of heat and the pressure wave as the fuel fumes ignited in an enormous roar, and the vehicle below exploded in a shower of shattered glass and splintered metal.

## Chapter 45

Taylor hurried past the reception desk to where a huddle of employees sheltered. She dropped her weapon to her side and offered a hand to the first person she reached, a girl, barely out of her teens, wide eyed and trembling.

"Police. We have to get you out of here," she said to the group. "Line up by the door and when I tell you I want you to run as fast as you can towards my colleague by the gate. He'll direct you to safety."

No one moved.

"It's okay. I know you're scared, but we need to get you out of here."

The group flinched as another fusillade of gunfire rang out deeper in the building.

"What's your name?" Taylor knelt down. The girl's hand shook and her trembling lips moved, but no words came out.

"Come on. I'll help." With encouragement, the girl rose, gripping Taylor's hand as she led her to the door like a child. The rest of the group, under Taylor's encouragement, also formed up.

"After three?" She looked into the girl's eyes and smiled tightly. Shepherding her out the door, Taylor flashed a look over at the adjoining warehouse block where a serious amount of automatic gunfire was being exchanged.

"Go! Go!" She pushed the girl the first few steps and then she broke into a cowering run towards Macpherson, who was waving maniacally from the barrier. Taylor turned to the next in line and did the same again. As their colleagues bolted towards safety, the rest needed no encouragement to dash headlong across the car park.

Another crash of weapons rang out.

"Follow your colleagues, straight to the gate. No looking back. Okay?" said Taylor, lining the next two up at the door. Counting down, she then hustled them out.

"Is there anyone else in the building, anywhere people may be trapped?" Several blank stares and then an older gentleman nodded. His expression bleak.

"The packing and distribution area. We…" There was hesitation in his voice.

"Where?" said Taylor.

He pointed to a point beyond where the fallen body lay, blood now pooling from his fatal wounds.

"There are packers. We were told they are migrant workers…" His explanation ended abruptly as a shrill bleeping began to emanate from the fire alarm panel on the wall beside reception.

Taylor held him by the elbow as another worker sprinted for the gate.

"How do I get over there? Is there another way?"

He manoeuvred her to an A4 printout of the complex framed on the wall and traced a route through the office space and production plant. As he pulled away, she gripped his elbow and pointed at the pass around his neck.

He removed the access ID card, and she ushered him out the door just as the sound of an enormous explosion tore through the building.

As she was shaking the concussive blast from her ears, the fire alarm system came howling to life, klaxons and flashing beacons erupting in a wall of sound then, a split second later, the power went off.

❖ ❖ ❖

Shepard pulled aside the hatch and looked inside. Even though the power was off, there was still enough light coming from the ruptured skylights to see the women huddled on the floor away from the door. Slamming the hatch shut, he reached down, unlatched the locking bar and hauled the door open.

Terrified screams rang out and as one they scrambled away from him.

Snatching the mask from his face, he let the rifle hang on its sling and gestured that they rise, offering what he hoped was a friendly smile. None did. The majority cried, and those that didn't were seized by shock and fear.

"It's okay. Come with me. I'll get you out. Do you understand? Out?" he said, gesturing for them to herd out.

Pained cries called out from below as did the gruff shouts of re-organisation. The column of black soot and smoke that mushroomed up into the ceiling was filling the mezzanine space.

"Come on, we don't have time to debate this," muttered Shepard, taking a step into the room. He held his palms out. "Friend. Go, shoo, vamoose. Allez. Yallah."

One woman spoke, pointed to him and to his weapon, and then offered another rapid but incomprehensible phrase at the rest of the group.

"Friend." He pointed to himself and then out the door. "Bad men coming."

"I understand you."

Shepard pivoted to a young woman hugging her knees to his right.

"Thank God. Can you tell them we need to go? Right now," he said.

A secondary explosion from the burning van emphasised his point. Dust and flecks of oxidised steel coating drifted down from overhead.

The girl stood up and spoke. Shepard could see some faces react sceptically.

"Where are you taking us?" she asked.

The smell of burning was overpowering.

Good bloody question, sister, he thought, backing out of the door to check the stairs and mezzanine, but the group below remained preoccupied with their injuries and forming a strategy.

"Look, I don't know. But there's a fire now, and the police will be coming. They'll sort it out. Okay? The police, do you understand?"

She looked fearful at the prospect.

"For God's sake, come on!" snapped Shepard, losing patience.

A section of the racking had caught alight and the black smoke from the burning vehicle was getting out of control.

"You can wait for them to come and get you or you can come with me. The only other option is to stay here and burn to death."

"They took our money. Our documents," said the girl, conflicted but her eyes wide on the dancing orange light outside the room. Inside, several women coughed as the cloying sooty smoke built up.

Shepard shrugged.

"Miss, we need to go."

Two rounds cracked into the door frame behind him, splinters peppering his neck as he spun to face the shooter. A third shot missed, and more screams erupted around him as the stray bullet thudded into the external cladding.

Shepard fired low and blind, the high calibre rounds shattering packing crates. He caught the flash of scrambled movement, the shooter's eyes feral in the darkness as he burst from cover. Shepard lined him up and squeezed the trigger. His three-round burst found its target, and the gunman tumbled over the edge of the mezzanine.

❖ ❖ ❖

Taylor stepped around an overturned chair and moved with her weapon raised through an open-plan office space.

It was the usual fare, laptops in docking stations, PC monitors and bookcases full of revenue reports and order books. Plastered on the walls were mouth-watering images of overflowing restaurant tables, flaming barbecue pits, and glistening joints of meat.

Strategically placed emergency exit signs and the flash of sounder strobe units illuminated the darkness, and Taylor's eyes sought movement in the shadows, her hearing deafened by the ear-splitting electronic sirens.

Reaching a set of magnetically locked double doors, she swiped the access card. Nothing happened. A red LED glowed on the door's slimline lock and she gave the kickplate a testing shove with her foot, easing it open a crack. Shouldering the door aside, she entered a corridor, the howl less but still disorientating when added to the out of sequence flashes from the strobes.

Moving quickly, Taylor passed a meeting room, an admin storage space, and a kitchen, the double porthole windows affording a glimpse of abandoned lunches and spilt tea. As her focus returned to the corridor a door ahead swung open violently, a red strobing light showing a face as equally surprised as she was.

"Police!" she shouted over the din.

The figure, recovering, raised a stubby submachine pistol.

Taylor squeezed the Glock's trigger. As her first round hit centre mass she took a step forward and fired off another shot, catching the gunman high on the left shoulder. The muzzle flash and thundering discharge of the man's weapon briefly drowned out the alarms, sending clouds of plaster and chunks of suspended ceiling tile showering into the air.

Taylor kicked his weapon away and knelt, feeling for a pulse. The man choked. There was blood on his lips, and his eyes were wide as he fought for breath, a wet whistle sounding from his chest.

"Taylor to Control. Armed suspect requiring immediate medical attention. Secondary corridor from main administration area. Be advised the building is not secure. Repeat armed suspects still at large. Any units receiving proceed with caution." She lifted her thumb from the push-to-talk.

There was a bleep and an urgent buzz of reply in her ear, but it was lost in the wave of alarms.

The door had come to rest against the gunman's legs. She eased it open and stepped over the body, moving into a cavernous production space. The smell of detergent and disinfectants mingled with an overpowering smell of five-spice and broiling meat. Tall vats and cylindrical mixing and chopping machines were arranged in rows along each side of a gully protected by a wire mesh step-plate.

Taylor moved through the centre channel, eyes darting between the cylindrical gravity fillers and industrial ovens. Reaching the other side without incident, she pushed through a set of rubber crash doors and into another corridor. Catching her breath and her sense of direction, she thought back to the building layout and the hasty instructions of where to go.

Mercifully, the fire alarm sounders warbled to a stop, replaced by an intermittent and much less intense single long bleep every fifteen seconds.

So far, other than the gunman, the plant was empty. No staff. No contractors.

Nearby gunfire punctured the silence. Briefly checking her weapon, she moved on, mentally placing herself somewhere in between the administration block and the site of the explosion. As she rounded the next corner, she shoved through a set of crash doors into a packing area.

A long conveyor wound through the space; underneath folded packing material and plastic boxes were stacked ready for use. As she moved towards the opposite side of the room, a column of dishevelled figures, led by a bearded and armed man crashed through the set of rubber swing doors directly in front of her, blocking her path.

## Chapter 46

"Police! Put your weapon down."

Taylor flinched and let out a shrill scream of surprise as the heat and zip of incoming gunfire swarmed past her head. Chunks of wooden framing, packing crate, and the sharp report of rounds pinging off the conveyor assaulted her senses.

As the throaty roar of automatic gunfire erupted nearby, she scrambled for cover. The bearded man raised his weapon, unloading towards the gunfire.

Taylor rushed around the edge of a full-height metal rack, fighting palpitations and racing breath as more gunfire struck the uprights, muzzle flash highlighting the two shooters weaving towards her between the concrete stanchions and the framework of machinery and chutes.

Risking a look, she saw the bearded figure lunge forward to take cover behind an electric pallet truck and charging station. Rising above the machine's bodywork, he leaned on an elbow and thundered off a long burst towards the approaching gunmen.

The air stank of cordite and burnt paper. The group of women cowered and cried where they crouched in the cover of an alcove formed under a section of empty racking to the left of the double crash doors. Taylor ducked as another round buzzed past.

What the hell have I walked into? She thought, seeking options and stunned by the onslaught.

The bearded man had dropped his back to the cover afforded by the solid truck and dropped out an empty clip. He slammed a replacement home, gave it a slap, then racked the assault rifle and spun around the side to unleash another fusillade.

Taylor's ears rang with the sound of gunfire. Sensing movement to the right of the door she had entered, she caught sight of a crouching figure darting forward, raising a pistol towards the man and cowering women.

She leapt up, taking a modified weaver stance, and drew a bead, lining up the two luminous rear sighting dots with the single front aim point to form a tight row. She was on the edge of effective range, but she squeezed off two rounds. Both missed but forced the man to his right. His aim changed to target her, and both weapons fired at the same instant.

Taylor flinched as shrapnel peppered her cheek. When she looked back, the man was down, his face contorted and a bloody hand putting pressure on a wound where his shoulder joint met his chest.

The bearded figure continued to fire controlled bursts downrange of his position, his face streaked with sweat and soot. The women trapped in the middle of the mayhem were in a similar state.

Taylor had been on enough brothel raids and container lorry seizures to recognise the journey those fearful faces had been on. What she couldn't explain was why the two conflicting groups were playing out a gun battle over them inside an Albanian front business.

As more rounds zipped close, Taylor sought new cover, spotting the protected corners of a small administration space. A PC, printer, and rolls of labels sat atop a unit made from pallets and steel slip-plates and it offered more protection than the shattered shelving around her.

Just as she moved clear, a heavy kick in the chest lifted her off her feet and slammed her against the floor. The room spun, and she tasted dust and blood in her mouth. Her vision darkened, panic seizing her as she tried to breathe but couldn't pull in any air.

❖ ❖ ❖

Shepard sensed rather than heard the impact. He twisted from his position to see the police officer take a bullet and crash to the floor. The gunman responsible rushed from cover with his face contorted in rage whilst incongruously wearing a Simpsons tee shirt and patterned Bermuda shorts. The shooter swept his pistol towards the group of women, the bark of a shot winging one but sending the entire flock out from their flimsy cover like starlings fleeing a sunset bridge, their voices pitched in fear.

Shepard aimed and squeezed his trigger.

The two shots overlapped above the heart line while the third caught the man in the shallow dip of his chin. Blood and brain matter sprayed the concrete pillar that arrested his forward momentum as he fell.

Best laid plans, thought Shepard.

The kinetic crash and burn of the drug stash had now descended into yet another asset extraction under fire. He had liberated enough Yazidi women and girls from captivity in and around Mosul and Kirkuk to know their look; it was feral fear. He could guess the rest. There was always some asshole willing to exploit human misery, and these women had either been sold into slavery or tricked into paying some extortionate rate to trade the deprivation of wherever was home for the false luxury of the EU.

Shepard pushed up to a kneeling position. Bullets thwacked into the wooden pallets and zipped past him but he was calm in the face of the onslaught, unloading the rest of his magazine across the conveyor, suppressing the return fire for the few seconds he needed.

The police officer had rushed into the packing hall as he had been heading out. What he couldn't work out yet was where the rest of the Armed Response Unit was.

Shepard darted across the gap and flipped her onto her

back to assess the damage. Her eyes stared straight up, she was sheet white and she didn't seem to be breathing. Lifting her fallen Glock, he shoved it into the side panel of his webbing, then grabbed the collar of her body armour and dragged her into cover.

He pushed a hand up under her body armour, fingertips searching her ribs, over her stomach and along the breastbone for wounds.

She gasped. Her eyes squeezed shut and her hand snatched out to grab his wrist.

"Relax. You're not my type, love," said Shepard. He pulled his hand out. No blood. "You're all right. Can you breathe?"

Taylor gave an unconvincing nod and rolled onto hands and knees, trying to suck in air and lower her heart rate.

"It'll hurt like hell in the morning," said Shepard, returning his attention to the approaching enemy.

"It's stinging a bit now, thanks." Taylor rubbed the indent and scorch mark that the impact had left on her chest plate.

The sharp bbrrraaat, bbrrraaat of submachine pistols sounded from locations to the left and right of their cover. Incoming rounds buzzing like hornets to ricochet around their position. Shepard aimed his Kalashnikov and returned fire.

"You on your own?" he shouted, brass cartridges chinking off the ground.

Taylor smiled weakly.

"Fuck's sake." Shepard ducked below cover, glanced at the pale face and grinned despite the situation.

Taking an elbow, he emptied his magazine at one of the darting targets, a grunt and falling shadow suggesting he'd at least wounded the man.

"We have to move," said Shepard.

"Give me a second." Taylor blew out a breath and felt the ground swim beneath her.

Beyond the intermittent hoot of the fire alarm and the ringing in his ears, Shepard could pick out the two-tone blaring sirens of approaching first responders.

"We don't have a minute." He dropped the AK to hang on its sling and hoisted the police officer in a fireman's carry.

Taylor felt a wave of nausea as he upended her. The man paused by the cowering group of women to exchange words with one before ushering the rest back into the corridor from which they had come. Taylor could smell cordite and sweat off the man, but as soon as the crash doors closed behind them, the smell of burning diesel and smoke overwhelmed her.

"Left!" boomed Shepard as the group struggled through the smoke-filled corridor.

"Left, left, left." The assault rifle banged against his hip as he shifted the weight of the police officer.

He heard the heavy crash as one woman shoved the emergency exit bar and swung the doors wide, sunlight and cool air streaming in for a second only for it to darken a heartbeat later with the outpouring of smoke.

They entered a courtyard, framed on all sides by metal cladding rising to a patchy blue sky, dirty smudges of grey cloud that spoilt the overhead azure joined by a growing pillar of thick black smoke.

The women huddled in the centre of the outdoor space, three of them aiding a fourth who was in shock and bleeding from an arm wound. Shepard paused beside the trio, nodding and giving a smile of approval at the hasty dressing fastened above and over the wound. She'd live. For how long though was the trouble. The exit had corralled them in the small overlap where the three separate arms of the business met to form a lunch garden with no immediately apparent means of escape.

## Chapter 47

Elaine Weir stooped to pick up a stuffed pug pup from the footpath, then shoved the toy back into the pram beside her daughter. The little girl grabbed it by one ear and began chewing the other.

"Don't do that to doggie," admonished Elaine, glancing away as the noise of sirens and the flashing lights of police Land Rovers and estate cars sped along the main road past the mouth of the estate.

"Nee-naw! Nee-naw!" Freya squealed with delight, shaking her pet pug to within an inch of its life before letting it fly from buggy to footpath again.

"For goodness' sake, Freya!"

As Elaine wheeled the pushchair forward, her attention fell on a familiar figure who blocked the path ahead. He stooped to pick up the toy.

"Hiya, Freya! Remember me? Uncle Billy?"

Billy Webster waggled the toy in front of the girl's squirming hands, her face squashed in delight at the game.

"Doggie, doggie, doggie!"

"What's happened to you, Barney? Talking when you should have been listening?" said Elaine, looking over Webster's shoulder to where Barney Murray shifted nervously from foot to foot, his hoody drawn up to cover his head but unable to mask the blooming black and purple eyes.

"Give her the teddy back, Billy. I'm late for work. I have to get her dropped to our Jacquie yet and then get in before my da hits the roof."

Webster waggled the toy playfully before shoving it into the greedy hands, but he didn't move.

"Sure you don't work today, so why the excuses?

Somebody to see?"

"Billy, I don't have time for your messing about," Elaine snapped, impatient at the delay.

As she made to move past, Webster stepped in to block her. Murray doing likewise, she made to swerve around. Open mouthed and with her temper rising, Elaine only half noticed the red van pull up beside the kerb.

"You off to see your boyfriend, Elaine?" said Webster.

"Boyfriend?" She half laughed, confusion furrowing her forehead.

"Don't be acting stupid. Your boyfriend. The one we saw you with in Fearon that time."

"Tom…" Elaine snapped her mouth closed.

"Tom, is it? Where do we find Tommy boy then?" said Webster, a cruel smile on his face.

"I don't know. I…"

Webster smiled at the child chewing on the ear of her stuffed animal. When he looked back at Elaine, his eyes were flinty.

"Don't fuck me about, Elaine. We heard from Swampy that one of his punters got a kicking in your da's shop. You telling me that wasn't Tommy? Because it sounded very like him!"

"He's not my…"

"Where does he live?"

"I don't know."

She glanced back up the street, trying to figure out what was going on. The side panel door of the van parked kerbside was open and revealed a gloomy interior, its floor covered in an old cutting of oil-stained carpet.

Elaine jerked the pushchair back violently as Webster reached for it. Somewhere there was the slam of a car door and the sirens continued in the distance. She searched the street, but there was no one.

"Billy!" She screamed as he grabbed the front forks of the

buggy and jerked it from her grip, Freya wailing in fright and confusion.

"Barney! Fuck's sake, grab her will you," barked Webster as he shook the buggy free from Elaine's grip.

"What are you doing?" Barney Murray took a few paces forward, the panic rising in his voice and disbelief on his face as Webster shoved the pushchair complete with wriggling and screeching little girl into the van.

"We can't just leave her, can we?" he snarled.

Elaine Weir clutched at her stomach and screamed.

"Help! Please..." Webster stepped back out of the van, Freya crying uncontrollably for her mother.

Elaine stepped back from Webster and Murray, frozen on the path, looked past her.

It was only then she realised the trap, just as thick arms wrapped around her and propelled her forward. Her legs thrashing, she got a purchase on the door frame and for a moment felt the joy of resistance.

Then the blinding flash of pain across the crown of her head loosed the foothold, and she was pitched into the van beside the buggy. The door rasped closed and plunged them into darkness, and as the van sped off, she was thrown from her feet into the panel-work.

The only sign of the disturbance was a stuffed pug pup lying in the gutter.

## Chapter 48

The first two doors were fire escape exits with no means to open them from the outside. The third option was a half and half opaque glass panel door with a fat powder-coated handle and key lock.

Shepard reached out and twisted. The locks disengaged, and the door fell open.

Shifting the police officer on his shoulder, he peeked in. The corridor beyond stretched for ten metres in either direction. Strobes flickered on polished floors and reflected from poster-sized renders of haute cuisine. There was no sign of life.

He drew the Sig from the drop holster and called for the women to follow, steering them along the eastern route which led, as far as he could tell, towards the front car park but moving at a diagonal to the front gate. After passing through several doors, the corridors became more industrial, walls covered with crash pads and Acrovyn cladding before they opened into a larger production space.

Shepard paused and scanned the area, listening again for signs of a pursuit that seemed to have been abandoned. Whether that was because of the fire that had gripped the area following the van explosion or because of the arriving emergency services he couldn't guess and didn't care.

Illuminated fire exit signs marshalled the route out of the plant and he led the woman through the vats, gravity feeds, and huge ovens. Reaching the other side without incident, they moved into a Goods-In area.

The four roller shutter doors were closed, each with a single emergency exit alongside. Two forklifts charged beside pallet trucks and there were scores of plastic-wrapped cubes of unpacked deliveries cluttering the space.

Shepard set the police officer down against one of the blocks.

"Don't be doing anything rash. Get your breath back."

Taylor blew out a breath and nodded, her chest was killing her as pain continued to radiate out from the site of the bullet's impact.

"How is she?" Shepard approached the group of women who had laid their friend on the ground. The woman was pale. Her lips quivered and when he checked, her pulse was thready. The wound had soaked the dressing and the material of her long-sleeved tee shirt with blood.

"She's in shock," he said. The concerned and frightened faces looked at him expectantly.

"The police lady will help you from here, okay? She'll know what to do." Shepard nodded across at the recumbent Taylor.

The girl who had first spoken to him grabbed his arm.

"The men? They will come for us?"

"I don't think so. The police are here now, so I have to go."

"There are more of us!"

Shepard looked at the pleading eyes. He'd done enough, far more than he should have got embroiled in.

"Tell the police lady." He indicated Taylor again. She nodded once and returned to hold her friend's hand.

"You want to tell me who you are?" said Taylor.

Shepard crouched beside her and tilted her jaw to look into her eyes. The colour was coming back into her cheeks.

"I'm just a good guy doing bad things to bad people, officer."

"You expect me to buy that? Who are these women?"

Shepard shrugged.

"Mules. Slave labour. Who knows? That girl over there speaks English." He jerked his chin towards the girl. "She says there are more of them. Look, we need to part ways. Your mob is outside and I expect any of the crew that were in here have tried to leg it. There's a production bay on the far side of the building we came from, and I saw them cutting a large quantity of drugs. If the fire hasn't taken it, you'll have quite a haul. Might get you a promotion."

"It might take the heat off me charging in here without back-up," mumbled Taylor.

Shepard grinned.

"You've the heart of a lion."

"And you're under arrest," said Taylor, looking up at the soot-blackened face. The grey eyes that looked back were amused but resigned.

The packing case was obliterated inches above her head and Shepard shoved her down, throwing himself over her.

Bbrraaat. Bbrraaat. Bbrraaat.

Shepard snatched for the holstered Sig. From the corner of his eye, he could see the MAC-10 toting guard he had first seen outside bearing down on them, calmly dropping a clip to clatter on the floor. His clothes were blackened and the plasters on his face had slipped, revealing nasty wounds to his nose and lower lip. He slapped home a new clip, marching forward and taking aim.

Shepard felt the officer tug and jerk below him.

They were caught up in each other's limbs and tangled in his webbing. He couldn't clear his arm to fire.

Shots rang out. Shepard twisted his head away, the heat of rounds and assault of noise ringing in his ears until the sound of a slide lock-out ended the volley.

Taylor dropped her Glock to the floor and slumped back.

Shepard twisted off and observed her handiwork.

The gunman lay folded over on the ground. Five bullets grouped from stomach to upper chest. He was dead.

Taylor clunked her head back against the packing crate,

blood trickling from a cut on her temple.

Shepard looked down at her arm where it lay across his.

"I said, you are under arrest," she said.

The peal of sirens and the scrunch of tyres sounded from behind the roller doors. Inside the building, there was more movement, muted shouts and heavy footfalls.

"Armed police!"

Shepard looked down to where his wrist was securely fastened to the slender feminine one beside it by black anodised speed-cuffs. As he looked the woman in the eye, she returned a mischievous glint.

"You have got to be kidding me?" he said.

## Chapter 49

Chaos was an understatement.

If the scene outside the Corners resembled the Alamo, then this was the Normandy landings. Macpherson directed another ambulance past the cordon and pointed towards a small print works staff car park which had become a hastily arranged triage area.

The beetle black bodies and helmeted figures of the armed response team exited the admin area and moved back to the forward assembly point, one raising his voice in an authoritative request.

"Can we get the paramedics up here, please?"

Macpherson ducked under the tape and rushed forward to meet the armed officer.

"We've a colleague in there," he said.

"I know, sir," the officer raised a placating palm. "We need the paramedics up, there's a casualty inside. Can I ask you to let us… Oi!"

Macpherson, hearing enough, stepped past and jogged to the admin building.

The wind had turned and the column of smoke from the warehouse blaze was now drifting across the forecourt and over the industrial estate. As Macpherson hauled open the door, two fire tenders rolled up, their horns blaring and sirens flashing.

"Ronnie!" Macpherson tipped aside an office chair and briskly walked through the gloom, stumbling to a stop as he found the body of a man, gunshot wounds to chest and shoulder. Macpherson grimaced and moved on, lost in the maze of intersecting corridors and rooms.

"Ronnie!" he called. "Ronnie!"

Then he heard crying ahead.

"Armed police!" The challenge rang out from a young officer stationed alongside a group of women.

"Relax, son," said Macpherson, holding up his warrant card. "Do you mind pointing that somewhere else?"

The officer cradled his Heckler and Koch G36 carbine in the crook of his elbows.

"This lady's been shot. Team Lead has gone for the paramedics."

"I spoke to him outside. Get the roller door up, will you?" said Macpherson, nodding his understanding.

"Power's out." The officer shrugged.

"That's why there's a bloody chain attached to it, son. Get it open, then they can drive right in."

Macpherson knelt beside the injured woman and her two carers.

"Hang on in there, pet. You'll be in the hospital with your feet up and a tea in your hand in no time," he said, patting the woman on her good shoulder. "Any sign of anyone else?"

The armed officer was manhandling the manual lifting chain from its out of the way hook.

"No, we found them huddled here."

"He took her!"

Macpherson spun around to look at the group. One of the women sat up on her knees. She was dishevelled and dirty, maybe twenty years old but certainly not much more.

"Who took her?" snapped Macpherson.

"The man who saved us. He took the police lady." She pointed over Macpherson's shoulder between the racks of stacked goods.

In the distance he could just make out the flash of daylight where a door stood ajar, swaying open as it caught a draught of wind.

## Chapter 50

Gordon Beattie put down his coffee cup and dabbed his lips with a folded cotton napkin. The prickle of sweat erupted along his brow and down his spine.

"Mr Beattie?" His minder for the day, Jock Hayes, prompted him for a response, but his whispered words were still ringing in Beattie's ear.

Not now. Not fucking now. Beattie excused himself from the company of the four bank executives and the CFO of Finnrock. In the background, the soothing notes of Beethoven's Für Elise played from the integrated Bang and Olufsen sound system, but it was only when they were out of earshot he spoke.

"Which one, Jock?"

Hayes led him down the plushly carpeted hallway and held open the door of the meeting room that overlooked the River Lagan and the imposing figure of the Belle on the Ball. The twenty-metre-high Beacon of Hope in Thanksgiving Square stood proudly atop the globe holding her hoop aloft, the statue's stainless steel and cast bronze spirals aglow in the sunlight.

In the middle of the table sat a spidery conference phone which Beattie ignored, instead accepting the mobile phone Hayes removed from his jacket pocket. Beattie stabbed at the buttons.

"Amir?"

"Monster? They are saying it's chaos. Somebody hit the delivery. It's gone."

"All of it?"

"All of it. My fucking units are on fire and Bekim is dead. The rest are in hospital or have been arrested."

Beattie sat on the edge of the conference table, stood, pacing to the window and looking out over the ribbon of green-grey water and across to the Waterfront Conference Centre and the High Court.

"You can't put this on me, Monster…" Amir Kazazi was ranting, but Beattie wasn't listening. His mind was in free-fall. Fifteen million of product snatched away and his ultimate prize slipping under the rippling water of the Lagan.

"Amir, clear out and keep a low profile. I'm going to need you when I call. This isn't over."

Beattie flung the phone against the window and doubled up in a bellow of rage and frustration.

"Get me that!"

Jock Hayes crossed the room and picked up the handset, placing it in his employer's hand before returning to reset the blinds.

Beattie kicked over a chair as he waited for the phone to connect, wiping a hand over his sweating face and smoothing down his hair.

"Freaky, it's me. Have them clowns got that wee girl yet?"

## Chapter 51

"You'd think you'd be grateful. I just saved you back there."

Shepard set the police officer on her feet and they both looked back down the hill to the chaos below.

"Resisting arrest isn't doing you any favours," said Taylor.

Shepard pointed a finger at her. Sweat sheened his face from the exertion of carrying her from the plant and up the steep escarpment back to his motorcycle.

"Listen here, lady, I did you a favour. Have you any idea how much shit I've just taken off the street?"

"What do you want, a citizen commendation? You're charging about there with a bloody assault rifle."

"It's as well I am, or you'd be dead!"

"I think you'll find it was me that kept you from earning a hole in your skull."

Shepard jerked his wrist, tugging her off balance.

"Give me the bloody key!"

"No!" Taylor jerked back. It was a petulant gesture and only served to hurt her own wrist.

An arcing jet of water shot up from one of the fire appliances to douse the burning warehouse. The fire had spread up from its seat to lap along the roofline of the warehouse, but so far it hadn't got a grip on any of the other units. Through the tree line and brush of the escarpment, they watched one of the roller shutters lift and an armed officer step into the lot, hand on throat as he radioed in. Soon after, the blip and wail of a siren started up again.

"Who are you?" said Taylor.

"It doesn't matter who I am," said Shepard, his arm outstretched and rummaging in his rucksack for a means to unshackle himself.

"Well, do you have a death wish or something?"

Shepard huffed a laugh as he pulled out a small flat-edged screwdriver.

"Wouldn't be the first time someone asked me that."

"You know we can protect you? I know that warehouse was just a front. If you give them up, we can talk about a deal."

"I don't work for that crowd. Will you not give me the key?"

"What's it worth?"

Shepard glared at her.

"Did you shoot up the Corners Bar too?" said Taylor.

"No comment." Shepard gave her a sarcastic smile and returned to looking in the rucksack, finally determining there was only going to be one way out of the situation.

"That's a nice bike," said Taylor, noting the absence of licence plates.

"Didn't have you down as a petrolhead?"

"Are you one of Beattie's thugs?" said Taylor.

Shepard spun round.

"How about you stop with the third degree for a minute?"

Taylor shrugged and Shepard blew out a breath.

"No. I'm not one of Beattie's thugs, but I'll tell you what. If you let me out of this bloody cuff, I'll make sure Gordon Beattie gets what he deserves."

Taylor scowled.

"What? It's not like your face hasn't been in every paper and on every news channel over the last couple of months. I saw what you tried to do. Honestly, it sounds like you got screwed over and I'm sorry about that, but I'm not sitting about waiting on the creaking gears of justice to wind up anymore. It's time his past caught up with him."

"That's what that is all about?" Taylor pointed her free hand to the ambulances, blue strobing police cars and crowds of people making their way south from the cordon which now sealed off the factory gates.

Shepard heard shouting from the compound below, but the words were snatched away by the wind and the rustle of the trees.

"What did he do? Screw you on a deal? Put a price on your head?"

"Let's just say he took something from me."

"So what was that back there? You taking something back?" sneered Taylor.

"I'm nothing like him."

"The man running riot with an assault rifle? You could've fooled me."

Shepard's mobile buzzed in his breast pocket.

"You going to get that?" Taylor nodded down.

Shepard squinted at the screen. There was no caller ID. He pressed the end call button. Almost immediately it rang again. He swiped to answer.

"Hello?"

"Tom?" The voice was tense, sobbing. "Tom, they want to talk to you…" A ragged shuddering breath sounded on the line. "They made me call. They have Freya…" There was an anguished sob, then the sound of disturbance.

"Elaine?" Shepard gripped the phone, trying to refocus. Taylor's eyes narrowed, close enough to hear every word.

"Is that you, Paedo? You remember me, don't ya?"

"If you hurt her or the girl…"

"Aye, big man, you'll what? I'm making the threats here. We know about you, so keep your phone on and we'll tell you where to find her."

The line went dead.

"Fuck!" roared Shepard.

"What was that all about?" said Taylor.

Shepard gritted his teeth hard and screwed his eyes shut,

feeling the anger build.

"Hey, tell me?" Taylor shook her wrist, which in turn jerked his. "Is she in trouble?"

"Ronnie!"

Shepard's head snapped round. He could hear the jangling of the fence, and the struggle of someone peeling apart the damaged section below.

"Look, I'm sorry," said Shepard, his voice almost a whisper.

"Ronnie!"

Taylor glanced down the hill but couldn't see Macpherson. She looked back at the man she was shackled to, a narrow crease between her eyebrows.

"Sorry for what?"

His hand gripped her forearm as he reeled her in, firm and controlled, as if for a dance. His other arm swept around and under her chin in a choke, the vicelike grip of the rear hold compressing her carotid artery and the vagus nerve.

Taylor kicked out her feet, struggling to find release, but almost immediately felt her vision darken. The last thing she heard was another of Macpherson's shouts from somewhere far below.

## *Chapter 52*

"Is she okay?" DCI Gillian Reed stalked across the ambulance bay lobby to the nurse base where Macpherson was in conversation with a small woman in baby blue scrubs.

"Aye. Tough as her old man, that one," he said, nodding in acknowledgement.

"Oh, sorry, ma'am. I didn't realise you were here, would you like mine?" Erin Reilly, approaching from behind a pillar, passed across a plastic beaker of tea to Macpherson and offered the other to the detective chief inspector.

"Drink your tea up, Erin. I'm not staying. The chief super and the ACC are having a canary back at base. Is she awake?" Reed addressed the last to the nurse, who nodded.

"You can go in for a wee minute if you like. All things considered, she's right as rain to go home. We're just waiting on the pharmacy to send up some pain relief."

Reed smiled her thanks and allowed Macpherson to pull back the curtain to bay four.

Taylor looked haggard under the harsh lights, propped up at an uncomfortable angle and holding a swab of cotton on her inner arm. Her face was pale, her eyes red, and her blouse sleeve was bloody.

"Inspector Taylor. Good evening, you know I'm in two minds whether to write you up for a commendation or issue you a misconduct notice." Gillian Reed put a comforting hand on her inspector's wrist. "What were you playing at running in like that? You should have waited."

"I know, ma'am. I just… I don't know."

"At least you're in one piece, which is more than can be said for some. Have you handed in your firearm?"

"She has," said Macpherson.

The detective sergeant had graced the top of the escarpment in time to see the billowing dust cloud and hear the throaty roar of an escaping motorcycle. He'd found Taylor on her back, gasping for air but otherwise unhurt, her unloaded weapon beside her.

At once berating her and thanking God she was okay, Macpherson had pulled her head onto his lap and called in their position, but paying no heed to his complaints nor the hindrance of her injuries, Taylor had declined a blue light and so the two had walked back down the hill to the forward staging area where she had been triaged and handed her weapon over to the firearms officers to be secured for forensics. She was then taken to the Royal Victoria Accident and Emergency department in the back of a PSNI squad car, Macpherson at her side.

"Good. You know the drill. You'll be administrative until we have investigated the incident. The crucial thing is to get your version of events ironclad and cooperate with the investigating officers, okay?"

"Yes." Taylor nodded wearily. In the back of her mind, she'd known this would happen. A great big handbrake on progress while it could be proved she wasn't a trigger happy maniac in cop's clothing.

"Are the women and girls alright?" she said, shaking off the thought of being confined to barracks.

"They're fine. They are being assessed, but at the minute it looks like the usual. Paid for surreptitious entry into the European Union but duped to end up the victims of a trafficking ring. MacDonald's team are looking into the owners of the production plant now."

"I'd like to get back at it as soon as possible," said Taylor.

"Veronica, I know you do. With what we have found and the initial testimony of these women, I don't see a problem getting you reinstated to full duty asap. However, the only thing you are going to do today is take the co-codamol that the nurse has prescribed and the rest of your shift off. Tomorrow, too. You've been shot and strangled. You know how it works, write up your report while it's fresh and then get away home."

"I'm fine." She waved away the beginnings of Macpherson's scowl. "I am. There's nothing stopping me answering phone calls and mining the case database." She sat up straighter, grinding her molars to curtail the wince of pain. "The plant is a subsidiary for a front company owned by an Albanian gang. I should have received an intel packet from Juliet Sommers by now," she said, articulating what she knew in an attempt to prove she was fit for duty.

"Albanians?" said Reed.

"Amir Kazazi is the head man. We've also identified another member, Bekim Nishani. Nishani has been mentioned a few times in connection with Rab Millar's murder. The guy who…" Taylor drifted off a second. The guy who what? She put her thoughts back in order.

"I think the unknown from the plant was also behind the Corners, maybe Millar too."

"What?"

"On the hill…" Taylor screwed her eyes shut. "I can't remember exactly, but he mentioned Gordon Beattie."

"Veronica…"

"He took a call. If we can get a search order for cell tower comparisons from the attack on the Corners and cross match it with hits from around Signal today, we could strike lucky."

"DI Taylor…"

"Whoever he is, I think they have baited a trap to stop him…"

"Veronica!" Reed raised her voice and Taylor stopped.

"This isn't a debate. Write up your version of events and then home. No speculation. No suppositions."

Reed turned to Macpherson.

"God knows why, but I'm putting my faith in you she does what I've just said."

## Chapter 53

"Twenty minutes."

"You'd better be or I'll be up there after you and you'll wish you'd taken that bullet," grumbled Macpherson, turning to look out the windscreen as Taylor slammed the Vauxhall's door with a smile.

She keyed in through the code lock on the back entrance and took the stairs to the CID suite, feeling the strain and the swelling bruise on her chest with each step.

The incident room was busy. It had expanded now, with a corner being set up to deal with the evidence and analysis of the day's events in Mountainview Crescent. There were already several scene photographs pinned to the boards, including a few more gratuitous ones of the dead men, and a uniformed constable stood at a printer, lifting out headshots for each of the women. Phones rang and the urgent murmur of conversation thrummed as the swing shift and uniform officers hurried between duties, ferrying collated reports and transcripts, and snatching up receivers. There was an air of professional urgency. Overseeing it all, Phillip MacDonald stood, hands on hips, his sleeves rolled up and his striped tie loosened, the weight of the week evident in his posture.

Taylor avoided him, eager to escape another debrief, and logged into her PC. As the server booted up, she found the intel report on Kazazi had arrived and forwarded it to MacDonald, then opening a new mail, she fired off a quick message to Diane Pearson requesting an update if it turned out any weapons used at Mountainview matched those from the Corners attack.

Taylor took a long breath and loaded her after-action report, recalling the events of the day from arriving at the vehicle barrier to waking up gasping for breath with Macpherson swearing like a sailor in her ear. She stuck to the facts. Recounting the three men she had shot and documenting her own injury and aid from the unidentified male, detailing the flight from the warehouse and compound and his insistence he was not part of either gang but harboured a grudge against Gordon Beattie. She read over it twice, both times considering if deleting the references to Beattie may be better, but in the end, she left it as it was and hit send.

She was moving the cursor to log off when a mail dinged in from Jack Collins, reminding her that the invitation to question the lawyer wasn't open indefinitely. He had attached a summary of what had they had gleaned so far from the initial questioning, interviews with his spouse and his financial records and medical reports. Without reading, she downloaded them as PDFs and sent them to her own secure cloud account so she could review them from home.

A quick skim through the rest of her inbox rewarded Taylor with an email from Deborah Sall listing clients who had shared Sanctuary accommodation with Lena, and a report from Carrie on what she had gleaned from Companies House on Miltek and its recent acquisitions. She downloaded these too, and tasks complete closed down the PC and flicked off her lamp, sneaking back out before anyone noticed her.

❖ ❖ ❖

Gillian Reed let out a slow breath and adjusted her jacket, then knocked on the door. Without waiting for a reply, she opened it and walked in.

ACC Ken Wallace and Chief Superintendent Law sat diagonally opposite each other on the breakout sofa seating of the chief super's office, a carafe of water and two tumblers between them.

"Gillian. Any news?" said Wallace, remaining seated.

"The scene is secure and forensics are going over the building, but it's as the initial report states. Fire damaged a section of the distribution centre and there are at least seven UI males shot dead with a significant quantity of narcotics seized."

"The civilian casualties?"

"Minor injuries. One woman received a GSW and is undergoing surgery to remove the bullet. She should pull through."

Ken Wallace uncrossed his legs and stood, taking a deep nasal breath as he paced to the window and peered out. After several moments, he turned to look back at his colleagues.

"These women? Have we any updates on the circumstances of how they came to be there?" He leaned back on the sill and crossed his arms.

Reed moved to one of the single chairs and sat.

"A request has gone out for an interpreter so that we may collate statements officially. Unofficially, one of the group has undertaken the role in the interim. She claims she was duped by what appeared to be a legitimate advertisement for work with Signal Meats on an internet jobs board. The others had paid to be smuggled across jurisdictions for work or to claim asylum. She confirms, like herself, most of the captives are from the border areas between Bulgaria and North Macedonia, and all had passports and identifying documents seized by the OCG. This group was unpaid labour, but she claims another group had recently been moved on to forced sexual exploitation."

"The gunmen?" said Wallace.

"At least one remains at large and of the seven dead we are trying to match to known offender profiles."

"This has got completely out of hand," said William Law. He held a legal pad on his knees and scribbled bullet points of Reed's report. "This has now escalated beyond anything we expected. For goodness' sake, I warned you at the start of the week we did not want this descending into an all-out turf war and now look. This is going to call for a multi-agency task force and you know the strain that will put on budgets when…"

"William, we all know where we stand with budgets and we just have to work with it. What's done is done. The immigration service, NCA and the Police Ombudsman's office will all be involved in this so can we just set up designating reporting lanes and contact points," said Wallace, waving a dismissive hand and moving back to the seats but not sitting.

Law frowned but gave a nod of compliance.

Gillian Reed considered her next topic carefully. She could fully anticipate William Law's reaction and had considered withholding until she could sleep on it, but her intuition and Wallace's acknowledgement it may come up through inter-agency findings or forensic reports tipped her hand.

"Sir, Detective Inspector Taylor believes the gunman at large may also be the individual responsible for the attack on the Corners Bar and the murder of Robert Millar."

"Ridiculous. How can she know that! I've her report here." Law flicked through his notes. "Are we to believe he's some sort of vigilante?" Law gave a scoffing laugh. "It's nonsense. Where did he get access to the weaponry and his intelligence for a start? This is part of a group feud." He emphasised the point, stabbing his legal pad before flicking back a few pages to a heavily inked report.

"It's a blessing Veronica Taylor is on administrative pending investigation because…" He raised a hand to ward off Reed's objection. "I have it here in front of me, Gillian. She was shot and I quote 'suffered a period of unconsciousness arising from strangulation.' This at the hands of the man she claims saved her and this group of refugees or whatever we are designating them." He threw his hands in the air and gave a dramatic shrug. "I'm not having the investigations into any of this week's events dissected by the DPP because Taylor jumps to conclusions and is likely too stubborn to take the mandatory rest period while under investigation. I shouldn't need to remind you how many claims for stress and burn-out are hanging over the department already."

"Sir, Veronica Taylor might be impulsive and prone to following her gut, but no more so than any of us would have been at her stage in our career. She has shown extreme courage, twice this week, and she gets results. We are better off with her on board."

"Your opinion," said Law.

"What have we got on this man who she claims aided her?" Wallace moved again to perch on the edge of Law's desk.

"Precious little. IC one male, mid to late thirties. Diane Pearson's team has the handcuffs and Taylor's firearm to try to lift prints or a DNA sample to run against the database."

"We won't hold our breath then," muttered Law.

"Sir," said Reed, addressing ACC Wallace, "Taylor believes this man's motive extends beyond these attacks. He referenced Gordon Beattie as a target."

"Oh, for the love of..." Law dropped his pen onto the pad. "Can we ever move past that man!"

"William, be quiet for a minute," snapped Wallace. Law picked up his pen and shook his head in silent irritation.

"Was there a specific threat?" said Wallace.

"Not in her report, sir. He said that given the legal route against Beattie had failed, he would pursue action against Beattie by his own hands."

Wallace pursed his lips, a deep line furrowed between his eyebrows as he considered the news.

"Have you notified him?"

"No," said Reed.

"Leave it with me. I've already spoken with his legal team regarding him helping quell the recent tensions, so I'll advise Mr Beattie of the threat myself. If in the meantime, anything turns up on this gunman, vigilante, I want to know straight away." Wallace looked at her, waiting on a response.

"Yes, sir." Reed nodded and Wallace, now satisfied, sat back down on the chair he had vacated and took a sip of water.

"We'll let you get back to it, Gillian. Keep me informed. We're going to have to put our heads together here on how to bring the various branches involved together," he said.

Law nodded, saying nothing nor looking at Reed.

Reed gave a tight smile and stood, then left to return to the incident room, neither offended nor surprised at the dismissal. She knew Wallace and Law were of the old brigade. Happy to accept her input when it suited, but covetous of the political positions their own roles afforded them. Law was particularly eager to be acknowledged as the figurehead when success was in the wings, and when not, well, she wouldn't be surprised if he was plotting to jettison any blame onto her and the team rather than confront the surgical precision with which he had wielded his pen in cutting resources and funding to her officers on the front line.

She hadn't made DCI without understanding this was all part of the game, but it didn't mean she had to like it.

## Chapter 54

Taylor winced as she shrugged on a hoody and padded barefoot to the kitchen where she collected a fat bowled glass from the counter and a bottle of Casillero Del Diablo from the wine rack. Returning to her spot on the sofa, she cracked two co-codamol from a foil packet and knocked them back with a slug of the wine and the hope it wouldn't be too long before they kicked in and nudged the edge off the dull ache on her breastbone.

The television flickered mutely in the background as she waited for the early evening news reports to come on. Not so much to review the day's events, but to see who the talking heads would choose to blame for a running gun battle and a trafficking ring operating under the nose of local authorities.

She swirled the wine and took another sip. Her chest hurt and she tentatively touched it, considering how fortunate she had been and that a bruise was a small price to pay. She had been lucky.

The consequences of running into the building hadn't been a total afterthought, although now she found herself confined to base, stuck on phones and collating case data, regret was rearing up and not for the first time she wondered why they issued firearms if the consequences of using them felt like a punishment.

Her laptop chimed to life and on entering the passwords to get into her accounts, she clicked the tab to download the files on Bryce Baxter. As the pop-up appeared and began the countdown, her thoughts turned again to the loop connecting Millar, Lena Borodenko and the Corners Attack to Baxter, his company, Sanctuary and finally Morrow and Burke. There was a thread there, she was sure of it, but the unpicking was proving difficult.

Flipping open an A4 spiral pad, she drew a mind map, Millar in the centre with squiggled spider legs leading off his name to Miltek, his Albanian connections and Gordon Beattie. Carrie's report had identified eight properties purchased by Miltek that the business still held and another four offloaded to an affiliate company of which the Miltek board was nominated as a minority shareholder.

The process helped her visualise and hypothesise, allowing her to make intuitive leaps that might lead to a new train of thought or an insight that opened a new line of questioning. To the right-hand side of the page, she drew and circled a large question mark that represented the latest piece in the puzzle. Who was the mystery man disrupting organised crime and what were his motives? From the question mark, she drew two lines, marking the connected boxes as 'Personal' and 'Professional'.

Her phone chimed. Macpherson checking she was alright. She replied with an affirmative and an emoji which she knew he hated and dropped the handset onto the sofa, pulling the laptop forward to read the reports after Sunday's incident.

She had been on her way back to barracks when a car jumped the lights at the end of Victoria Street and Queen Square and she saw there was a tussle happening inside, the flurry of arms and erratic driving threatening to see the car mount the pavement or swerve into the oncoming lane. A patrol vehicle and a second car roared out of High Street in pursuit, and she jammed on her blue lights and followed. When the driver took another wild turn into York Street, swerving at the last minute to go the wrong way down North Street, Taylor picked up pursuit. The car eventually ran out of road and mounted the kerb, crashing into a set of traffic bollards set at the entrance to the Rosemary Street pedestrian precinct. As Taylor jerked off her seatbelt, the driver stumbled out and made a run, swerving her in an attempt at escape through the honking traffic in Waring Street. The cries of a child and the whump of the crashed car catching fire distracted Taylor from pursuit.

The rest had played out in a blur. Fighting the rising heat, she had pulled open the rear passenger door and hauled out a hysterical woman and baby, both stinking of accelerant. Soon after, the scene was chaotic as fire, ambulance and police services jammed up the junction with Taylor remaining a reassuring presence at the woman's side until the call had come in about Millar.

Bryce Baxter was apprehended and taken to Musgrave Street, where it was established he had been drinking. Cautioned for driving under the influence and several driving offences, he was held on suspicion of assault occasioning actual bodily harm. His defence was that he was trying to get his wife to hospital following a severe bout of mania where she had threatened him and their child. Reading the scene notes from the follow-up at their home, there had certainly been a domestic disturbance.

Taylor skimmed the rest. Baxter was treated by a custody medic for minor cuts and whiplash, given paracetamol for the short term, and then he clammed up.

Blood tests confirmed he was over the alcohol limit, at which point he advised he required his blood pressure medication. Sequestering his GP medical report confirmed a repeat prescription for doxazosin and one for Gemifloxacin.

Clicking open Google, she searched for both drugs.

Placing the largely untouched wine on the coffee table she studied the open A4 page of her mind map, letting the wheels spin as her attention flicked between it and Baxter's case report, her eyes catching a single line that she had missed on her first skim through. She paused and read it again, then clicked open the email list from Deborah Sall, scanning the information until she found what she needed. The link cut an arrow into the heart of one theory. As she considered the implications she clicked back to Carrie's financial findings, and found muddled in amongst the entries a name she recognised.

After a moment's thought, she took the wine goblet to the kitchen and sloshed the contents into the sink, rinsing away the residue before grabbing her mobile, thumbing through her contacts list.

"Jack? It's Ronnie Taylor. I need another favour."

## Chapter 55

Bryce Baxter was red faced with sweat beading his upper lip and he fidgeted every half minute or so, fussing his feet, or shifting in his chair.

Taylor looked from him to his solicitor, a willowy woman in an expensive skirt suit. The nib of her pen hovered over an open moleskin notebook as she spoke.

"What has this to do with any of the charges against my client, Inspector?" Her voice was crisp and tinged with the air of superiority. "I mean, you didn't drag us in here just to evaluate his ongoing health conditions?"

Taylor smiled with one side of her mouth and blinked away a retort, settling back in her chair. Jim Collins picked at the edge of a supermarket brand notebook looking as frayed as the page ends.

"You're looking a bit peaky there, Mr Baxter. You keeping up with the heart tablets?" said Taylor.

Bryce Baxter began another routine of left foot, right foot, shoogle in the chair.

"I've ready told him." He pointed a finger at Collins and then at his own chest, right about the spot where Taylor's bruise pulsed below her denim shirt. "I'm the victim here. Me! It's Jacinta is the one needs to be locked up. For her own safety." He dropped the finger and ran a hand through a floppy fringe, his hair the colour of straw left too long in the sun.

"Your wife?" said Taylor, nodding at her notes.

"If we could move past stating the obvious, Inspector." The willowy woman tapped the heel of her pen against the smooth cream pages of her book.

"How long have you been married?" said Taylor.

"Nearly two years," said Baxter, cutting over the tut of his brief.

"And your son is what age?"

"He'll be coming eight months in August." Baxter frowned at the questions.

"Nice age, still learning new things, huh? How did you meet your wife?"

Baxter looked to his solicitor who raised her eyebrows, then nodded.

"I met Jacinta through work."

"She was a colleague?" said Taylor, frowning.

"She was a colleague. Sort of. She was a liaison officer between her employer and Harper, Baxter, Brooke."

"Which is your father's business?"

"Yes. Inspector, what's the point here? She was a housing officer, and her role was to draw up sale and lease agreements for her clients and liaise with our office on contract completion."

"A housing officer for Morrow and Burke?"

"Yes," said Baxter.

"And before that?" Taylor cocked her head as she waited for the reply.

Baxter's solicitor cleared her throat.

"Inspector, can we stick to anything relevant to the charges against my client? I hardly think Mrs Baxter's employment history has any bearing on…"

"You claim Jacinta has been suffering post-natal depression which has now manifested into violent outbursts," said Taylor, drowning out the words of the now scowling solicitor.

"Yes. I've been through this." Baxter looked to Collins, who nodded in confirmation.

"DI Taylor is just confirming what you told me, but if there is anything you left out or wish to change, you may," said Collins.

"I'm telling the truth," said Baxter indignantly; his brief laid a palm on the table and shook her head at him. Baxter fell quiet.

"Mr Baxter, your neighbours have made several noise complaints over the past three months. At one point officers attended your home on reports of an ongoing fracas." Taylor set out a page with the times and dates of the calls and summary reports. "My colleagues have some concern you and your wife were arguing a lot and there was a suggestion during her interviews she has tried to leave you several times."

"Leave me? She'd never leave me," Bryce Baxter scoffed.

"You seem fairly sure of that?" said Taylor.

Baxter retreated from his arrogant outburst.

"Why would she? We have a child and she wants for nothing."

"Very different circumstance than those she used to be in," said Taylor.

Baxter blinked and looked away.

"You were introduced to Jacinta through one of your other clients, weren't you?"

"Inspector…" Taylor offered a conciliatory hand to the solicitor.

"Okay, we'll come back to that. Explain what happened on Sunday evening?"

"I was out in the afternoon and when I arrived home, she flew into a rage. I found her upstairs wrecking the house."

"So she was already in an agitated state?"

"Yes!" snapped Baxter, throwing his hands in the air.

"Is one of the side effects of your medication a reduced stability of mood, propensity for sudden anxiety or feeling agitated or angry."

"I don't know," spluttered Baxter.

"You never read the leaflets?" said Taylor.

He placed both hands on the table.

"No. Not really, do you? You just take them. For God's sake, I didn't buy them off the internet, they were prescribed."

"Inspector, can we get to the point of why my client's heart medication is of a sudden interest to you," said the brief, her lips then pressing into a tight line of impatience.

Taylor drew out a printed pamphlet and turned it to face them.

"I'm not interested in his heart medication. I want to know about this."

The printout was of a patient information leaflet for Gemifloxacin, a broad-spectrum antibiotic.

Bryce Baxter flushed as the solicitor eased the paper across, skimming the details.

"It's an antibiotic, prescribed by his GP. Your point?"

"Mr Baxter?" said Taylor.

Baxter's dance began again. Right foot, left foot, shoogle in the chair.

"It's treatment for a sexually transmitted infection, isn't it?" said Taylor.

Jim Collins shot her a look, and the solicitor held up her hand to forestall Baxter's answer.

"I don't see how this makes any difference and as we've been over everything else with your colleagues, I believe it is time to end this." She closed her book and raised an index finger at Baxter.

"You know Robert Millar, don't you, Mr Baxter."

"Who…" began the brief, but Taylor held up a hand to quiet her, the solicitor casting a frosty glare.

"Would you like to tell us the nature of that relationship?"

Baxter leaned forward and frowned at the patient leaflet with glazed eyes.

"He was a client."

"You're aware he died then?"

"It's hard to miss the news, even when you're stuck in here," said Baxter.

"What about Lena Borodenko? Is that name familiar?" Taylor watched as the muscles of his jaws flex and he sat back.

"Inspector, if perhaps you can offer a suggestion why these people would have any bearing…"

"You met your wife through working with the Sanctuary organisation, isn't that correct?" said Taylor.

"What has…"

"She was introduced by one of your Sanctuary clients, Lena Borodenko. They shared the same accommodation."

"I still don't see…" Baxter's eyes narrowed as nervousness was overcome by fear.

"Court records show your firm represented Lena at her hearings and with her other legal problems. Now, it wasn't your name on the submissions but you did sign off on her case when it came to final accounts."

"We might have an exclusive arrangement with Sanctuary, but I can't remember all my past clients," said Baxter.

"Surely you'd remember her?"

Baxter flushed.

"I know your wife was leaving you because you were sleeping with prostitutes, so, is that where you were on Sunday, rekindling that prior relationship with Miss Borodenko?"

"I must object to this…" said the solicitor.

"That's the reason for the fight and the reason for the antibiotic, isn't it? It's the treatment for more than one particular ailment but it's not the first time you've been to the GP for similar prescriptions, is it?" Taylor waited for the man to respond. He didn't.

"That's what this latest row was over. Jacinta had endured

enough." Taylor pulled a section of printed paper from her notes. " I've just spent the last two hours at a women's refuge hearing the side of the story you pressured her to keep hidden. The first case was eighteen months ago with another just after the birth of your child, so I'm guessing once bitten, twice shy didn't cut it for you."

The accusation seemed to hang on Baxter like a yoke, pressing him down into the seat.

"Yes," he breathed. The solicitor scowled at the admission, flipping open her notes and staining the page with an indecipherable scrawl.

"Yes to which?" said Collins.

"Yes, that is the reason for the treatment and for the arguments." Baxter's face glowed in shame.

"Daddy won't be too chuffed, will he?" Taylor blew out a breath, pointedly looking at the solicitor who ignored her and continued to scribble. "Did you meet these women through Robert Millar?"

"Don't answer that," the solicitor snapped.

"Why not? It's a simple question."

"Inspector…"

"Well then let me ask this, have you ever heard of Havelock Holdings?"

"Can we stick to one line of questioning…"

"Were you with Lena Borodenko on Sunday?"

Baxter didn't answer, so Taylor took a punt.

"Did Lena Borodenko tell you she was pregnant with your child?"

The blood left Baxter's face.

"Did you then go to Rab Millar, your client, her employer and tell him to fix it?"

"Inspector!" Baxter's brief snapped her notebook shut. "Please. Perhaps this might be a reasonable time to ask for a break? I'd like to clarify some things with my client."

Taylor nodded. Satisfied that for perhaps the first time on the case, she was on to something credible.

## Chapter 56

The Jaguar XJ swept along the tree-lined avenue past well-maintained hedgerows, wrought-iron railings and automated gates. A few cars, luxury models one and all, sat kerbside, but mostly they were ensconced behind the secure facades of each detached red brick house.

"Just a moment, sir." Malcolm Howard's driver indicated and pulled over.

"What is it, Adrian?"

"Not sure, sir. Stay in the car a moment, please."

The large executive car purred as it came to a halt short of the high black gates that protected the threshold of the Howard residence. Ahead and barring the entrance was another vehicle. Adrian, Howard's regular driver, exited the car, the interior light illuminating and a bright warning chime sounding as he did so, the door closing behind with an expensive clunk. Almost immediately the rear passenger door opened, and a figure folded himself in beside Howard.

"Christ. What the..."

"Evening, Councillor. I enjoyed your speech the other day."

The driver's door reopened and a new driver climbed in, knocking the car into gear and, taking direction from the man now luxuriating in the leather upholstery in the rear passenger seat, moved off.

As the Jaguar passed the blocking vehicle, the carriage lights beside his front door came on and Howard saw his wife's face in the window, concern or consternation on her face, he couldn't decide. Adrian was climbing into the passenger seat of the blacked-out SUV. Howard swivelled his head to further decipher the scene now behind him.

"Where are we going? Where's Adrian going?"

"Relax, Malcolm. We're going a quick run. Your driver will meet us later and drop you back home." The man's smile was generous but devoid of any warmth.

"Are you insane? Even if the curtain twitchers on the road missed that stunt, what the hell am I supposed to tell my wife?" Howard spun on his new passenger and thumped the headrest in front of him.

"How is Daphne? Keeping alright?" said the man, disinterested at the show of aggression.

"Let's hope she hasn't already phoned the police, of course. Christ, that's all I'd need," raged Howard like a tempestuous child, his ravings falling on deaf ears as his fellow passenger gazed out the window as the prosperous suburb flashed by.

"I don't think she'd be one to call in the law, Malcolm. The women's section at Maghaberry wouldn't suit her social aspirations. Anyway, I heard the recycling centre was doing a fair trade in her gin bottles lately but I suppose when you're married to such an illustrious legislator who's working all those hours in the public interest, it must get lonely knocking around that big house on your own. What's another half hour to her?"

Howard's lips twisted, his teeth bared as he ground out a retort.

"Fuck you. I told you discretion was paramount if I was to play my part in this, Beattie." Howard slumped back in the leather seat, staring at the roof.

Gordon Beattie ignored him. The car accelerated through traffic onto the A55 ring road, on one side the manicured lawns of a public park and on the other rows of white stucco apartment blocks. The traffic was light for a Monday afternoon and the car made brisk progress. They swept in silence onto a roundabout, the second exit taking them onto the B170 where they climbed uphill; a glimpse of the illuminated Parliament Buildings flashed between the trees as they climbed higher, leaving the city in their wake.

Beattie fished inside his overcoat and removed an envelope which he set on the armrest between them.

"I think if you are going to lecture anyone on discretion, Councillor, you'd better have a word with the wee man downstairs."

"What's this?"

"Call it an incentive to realign your focus for the next few days."

Howard stared at the envelope. Indecision gnawed at him but inquisitiveness won over. Tearing it open along the seam he dared peek in then withdrew a glossy eight by ten.

"How did you get these?"

"Does it matter?"

"It does to me! Is that bitch in on your scheme?"

"Now come on," said Beattie. "How I come about my source material is irrelevant, but as a matter of fact, no. She is not in on my scheme, and I guess she would be equally mortified if those found their way on to the editor's desk at the Sunday World."

The photographs were not grainy black and white's that could be argued as indistinct or easy fakes. They were a mixture of both wide-angle and close-up high-resolution photographs. Full technicolour pornographic stills from his trysts with Jane Richards. Howard returned the pictures to their envelope and placed them into a back pocket of his zipped folio case.

"Is it too much to hope that these are the only copies?"

Beattie sniffed. The cool look answer enough.

"Malcolm, I never intended to resort to blackmailing one of my partners."

"Spare me, Beattie. We were never partners."

Beattie snarled, and for the first time, Malcolm Howard

noted the agitation behind the nonchalance of his tone and the redness in his eyes.

"I've had it up to here today, Councillor. I've too much at stake, and you are an integral part of this. The plan has changed and because of that, I need people I can trust. The question I am asking myself is, can I still trust you?"

"Is there honour amongst thieves you mean?" Howard scoffed.

"Malcolm, let's not beat about the bush. That is exactly what you are. A thief. A damn good one, I have to say. You might not like it, but you just wear a different mask to mine."

"We are not the same," said Howard.

"Really? Well, I suppose not. You're cheating on your wife, and deceiving friends, colleagues, and the people and organisations who blindly put their faith in you. You, my old mucker, are the lowest of the low. You portray one face and hide the truth of the other."

Howard looked winded, the movement of the vehicle and the stuffy atmosphere choking him. Absent his tie, he unbuttoned his shirt another notch and stretched out the collar.

"On the other hand, I am who I am," said Beattie. "My mistakes are there for all to read and discuss. The difference between us is, I have made it to the position where people don't care anymore. They're happy to just reach out and snap up the donations. It's hard to hate the man building schools and community centres." He looked out the window at the passing countryside as he spoke.

The Jaguar indicated, taking a slip road, the suspension doing its best to cope with the rutted concrete lane before it drew to a stop. Beattie let himself out and cool air rushed into the cabin. Howard shivered, aware suddenly of just how tightly he gripped the folio and the feeling of his shirt stuck to his back. His door opened and Beattie's man peered in.

"Sir?" He presented a palm. Howard could smell stale smoke on his breath as he got out and walked across to stand a few paces behind Gordon Beattie.

"Are you committed to this?" said Beattie.

"Of course I am," said Howard with a tut.

"I need fifteen million and I need it to be untraceable."

Malcolm Howard felt the cramp of vomit in his gut.

"I can't just…"

"You bloody can't or won't?" roared Beattie, rounding on the councillor. "You established the procurement lines for my companies, organised the renewable contracts into shell companies that you control." He let the words sink in. "You've actively diverted capital funds to projects that don't exist, and you've benefitted from all this up until now with zero hassle from me. Now you are going to step it up and get me a liquid fifteen million."

"When you start moving that sort of money people notice. What if someone decides to excavate the paper mountain? All that comes back to me. I may well be two-faced and greedy but I'm not bloody reckless!"

"You've been defrauding the public purse for years and gotten away with it, Malcolm. Where's the sudden worry come from?"

"I am playing the system as the rules allow," Howard protested. "It's why I have no problem taking my cut and how you've managed to get your dubious funding and your dirty cash washed despite your problems, so don't pretend you've been doing me a favour."

Beattie looked out across the darkening sky. His head was banging, the pressure in his sinuses painful. He was too close to throw in the towel and let the victory slip away.

They stood on a high outcrop, a deep crater hewn in the earth many feet below them. Industrial machinery lay quiet for the night in the depression below, the tyre tracks winding in concentric circles around the lip and meandering into the huge breaking sheds. A few lights remained on in a two-storey prefabricated office complex in the distance. Forestry and reservoirs spread out beyond that before the myriad of a hundred thousand city lights cast an orange glow into the heavens, the black sliver of Belfast Lough slicing through the middle.

"The thing about pressure is you don't notice it at first, it creeps up until there is no escaping the crushing grip. The key to survival is knowing when to release the safety valve or bring to bear a greater pressure," said Beattie, turning to face the pacing councilman.

"Are you threatening me?"

"You're thriving on the scraps I throw you. I don't hear you whining when it's all going well and you've lady muck on her back! Suck it up, Malcolm. Arrange the money."

"You're a two-bit backstreet shit, Beattie," sneered Howard. "A predator. Those photographs show your true nature. Just because you wear a fancy suit and play businessman doesn't…"

The words died in his throat, a choking gurgle escaping his mouth. His eyes bulged in terror as Beattie moved with shocking speed and lanced a stiff fingered jab to his throat. Grabbing the lapel of his jacket with the other hand, Beattie pivoted the gagging Howard around on unsteady legs and shoved him backwards over the precipice.

Howard's arms pinwheeled, his feet scrambling for purchase on the shale surface as Beattie's strong grip held firm, preventing him from plummeting to a messy death on the rocks below.

With a sudden reversal of movement, Beattie tossed him safely onto the filthy ground.

"I have the power to end you, Councillor. I'm not talking about having you smeared all over those rocks and then disappeared into the crushers either." Howard scrambled away from the edge, pale at the threat.

"Once I've let the lads teach you some respect, I will ruin you. Your family will disown you and they'll be left with nothing once the Assets boys get stripping away. Your wife will be destitute if she doesn't follow you into the cells and you can forget your mother seeing out her days in that fancy old folks home. Your peers will be appalled, and the press will have a field day. You will be going down for a very long time. If you've any notion that the time will be easy and you'll be tucked away in a wing of your own, think again." Beattie loomed over the fallen man and grabbed him by his collar, dragging him to his feet. Howard's knees scraped along the ground, his shoes scuffing as he tried to get his feet under control as Beattie propelled him against the boot lid of the Jaguar.

"You think you're the only player of significance I have in my pocket. I have police. I have judiciary. I have industry. I own the fucking prison bars you'll be languishing behind. You are a cog, Malcolm," hissed Beattie.

The boot of the car swept open with a quiet click, the interior swathed in blue polythene tarpaulin.

"I'm sorry. I'm sorry. Don't do this…"

"Why not?"

"I'm useful. You know I am," begged Howard.

"You're an irritant and a liability. I need that money and if you won't get me the money, then you're no good to me!"

"Please, don't do this."

Beattie released his grip and Howard slumped against the car, breathing heavily. A set of headlights swept over him as a vehicle made its way down the rutted lane towards them. The sound of Beattie's laugh was cold.

"You really are a spineless bastard, Malcolm," said Beattie.

Howard's head slumped forward in shame, his cheeks

burning. He shivered uncontrollably as adrenaline overloaded his central nervous system.

"Can you make this work?" said Beattie with finality.

"Yes," croaked Howard, feeling a surge of bile rise.

"Get your shit together, Malcolm. No more fucking distractions."

"I swear."

"I need your head in the game. I lost an associate this week and a fortune today, the profit of which was going to pay you back the money you offset from your pet project."

"I'll sort it. Give me until the end of the week."

"You have forty-eight hours to get the money authorised."

"I can't get that in two—"

"You'll get it or I swear to God…"

"The Sanctuary funding was for eight hundred grand!" protested Howard.

"So do your magic. You'll get your cut plus three per cent."

"There's procedures. I need time to circumvent them. I'm telling you transactions of that magnitude will come under scrutiny and I'll end up with an oversight committee…"

"Don't worry about an audit."

Howard's mouth opened and closed. He couldn't find any words.

Beattie straightened him up and dusted him down, then opened the boot again so that he could see his alternative.

Howard tore his eyes and imagination away, now able to see the second vehicle was the one that had blocked his driveway earlier. Adrian stepped out with no apparent concern. Beattie nodded in passing, stopping as he made to enter the rear seat.

"Don't disappoint me, Malcolm," he called.

Howard, no longer able to control the build-up of tension vomited violently, clinging to the boot of his car as Beattie was driven off.

## Chapter 57

Elaine Weir shivered, her back pressed against the damp brickwork of a windowless room, exhausted but alert, her tears cried out, but still trembling with emotion.

Somewhere beyond the black door with its peeling paintwork, she could hear the mewling cry of children. She tried to pick the sound of Freya's from the chorus and on at least a few occasions gasped and cried out in futile desperation as she heard her daughter's cry.

She did not know where she was. Occasionally a low vibration rumbled through the floor. Perhaps heavy traffic passing a short distance away, the sound though was absent, suggesting they were a distance from a road, perhaps even under one. She had glimpsed sky through a rapidly closing shutter door as they had hauled her out of the van and into a factory or warehouse, a cavernous space of dusty purloins and high vaulted ceilings, with the smell of fuel and the sea in the air.

The events played in a nightmarish loop. The darkness as the door slammed closed and the disorientating journey in the racing van, Billy Webster cruelly separating her from her child once he hauled the side door open. Telling her she could see her daughter again once she'd made the call.

That call had been hours ago, and since then there had been nothing but the intolerable gnawing of fear. Elaine rubbed away tear tracks.

She wasn't alone but sat apart from the other women locked in the room with the black ghosting of mould on the ceiling and a bare concrete floor. No one had responded to her pleas. They all recoiled as she begged for her child's return, each with their own pain stamped in soulless eyes and wrapped up in their own nightmares.

She rocked back against the damp brickwork, her index finger clamped between her teeth. A single tear rolled down her cheek.

She stood up at the sound of approaching feet. There was a rattle and rasp as the door was unbolted from the outside and then with a sudden precision and violence, another woman was thrust into the temporary cell.

She slumped to her knees and sobbed as the door closed behind her. Elaine waited to see if anyone would go to her, but they didn't. The woman's face was bruised, a purple halo around her eyes turning amber at the edges, and she had a nasty cut on her nose. Elaine pushed off the wall and wrapped an arm around her, guiding her to her feet and across to her space against the wall.

"You'll be alright," she said soothingly, as though talking to her daughter. Knowing the lie but unable to face the truth.

The woman held her hand. Her nails were chipped and knuckles scrapped.

"I am Lena," she said.

Elaine Weir nodded, a hundred questions for the woman, but asking none.

## Chapter 58

Shepard picked up the phone, checked the screen, then threw it down on the sofa again.

He towelled off his damp hair and pulled on a fresh tee shirt. His clothes from the raid on the production plant were now flopping about in the soapsuds of the washer-dryer, the weapons stripped, cleaned and oiled, ready for use again.

He crossed the room and peered out at the burned down hulk of the maisonette flats. The area remained cordoned off with fluttering tape, although the Škoda Octavia police cars and their occupants had now gone.

As he watched, a team of council workers pulled up in a low flatbed lorry. Disembarking in hi-vis coveralls, they began clearing ash and debris from the path and the road outside the ruins. They crisscrossed the road, using a truck-mounted bowser to hose down the blackened paths, pausing as a recovery truck pulled in, its blinking yellow lights strobing across the wet walkways. It stopped and, after a brief word and direction from one of the council workers, drove around to the rear of the premises, a large claw-mounted arm ready to pluck the burned-out wreckage of Harry Carruthers' van from where it lay.

Shepard crossed back to the sofa and checked the phone again. No calls. Putting the edge of the hard plastic to his forehead, he cursed.

Since receiving the call, he had carried out several counter-surveillance sweeps before returning to the lock-up and then to the flat. He had known his actions would put him at risk and in a way he welcomed it. That was the point. To amp up the pressure and force Beattie's crew to lash out. To make a mistake and offer him a shot at bringing down the house.

Now, with it likely one of the kids working the stash house across the street had ID'd him, it was time to leave the flat and set up a new base of operations.

He gripped the phone and closed his eyes. In taking the woman and her daughter, they had made a mistake. He didn't know Elaine Weir; he didn't have any feelings towards her either way, bar his ingrained moral code to step in to champion those unable to defend themselves. He didn't know why he did it; more often than not he put it down to being in the wrong place at the wrong time, although more recently he realised it was a position he put himself in. Removed at a cautious distance but close enough to engage as threats would arise. A sheepdog circling the flock.

One thing was sure, waiting was not a viable option. Not only did the inactivity ramp up the feelings of impotency, but it also meant that Elaine and her child were at greater risk of coming to harm. Shepard's mind went back to the young woman at the nightclub, the extent of her beating, and the vile threats Millar had been making.

The driver of the recovery truck had lowered the stabilising arms and unhooked the controller, stepping around the chassis for an unobstructed view. A group of youngsters on their mountain bikes had gathered at the fringe of the car park to watch and hurl abuse.

Shepard's TETRA radio murmured from atop the drawers and his thoughts turned to the raid. The police officer's face stared out from his open laptop. Detective Inspector Veronica Taylor. Lauded or vilified depending on which article you read. The column inches leaning towards her being a fine officer with an exemplary track record with one stain, her failure to put away the kingpin, each article referring to the cat and mouse between her and Gordon Beattie.

It took some guts to come charging in with no hesitation, knowing it would put her on the bench until her actions were picked apart to satisfy official bureaucracy. One thing was for sure, she was on the same path as himself, gunning for the scalp of Beattie and his organisation. Shepard's problem with her was one of trust.

He sat down on one of the kitchen bar stools, plugged the phone into the USB cord, and launched the tracking app and an open window.

Gordon Beattie had surrounded himself with a web of advisers and had the influence to disrupt and usurp investigations into his businesses. Only Taylor had come close. Thumbing through the open dossier on Beattie and some of his closest cohorts, he considered what use it would be to Taylor. Would she have the stomach for the shit that would rain down if she used it, or would even the hint of acting on it end her career?

The two vehicles from the stash house were still transmitting. The one from the food production plant now blinked from a housing estate that bordered onto the major arterial routes through the east of the city, the other from an industrial unit set within the larger sprawl of the city's docklands. It would be a total presumption that either location was where Elaine Weir was being held, and it would be a risk to even try to find out. Shepard looked again at the phone, frustrated by the knowledge he would have to wait. He passed the time by preparing himself for the summons that would come while figuring out how walking unarmed into the mouth of the beast could end with Gordon Beattie atoning for his crimes and Elaine Weir and her child walking away unharmed.

He looked into the detective's eyes staring at him from the laptop. Whether or not he trusted her, his option of going it alone seemed to only end one way.

## Chapter 59

"So he's admitting to the charges?" said Macpherson.

"He is. His wife had confronted him over another infection and financial statements in her name that she wasn't aware of. The accounts are associated with an investment company Carrie linked to Miller and Miltek through the paper trail. Baxter, by his own admission, says he freaked out when she cornered him. I think he knew it was all unravelling and it was only a matter of time before we were at the door anyway."

Taylor sat at her desk. Macpherson opposite frowned as he made a mess of cutting into a fresh scone with a flimsy plastic fork, a small foil pack of butter, and jam at his elbow.

"Do you want half?" he said.

Taylor declined and lifted the coffee he had brought her.

"You should be at home," he mumbled through a mouthful.

"I can't sit in the house and I might as well be useful in here."

Macpherson slugged some tea, brushing crumbs from his lap.

"And he says he knew nothing about Lena's punishment beating or where she is now?"

"He's adamant on that. Agrees he confronted Millar once he found out he'd caught a dose of the nasties but Millar gave him short shrift and sent him packing. He couldn't have had any contact with Lena since because he's been in custody from Sunday night."

"We're no closer to finding her or finding out if he's the baby daddy."

"That revelation caught him off guard, but he's sticking to

not having seen her since her time in Sanctuary," said Taylor with a disbelieving shake of the head.

"We're certain that he didn't go back and have a crack at Millar?"

"He wouldn't have the balls for that and the timeline doesn't fit. It's a pity we've no CCTV from Speakers Square."

"Aye, I was thinking about that," Macpherson tapped his nose. "I might be able to help."

"How? You can hardly change the batteries in the Sky remote."

"Do you want to know or not?" Macpherson scowled. Taylor, smiling, raised her hands in surrender.

"The Crab and Keel."

"The seafood place?" said Taylor.

"Best surf and turf in the town."

"You're an egg and bacon soda man, since when did you eat in Michelin star restaurants?"

"I'm not a complete heathen. Anyway, long story short. It's across the square from the apartments and I play poker with the manager. It's a punt, but he's going to set me up with copies of their CCTV that covers the street."

"Happy days. Fingers crossed then," said Taylor.

"Yeah, if anything, it might prove this Baxter's a lying piece of shit and he couldn't keep away from the place."

"Maybe. Now, what are we going to do about our other problem?"

"Mystery man?"

"Tom. I think? I overheard most of the conversation. The woman who phoned him was called Elaine. I got the feeling she was in trouble."

"Trouble that comes from knocking about with men who shoot up the bars and businesses of organised criminal gangs. She'll be no better than him," said Macpherson, aiming the crust of the scone at his inspector.

Taylor drained the rest of her coffee and slung the plastic beaker into the bin at her feet.

"My head hurts trying to put this together. He has an axe to grind with Beattie, I'm sure of that."

She got up and considered the disjointed pieces on the extended incident board. Her desk line rang, and she picked it up.

"Taylor."

"Veronica. It's Diane Pearson."

Taylor hit the speaker button and waved Macpherson closer.

"Go ahead, Diane. I have Doc with me here."

"I've the preliminaries back on the brass from the firefight. It looks good for a match on the Corners shooting."

"How long before we can say that's a definite?" said Macpherson.

"Another twenty-four hours. We've also got some fibres from the teeth of your cuffs. Not much, but again we'll be running them against what we got from the scene in Risky's nightclub and the Corner Bar."

"Thanks. You'll keep me updated," said Taylor, blowing out a sigh that it wasn't more.

"Absolutely, but I have something else."

"Okay?"

"We caught a match on the cartridges recovered from the street outside the Corners."

"We're all ears here, Di, spit it out," said Macpherson.

"Well, I hope you're sitting down. I'm ninety-five per cent certain they match casings we collected at the scene of another murder."

"Which one?" said Taylor, leaning forward on her elbows in the expectation of a new lead.

"Martin Coleman's."

❖ ❖ ❖

"Did I not tell you to go home?" Gillian Reed slid her keyboard away and motioned for Taylor to sit.

"I'm fine, ma'am."

"That's not the point, is it? I don't want to give the chief super any reason to question you over decisions or strategy that you make or sign off on that might come under the scrutiny of the DPP at a later date. Veronica. You were shot, and you killed a man. Several men."

"I know, decompress and recuperate. I've been through the training courses, but with respect, we both know the investigation is better served with me being here."

Reed shook her head and set her glasses on the table.

"I've just had an email from Leonard Gilmore. He's pressing ahead with the charges against Baxter," she said. Taylor nodded.

"He's admitting the attack on his wife. Connecting him with Rab Millar is a bonus, and I'm sure he'll break and confirm my suspicions about Lena. I've requested his accounts be scrutinised and I'm expecting to find a connection to the Miltek property deals and a trace of embezzlement or laundering."

"Good, keep me informed," said Reed. "Was there anything else?"

"I've just been on a call with Di Pearson."

"Oh?"

"A weapon used in the Corners Bar attack is likely to prove a match to the one that murdered Martin Coleman," said Taylor. Reed held her composure.

"Close the door, Veronica."

Taylor stood up and did as requested.

"Who else knows about this?"

"Just Doc."

"Okay. I expect you're bringing me this for a reason?" said Reed.

"We've been looking for a motive for Rab Millar's killing. I didn't think it was inter-rivalry. Same with the Corners attack and Billy McBride. But now we have one thing connecting all those players. It's Gordon Beattie."

Reed pursed her lips.

"Go on."

"We know Beattie came to prominence after the death of Coleman," said Taylor.

"Agreed, but he also wasn't in the same county where the hit was carried out."

"That's what the reports say, that both he and Billy McBride had solid alibis for the night. But if Freaky Jackson was in the Corners Bar when it was attacked and his back-up was outside with this firearm, then sometime after the Coleman killing the murder weapon made it into the hands of Beattie's crew. Maybe he didn't pull the trigger, but what if he placed the gun in the hand that did?"

"I can't see Gordon Beattie being behind the hit on Coleman, Veronica."

"It wasn't weeks after, Beattie put McBride on the boat to England."

It was difficult given the passage of time for Reed to give a solid assessment of the hypothesis as she had been a junior rank serving in the north-west at the time.

"Beattie had to be seen leading the hunt for who murdered his mate, and McBride isn't the type to keep his mouth shut, so it's only a matter of time before someone fills Beattie in that McBride is chatting about their arrangement. McBride is already public enemy number one so Beattie takes action, he has McBride exiled, and keeps the murder weapon as insurance. Taking the glory and the crown," said Taylor.

"I'll have to take this to ACC Wallace. He's only after setting up a meeting with Solomon Reeves to tell him you think Beattie's in the sights of this mystery shooter."

"He's the missing piece. Millar, the Corners, the drugs den on the Fearon Estate and now today. All these are linked to Gordon Beattie's underground activities."

"Veronica, you need to be wary here. Beattie is fresh off the hook…"

"That's why this fella has come out of the woodwork. We couldn't nail Beattie to the wall, so he's going to do it for us."

"Getting him off the streets is as much of a priority as any of the rest of this," said Reed.

"Agreed. Did you consider the RIPA? If we can match the phone data to cell towers, we might get a hit."

"I'll have it taken care of. In the meantime, if you can't take my advice and go home, see how we are coming on with tracking down this Jackson character."

"Ma'am." Taylor stood and as she pulled the door open, Reed spoke, her tone firm.

"Keep this Coleman thing under the radar, Veronica. Understood?"

## Chapter 60

Taylor made her way back to the CID floor and as she skirted the incident room could see Erin Reilly tucking a strand of hair behind her ear as she spoke animatedly to Macpherson. Chris Walker hovered over her shoulder, batting Macpherson's hand away from a packet of Tayto cheese and onion potato crisps.

Macpherson raised an eyebrow, and she shrugged.

"Erin, what's up?" said Taylor, approaching the trio.

"The blood on the couch at Webster's address isn't human. That's the first of the good news."

Taylor sat on the edge of the desk and waited.

"Once we established we hadn't a murder scene, the search team went to town. Apart from the SIMs and burner phones Chris and I recovered, the dog found a cache of cocaine and cash hidden in a manufactured recess in the hot press. They also recovered a couple of knives and a deactivated firearm. The sort of thing you hold up the corner shop with."

"Good. That's one more thing to have them up on, but, are we any closer to finding the buggers?"

"No. They're still in the wind, but we have been down in the dungeon with the tech team all afternoon cross-matching anything we can get from the SIMs. The hope was to get a hit on another active burner."

"Did you get one?"

Something in the excited expressions told her they had. Macpherson had his elbows planted on the table and his chin on his fists.

"Better than that. Someone got sloppy. We have a call to a registered mobile number and it flagged up as someone you know," said Reilly.

"Me?" Taylor looked at each of them with a confused expression.

Reilly nodded as Walker filled in the missing detail.

"Bryce Baxter, and it gets better. I took a run upstairs and had a word with Jim Collins. He agreed to sign over Baxter's mobile for a quick look and there were dozens of calls between Baxter and the burners, so he certainly had some link to Jackson's crew."

"He's a solicitor, might be he was the man to keep them right if they fell foul of the law," said Macpherson. Taylor shrugged.

"Erin, get this to Jim and see if he can squeeze anything else out of Baxter. If we have him tied to Jackson, get his explanation, and sit in because he may spill locations we can run down."

Reilly gave a thumbs up.

"Guv, on the evening of his arrest, Baxter made four calls in the space of half an hour," continued Walker.

"To this crowd?" Macpherson waved a hand across the desk, indicating the SIMs and mobile phones.

"No, Sarge. To Daphne Morrow of Morrow and Burke."

Taylor walked away from the table and looked up at the incident board, again trying to form the pieces together in her head.

"Could have been innocent?" Macpherson said, again playing devil's advocate, but the tone in his voice hovered somewhere very close to sarcasm. He shrugged. "You've just landed home to a row with the wife who has found out you've given her a dose, and have been using her name to stuff a few dodgy bank accounts. Who are you going to call? The local real estate agent?"

"Jacinta Baxter used to work for Daphne Morrow," said Taylor, half to herself. She turned back to the desk.

"I'm not going anywhere, so I need you lot out on the

ground. Where's Carrie?"

"Still with fire investigation. She was hoping she could liaise with Di Pearson over the trace drugs they found in the van and what they are getting from the factory to see if she can link them to the same batch," said Walker.

"Thanks. Doc, I want you to pick Carrie up. She's been to Morrow and Burke before, so she should sense if there's been a seed change in attitudes. Ask about that wee girl, Rachael, too. Erin, Chris, I need more proof off those phones. Especially if any other SIMs have links to Morrow, her business or anything else associated with Millar, Baxter or Gordon Beattie. Call patterns, dates, geo-locations if you have them, the heap. We need to pinpoint Freaky Jackson and his crew before our man with the machine gun does and we're playing catch up for the fourth time this week."

*Chapter 61*

"You can't park here."

"Carrie, we're the police. It's a perk of the job."

Macpherson had bumped the passenger side wheels of the Mondeo pool car up onto the footpath between a dented dustbin and a Saab convertible. Its broad backside however extended into the single lane of traffic forcing cars to swing out over the central white line and as he flung open his door, the backwash of hot exhaust from a passing silver van swept over him causing a momentary splutter.

Cook, exiting onto the footpath, faced no such dangers. Just the squeeze out of the door, which was impeded by the council bin.

"You'll get a ticket."

"Carrie." Macpherson opened his arms wide then dug in his pocket for his warrant card, which he waved. "We're engaged in the line of duty."

"Won't matter round here. They'd book their own granny. Come on, it's up the street a bit. Sarge?"

Macpherson stood looking in the window of a home bakery. He pointed at a selection of iced German biscuits.

"Remind me to pick some of them up on the way back out. It's a wonder the ones they sell in the canteen don't have a health warning. I broke a tooth the last time I bit into one, you know."

Cook grabbed him by the sleeve and under protest he allowed himself to be dragged away.

❖ ❖ ❖

"Not here?" said Macpherson, voice rising in surprise.

The vacuous expression looked back before momentarily breaking into a smile.

"Morrow and Burke. How may I direct your call, please?" The bright red lips smiled into the microphone of the headset as manicured fingers danced across a telephone console. "One second, Ms Neill. Transferring you now."

The same receptionist from Carrie Cook's previous visit repeated her unhelpful answer.

"No. Ms Morrow is not here."

"Do you know where she is?" asked Cook.

"I wouldn't be able to help you with that. No."

"Are you not supposed to be helpful? First face of the business and all," said Macpherson, plunging hands into pockets.

The receptionist just cast her blank expression on him and then returned to typing. Cook was unsure if they taught the look to deal with aggrieved clients or it was a dangerous dose of Botox.

"Is Miss Sharp available," asked Carrie, a polite and patient smile in contrast to Macpherson's scowl.

"She is not."

"It's very quiet in here today? Is it a bank holiday or what?" said Macpherson.

The receptionist didn't look up as Cook followed Macpherson's gaze into the office, which several days earlier had been buzzing with activity but now was serenely quiet.

"Is Rachael working today?" asked Cook, turning back. Macpherson was thumbing through a selection of marketing material and periodicals, his attention piqued as he selected a brochure with Daphne Morrow on the cover and advertising a selection of warehouse units for immediate let.

"Can I help you?"

Cook turned towards the voice. Macpherson returned the brochure and rocked up on the balls of his feet.

"And who might you be, sir?" he said.

"I could ask you the same thing."

Cook recognised the work supervisor who watched the desks in the rear space.

"We're the police, mister?"

"I recognise you from earlier in the week, Constable. What's this about?" He pointed at Cook but spoke to Macpherson, who stepped forward and introduced himself.

"Detective Sergeant Macpherson. My colleague here was following up on some information your office promised regarding certain property deals and a dead man, but you don't seem to be in a hurry and she's too polite to badger you. I tagged along because I thought my bluntness might get the ball rolling, so to speak. What's your name, sir?" He reached out a big paw but didn't offer a smile.

The man stood his ground and looked at the outstretched hand, nonplussed at the statement.

"Is that relevant?"

"It's just so when my superiors ask how the enquiry into dubious property dealing by a dead gangster and a top-end leasing firm is progressing, then I can note in my report that I spoke to a figure of authority."

"I'm not a manager here."

"Really?" said Cook, surprised.

"I'm afraid so." The smile was nearer a sneer as he nodded. "Miss Sharp is otherwise engaged today, and Ms Morrow has been off ill. If you leave some details, I'll make sure they are both notified so we can get your enquiry resolved. I'm sorry you had to call all the way out again." He smiled again, but it was just a muscle movement. There was no intent behind it.

"Oh, it's no bother." Macpherson stepped away from the interaction. "We can call anytime. It's much more helpful if you can cooperate. Once we apply for warrants and that, well, you know. It gets messy."

The other man stared at Cook with the same studious glare he'd given the office staff a few days previous.

"Can I take a copy?" Macpherson pointed to a company newsletter.

"Be my guest. Our agent contact details are inside if you see anything you like. We have some nice property that you might be able to afford on a police officer's salary."

❖ ❖ ❖

"Cheek of the bugger."

Macpherson gunned the Mondeo past the old Moravian Church and King William Park, jumping the amber light onto Belfast's Golden Mile.

"Eight grand I paid for our house. Eight grand! Do you know what it's worth now?"

Cook concentrated on the traffic in front as he looked at her from the driver's seat, shaking her head.

"Aye, well. Neither do I but it's a damn sight more than eight grand, I'll tell you that," huffed Macpherson, his eyes switching back to the road.

"Do you know where you're going?" said Cook, gripping the overdoor handhold as he swerved around a bus and then dabbed the brakes as he was met with a line of stationary traffic. Red tail lights glowed as far as they could see.

"Of course I know. I checked before we left the station." He indicated right, avoiding oncoming traffic around the Istanbul Food Market and pulled onto Botanic Avenue, heading towards the leafy streets of South Belfast.

"That was one way!" Macpherson shook his head at the complaint and opened his mouth to speak.

"We're the police," muttered Cook in a mock impersonation. "So, you dug out the address just in case?"

"Carrie, I've been a copper since you were…"

"In my nappies, you said. Repeating yourself is a sign of old age you know?"

The dome of the Palm House in Botanic Gardens blinked into view and then was gone, hidden by the trees of the park and the facade of the McClay Library. Macpherson swept left past the Union Theological College to shortcut through the tight streets of Victorian terraces making up the Holy Land. Cars parked kerbside narrowing the tarmac like an Ulster fry narrowed the arteries. A pedestrian jumped back to safety between parked cars at the last second as the Mondeo roared on.

"Do you think she's really sick?" said Cook.

"We're going to find out. If this bloody traffic will sort itself out." Macpherson leaned on the horn as he crossed the Ormeau Bridge, throwing up a hand as he was cut up, narrowly avoiding a collision. He craned his neck to get a better view of what was going on ahead. "Aye, might of known it'd be you lot!"

Ahead, a group of Lycra-clad cyclists, three abreast and oblivious to the chaos behind, clogged the inner lane.

"Watch out!" shouted Cook., as he pulled across the central white line and floored it past the bikers, a silver Renault swerving into the bus lane to avoid an impending head-on disaster.

"Relax, Carrie. I did a course in high-speed pursuit." He looked across at her again. "This is a walk in the park."

Cook said nothing, her grip firmly secured on the door handle, her eyes scanning the Morrow and Burke newsletter on her lap. She had it open at the first page, showing a pitchy sales blurb on a new serviced apartment development alongside a set of glossy photographs. Several well-dressed figures sat around a polished walnut table. One of the women was one of the Stepfords she recognised from her last visit to the management company, another was Jane Richards from Sanctuary. The photograph identified her neighbour as Frank Poulter from the Ethical Banking Trust, then there were a few faces she could place as Belfast City Council members but only one woman whose face she could pair with a name.

Sweet treats and china cups sat at their elbows. It was a self-congratulatory piece on Morrow and Burke's continued support for Sanctuary and the announcement of a further bespoke development: a new residential scheme to be built in tandem with support from both the council and a private equity team supported by Poulter and the EBT. Just one person was missing from the image. Daphne Morrow.

"Why would they say she was at this meeting yet she's dodged the glory photo?" said Cook.

"You know what these people are like, Carrie. Secret squirrel."

"She wasn't there was she?"

Macpherson pulled a sceptical expression in response as he slowed the big Ford to a more sedate pace as he turned off the country-bound A24 and into the tree-lined Hampton Park. Gnarled tree trunks and broad branches shaded the road and offered seclusion to the detached, red brick, Edwardian properties set back from the grass verges and footpaths. Large gates closed off most of the houses, their original wrought-iron gates refurbished and framed by ten-foot pillars. Others had chosen more modern and automatic affairs with ornamental knockers and video intercoms.

"Here we go," said Macpherson as he pulled up on the verge.

There were two entrances to the Morrow-Howard home. The vehicle gate, with a letterbox inset, was closed, while halfway along the perimeter a pedestrian gate was ajar.

The property was surrounded by a waist-high wall in the same shade of dark cream as the gate pillars. A gloss black decorative iron fence was inset into the wall, behind which a well-tended hedgerow screened the lower aspect of the house from prying eyes. A crushed gravel path wound its way through raised borders and an immaculate striped lawn. Both gates had an intercom station.

"You ringing?" asked Cook.

"Gate's open. Come on."

Macpherson eased the garden gate aside and crunched up the path.

The double front entrance doors were the same gloss black as the gates and wide open. Sunlight filled the porch, and the original decorative copper detail in the window panels of the inner doors glowed.

Macpherson gave the glass a rap. He could see into the hallway. The walls were decorated in a thick yellow damask paper which perfectly coordinated with the gold wall-mounted lights, mirror and a chandelier with an oak leaf design that matched the trees dotting the grounds. An unlit but set fireplace dominated the hallway. Brass tongs, scuttle and bellows stood ready for use on the tiled hearth next to a pyramid of dried logs. To the left of a broad staircase was a table holding a glass vase of orange lilies. Beside the table stood a travel bag. He rapped a second time, calling out.

"Hello?"

From somewhere inside he thought he heard a door slam, or something heavy topple.

"Keep an eye here, Carrie. I'll have a juke around the back."

"Have you a landline number?"

"No. It's unlisted. I'll be back in a sec. Give them another shout there in a minute."

"Watch they've no hounds round there," she warned, miming a snapping mouth with her hand.

Macpherson shook his head. It wouldn't have been the first time a homeowner had removed an overzealous ankle-biter from the hem of his trouser leg.

He negotiated a small patch of grass, and then his footfalls crunched through more gravel as he rounded the rear where a conservatory overlooked a long lawn surrounded by the same high hedgerow and screening trees. Inside, an indoor palm sat between two white sofas and a set of dining furniture. The whole floor space was white tile with black accents. The property reeked of wealth.

Macpherson scanned the garden for the lady of the house, but there was no sign of anyone, just the sound of the breeze through branches and the trill of suburban songbirds. Even the hum of traffic was so dulled as to be non-existent. A MINI Countryman was parked opposite another gate that split the hedgerow and led to a lane. Gathering his bearings, Macpherson surmised it was some sort of forestry track that would lead to one of the adjoining roads or the golf club, two hundred yards away beyond the dense tree line.

He reached out to try the handle on the conservatory door, and it opened. Presenting a problem. Procedure said no. His curiosity, however, was most definitely saying yes.

*Chapter 62*

Taylor checked her watch and cracked out two co-codamol, flicking the pills into her mouth and taking a swig of coffee to wash them down. She instantly regretted it, the liquid long since having gone cold.

She hadn't heard from Doc or Carrie, and with Walker and Reilly deep into a trawl through call records, she rose from her seat with a copy of Diane Pearson's initial ballistics reports and made her way up to the canteen where she ordered a fresh orange juice and cereal bar before descending via the rear stairs to the old admin block. The carpet tiles gave way to tired linoleum as she followed her nose to the records room.

She flicked on the desk lamp and tried to ignore the flickering overhead lights, the static hum and clicks sounding as though the ghosts of the case files were trying to manifest their venting voices through the tubes trapped electrons and gases.

A younger Gordon Beattie stared up from the file. Age had improved his looks. In the picture he was gawky, a lot thinner, and absent one of his trademark four grand tailored suits and designer ties.

Macpherson's initials were recently marked in the margin of the title page alongside a long list of others. She had not really quizzed him on his findings, concluding from the shrug and the brief synopsis that it was a dead duck.

She scanned the signatures and the dates from the original enquiry to a second review, then an independent review by the assistant chief ombudsman and a few passing inquiries by officers who she knew had worked the Loyalist gangs each side of the Good Friday Agreement and through the later feuds. After years of dust came the fingertips of the HET. She scrawled her own mark into the ledger.

Flipping through, Taylor paused when she got to the ballistics report, pulling out a page and comparing the document with Pearson's recent findings.

The original document had a succinct summation, both from the then state pathologist, Professor Eamon Fitzmorris and the director of forensic science. Death was a result of gunshot wounds to the back from close range. Bullets retrieved from the deceased consistent with the 9x19mm Parabellum cartridges retrieved on scene. None of those matched any other killings before or had since, nor was the rifling consistent with any weapons reported stolen or missing from security force personnel or police armouries. There were no prints and no witnesses.

Macpherson's shrug seemed to bear fruit as she flicked through the rest of the file. Both of the men considered suspects had ironclad alibis. She paused as her eye was drawn to a familiar signature on one of the appendix documents.

William Law. The years and the promotions had added a degree of elaboration to his spiky signature, but she recognised it. The sticker upon which it resided had been attached to the upper right corner in each of half a dozen black and white eight by tens. The pictures showed a gloomy sky, in the same shade as the potholed road, and overgrown embankments hemming in a vehicle. Police officers surrounded the wreckage and warning tape, broken from a fence post was caught mid-flight in one shot and limp on its mooring in another. Raindrops peppered one image, and the blacked-out rear windows of a mortuary van stared out morosely from another.

The brief report ran to a page, and she looked back at the pictures, something nagging, but not sure what. A profile of a younger William Law was out of focus in one shot, standing next to the vehicle, a late model Vauxhall Vectra. Interior shots of the burned wreckage showed the remains of a burnt child seat, and her mind drifted back to Baxter. Taylor skimmed the report again, re-reading more carefully, but she couldn't find any information on the vehicle, its occupants or the accident other than the sanitised version. Her interest piqued, she looked at the last image again, seeing what had bothered her.

Taken from a low angle near the front of the vehicle, it caught the bubbled paint, scorched bodywork and tyres melted to the road. There was a partial plate visible. What caught her attention was the configuration. It wasn't local.

## Chapter 63

Carrie Cook rapped on the glass, a dull resonance echoing in the spacious hallway beyond.

"Hello? Ms Morrow. It's Detective Constable Cook, are you home?" she called, looking around the porch for a doorbell or intercom, but there was none. Nor was there any sign of her sergeant returning from his expedition round the back of the property.

She heard the rumble of tyres on tarmac and the low growl of an engine on the road, but because of the hedgerow and the fence, she couldn't see anything. The sound passed on down the road and out of earshot.

Looking back into the hall, she strained to make out any movement or hear anything from within the house.

Her eyes kept straying back to the selection of documents placed on the table beside the vase of blooming orange flowers. They could be the morning's mail, a wad of bills or, she surmised, they could be travel documents. The luggage for the trip sat by the balustrade as though ready to go as soon as the owner descended the stairs.

Carrie pulled out her mobile and selected Macpherson's number.

❖ ❖ ❖

Macpherson pushed the door open with a nitrile gloved hand and stepped into the conservatory, which opened through an archway to an expansive kitchen, the opening framed by two stained glass windows. From his vantage point, he could see a modern double refrigerator next to a set of traditional Victorian style cupboard units and a range with multiple hotplates. The smell of fresh coffee accompanied a sweet, yeasty aroma which set his stomach grumbling, a warm and buttery scent like croissants just lifted from the oven.

His shoes crunched on the tile floor, the gravelly residue from the outside stones rasping on the polished surface. Making his way into the kitchen, he found no sign of life. No telltale mugs or plates. The sink was dry and the worktops that aligned around a kitchen island sparkled.

Three other doors led off the kitchen. One he expected led to the hallway, the other to a morning or dining room. The third, by its position and determined by what he had gleaned from the layout, was a utility or muck room leading out to the lawns.

The shrill triple note of his mobile rang, startling him into a flurry of movement to dig the phone from his pocket.

"Carrie?" His whispers were harsh in the silence.

"Where are you?"

"Hang on, I'm in the house. I'll be out in a second," he said.

"You're where!" Cook's tone was both admonishing and incredulous. "For God's sake, come back round here. You know…"

"Hang on, I hear someone." Macpherson moved the phone away from his ear. He was sure he'd heard something from the muck room which led to the double garage. He thought of the luggage, making a summation Ms Morrow may be loading a car.

"Doc?" Cook's tinny voice whispered from the phone.

Macpherson placed his ear to the door. Something scraped in the distance. He opened the door and walked into a well-appointed utility. A steel sink and draining board sat over a washer and separate dryer. A matching pair of his and hers wellington boots stood by the side of the door that led to the garden, and a dog's leash hung from a hook. He looked around warily. No sign of the dog. The same brief scuffle and a thud sounded from a door opposite.

"Ms Morrow? It's the police."

He moved down and opened the door. The garage smelled of fuel and cut grass. A ride-on lawnmower was parked against a wall and there was a workbench full of tools, car cleaning products and utensils. Stored underneath was the usual detritus of old packing boxes and household items that might come into favour or be of use in a dire emergency. An old vacuum cleaner for the car, light fittings with no bulbs, and pots of open paint, hardened drips of colour bleeding down the side from previous use.

Morrow's car was parked up in the centre. He reached out to touch the bonnet and it was cold.

The sensation of the metalwork on his palm was the last thing he felt before the blow struck his head and he dropped the phone.

## Chapter 64

Taylor inputted a new date range and waited for the search to throw up any new results. As the tab updated, she glanced at her phone again. The screen was dark, which meant radio silence. She picked it up and tapped Macpherson's number.

"The number you are calling is busy right now, please hang up and try again later." Closing the call, she did the same for Carrie, getting the same result.

The search screen began to scroll with images and headlines for the range she had selected, the results dominated by bold copy regarding the death of Martin Coleman, the Loyalist feud that threatened to ignite in the aftermath, and the rhetoric from each side of the political divide pouring fuel on the flames as they battled for dominance in the upcoming election to decide the balance of power in the fledgeling executive government.

None of that interested her though as she tiptoed the mouse along the bylines and the sub-headings, looking for something else. Something blinded by the bonfire of the murder of gangster number one. Share prices were in discussion, as was the conversation on the fifty greatest football players of all time prior to that summer's World Cup. Another drug scandal in a cycling race and a UK government minister outed with his mistress, leaving him not so much shamefaced as belligerent. Finally, between a section on roosting seabirds and flooded farmland, she spotted an inch of print.

'TWO DIE IN TRAGIC ROAD ACCIDENT.'

The piece was flimsy. Although succinct in the headline, it didn't offer much more, but it was a start. A mother and child dying in a tragic accident. Their car losing control on the slippery descent to a coastal beauty spot before catching fire. There was no mention of the other events which had transpired nearby.

Taylor spent another ten minutes flicking between news archives and websites until she landed on something with a bit more meat. The first, written by a reporter from the local newspaper, contained the bones of the story.

The woman named as Cara Shepard was a visitor to the province. There to visit family and the graves of her dead parents. Her only child Thomas died alongside her in the accident. There was scant mention of a husband who from the report had been working abroad at the time and was flying back to the UK for the return of the bodies and funeral.

The tragic tale became more fleshed out as it was picked up by the Belfast Telegraph six weeks later, although even then it was relegated from the front pages and at no point mentioned Coleman or the furore that had been going on a half mile away. Alongside an approved picture of the accident site was a picture of Shepard and her child smiling happily into a camera, ice cream dripping from the child's nose. Another photograph showed a funeral. Taylor read the copy. Cara Shepard nee Maguire, only surviving daughter of Eugene and Mary Maguire. Taylor knew the name, but a side note regarding the bombing of Skipper Street and the death of her siblings and her father's connections to the Republican movement added a few details she did not. The picture the reporter had chosen of Maguire himself showed an ill old man.

Cara was in the foreground of the next shot, a long lens job from an associated press photographer. She leaned on the arm of a tall dark-haired man, one arm looped through his, a white rose in the other. She was pretty, auburn-haired with flawless skin, the redness on her cheeks exacerbated by tears and the wind whipping across the city cemetery. Taylor's breath caught as she scrolled further. The couple had manoeuvred away from the coffin to allow fellow mourners in to pay their respects, both faces staring down the barrel of the photographer's camera.

Taylor snatched up her phone.

## Chapter 65

Beattie surreptitiously wiped his palms on the arms of his suit jacket as two blacked-out Mercedes pulled into the forecourt. He stood on the leading edge of a loading ramp, dark clouds rolling from the Irish Sea into the mouth of Belfast Lough, mirroring his darkening mood and his trepidation. The men inside the vehicle were not to be trifled with.

"Shall we?"

Beattie turned his head to look at John Barrett who was, as ever, the image of an impeccable and unflappable old Etonian.

"Relax, Gordon. These men want to do business. They would not be here otherwise."

Barrett's words made sense.

His displeasure at the predicament Beattie had brought to him had played out with a minor expression of disappointment, a sniff and downturn of the mouth, then a heartbeat later Barrett had made him an offer.

Beattie, with no option but to accept, admired the man for seizing the opportunity. He hadn't arrived at his own position by dwelling on or reliving past failures. They were something to learn from, a valuable experience, and the controlling fifty-one per cent share of something as lucrative as what they were about to seal was generous and better than the bullet that normally followed failure. No one wanted to see bodies and headlines just as the ink was being put to a new deal. The spotlight brought interest, and interest was bad news for business.

Jackson and his lads had secured the girl and baited the trap for the bastard who was picking the scabs off recent wounds and stirring up the mud covering old ones. It wouldn't be long before he addressed that, and if the ruthless bastards in the Mercedes were there to see him do it, so much the better. It would help cement his reputation and his commitment to getting his hands dirty.

Barrett's security detail was hidden discreetly by the front of the administration building, while Beattie's own security, comprising Jock Hayes and Harry Carruthers, stood equidistant from them and where the cars carrying the representatives from the Hijos de la Muerte Cartel had stopped.

Driver and passenger exited the first vehicle, making no attempt to hide the fact they were armed, snub nosed Ingram submachine guns hung on short slings over their jackets. They opened their adjacent rear doors, and the passengers alighted.

The first man was Latin American, with a neatly clipped black beard, growing grey around the jawline. His receding hair was cut short and thin on top. His suit was the colour of burned ash and he wore a black shirt and suede shoes. His partner was younger. Dark eyes and complexion suggested a mixed heritage. His hair was thick and wavy, styled with product, and his pinstripe navy suit and blue Oxford shirt matched the gleam of luxury on his wrist.

"Gentlemen. Welcome. Pleasant journey?" Barrett strode confidently forward.

"Apart from the weather, yes. I don't know how you live in these climes. I look forward to my hacienda and my hammock in the heat of the afternoon." The older man spoke English with little trace of an accent.

The second car's rear passenger door opened in the same instant as the driver's. The driver, a short redhead in a dove grey suit, fought to grip the handle as the door propelled open, and a tall, black man stepped out, his head shaven clean and sporting a neat jet black beard. He towered over the roof of the Mercedes, and Beattie wondered if they had folded him in.

He wore a debonair maroon wool suit and waistcoat with a crisp white shirt and matching tie, with a ruby tiepin studded in the centre. His eyes alighted on Barrett and his face broke into a smile.

"John, you bastard. I have missed you." The man strode forward and took Barrett by the shoulders, kissing him on each cheek.

"I need some more of that whiskey you sent me. It did not last a crack, as you say. Good to see you, my friend."

"General. It's good to see you too. These fine gentlemen you know," said Barrett, indicating the cartel representatives. Each man pumped the general's hand enthusiastically. Barrett turned his hand to Beattie.

"And this is the gentleman furnishing our operation, General. Gordon Beattie. Gordon, this is General Baba Sunday."

Beattie nodded a greeting as Sunday appraised him. The eyes were warm and bright. Beattie hadn't a notion who the man was or why he was there, and for the first time, he felt a knot of unease.

"Whiskey will come later, Baba. First, let's conclude our business, and see you all back on the road home safely. Shall we?" Barrett proffered a hand in the direction of the administration block with a predatory grin. Beattie felt a chill as it landed on him and he turned to lead the way.

❖ ❖ ❖

The men who had moved them from the cell were new. Elaine had noted the previous group had been local, a mix of northern and southern accents, but all were white. Several of the men who now herded the frightened cohort of women through the bowels of the old building were black and spoke in a language she couldn't understand, and they laughed as they prodded them roughly along, as though the task was as mundane as shifting boxes or herding cattle.

They exited a dull corridor smelling faintly of cabbage and old fish into a larger space. A similar mildewed ceiling and peeling paint greeted them but the back wall had been retrofitted with floor to ceiling cages. The enclosures were wire-framed and spot welded, and the tools of construction remained strewn about: a grinder, lengths of cut down angle iron, bolts, a club hammer and a long-handled crowbar. Old newspapers had been discarded on the floor of each, the doors open and hooked on a latch. The laughter stopped as the men began to shove three and four women at a time into spaces fit for two, raising their voices and tempers. The translation of the orders and the crying protests were lost to both parties.

As Elaine passed each of the cages, she could see both desperation and resignation, knowing in the haunted looks this was no new experience for some. She still had not seen Freya, nor the other children she had heard earlier. Her stomach knotted and her skin crawled as a leering face grabbed her, shoving her towards the open door of her pen. She tripped, and he laughed, slamming the door. It closed on her ankle and she cried out in pain, as his laugh became staccato barks of anger, and she felt herself dragged from the doorway into a corner. Blinking away tears, she looked at the faces of the women with her. One was the girl with the broken tooth and the other almost a babe herself. The youngster was raven-haired, her expression resolute. She pulled a blanket off her shoulders and offered it to Elaine. The cruel cuts to her wrists red raw against her pale skin.

❖ ❖ ❖

Gary Webster winced as he chewed the cuticle of his index finger, his teeth drawing blood. He was getting a cold sweat on and knew it would not improve without a decent hit of gear. His problem: like a sailor stuck in the doldrums with water all around but not a sip to quench his thirst, was that he found himself sat next to crates of pristine cocaine and parcels of packaged heroin which he couldn't touch. He looked across at Barney Murray who looked sick too.

"Pull your fucking selves together, will you?" said Billy Webster, slumping down on the edge of the rough-hewn bench beside his brother.

They were sequestered in a sectioned-off area of the main warehouse. Several cardboard cases of energy drink, cola and beer had been torn open, and an empty beer can in front of the younger Webster overflowed with crushed cigarette butts.

"Where's Freaky?" said Barney, straightening himself up from his slouch, his complexion as grey as the concrete floor.

"Dunno. Was over there a minute ago with one of them ones," said Billy, picking up a cola. It opened with a hiss and he sank half straight down, gesturing at a separate table of black men. They were all in smart dress of slacks and shirts, their sleeves rolled up, their attire not hiding their tough looks or scarred faces and homemade tattoos.

"Who are they?" whispered Barney.

Billy Webster shrugged. "Who cares. They must be part of this deal. I wish they'd hurry up and phone this Tommy fella, the bastard. I'll fucking slot him myself for making us look like tits." He slammed the cola onto the table, drawing an irate eye from one of the crew nearby.

Gary Webster hissed a sigh and stood. "Alright, big fella?" He smiled at one man rolling a joint.

"What's up, boy?" He spoke in a thick West African accent, his head shaven to stubble. Two of his back teeth were missing.

"Roll us one of them, will you, mate?" Gary Webster leaned in. "Don't mind my brother. He's tense, probably needs one of these, you know?" he added with a conspiratorial wink.

"Take this one and relax. The general is here now. It won't be long."

"General?" said Webster, accepting the spliff with a thumb of thanks. The other man laughed.

"Smoke your dope. Once the trucks arrive, we'll have to load them up. I'll tell you when we need you."

Webster nodded his thanks again and walked back to his brother and Murray, sitting down and sparking a light.

"Who's this general? And what trucks? Do you know what the craic is here, Billy?" Gary blew out a thin cloud of smoke.

"I know fuck all, is what I know, and I don't want to know, either. I just want your man's balls in a vice."

Gary Webster rolled his eyes and took another drag on the joint. Barney Murray scooted forward.

"What's going to happen to Elaine?"

Billy Webster scowled at him.

"You fancy her or what?" he snapped.

"No!" Murray shot back. "We know her, and where's the wee girl?"

"All them kids gurning was doing my head in. I'm glad they're away," said Billy, spitting on the floor.

"I can't see this ending well," said Gary, hissing out a deep lungful of marijuana.

"But what about the kid? She's Graham's wee girl," insisted Barney.

"Barney, Graham's inside for another five years," retorted Billy Webster. "That skank Elaine knows it's us who took her. You think she's going to keep her trap shut after this? Wise up."

"If we give her the wee girl back. Tell her not to…" There was desperation in Murray's voice.

Billy Webster swigged the last dregs of his cola.

"Elaine isn't leaving here to tell anybody anything," he

said, crushing the can in his hand and letting it clatter to the ground before he kicked it away.

Murray looked at the younger Webster. Gary saw the pleading in his eyes and put the joint to his lips, drawing deeply, then he looked away, watching the cloud of exhaled vapour as it bloomed into the air.

## Chapter 66

Cook raised the phone to her ear and then dropped it to her side and stepped from the porch. The sound of tyres tearing through gravel and scattering stones echoed from around the side of the house.

She sprinted around the front of the house, hurdling a dwarf hedgerow and slaloming through a set of oversized plant pots with miniature cherry trees, and with one hand using the downspout for leverage, she sling-shotted around the corner in time to see red tail lights disappear down a tree-lined lane.

She sprinted after the vehicle but reaching the gate she knew it was hopeless.

Cook whirled around, but there was no sign of Doc.

There was a single door to the rear of the garage and another into the conservatory. A quick glance through the glass offered no sign of Macpherson or Morrow.

She unholstered her pistol. Holding it low against her thigh, she jerked open the garage door and moved quickly inside.

Macpherson was slumped against the front bumper of a pillar-box red Audi A3 Sportback.

The left-hand side of his face matched the bodywork.

❖ ❖ ❖

Taylor rushed into the incident room on her way to Gillian Reed but searching for Reilly and Walker first. She spotted Phillip MacDonald, who glanced up as she entered, frowning at her flushed face and concentrated expression. Then he spotted the files in her hand.

"Ronnie?"

She held up a hand as she spotted Erin Reilly, but before

she could speak, her phone rang. Macpherson.

"Doc? What's going on I've been... Carrie?" She listened to the rushed voice on the line, then stabbed the call end button.

"Erin, Chris?"

The two looked up from a spreadsheet of call comparisons.

"There's an ambulance on the way to Daphne Morrow's. Get a call in downstairs and get it out over the net to be on the lookout for a cream and black MINI Countryman." Taylor snapped out the registration recited by Cook. "Area of A24 and the Embankment."

"Got it." Walker jumped up, and Reilly twisted the screen.

"Guv. There's at least two dozen calls going back three weeks between Baxter and Daphne Morrow. Baxter has also been in touch with at least six other numbers contained on one or more of the burners. The request is in for his voicemails and landline calls."

"DI Taylor?" Gillian Reed broke stride as she passed the cubicles, William Law at her elbow, his cap tucked under his arm and his expression gloomy.

"The second you hear about Doc's condition you come straight in." Taylor jabbed a finger into the desk. "Same if any of the crews or ANPR pick up that car, okay?"

Reilly nodded.

"Phillip?" Taylor called across to MacDonald. "Have you got five?"

MacDonald raised a quizzical eyebrow and left his position scrutinising a screen over the shoulder of a DS, following Taylor as she moved to address the DCI and chief super.

"I think I have something."

❖ ❖ ❖

Taylor finished her synopsis and stood against the wall, her heart was thumping, and her blood pressure up.

"There was absolutely no connection to the shooting of Martin Coleman." William Law put his pen down on his notebook and then picked it up again. Twisting the cap off and then clicking it back on.

"I don't think this fella believes that, sir," said Taylor, striding forward and sliding the printouts from the Telegraph article across the conference table with a stiff finger. The blow-ups had blurred and distorted the image, but she was resolute in her belief.

"This," she pointed at the figure arm in arm with Cara Maguire. "Is the guy who hit Signal Foods, attacked the Corners and admitted to me he has a grievance with the Monster. With respect, is there something we may have missed at the time?"

"I can't think of anything," said Law, puffing out his cheeks.

"Well, I'm certain he believes his wife and child were caught up in what happened to Coleman.."

"This woman is Eugene Maguire's girl?" said Gillian Reed, picking up the print.

"Yes, and he has to be her husband. There's nothing about him in any of the articles," said Taylor. "I couldn't find anything in the national press regarding the funerals of the woman and child. The whole episode faded into nothing."

"I can run the partial registration and try to find a last known address for her. If we have that, somebody might know what became of the husband? Even if it rules him out of this," said MacDonald. He made a face that suggested he was fifty, fifty with Taylor's assessment.

Law clicked the pen cap again, his eyes sighted in the middle distance.

"There was a lot of noise after the death of Coleman. We were on the brink of devolution and securing a deal to bring an end to the Loyalist violence when a major player met a bloody end. It was a damned debacle." Law held up a palm as Taylor made to speak. "I'm not advocating it, but at the time there was something far larger at stake than a murdered hoodlum. We have to look at this from the wider perspective, Veronica. If the reporting of this accident has got lost between the cracks, don't be jumping to the conclusion that it was a conspiracy."

"I'm not saying it's a conspiracy, sir," said Taylor, exasperation in her tone. "I'm saying the story of a leading Republican's daughter dying at the same beauty spot on the same day as a leading Loyalist should have been a big sensation. It's barely warranted a mention. Now we have…"

"We don't know what we have," snapped Law. "Anyway, Maguire was a footnote by then,"

Taylor bit back a retort and sat down, worry about Macpherson at the forefront of her mind. Her concern was eased somewhat by the knowledge she was close to identifying both a potential motive and a suspect, that knowledge ramping up a familiar energy and excitement when something felt like it was about to break. Law's lacklustre contradictions seemed disingenuous considering the photograph staring up from the smooth polished surface.

"This woman's husband is targeting people with close links to Coleman. Why? How has he even joined the dots?"

"Beattie was picked up by a checkpoint miles away at the time, he's not connected," sighed Law.

"He has to be!" said Taylor, her patience ebbing away.

Law looked into her eyes and for a brief second, she saw a crack in the curtain of ambition, past the wall of seniority and command, and glimpsed the copper inside. Law noticed her shift, and finally, he nodded.

"I'll brief the ACC," he said.

"Now?"

"He's on his way back to headquarters." Law raised a single digit and prodded the printout. "I'll give him an hour and then phone him. That means you may get your skates on and find out everything you can about this man, Shepard."

Taylor was out of her seat before he finished the sentence and before he could change his mind.

## Chapter 67

"You may take that as the wholesale price. We are happy with the cooperation up to this point and with the infrastructure investment you have shouldered. We would however ask for an equitable deal on any shipping of product or services from our other partners wishing to use your route into Europe or Africa."

The group of men sat in relaxed fashion around a polished black glass conference table. The walls were lacquered in a matt black panelling and studded with wall lights. Each man was nursing a coffee and the whole deal had the sense of formality about it.

"Mr Beattie, in my country we see these obstacles all the time. Our Venezuelan brothers offer you a good deal." General Sunday gave Beattie a curt nod.

Beattie smiled, his coffee untouched, his eyes on the older Venezuelan.

"Señor Ruiz. I appreciate the offer. And please, my sincere apologies this meeting is not under better circumstances," he said.

Ruiz waved the apology away.

"The people John represents have complete faith in your abilities as a partner, and we are aware of your propensity in dealing with awkward issues. It is not a problem."

"Thank you." Beattie took a sip of the coffee, which had cooled beyond pleasant.

"You do of course have the final funds available for transfer?"

The younger of the two men from Hijos de la Muerte addressed Beattie. There was an edge to his words that suggested the offer from Pablo Ruiz could be swiftly revoked.

John Barrett rescued the moment.

"The consortium will stand over Mr Beattie's account until his own funds are clear, Sebastian. We have his contingency and are in no doubt of his ability to pay."

"Very good." The younger man put a hand into the air and snapped his fingers. One of the suited guardians moved forward, one hand holding the Ingram in place, the other depositing a briefcase onto the table.

Sebastian Hector Gutierrez unclasped the lid and popped it open, then he raised the screen of the laptop within and logged on. He turned it to face Barrett and Beattie.

"These are the schedules for the next three months. Bills of lading and consignment details of the agreed shipments. Once you review and acknowledge, we can move to payment."

Barrett removed his tortoiseshell spectacles and perched them on his nose, head bobbing as he appraised the facts and figures before him.

Beattie did a rough calculation and felt his stomach knot in anticipation at the level that he was about to step up to.

"This looks in order, Sebastian. Did you receive the encrypted algorithm?" said Barrett.

Gutierrez nodded and double-clicked an icon, entering a strip of memorised data before spinning the screen to Barrett, who reciprocated.

Gutierrez then passed the laptop to Ruiz, who added his own pass details.

"Everything seems in order. We shall await authentication of the transaction."

A small blue icon spun on its axis as the transaction bounced across the globe, each transfer receiving a handshake from its electronic counterpart, and the bar below the icon began to fill.

"Congratulations, gentlemen!" Baba Sunday boomed, a

broad grin on his face.

"May we discuss our business now, John! I believe you won't be disappointed with my wares and my men tell me that you have outdone yourself this time with mine."

Beattie was preoccupied watching the bar increase, each pixel representing the fortune that he now held a majority stake in.

His rapt attention was arrested however as Barrett spoke.

## Chapter 68

Shepard looked across the waste ground to where twin headlamp beams slanted through the dying light to illuminate the rotten iron corpse of a see-saw. The old slide beside it was cordoned off, its plastic surface splintered and wooden steps missing. The swings were wrapped up tight on crossbars by their rusted chains, and the wall that surrounded the play park was daubed in sectarian graffiti. The chain-link fence meant to deter entry chattered in the wind, decorated by a fluttering rainbow of cheap discarded carrier bags. A closer inspection of the benches and the area around the roundabout would reveal discarded bottles of alcohol and spent hypodermic needles. It had long since been a place of joy.

Spits of rain cut through the beams of light as Shepard pushed himself off the wall and into the glare. Two car doors opened as he approached, the two men who stepped out silhouetted by the headlamps.

Shepard opened his jacket, offering assurance he was unarmed.

"Where are they?" he said.

The man who stepped out of the glare beckoned him forward. He held a Berretta low against his thigh.

"Turn around and kneel down," he said coldly.

Shepard stood his ground.

"Is this supposed to scare me?"

The man waved the pistol in a circular motion to reiterate his instruction.

Freaky Jackson stepped from behind the gunman and sauntered up to come toe to toe with Shepard, his cruel eyes narrowing. Shepard continued to hold his jacket open.

"I'm not armed."

"Pull up the shirt and turn around slowly," said Jackson.

"You think I'm wearing a wire?"

"Just turn the fuck around, will you?" snapped Jackson.

Shepard turned slowly.

The fist that slammed into his kidneys wasn't totally unexpected. Even so, it blasted the breath from his lungs and dropped him to a knee.

Jackson stood on his leg and hauled his head back by the hair.

"You've some fucking balls you know?"

"Says the man who snatched a wee girl and her daughter?" snarled Shepard as Jackson jerked his head back.

"If it was up to me, they'd be finding pieces of you around this park for a week."

"Where's the girl?" said Shepard, eyes boring into Jackson's.

Jackson tipped Shepard's head forward and slammed a punch into the base of his neck. His teeth clattered together, the blow dropping him to the gritty tarmac, the rough gravel rasping against his cheek. Jackson stamped a heavy foot onto the back of his knee, following up with a flurry of kicks to the ribs.

Shepard rolled into a foetal ball as the blows continued to rain in.

"Get up." Jackson wiped a hand across his mouth and spat into the air. The tirade of blows abated.

"Get up, I said."

Shepard rolled onto his knees, breathing heavily. Blood dripped into his eye. Jackson grabbed his collar and hauled him up, propelling him towards the car.

"You're going to wish the Monster had let me just put you out of your misery."

Shepard said nothing, allowing himself to be led towards

the car. The gunman, watching from a careful distance, made no attempt to assist Jackson.

As he made to duck into the rear seat, Jackson swung another cheap punch, ricocheting his head against the door pillar. The flash of pain bloomed bright behind his eyes, and then Shepard felt the rasp of a rough hood being drawn over his head.

❖ ❖ ❖

The BMW rode an easy arc as it reversed and then drew off from the edge of the old park, slowing to negotiate one of the deep potholes that scarred the lane.

The play park was scooped into a depression at the end of a dead-end track. Overgrown trees and muddy verges eventually gave way to smoother tarmac and pavements that skirted business units, a derelict canning factory and an electrical substation.

As it passed the parked cars edged up on one side of the road, the passengers remained hidden behind the dark tint of the windows.

When the BMW's red tail lights rounded the next lazy bend, a small car pulled out of the line. Running dark for the first hundred yards, the driver observed the BMW indicating left, out of the lane and into the small suburban terraces that led to the main road of shops and brightly lit neon takeaways.

Holding back to avoid detection but close enough to keep in contact, the Vauxhall Astra shadowed the bigger coupe through the quiet streets until they both merged onto busier roads thick with the traffic of a second rush hour.

## Chapter 69

The Venezuelans and General Sunday toasted from thick-bottomed whiskey tumblers and a bottle of Midleton Very Rare sat uncorked on the table. The men's conversation was muted as they looked out of the de-cloaked viewing window across the warehouse below.

Gordon Beattie swallowed the contents of his glass in one go. The heat as it hit the back of his throat and the expelled fumes burned away the immediate tension in his stomach.

He watched a forty-foot transporter reverse into the loading dock, engine noise dampened by the thick viewport, but the vibrations felt as a slight tremor underfoot.

"Kids, Johnny. Fucking children?" hissed Beattie.

John Barrett raised his glass to Sunday from his position beside Beattie.

"A commodity like any other Gordon," he said, enjoying a sip of the vintage whiskey.

"They're not like any other, for Christ's sake."

Barrett motioned towards the laptop screen, the little blue bar well past the three-quarters mark.

"A bit late to be developing a conscience."

Beattie bit back a retort as Pablo Ruiz glanced back with the hint of a smile.

"There's a bit of a difference between five months and fifteen years."

"Not really," John Barrett shrugged. "Over here? Yes. But we're too soft. Half of Sunday's fighters are children, and they're vicious wee bastards too. Twice as bloodthirsty as the adults." Barrett stared at Beattie. "You were happy enough to let Millar recruit schoolgirls to turn tricks. What's the difference?"

"The difference is these are bloody children!" Beattie's hand shook.

"Do you know what the market price is for baby organs in China?" said Barrett. "A fortune. Buyers buy. Sellers sell. It's that simple, Gordon. No one is asking you to roll your sleeves up and snatch a child from a pram, although your client base is as likely to sell you their own for the cost of a gram," said Barrett, shrugging again, his expression one of complete ambivalence.

Beattie's knuckles whitened as he put his glass to his lips.

"Hijos have offered you a very lucrative deal. All you have to do is carry on as you have been with the added incentives and the majority shareholding. The people I represent will use your pipeline to assist in the distribution of these other revenue streams. I'm afraid that's the price you pay for your prize."

Beattie walked across to the conference table and hefted the bottle of thirty-five thousand euro whiskey, the neck of the bottle rattling against the lip of his glass as he poured a slug.

The warehouse space outside the window dominated his eyeline. Packing crates of ammunition and small arms sat stacked in a corner, alongside ten long crates, their markings identifying Chinese made Type 69 85mm rocket propelled grenades.

The weapons formed part of General Sunday's dowry along with a substantial sum of cash. The used denominations, cling-wrapped in large bricks, were being hand-balled out the back of the container lorry as the cargo Sunday was paying for was being herded along a pedestrian walkway at the far edge of the floor space. Marshalled by three women, the line of children walked hand in hand, younger ones carried awkwardly by older children. Their faces were pale and streaked with tears, wide eyed at the unfamiliar surroundings, the desire for understanding and the comfort only their parents could bring etched on small faces as they were guided through the open stable door of a Portakabin structure.

Somewhere under his feet, another group of women and girls would eventually follow the children.

*"White-skinned and red headed. Highly desirable, very lucrative. If there is anything left once the commandants are finished with them, they'll be sold to the troops."* Baba Sunday had rubbed his palms together in delight as he appraised his purchase, and his exuberance and his words continued to replay in Beattie's mind.

Drugs were one thing. Murder and militancy he had grown up with. The weapons were destined for organised criminal groups or dissidents, it was nothing new, and he could live with it. He had overseen the procurement of armament for his old comrades plenty of times. But the trafficking of minors bothered him, although Barrett had a valid point. The flesh trade was a string to the Beattie empire, a poorer subsidiary to the narcotics, but under Rab Millar, it had still been a lucrative one. His ears sang with the rush of blood in them.

*"Mr Beattie?"*

Running the positives through his mind, Beattie tried to offset his unease at the thought of what awaited the human cargo at their destination. His deal agreed on local rates at the Venezuelan dockside and the means to move tons of product across the Atlantic to the processing plant in El Jadida and then ship to Ireland and the UK all under his own steam. No middlemen, no charters, and based on the figures he could undercut any other competitor and still shatter the revenue ceiling. Earnings would be stratospheric. Competitors would have no choice but to buy wholesale from him, and factoring in a rate to move on the consortium's cargo, the stock just kept rising.

*"Mr Beattie?"*

John Barrett touched his arm. Beattie turned, his mind a million miles away. Barrett pointed at the open door.

Jock Hayes stood in the opening.

"Mr Beattie. You have a visitor."

## Chapter 70

It had taken longer than expected, but MacDonald had produced an address.

"Poole," he said.

"Poole. South of England?" Taylor moved her mouse and opened a window, launching a map app and inputting Cara Shepard's address.

"Samson Road." MacDonald held the sheet so she could see the postcode.

The screen zoomed in and Taylor dropped the icon of the little figure into the map so they now looked at a neat street of chalet bungalows. Using the screen arrows, she roamed the neighbourhood until she found the house. The garden was a little overgrown, but the place looked in good order otherwise.

"Can we run the property details?"

"Already done," said MacDonald. "It was mortgaged in the name of Thomas and Cara Shepard. The account was closed six months after the accident."

Taylor's brows dropped as she zoomed back out, swirling a circle with the pointer.

"Naval base?"

MacDonald nodded. "Details on the mortgage records show Mr Shepard as HM Forces. The wife as a registered general nurse, Southampton General. It's an NHS teaching hospital."

"Southampton was also McBride's last known address," said Taylor.

"Have we any word on that?"

Taylor shook her head.

"Nothing. They'll not be breaking any sweat. I expect we'll

only find out if they turn up a body."

"What do you think?" MacDonald sat down on the edge of the desk opposite.

Taylor blew a sigh.

"I'll have to send this up to the DCI. We won't get any further doing this." She pointed at the computer screen. "Let's see if she can get the ball rolling with military liaison. It's a long shot, but if Shepard served here, he could have had contact with McBride."

"It still doesn't give us a reasonable explanation for his grudge against Beattie though. If this is the right fella."

Taylor stared at the neat little house in the neat little street.

"I think the death of a wife and child is likely explanation enough."

"Ronnie, Beattie was miles away, and McBride had a hundred witnesses. We have no one for Coleman."

"So what does he know that we don't? We need to see his records…" Her voice trailed off as she considered the absurdity of the request. Her prevailing thoughts then turned to consider. If this was the same man, where was he now?

## Chapter 71

The Astra pulled up discreetly a hundred yards away from the building. The rain was more persistent now, and the wipers beat a slow heartbeat as they juddered across the windshield.

A tuck truck with hatch extended served a line of hungry truckers and shift workers deep-fried food in a narrow lay-by a hundred yards past the gate into the compound where the BMW had turned off.

From the Astra's spot kerbside on the opposite side of the road, the rear lights of the coupe could still be seen through the wrought-iron and barbed wire fence which enclosed the building. The name of the shipping company was emblazoned across the gable panelling in large blue and white print.

The BMW's rear doors opened and first one, then another man exited. Both were muscular and brooding as they manhandled their hooded passenger from the back seat, his hands firmly secured to the front, and led him towards a pedestrian door. It opened as they approached, and the warm glow of internal light spilled out into the car park.

As the door shut and the light blinked out, the watcher gunned the Astra's engine and peeled across the road, nosing the car through traffic towards the city and a pre-planned rendezvous.

## Chapter 72

Gary Webster poked through the remains of his makeshift ashtray and toyed with the butts of the two joints he had already smoked to the nub. His feet tapped and his legs were restless.

The sense of urgency brewing in the warehouse had increased, the group of foreigners having left and returned several times and with nosiness getting the better of him, Gary had firmly but politely been told to stop as he made to leave and observe the goings-on. The rumble of transport thrummed underfoot and he could see the man who had gifted him the joint unloading a forty-footer beyond the shoulder of the man who now stood guard on the door.

Barney Murray, slumped with his back against the wall, stood and stretched, equally restless for knowledge.

"Ask to speak to Freaky? Why won't they tell us anything? Go on, ask him, Billy," he said, shuffling across to look past Gary.

Billy Webster sat with his feet up and arms behind his head, staring at the ceiling in his third position. First, he paced in circles, second, he'd stop and glare at the man blocking his exit, then third, slump back feet up. Staring.

"I'm not asking him. Freaky will be back when he's back. Sit down."

"What about Elaine?"

"Barney, I told you to stop whining about the wee bitch. She got herself into this."

Murray leaned back against the wall and chewed on a knuckle.

Gary Webster triumphantly held aloft a decent discarded butt and sparked it up.

"You three. Time to make yourselves useful." The big man who had supplied Gary with his spliff a few hours previously strode into the room and waved his hand in a motion to follow.

"We don't take our orders from you, alright?" Billy Webster shot up so fast the chair overturned.

"Aboki, we are not enemies. Your boss man says to help, so you help. Alright?" The African's tone wasn't hostile, but it gave no room for further argument.

"Help to do what?" Making no attempt to right the chair and adopting an aggressive stance, Billy moved forward, elbows flared, chin up. He gave away about eight inches in height and twice again in reach.

"The general's merchandise is moving in an hour. It's time to get it loaded."

"Who's this bloody general youse are all bleating on about?"

"Do a good job and you might get to meet him." The big man smiled, gaps glaring in his tombstone teeth. He nodded at his compatriot as he led the three youngsters out into the warehouse, their eyes darting at the activity and the manpower scurrying about the place.

A second forty-foot curtain-sider had docked and was being unloaded next to where a refrigerated DAF box van lowered its tailgate onto the loading pier. As they navigated the cordoned off stacks of boxes and equipment, Billy Webster glimpsed Freaky Jackson and another of the Africans. Between them was the bearded figure from the stairs of Fearon House. The three disappeared from view as they passed through a set of crash doors.

"Did you see your man?" he said, turning. Barney Murray stumbled up short, his eyes on the floor, shoulders sagging. Out of his depth.

Billy Webster gave him a shove, looking back the way they

had come.

"Where the fuck is our Gary?"

*Chapter 73*

A billboard hung suspended from the ceiling showing the ruins of an ancient castle set atop a clifftop of emerald green moss. The grey waters of the Atlantic churned far below. A question was emblazoned across the advertisement. Getaway?

The check-in hall of George Best City Airport was busy. Travellers waited in the rows of ergonomic seating, carry-on luggage parked between them as they chatted or surfed on phones and devices. A few children slid playfully along the polished floors, while others lined up in the snake of a queue to complete their self-service boarding. Nearby, a separate queue formed at the Aer Lingus service desk to book last-minute seats.

"Madam. Can I help you?"

"Could you tell me the next available flight please?"

"I'm sorry, madam. Next flight to where?"

"Just the next flight. Spontaneous break." The woman adjusted the expensive Givenchy scarf and set a holdall on the floor before the check-in clerk, who smiled politely and rattled her manicured fingers across the keyboard hidden from the passenger's view.

"We have the nineteen forty-five to Schiphol?"

"That's fine."

"You're sure?" the clerk asked, never before having received such a request.

"Absolutely." The woman presented an Amex gold card and an Irish passport.

"No luggage today?" The clerk slipped easily into the usual patter.

"Just this."

Craning her neck to view the small case, the clerk motioned to the conveyor at her left elbow.

"Pop it on the scales, please." The red numbers illuminated for staff and passenger to see.

"Okay, that's you. Passport and payment card, please."

Five minutes later, with boarding card in hand, the woman paused as she passed the small WH Smith concession on her way to security. She bought a plastic bag from a dispenser to hold her liquid toiletries and glimpsed the late edition of the Belfast Telegraph. The headlines were dominated by pictures and copy of a gunfight and drugs seizure in the north of the city. She took a copy and paid for it, her interest in the article noted to appear on page four. 'LAWYER FACES ASSAULT CHARGES.'

Tucking the paper under her arm, she passed through the first yellow barrier, warning signs calling for attention. Passengers only beyond this point. No Return. Deposit sharps and explosives. Act Now!

Dispersed among the warnings, the corridor leading to security was festooned with advertisements: forty per cent off fragrances, Northern Irish beef and Shortcross gin. The last focused her mind on the dash through passport control to the Lagan Bar, where a gin would be the first thing past her lips. A double at that.

There was a garbled security announcement about abandoned bags, and a reminder to ensure awareness of belongings at all times. The queue edged forward, and she grabbed a long grey tray. She put in the bag, added her toiletries, scarf and sunglasses, and popped it on the conveyor and waited.

The security guard called her forward into lane two.

The guard's radio bleeped, and he responded. Confusion marking his face.

A commotion started at the back of the queue, then the

three operating conveyors stopped, red lights atop each X-ray unit illuminating.

"Step aside. Excuse me. Step aside, please."

Daphne Morrow thought to run, but there was nowhere to go. She was trapped between the airport security team and a short, bearded figure elbowing his way through the crowd. His shirt collar was stained with blood and an oversized bandage was plastered to the side of his head. Behind him and offering apologies, Morrow recognised the slim figure of Detective Constable Carrie Cook accompanied by a uniformed colleague of the Harbour Police who was speaking into his radio.

So close, and yet so far.

## Chapter 74

Daphne Morrow sat straight-backed with hands folded in her lap on the same chair in interview room four that Rowdy Burns had previously occupied. A plastic beaker of water stood untouched in front of her.

Taylor observed her on the wall-mounted monitor, Carrie Cook standing to her right, and Macpherson slumped into a chair only slightly more comfortable than the one occupied by the businesswoman.

Taylor rubbed her eyes, pressing her fingertips against her eyelids until light bloomed in the darkness. Things were falling into place.

"Cool customer," said Phillip MacDonald from his position behind Taylor. Morrow had shifted, adjusting her necklace and straightening her blouse.

"I'll confront her with Baxter's call logs. We know she's actively avoided assisting us and lied about her attendance at the housing meeting on the day of Lena's disappearance, and I've turned up a few other things she needs to account for." Taylor shook her suit jacket off the back of Macpherson's chair, as he stood up, sliding a thin manilla folder off the desk.

"Where are you going?" said MacDonald.

"In there with you."

MacDonald chuckled.

"Doc, sit back down. Neither of the pair of you are going in there. You have a conflict of interest given she thumped you on the head and you," he gestured at Taylor, "are stood down awaiting clearance for duty."

"Piss off, MacDonald. I'm going in there whether…" Macpherson took a step towards the door.

"He's right, Doc. Sit down," said Taylor. "Carrie, you go. We'll watch. You okay with that?"

"What are you up to?" said MacDonald, narrowing his eyes.

"Nothing, it's as you say, and I'm not jeopardising this over procedure. I can observe and offer you an opinion on what I see though, correct?"

"Whatever. Are you ready?" MacDonald looked at Cook.

Taylor nodded her approval, and Cook took a breath.

"I'm ready."

❖ ❖ ❖

Taylor watched the initial preamble with growing interest. Beside her, Macpherson sat forward on the edge of his chair, picking the edge of his bandages.

"Cool as ice," he mumbled.

"That's because she thinks this isn't going anywhere," said Taylor, downing the last inch of water before tossing the beaker into the waste.

MacDonald had paused, waiting for an answer on the reason for Morrow's trip to Holland.

She smiled, declining to comment. Content to wait until representation arrived.

Taylor's phone rang. The conversation was brief. She pressed a small button on the console as she hung up, and a small call light flickered on the data trunking inside the interview room.

MacDonald paused the interview, and Taylor watched him stand and disappear from camera view.

The observation room door opened.

"Representative's here," said Taylor.

"Okay. I'll grab them…" MacDonald turned to leave.

"Do you mind if I do it?"

"Whatever. Bring them in." MacDonald shrugged.

"Will do. Phillip, see if you can get her to relinquish her

phone," said Taylor.

MacDonald nodded, raising an eyebrow at Macpherson, who shrugged. Taylor squeezed between the two men and hurried down the corridor, taking the stairs to the ground floor, where she spotted the man straight away.

"Mr Baxter?"

Charles Baxter waited on one of the orange plastic seats, briefcase balanced on knees and a pen clamped between teeth as he fussed with a moleskin notebook.

Taylor couldn't see a resemblance. Bryce Baxter must have taken after the mother.

"DI Taylor. I'd have thought you…"

"Just fetching the VIPs and making the tea, sir. This way, please."

Taylor led him to the lift and hit the recessed button with a knuckle, then waited for the pleasant voice to tell them it had arrived.

"It's slow. Sorry."

Baxter Senior didn't reply.

"How are you getting on? You know, being a man down?" said Taylor, staring ahead. Watching the floors tick down.

"We'll cope. Your case against Bryce is by no means cut and dried." Baxter's tone was light and businesslike considering his son's involvement.

The doors of the lift finally opened with a ping, and Taylor offered the lawyer in ahead of her.

"Ladies first."

She smiled and accepted, waiting a beat to hit the button.

"Still, it's a bit of a mess," she said.

"I'm sure we can sort it. Jacinta, well, bless her but…" Baxter trailed off.

"Couples, eh?"

"You married?" Baxter looked at her sideways, taking a glance at her hand.

"Not me, sir. The job keeps getting in the way."

The faceless woman announced they'd arrived and Taylor stepped out first, leading the way to the interview suite.

"Quite a coincidence, all this. Your son in custody. Daughter-in-law's ex-employer calling you in now for this. It's all very tangled."

"Nature of business in such a small city." There was a swagger and bluster to the lawyer as Phillip MacDonald exited the interview room and approached.

"Mr Baxter. This way," he said, offering a hand.

"I'll need five minutes with my client if that's okay?"

MacDonald nodded at the request.

"Of course. Thanks, DI Taylor."

The two men turned their backs and took the first few steps to the door.

"I meant to say, sir. Congratulations."

Baxter stopped, turning back with a quizzical look on his face.

"Congratulations?"

"On the happy news, sir." Taylor mirrored the look. "I thought your colleague might have mentioned to you already."

"What news?" said Baxter, looking between the two detectives.

"Lena Borodenko. She's pregnant."

## Chapter 75

Shepard hawked a gob of bloody spittle onto the floor. His jaw throbbed from the blow which he had deflected slightly by moving his head in time with the swing.

Freaky Jackson stalked a few steps away, red faced, a sweat worked up, perspiration dappling his temples. He turned back with a snarl and launched a savage blow into Shepard's exposed stomach. He was naked, arms bound behind the office chair on which they had perched him. With no means to absorb the blow, Shepard convulsed against his bindings, the chair rocking wildly. Wheels that should have been there were absent, leaving it unbalanced on a spider-leg frame of toughened plastic.

The men from the car watched. Both smoked. Neither spoke.

"Have you got no questions?" croaked Shepard, sucking in a ragged breath, the inhalation stealing the throb in his jaw and replacing it in his abdomen.

"You're a smart fucker, aren't you?" sneered Jackson.

"Is that not how it goes. Few smacks and a few questions?" Shepard spat another gob of phlegmy blood. "If you're hoping a beating will open me up, you may as well get someone else in here because you're obviously only used to beating the women."

Jackson took three quick strides and crashed a brutal uppercut into Shepard's exposed jaw, the momentum snapping his head back and throwing the chair to the floor.

Shepard let out an involuntary yell as his full weight crashed down on his hands and arms, and the hard plastic spine of the chair jabbed into his arched vertebrae, numbing his legs. The tendons of his shoulders snapped tight, and he fought to alleviate the strain of the position, focusing on the single bare bulb dangling from the concrete ceiling and the twist of steel conduit feeding both the light and the room's electrical outlets.

The two other men in the room heaved his seat back upright. Shepard let his head hang forward, feeling blood rushing back into his hands. His teeth gritted in pain but he was feeling euphoric. He had sensed the old chair give a little.

Jackson drew his fist back to strike again.

"Wait."

Holding off the blow, Jackson turned to face the open door. The newcomer was a tall black man with a dour face and happy clothes.

"Come."

"I'll come when I'm through with this," said Jackson, wiping a hand across his mouth.

"Now."

Jackson read the man's expression and turned back to Shepard.

"Think on, dickhead. When I come back, I will be asking questions."

"I'll be right here," said Shepard.

"Youse two, get the car ready. He'll be going for his tea soon," said Jackson, grabbing his jacket from where it hung on a vice clamped to the edge of a rusted workbench. On top of the bench was a selection of dulled tools and bloody rags.

Shepard knew they weren't empty threats.

The slam of the door and rasp of lock echoed in the small room and Shepard aimed another bloody gob of spittle at the floor. He flexed his hands, trying to work the blood back into the digits while wondering how his plans beyond the walls of his prison were coming together.

## Chapter 76

Gary Webster mooched through a back corridor, having successfully slipped out of an open fire escape door. He didn't particularly know nor care where he was going, rather he sought a quiet corner to cook up the last of the crack he'd salvaged from down the back of the sofa in the flats, but as yet, had not been given two minutes to enjoy.

Whatever was going on in the warehouse, he was confident they'd not miss his input and lugging about crates and cartons wasn't for him.

"Hey, where are you going?" The clatter of the pallet truck forced the guy behind the forks to raise his voice.

"Piss, mate," said Webster without breaking stride. The fella was about the same age as himself, hair gelled, sleeves of a boiler suit rolled up. The pallet truck banged on over the hard floor and the lad jutted his chin over his shoulder.

"On up there. You can cut back into the main loading bays from the double door opposite. Right, right and left. Yeah?"

Webster raised a thumb in thanks and walked on.

The corridor dog-legged twice and he caught the whiff of the toilets before he saw them. The door handle was missing, and there were black palm prints on the door and frame. Shouldering it aside, he walked up to the stainless steel urinal, the floor awash with either piss or water. Soil pipe limescale stained the trough and an incessant trickle of water ran from the large cistern above. Once he'd relieved himself and as he was fastening his jeans, Gary heard raised voices and the urgent march of feet. Shifting the door closed, he waited as they approached.

One voice amid the crowd was unmistakable, and Freaky Jackson didn't sound happy. The exchange was drowned out by a rush of water from the cistern as the group exited through the double doors opposite. Webster waited a few beats and then peered out. With the coast clear, he continued his search for a quiet place to smoke.

The corridor had several doors on each side, the arrow hatch glass windows set in each reminding him of school. The rooms inside were racked out with shelves of plastic trays and hessian wrapped sacks.

He could hear more voices close by, separated from him by another set of double swing doors. He peered through the reinforced glass panel, eyes widening at what he saw. Cages. Women. Elaine Weir.

❖ ❖ ❖

"What do they want with us?" Elaine Weir clawed her fingers through the fencing of her prison, the wire cutting into her flesh.

"They are going to send us somewhere and then they will rape us."

Elaine Weir spun back.

"What!"

The young girl with the scarred wrists sat cross-legged, facing the door. She shrugged.

"They will rape us until we don't care anymore, and then they will put us in a brothel for other men to pay to rape us."

Elaine felt the earth tilt. The other woman standing in the corner nearby caught her.

"Come on, you're okay. Here, sit." She shot a glare at the younger girl. "We don't know that?"

"Really? What happened to your face?"

Lena Borodenko ignored the jibe, finally understanding that what she had believed for long enough was her choice was far from the truth of it.

"What's your name?" said Lena.

"Elaine. They have my daughter."

"They're traffickers. We are here to be sold on." The young girl had a resignation about her and Lena scowled, understanding that while she spoke the blunt truth it would do little to help them.

"Your wrists?" said Elaine, nodding at the bright marks.

"I tried to escape?"

"What happened?"

"They found me and brought a doctor. When I was better, they punished me for damaging their goods."

Elaine felt her eyes prick with tears, and her heart raced. The woman beside her stroked her back. The girl was young, too young to have led a life where suicide was the only exit.

The fear she felt for herself was eclipsed by fear for her daughter. Horrific thoughts she would never see her again flooded her mind. Darker images of what might happen to the youngster chilled her stomach to ice and, in the midst of it all, a snapshot of Tom and Billy Webster on the stairs in Fearon House burned in her mind.

Elaine stood up again, gulping a breath and wiping her nose on her sleeve. She grasped the cage again and looked out. There had to be fifty of them, each resigned to their fate. Most frightening of all, she realised from their submissive expressions most had endured something like this before.

## *Chapter 77*

Taylor had expected a reaction, but the sudden rise of blood to Charles Baxter's face made her seriously consider his head could be about to burst.

"Are you alright, Mr Baxter?" MacDonald edged a step closer, looking fearful the man was about to fit or fly into a rage.

"Why don't we all have a seat. I've a few theories I'd like to run past you and your client," said Taylor. Not waiting for an answer, she moved past the two men and into the interview room.

Cook stood in surprise as she entered, noted her inspector's face and relinquished her seat as MacDonald and Baxter filed in, the room now cramped.

"Ms Morrow, may I ask you to surrender your telephone and your handbag, please."

Daphne Morrow turned to look to her legal adviser, who had taken the seat to her right and was still no closer to composure.

"Ma'am?" Taylor slid a small tray across the table.

"Go ahead, Daphne," said Baxter, nodding once.

Cook gathered up the deposited items.

"Thanks, Carrie," said Taylor in dismissal. MacDonald took a breath and wondered how Taylor had hijacked his interview.

Taylor hit a button on the desk to start. A three-second warble sounded, followed by a long beep after which she ran through the preliminaries of time, date and attendees.

"You're a hard woman to track down, Ms Morrow," she said finally.

"A business like mine won't run itself."

"My colleagues tell me you've plenty of assistance."

"You verge on sounding like my husband, Inspector," said Morrow, smiling.

"Mr Howard?"

"Why keep a dog and bark yourself, is one of his more worn-out expressions," said Morrow.

"It's good that you do. Gives you time to take a bit of a break," said Taylor, shuffling some papers before pausing on one sheet. "Amsterdam, was it?"

"Inspector MacDonald, could we perhaps just clarify a few things?" said Charles Baxter with a wary glance at Taylor.

"I'm sure my colleague is getting to the point, sir." MacDonald looked at Taylor with a raising of the eyebrow and of his blood pressure, if the tip of his nose was anything to go by.

"Last-minute to Skipol. Any reason?"

"Last-minute business trip," said Morrow with a nonchalant wave.

"Same last-minute decision as when you pulled out of your commitment to the social collaboration scheme?"

"I was ill."

"I see, your office seemed sure of your whereabouts?"

"Inspector Taylor, my client's health is a personal matter and if she wishes to maintain a professional impression by keeping that to herself, it's her own business. I don't see how it impacts…"

"Do you have a contact or an itinerary for this Amsterdam trip?" said Taylor, ignoring Baxter's input.

"You've given us no reason to provide that, so if you could please get around to explaining why you have detained Ms Morrow," blustered Baxter, irritated at being ignored.

"Your client assaulted one of my officer's and was attempting to flee."

Morrow and Baxter sat stony faced at the bluntness of

Taylor's words, but neither leapt in with a denial.

"Where were you on Wednesday afternoon prior to DC Cook seeing you in your office?" said Taylor.

"I was at home, ill."

"Can Mr Morrow confirm this?"

"I doubt it."

"So no witnesses?"

"I was still in bed when he left."

Taylor pursed her lips and consulted her notes.

"DC Cook's report states you had another meeting to attend and no time for her questions. Doesn't sound like you were that ill?"

"The business won't run itself."

"Do you have issues with control, Ms Morrow?"

"If you want something doing, be prepared to do it yourself."

"What couldn't you leave to anyone else?"

"I prefer to handle major transactions myself, Inspector."

"I see. So what was so major it dragged you in from your sickbed?"

Charles Baxter breathed a sigh.

"Inspector Taylor, you have accused my client of assault. Did this alleged attack take place on Monday afternoon?" sighed Baxter.

"No," replied Taylor.

"So, is there a point to your line of questioning?"

"There is, and you might be able to help too."

Baxter's eyes narrowed.

"You know we are investigating the murder of Robert Millar?" she said.

Neither spoke, but Morrow dropped a brief glance at the tabletop and Baxter to the recording equipment.

"We know Robert Millar was the director of Miltek Refurb. Miltek being a client you both share?"

"I'm not at liberty to discuss my client portfolio…"

"Ms Morrow, you don't need to discuss anything. I'm already in possession of the facts."

"I don't know what facts you think you have, but I would be very careful where your next steps take you, Inspector," said Morrow.

"That sounds like a threat, ma'am."

"Call it an observation." A smirk broke Morrow's face. "I can't imagine the chief constable wishes the embarrassment of another investigation being drummed out of the courtroom and across the front pages?"

"I'd let me worry about that," said Taylor, slipping a page from her file. "This is a list of properties Miltek have purchased in the last twelve months."

"Where did you get…" said Baxter, peering over the top of his glasses at the papers.

"We had a court order approved to investigate Mr Millar's financial status so we could eliminate any of his recent business deals as a motive for his murder."

"You can't be suggesting I had anything to do with Robert Millar's death?" said Morrow, with an incredulous laugh.

"No. I'm not, but I'm confident I can tie the both of you to the operational end of Miltek's activities, which makes you both accessories," said Taylor.

"Accessories to what?"

"To the managing and the control of finances regarding activities connected to people trafficking, the forced coercion of vulnerable persons, financial fraud and tax evasion."

"That's ludicrous! Miltek bought up low-grade properties and then flipped them for profit. It's hardly a bloody crime, Inspector."

"I did consider Miltek was only a money-laundering operation. Given Millar's background, it made me think it was a simple attempt to legitimise illicit earnings."

"Where is the evidence, Inspector? Any transactions were scrutinised, and we have been completely transparent with the financial institutions involved," said Baxter.

"Millar didn't flip all the properties. He held a portfolio of warehousing facilities across the suburbs and into the dockland."

Morrow shrugged, disinterested.

"He also had several multi-occupancy dwellings," Taylor drew out a set of registration documents. "This three-block apartment at Morecross Weir in Annandale and two others in the city centre."

"If you say so," muttered Morrow, as Baxter eyed MacDonald, who also studied the papers for the first time.

"According to this, each of these properties also forms part of the Sanctuary scheme. Another client you both share."

"It's a small city."

"Tiny," agreed Taylor. "Which brings me to Jacinta Baxter. Your daughter-in-law."

Baxter blew out his cheeks and a notch crept between Morrow's manicured eyebrows.

"She's an ill woman, Inspector. She needs help, not my recriminations."

"You know Jacinta, don't you, Ms Morrow?"

"I'm not sure. I…"

"You do. She worked for you, April through September, eighteen months ago."

"We have a turnover of staff, I can't remember everyone who has come through the door."

"Easy to lose track when so many people come and go," Taylor sniffed and regarded Morrow. "I thought you'd remember her, considering you requested her through Sanctuary personally."

"My husband and I aim to see Sanctuary's guests find what help they can through our work placement schemes.

The charity has robust procedures in place to ensure the safety of all parties."

"I'm still surprised you don't remember her. My information shows she was a signatory in all the early Miltek deals, not to mention her significant investments in Havelock Holdings."

Neither offered Taylor any response.

"What about you, Mr Baxter, do you recall when you first met Jacinta?"

"I do not."

"But you must remember your son introducing her?"

"Maybe." Baxter shrugged.

"Did you not recognise her from the Sanctuary dwelling at Morecross Weir?"

Baxter reddened but didn't reply.

"That's where you first met Lena Borodenko, isn't it? You know her too, Ms Morrow."

"I've had enough of this. Are you going to sit there and pander to this or are you reining her in?" snapped Morrow, her ire aimed at MacDonald.

"Ms Morrow, I suggest you at least attempt to humour Inspector Taylor and her questions as any answers that you give may mitigate against her others that are coming down the line regarding why I have an officer with stitches in his head."

"As far as I'm aware, the law requires your officers to present a warrant before entering someone's home!" sneered Morrow with a disgusted shake of the head as she looked between both detectives.

"Your colleagues informed DS Macpherson you were ill and when he couldn't raise you, he entered to ensure your safety," said Taylor with a tight smile of apology.

"Rubbish!"

"Daphne," said Baxter in a low warning tone.

"Don't Daphne me. Sort this."

"Why were you really running, Ms Morrow?" pressed Taylor.

"I wasn't running anywhere as I've tried to explain…"

"If you think your safety is an issue, helping us can benefit you."

"You don't have a notion, dear," said Morrow, her words cold as ice.

"I think I do. Mr Baxter?"

"Get on with it, Inspector. Lay out whatever it is you think you have and we can discuss it."

Taylor caught MacDonald's glance. He gave a small nervous nod of his head.

The little light on the panel data trunking blinked and Taylor raised her palm to the camera. Now wasn't the time for a distraction.

*Chapter 78*

"John. I apologise for barging in like this, but Gordon has a problem."

Barrett waved the words away and offered the man a chair. The three of them had moved to the managing director's office, and the newcomer stood beside a bookcase of periodicals, manuals, and procedural documentation bound in thick white binders. Barrett sat at the head of an ostentatious meeting table surrounded by a collection of leather armchairs.

Barrett dismissed his security detail, who exited and pulled the heavy walnut panelled door closed behind them. He bade Beattie and the other man to sit.

Gordon Beattie undid his suit jacket and remained standing as he waited for an explanation, the newcomer's presence a discomfort.

"There's a missing persons report out for a girl and her youngster," said the man, taking a seat.

"So?" Beattie shrugged.

"So, I know you have her here, which means it won't take long for someone else to find out."

"She'll go home once she's served her purpose."

"It's not as simple as that. I've a witness who has placed one of your lads at the scene."

"Who?"

"One of the Brothers Grimm."

Before he could reply, a knock on the door interrupted them. Barrett barked a command, security ushering in Freaky Jackson.

"What the fuck is he doing here?" Jackson pointed an accusatory finger at the newcomer, his hand balling into a fist.

"If you don't mind taking a seat, our guest is in the middle of his explanation." Barrett pointed to a black fabric chair positioned near the bookcase. Jackson snatched it up in one big paw and deposited it awkwardly on the fringes of the other seats around the table, squeezing his bulk into the frame.

"Go on, well. Let's hear it?"

"Freaky!" admonished Beattie.

"The call identified one of the Webster boys. It will have to be sorted."

"They'll lie low for a while," said Jackson. "The wee girl will get her orders to keep her trap shut."

The visitor cocked his head and smiled politely, giving a glance towards Barrett, whose hands steepled. His mouth turned down as he decided.

"The girl and her daughter will join General Sunday's contingent. Gordon? One assumes these brothers are ten-a-penny and are expendable?"

"Wait, a fucking minute here…" Jackson half rose, taking the fabric and wood frame chair with him.

"Freaky, sit down," snapped Beattie. "They knew what they were getting into. The young one's a junkie, that's a liability straight away. See that it's taken care of."

"I can give them the cash to get out of town?" said Jackson.

"No, Freaky, you'll put them down. There can't be any more witnesses to this," said the visitor, his tone cold.

"Who the fuck are you to be telling me what to do?"

"Freaky!" Beattie's voice was raised in anger, but before he got further the newcomer butted in.

"If you don't have the stomach, I'll have one of my own do it." He turned to Beattie. "You have bigger problems to consider."

"What problems?"

"We have identified the thorn in your side."

"Have you now?" said Beattie.

"Who?" John Barrett leaned in, interested.

"Thomas Shepard. He's a decorated Special Forces Operative. Iraq, Afghanistan, and more recently he's been engaged in the anti-Assad operations in Syria."

"What's he want with me?" Beattie frowned, confusion on his face. Another painful surprise on a day of them.

Barrett sat back and considered the news before speaking.

"If you were to make an assessment? Is there a wider agenda here? By which I mean is this Shepard on assignment?"

"I don't believe so."

"You don't believe so," echoed Barrett, irritation creeping into his tone.

"No."

"But you can't be sure?" said Beattie. Suddenly the room felt tiny. Jackson looked at him, Beattie returning the gaze. He had a name now, and whatever Shepard wanted, they would soon make him talk.

"If it's any consolation, I'm confident his agenda is personal rather than any action by the security apparatus."

"It can't be personal? I've never heard of the fella!" said Beattie, feeling sweat trickle down his back. Jackson's expression was hostile as the visitor uncrossed his legs and spoke.

"You haven't, but six years ago the pair of you and Rab Millar murdered his wife, and I helped you cover it up."

## Chapter 79

"The address at Morecross Weir is one of Sanctuary's sheltered living schemes. Lena Borodenko and Jacinta, then Conway, were both living there, and that is where you met both."

Neither of the two faces across the table offered any acknowledgement of her words.

"Miltek was not in the business of purchasing property for financial gain. Rab Millar was running a domestic slavery ring, and to expand he needed the one thing you both have access to, vulnerable persons and vacant property."

"Preposterous."

"It might be if it wasn't for Havelock Holdings."

MacDonald looked uncomfortable but held his tongue. This was segueing into dangerous territory which would entangle him as much as Taylor if she didn't negotiate it safely.

"Millar got wind the pair of you were skimming the cream off larger government grants and decided he wanted a taste. That scam changed when Millar appointed you directors of Havelock Holdings. That company laundered the proceeds from his brothels and drugs, channelling it back into real estate."

"Inspector Taylor, I assume you have proof to back up these spurious allegations?" Baxter was smiling. It was bravado. His right foot tap-tapped. Like father like son.

"I'm getting there."

"I've had enough of this."

"Ms Morrow, can you please take your seat or I'll arrest you for assaulting a police officer," said Taylor, indicating Morrow should retake her seat.

"Your husband, along with Harper, Baxter, Brooke, and the Ethical Banking Trust are all significant partners in Sanctuary's success. It won't take too much digging to find that the appointment of Morrow and Burke to assist the organisation was because of personal relationships rather than the accepted tender practices."

Baxter pursed his lips but said nothing while Morrow fumed in silence.

"First you let Millar blind you with talk of profits, and then you happily sat back and accepted his payments."

"Inspector MacDonald. Are you going to put an end to this nonsense?" said Baxter.

"Rab Millar set you both up as integral parts of the Miltek dealings. It was a means to target and exploit vulnerable young women and children," said Taylor, ignoring the interruption. "Morrow and Burke have benefitted significantly from the labour provided by these young women under the guise of employment training and reintegration into work. Mr Baxter, your company has exclusivity on legal issues arising. There's even a significant tax benefit, isn't that correct?"

"Whatever tax exemptions we claim are ironclad."

"Maybe."

"Definitely," said Baxter.

"Not when it comes to this." Taylor reached to the floor and collected a thick blue folder.

"These are offshore transactions from a prior investigation into Gordon Beattie Holdings. I'm sure you are both familiar with the man?"

Neither Morrow nor Baxter answered.

"I got to thinking, what hold Millar could have over you to stop you turning him in or shutting off the tap if the pressure got too much, so I went looking. Havelock Holdings facilitated a cash sum through a network I know is associated with laundering Gordon Beattie's dirty cash. Not all of the money from that transaction came out the other side, but you both appropriated a tidy sum from that deal. Now this," Taylor slid out another spreadsheet. "Shows that exact sum routed through the Cayman Islands to a bank in Riga that we can link to Havelock. So, here's what I think. Millar had you embezzle that money because he knew it implicated you in a crime, and, if Gordon Beattie ever found out you stole his money, prison would be the last thing you would be worrying about."

Baxter swallowed, while Morrow for once lacked her front of brash arrogance.

"You can thank your son for bringing the final pieces to my attention."

"Bryce?"

"Bryce met with Rab Millar on the day of his death, his excuse being he contracted an STI from one of Millar's girls, but that wasn't the case. He was there because of Lena Borodenko. I guess the apple really didn't fall far from the tree."

"I don't know who that is?" said Morrow.

"You rent her the penthouse suite at Speakers Square, Ms Morrow. You've both been there. One of the many parties Rab Millar had after events at the Thirty-One Club wound down."

Baxter said nothing, but he didn't have to. Taylor slid out CCTV stills from the Crab and Keel which Macpherson's poker contact had helpfully provided.

"Bryce didn't get an STI from Lena. The calibre of clients Millar had her servicing meant she was tested every week. Bryce got his kicks further down Millar's menu and that's where he heard Daddy's favourite girl was pregnant and I don't think he'd planned on splitting the inheritance with an illegitimate half-sister." Taylor continued to present stills, timestamped over several months.

"It took a while longer than I thought but he talked in the end. Do you want to confirm why Bryce called you seven times on Sunday evening, Ms Morrow?"

"I haven't spoken to Bryce in…"

"We have the call logs, so don't bother denying it. What I couldn't get my head around was why would he be phoning you? His wife had just discovered her husband was playing away, again, and his father's favourite lady friend was pregnant. Not to mention Jacinta's discovery of those Havelock Holdings accounts. So I'm left thinking, of all people, why you?"

Morrow shrugged.

"He phoned you to make the problem disappear," said Taylor.

"And how was I supposed to do that?" Morrow scoffed.

"How you always do it, by using Millar's pipeline."

Taylor took a breath and flipped open her notes. It had all slowly fallen together after the visit to Sanctuary. Her interview with Bryce Baxter and then the subsequent conversation with his wife gave some flesh to the bones, Macpherson's CCTV and Carrie's dig through the financials packing on weight.

"Bryce needed his wife to disappear. She knew the truth because you both plucked her from the middle of it. Was the Riga deal what you had to pay for her liberty? Or was that just to ensure your compliance?"

Baxter's discomfort was now as dynamically pronounced as his son's.

"You put the girls from Sanctuary to work as domestic servants and sex workers, and when they'd fulfilled their usefulness, Millar had a route to ship them on and squeeze out the last profits by giving them to the Albanians."

Morrow's face pinched, Taylor's insights stinging.

"Millar evidently told Bryce he would deal with

Borodenko, but when things blew up at home, Bryce needed your help to ship on Jacinta and the child because she threatened to blow the whistle on your whole sordid scam."

"Nonsense. You haven't one slip of evidence we know anything about that."

"Actually, I do. We have a group of women rescued from a meat processing factory, and specialist officers have been questioning them. Aside from the routes they took to get into the country, their supposed sponsors, and their travel documents, they've been giving descriptions and additional information regarding others who remain missing. We have raided a property and recovered documents. One of those still missing is Rachael Petroskovia, she's fifteen years old. We've got copies of her formal identification and DC Cook confirms she worked at Morrow and Burke."

"We offer these girls a chance. I don't know every personal circumstance."

"I'll keep digging up evidence now I know where to look Ms Morrow, so I can only advise you to make it easier on yourself and start cooperating. Where is Rachael now?"

"I couldn't tell you," said Morrow with a petulant wave.

"Lena Borodenko?"

"No." Morrow shook her head.

"Is this your car?" Taylor slipped an eight by ten from the pile in front of her.

"Item Alpha Echo One One Four. A CCTV grab of a red Audi A3. Registration number Sierra Golf Zulu Fifty-one Twenty-seven."

"It looks like my car."

"The car in your garage that forensics are right now taking apart. So, will they find evidence of Lena Borodenko or Rachael Petroskovia inside?"

Morrow glared at Baxter, the conversation passing over him.

"Charles?" she snapped.

"Mr Baxter, this is your client and Lena Borodenko leaving the grounds of the Belfast Royal Hospital."

"Yes. It would seem so," said Baxter, looking at the CCTV grab, dazed and preoccupied.

"Ms Morrow, you were fleeing the country because your secrets were about to spill out and you needed to get ahead of Gordon Beattie."

"No."

The only sound was the quiet hum of the recording equipment and Baxter's slightly strangled breathing.

"Pregnant." Baxter's words came out in a whisper.

Taylor said nothing. Morrow's jaw clenched.

"Where is she, Daphne?"

"Oh, for Christ's sake! What is wrong with you? If your useless son wasn't enough to put up with now you've gone starry eyed over that slut!" The dam holding Daphne Morrow's patience burst.

"What did you do with her? If she's carrying my child…" Baxter's words had no sting. A tremulous shock rippled through him as he drifted off.

"Have you any idea how many other old fools Millar had her turning her tricks for? Don't be so naïve, Charles."

"Ms Morrow, do you know where Lena Borodenko and Rachael Petroskovia are?"

Morrow glared at the two detectives, her eyes slits of menace, her nostrils flared, and when she spoke, the tone was hard as flint.

"No. Comment."

Taylor nodded slowly. Baxter mouthed another appeal, but Morrow interjected before he could get the words to form.

"I want another solicitor."

## Chapter 80

"Back!"

Elaine Weir moved against the far wall of the cage.

"You. Get away from there, step back," snapped the guard.

Rachael Petroskovia moved away from the door.

The guard had for the last few hours patrolled through the converted kitchens leering at each group of captive women, at one point taking obscene pleasure in forcing one of the captives to relieve herself on the cage floor rather than grant her the opportunity of privacy or at the very least the upturned plastic bucket he used as a stool.

He loosed the shackle and pulled at the door.

"Out, it's time to move you pretties on." He licked his lips, one hand on a cruel wooden baton slipped through a loop on his hip.

"Where's my daughter?" said Elaine, her knuckles tight white pebbles under stretched skin.

"Get out. Come on, don't have me drag you." He drew the baton and struck the cage. "Out!"

Rachael backed away at the onslaught, Lena reaching out to grab Elaine's hand. She nodded, speaking softly.

"We have to go." Elaine shook her head. Tears staining her cheeks.

"No. Not without Freya. Where's my daughter!" she screeched, her face twisted in fear and hate.

The man shoved the door wide, hitching a hook to ensure it didn't slam closed behind him. He turned back, contempt and anger on his face.

"Jesus!" Elaine Weir closed her eyes as the blow struck.

The guard slumped against the cage and slid in a jerky motion to the floor.

"Get the fuck away from us!" Lena Borodenko stood in front of the two other women. A murmur rippled through the holding area, the women rising to their feet.

"Shut up. Shut the fuck up!" Gary Webster dropped the long crowbar to the floor with a resounding clang. "Shut up or they'll hear you."

"Gary?" Elaine released her grip, but Lena held her back.

"This bastard beat me." When she spoke, her missing tooth was exposed.

"I'm sorry. I am. He…"

"Gary, where is Freya. What have they done with the kids?" Elaine pushed forward and grabbed Gary by the shirt front.

"They have them in the warehouse. Elaine, you have to go. Billy shouldn't have got you mixed up in this."

"I'm not going without Freya," hissed Elaine, stepping back.

"For God's sake, will you just come on!" Webster reached in and made a grab. Lena rammed her fist at his face, but the blow lacked strength and glanced off the top of his head.

"Come on! I'm trying to help you to get out."

"How do we get out? Are you going to just walk us out the door?" said Lena, blinking away angry and frustrated tears.

"I'm not leaving without my daughter," said Elaine.

"You're not leaving at all. Gary, close that cage. What the fuck are you thinking?" Billy Webster scowled at his brother, the door behind swinging closed after Barney Murray. "Well? Are you going to answer me?"

"Billy, look at this?" Gary stepped from the cage and did a pirouette, stopping to gesture at the human cargo. "You know what's happening here? You know what's going to happen to them wee kids?"

"I don't give a shite. This is my chance to move up, Gary. No more picking up Lenny's shite. No more Fearon Estate."

Billy pointed down at the prone figure. "Did he see your face?"

"Billy. We aren't doing this. Elaine, come on."

The older Webster pulled out a knife.

"Stay in there, you bitch. Are you off your head, Gary? What do you think they'll do to us when they find out what you've done? These people don't fuck about."

"Elaine." Gary motioned for her to move out.

"Stay inside!" Billy roared, the knife flicking between Elaine and his brother. "Barney, help him with your man, we need to get rid of him before he wakes up and squeals."

"Billy?"

Webster swung round.

"I'm getting sick of repeating myself. Get rid of him!"

Barney's head bowed in submission. Billy Webster grinned, spinning back to his brother and taking a pace forward, the knife out. "We need to fix this now, Gary."

The blow to his back sent him stumbling, and Gary stole the chance, snatching at the blade. It sliced into his palm.

Billy Webster lashed out with a headbutt, fighting for control over the knife, the blow splitting the skin above the younger Webster's eyebrow.

Gary's arm reached around his brother's neck, his hand slick with blood as he tried to force his older brother off balance. Barney Murray jabbed blows into Billy's back again, a lifetime of subjugation unleashed in a furious frenzy. Billy kicked back, dragging a heel down Barney's shin, but the blows continued unabated.

The brothers were nose to nose, snarls and snot as they fought for an advantage and the blade seesawed between their bodies.

Gary's hands were numb, and his grip loose, too much of his own blood making the hold tenuous.

Billy threw a shoulder and met resistance. Gary Webster

angled his stance, fighting against the pressure, and then the blade slipped home. Billy roared as he drew the blade out and thrust it home again, Gary feeling the short sharp punches as the knife stabbed him. The last blow grated on one of his ribs as it exited. The fight left him and he slipped to his backside, holding his belly, his victorious brother standing over him, shock on his face, eyes wide at the damage he had inflicted on his only surviving family.

Wrapped up in his moment of victory, Billy Webster didn't see the club hammer descend nor feel the blow that shattered his skull.

## Chapter 81

"Can you make a case out of that?" said MacDonald.

"We're eighty per cent there at the minute. We've had the link between the slush funds and the bank in Riga for months but didn't know it would connect to this." Taylor sighed and sat. "Morrow was handling property deals linked to Millar's criminal enterprise and Havelock Holdings was laundering the proceeds which came from the exploitation of the women procured from Sanctuary. Both of them are up to their necks in it. Look at him. He's ready for a doctor."

MacDonald knew how Baxter felt. He loosed his tie a notch, then rolled up his sleeves as he put his thoughts in order.

"I've thought this was incestuous from the start, but the coincidences keep stacking up, and these prove it." Taylor slid across the financials on Havelock, the ties to Miltek and the records from Companies House on the directorship appointments of Morrow and Baxter. Land and Property Service had also issued their search on the Miltek portfolio, and it linked each of the addresses through Havelock Holdings to Sanctuary via Morrow's property agency.

"Dirty old bugger." Macpherson stared at the screen showing Baxter, stewing in another interview room.

"Stop picking at that plaster," said Taylor, nudging her DS on the shoulder.

Macpherson tutted and rustled his pockets until he found the tail end of a roll of mints.

"Can we charge her for assault at least?" he huffed, crunching down on a Polo.

"We could charge you for breaking and entering," said MacDonald.

"I didn't break anything," said Macpherson, crunching a mint. "I thought I heard a cry for help," he chewed under the sceptical glare of the two DIs.

"Based on what you've got, we can push her on the Borodenko girl. The key thing is getting her to open up quickly. Are you still of the opinion she's palmed them off to this pipeline?" MacDonald clicked the mouse and split the screen so they could observe both Morrow and Baxter.

"Why wouldn't she? It's what Millar had her set up for. Groom them, push them through the labour funnel and then discard them for a few quid once they'd outlived their usefulness. Borodenko raised the foreign connection, and we still haven't accounted for all the Albanians from Signal Foods. We know prostitution and people trafficking is their forte, so that has to be the route. Searching these properties is a starting point."

"What about Sanctuary?"

"I want to bring in their director, Jane Richards. Last I saw her she was very cosy with Morrow's husband," said Taylor. "I'd say it's a fair bet he helped to get his wife in the door with them."

"Christ, this is going to set the chief super's underpants on fire," said MacDonald.

Macpherson laughed as there was a knock on the door.

"Sorry," Chris Walker apologised, half in, half out of the room. "Guv, you're going to have to come with me."

"What is it, Chris?" Taylor nodded at Macpherson and he swept his sweetie wrappers off the table.

"There's been a walk-in. You need to come downstairs and see this for yourself."

❖ ❖ ❖

"Jesus Christ." Macpherson held up his hands in surrender, stealing a glance at the old man in the corner. "I'm sorry, Father."

Father Michael Keane waved the apology away.

"Son, you lot have said worse in front of me than that over the years. No offence taken."

There was a small interview room off the main station reception, a box room of whitewashed walls, a single school-style table and four plastic chairs, the walls festooned in community safety posters and wary warnings for vigilance. Taylor, Macpherson, and their visitor stood staring at the table's surface.

"I told him to come forward straight away and tell you his woe. But he told me it was his way or no way. He needed to be sure where they were keeping the girl."

Taylor looked at the cling-wrapped and broken down pieces of an AK-74 assault rifle and boxes of ammunition.

"Father..."

"Michael. Michael Keane. Here, he told me to give you this too." The priest dug in his frock coat and drew out a clear plastic ziplock bag, inside which was a mobile phone.

"What's this?" Taylor said, her mind reeling, still focused on the firearm she had last seen being unleashed inside Signal Foods.

"I'd call it a confession of sorts."

Taylor dug in a pocket and retrieved a nitrile glove. Snapping it on, she slipped the phone from the bag and tapped the screen. The photo icon flashed with a recording. She angled it so Macpherson could see, and hit play.

The image was erratic until it focused selfie-style on a familiar face.

"*Inspector, I'm sorry for what happened on the hill. Father Keane is an old friend and had no knowledge of my actions. He tried to dissuade me from this course when I asked for his help. I didn't listen to him either. I can be stubborn that way.*" The bearded face broke into a tired grin. "*Long story short, a young woman and her daughter have become involved in something I started against an old friend of yours. I don't imagine I have to spell out who that is. By now Father Keane can tell you where they've taken me, so round up the troops because once I have what I want, you are welcome to the rest of the whole rotten barrel."*

## Chapter 82

The club hammer thunked heavily to the floor, a spark glimmering against the concrete.

"Gary, Gary." Barney Murray slid to his knees and hauled the younger Webster to an upright sitting position. Webster's face was porcelain white. The blood from the nick on his eyebrow had clotted in his right eye and he raised a hand to brush away the crusts but winced.

"How do I stop the blood? Gary, you're bleeding."

"Is he dead?" Elaine Weir stayed back, holding onto the cage and peering at the supine Billy Webster, the back of his head misshapen like a badly risen loaf.

"Gary?" said Barney, desperation in his tone.

"Found a set of balls, Barney?" Gary Webster choked back a sob and clutched the wounds in his abdomen.

"I… I didn't mean to…"

"Fuck him, Barney. He was a nasty bastard. He'd have done it to you." Webster lifted a bloody hand towards the girls. "I'm sorry. I didn't know this was… I should have done something…"

Lena Borodenko squatted down beside the boy. Reaching out, she took his hand.

"It's okay, shush, we'll get an ambulance."

Webster smiled.

"Aye. Tell them I need morphine will you, a dirty big dose of it." His voice rasped as he struggled to breathe against the pain.

Rachael bustled over, with a wadded strip of blanket from th e cage. Murray moved aside, and she pushed the material over the wound. Webster moaned in agony.

"Press it down. No hard," she pushed Murray's hands

onto the wound. "Now keep up the pressure. We have to go." She tugged at Lena's shoulder.

"I'm staying with him."

"We have to go!" the younger woman implored. "Do you know how we get out of here?" she said, looking down at Murray.

"I…"

"Barney," Elaine stepped from the cage, frightened, her steps wary as she approached.

"Where is Freya? I can't go without Freya?"

"We have to go. We can call the police." Rachael glanced about the space. The guard remained unconscious. Billy Webster was dead and his brother was dying.

"They will come. We have to get away from here or you'll never see your daughter again."

"I'm staying with him." Lena Borodenko's tone gave no more room for argument. She swapped with Barney in putting pressure on Gary's stab wounds. "Go. Let these women out and all of you go."

"We stand more of a chance if it is just the four of us. We'll send back help," hissed Rachael.

The low murmurs of the other women were growing into frightened questions. Questions Elaine couldn't understand.

Rachael Petroskovia barked back, and the next exchange between the women was angry, the noise becoming loud. Too loud.

"We have to go." Rachael stalked across and took the baton from the guard.

"Take the knife too," said Barney. "They have guns." The course of his actions over the last few minutes was starting to hit home and with the realisation the shake of shock.

"Barney, I need to find Freya," said Elaine.

"We have no time." Rachael wiped the blade on Billy Webster's back and offered it to whoever would take it.

"Barney," Gary Webster's voice was low. His eyes flicking to the right. "Take them out that way. I passed a fella with a pallet truck so there must be a loading door." He grimaced and Lena swapped the now soaked wad of material for another, her free hand stroking damp hair from his face.

"Go. Go now while you still can," she ordered.

❖ ❖ ❖

"What do you mean he's here?"

"Freaky picked him up." Gordon Beattie looked at the police officer who he had known for most of his adult life.

The rise to the top of their chosen echelons was down to a mutual understanding that they needed each other. Beattie for the damage that could be wreaked by taking competitors off the streets and interrupting their business; that action made possible by having someone trustworthy enough on the inside to act on his intelligence and use it to advance their own career to the point where the information that flowed back was just as useful to Beattie himself.

There remained times though when the forces of law and chaos were still diametrically opposed.

"Looks like I'm doing your job for you again," said Jackson, with a sneer. "Relax, he's not going anywhere. I've locked him in a storage room downstairs."

The policeman thought of the ramifications and the potentialities that could slip out of control. The crawling legs of guilt crept through his belly, paranoia chewing him from the inside out like the larvae of a jewel wasp.

"What if I'm wrong and he is operational? Have you any idea what that means? He could have been under surveillance the whole time. John, you need to clear this place now."

John Barrett looked to each of the men, knowing it would reflect badly on him, and by proxy all present, if the situation disrupted the consortium's deal, much less subjected it to a raid.

He had granted the general and the cartel assurances of security. Losing face would require recrimination, fiscally and viscerally. It was, he thought, unprofessional that those vehement assurances were now being abandoned by the man who had claimed them impenetrable in the first instance. The fallout would be greater still if it was found that an agent of the state had infiltrated such an internationally significant deal.

"We are in the middle of the transfer," he said. "It will take as long to abort as to wrap it up, and I'm not prepared to lose face with the cartel nor General Sunday over 'what ifs'."

Gordon Beattie rose to his feet.

"Let's clear this up then. Freaky, take us to him." He nodded to the police officer. "We need to ask the bastard ourselves what he's been playing at and who, if anybody, he's working for."

## Chapter 83

"...the corner of Harbour and Cargo Road." Taylor spoke into the car's TETRA radio as Cook spirited the Vauxhall through a set of red lights, grille lights flashing neon blue and white.

Macpherson flopped against the rear passenger door and braced himself with one hand on the seat and the other on the grab handle.

"Christ, Carrie. Let's get there in one piece." His words received a coy wink in the rear-view mirror. The three passengers juddered as she hit a section of speed ramps hard enough to get the mud flaps and the sump tank protesting.

"All units, rally point Echo is the car park at Edgeware Removals and MBC Engineering. Secondary rally, Delta, is along Container Row next to ABG Tooling. The target building is Hoey International Cargo. Low key approach. ARV to advise when on scene," said Taylor, continuing her brief.

Cook took a left and right turn on two green lights, negotiating the light traffic on the Harbour Estate and keeping the western side of their target building in sight between the other industrial units. Pulling up in the forecourt of a dozen roller-shuttered warehouses, the car was masked by a low hedgerow.

Taylor placed the TETRA into the central console. The last few hours had been a blur. ACC Wallace was in meetings and the chief super was somewhere in transit between Musgrave and Headquarters.

After intense lobbying from herself and MacDonald, helped by the fact Hoey Cargo was another Miltek property they had tied to Morrow and Millar and identified on invoice documents seized from Signal Foods, DCI Gillian Reed had signed off on the operation to seize records and carry out a search as part of the ongoing investigation into the drugs and trafficked women found at Mountainview Crescent Industrial Estate.

"All units standby. Vehicle exiting Delta," said Taylor over the comms, watching a white van exit under a raised barrier. "Sierra Seven, have him pulled in at the port exit."

Confirmation from Sierra Seven buzzed over the comms channel.

Unmarked observation had provided intelligence that the yard was busy with freight loading, and the admin area had several vehicles parked up. There was visible foot traffic around the perimeter, but no overtly suspicious activity. The initial search teams would roll up to the gate with their warrants and conduct the search of the premises and seize physical and soft records in relation to Signal and Miltek.

Taylor's group, stationed at the exit of the ferry-side facility, was to ensure that once the team went in, nobody made a hasty exit from the rear.

Taylor, clicking her thumbnail against her teeth, watched and waited.

A refrigerated forty-footer backed towards one of the large loading bays. The shutters rattled up as it approached, the warm yellow glow of sodium lights leaking from the building's interior.

As the driver jumped down from the cab, the comms chirped confirmation the search team was inbound.

Game on.

## Chapter 84

"Do you know where you're going?"

"I've never been here before!" hissed Barney Murray. "It might be down here."

Murray, Elaine Weir and Rachael Petroskovia walked down a narrow concrete corridor, with lagged pipework and a strong tang of saltwater and sewage. The path descended from the converted kitchen area and dog-legged, widening slightly on the turn, the walls pockmarked and scored by the passage of cargo.

So far it seemed their escape had gone unnoticed, but now they were lost in the labyrinth of the building's undercroft.

"What was that?" Elaine grabbed Barney's elbow, dragging him to a stop.

"Come on." Rachael strode ahead. "It's only a matter of time before they find out we are missing. There must be a fire escape somewhere." She pointed to an illuminated emergency exit sign, where a little green man fled through a door.

"Rachael, just stop a second!" Elaine raised her voice, the echo alarmingly loud.

Then they heard it. A series of low shouts and the warble of an electronic sounder.

"Christ. They know, run."

❖❖❖

Shepard strained against the bonds and felt the chair flex some more. Tipping forward, he braced and pressed up into an uncomfortable bent crouch, the chair an awkward shell upon his back. He shuffled backwards a few paces, one chair leg catching the floor and crashing him back into a seating position. Sweat dripped in his eyes. He was a little closer to the wall, close enough to smash against the bare block. It would be hell on his hands and arms, but if it freed him, he'd get over it.

Years in the field, Special Forces selection, and hours of putting trainee recruits through the grinder had sharpened his internal clock, and the seconds were ticking down. If Jackson came back and they got the answers they needed, it wouldn't be long until he was dead in a ditch.

He'd hoped to have orchestrated a very different one-on-one with Gordon Beattie but with the complication of Elaine and her daughter he had played the hand dealt and in doing so would look the man in the eye and have him face what he had done in the name of climbing his corrupt ladder, and for dragging yet another two innocents into his orbit.

It had to be done before Beattie made an escape or before the cavalry arrived and took the opportunity from him. Michael Keane's involvement had been his back-up plan, and if timed right, Beattie would be dead and he would slip away in the chaos as the cops raided the facility and dismantled another of Beattie's sordid legacies.

Hours had passed since his arrival, and it was a half hour since Jackson had grabbed his coat and left. A drip of sweat hit the floor between his feet as he pressed into the shambling crouch, then exploded backwards against the wall. He felt a searing heat of pain as his weight and momentum were arrested by the rough cement, replaced by a surge of adrenaline on hearing the crack and splinter of plastic.

He landed heavily on his back, then rolled onto his side, his arms still strapped to the chair and the shards of the shattered spine and headrest bit into his skin as he stood.

Stepping over the sharper splinters and exposed bolts and screw tines, he shrugged off the remaining bonds to stand naked and bathed in a sheen of sweat under the glare of the single bulb, catching his breath and rubbing feeling back into his hands; he had no time to prepare when the door slammed open.

❖ ❖ ❖

"No, this way." Barney bundled the two women around a corner and up a short flight of steps.

"We should follow the signs," said Rachael.

"The signs are leading you to the main exits. There'll be too many people about. Come on, down this way. I heard…"

Elaine Weir squealed in fright as two men rounded the corner fifty feet ahead of them.

In the second of startled panic that caught them all unawares, Rachael grabbed Elaine by the wrist and dragged her into a side corridor, Barney's feet flapping hot on their heels.

Raised voices shouted in their wake.

The corridor dog-legged, and then another passage fed off in the direction from which they had come. Rachael charged on, doors along one side flashing past as they ran.

"In there. There, any of them. Get in," gasped Murray, pointing at a set of doors.

There were wooden pallets stockpiled along the walls, and he tipped a tall stack across the corridor as the girls gained a lead on him.

"Come on!" shouted Rachael, darting a look behind.

"In there!" Murray muscled to the front, halting the women's motion and dragging open a storage room door.

A minute to let the guards rush past, then they would double back and find another route. He shoved Elaine Weir through the door first, his heart pounding, hoping it wasn't too late and the pursuers would miss the door closing.

His heart plunged as Elaine screamed.

## Chapter 85

"…confirmed at entrance. Charlie Seven Four. Standby."

Taylor craned forward in her seat and clicked the button to drop the passenger window. The Vauxhall was stuffy, and the windscreen had fogged.

"Sure, you can't see through the bloody building, anyway. You're only straining your eyes," said Macpherson.

Carrie Cook flicked the blowers on and cool, then warm air hissed from the window vents. Macpherson manoeuvred between the two front seats, one arm pulling on Taylor's headrest.

"You any snacks in here?"

The TETRA warbled from its position in the centre console.

"Charlie Seven Four. All units. Barrier still down. Proceeding to gatehouse on foot."

A dozen external floods illuminated the rear facade, picking out pools of light along the access road to the rear gatehouse across from the secondary position. Taylor keyed the comms.

"All units be advised. Possible egress of subjects position Delta. Exit route illuminated. Wait one."

In the air from across the yard, a faint warning horn warbled.

"What's that?" said Macpherson, brows down, concentrating on flickers in the pools of light.

"Fire alarm?" said Cook.

"No. What's that?"

Taylor followed his outstretched finger pointing at eleven o'clock from their position, about a hundred yards from where the big truck had backed into the loading bay, and a small rectangle of light bloomed on the wall, movement flickering between shadow and the light cast by the floods.

Taylor opened her door and climbed out, aware that Cook and Macpherson had followed suit.

"Christ the night." Macpherson reached back in to grab the comms.

Taylor was off and running.

As the figures moved under a shaft of illumination, she could make out a score of individual faces, and at the head, bloodied and stooped under the weight of a young man was Lena Borodenko.

## Chapter 86

John Barrett's aide nodded and exited the director's office, closing the door behind him.

Barrett stood, his jaw clenched and blood pressure hissing in his ears.

He lifted the glass of water from the desk and slugged it back, then took a deep breath. The consortium would be unhappy. There was no doubt about that, but the level of wrath that would descend would wholly depend on the next few minutes and how organised a retreat he could beat.

He hurried across the plush carpet and clicked open the adjoining door, exiting through the PA's office to another small hallway and then back into the viewing gallery.

A low tone from the tannoy system announced his arrival.

"John?" General Sunday had the neck of the exquisite whiskey against his glass, his smile dying as the alarm sounded.

The Venezuelans were quicker on the uptake. Ruiz removed a mobile phone from his pocket and Sebastien Gutierrez snapped closed the lid of the laptop, securing the binding of the carry case.

The main double door to the office opened and Barrett's security detail entered, weapons in hand.

"Gentlemen, there's no need to be concerned. It's unfortunate, but we must abandon our business for the moment. If you'll follow Derek, we have a contingency to return you to the airport."

Sunday necked what he had in his glass, stoppered the whiskey and with the bottle in a fat hand, headed to the door.

"Where's Gordon?"

"Mr Beattie knows his way out, General. Now, please.

After you."

❖ ❖ ❖

Murray blinked in shock as he was confronted by the man, naked apart from a triangle of plastic bound to his wrist. His face was battered and bloody he had a fresh wound to the right-hand side of his chest, and the rest of him looked like it had been hit with a power sander.

Scar tissue ran from calf to thigh on his left-hand side and two deep pockmarks pitted the torso, one low on the left of his stomach, the other high on his right pectoral muscle.

It took a few heartbeats to recognise him as the same man he had seen on the stairway at Fearon House. The same man he had seen fire a rocket into the Blackshaft Terrace crack house and likely the same man who had butchered Rab Millar and blitzed the Corners Bar.

He didn't have time to think of anything else as the two pursuing guards rushed into view.

❖ ❖ ❖

Shepard squinted in surprise as Elaine Weir tore through the open doorway, her shock at the sight of him audible as another girl rushed in behind. He recognised the last figure as the kid from the crack house.

Angry shouts sounded outside and as the kid in the door froze, Shepard moved.

Sidestepping to the workbench, he grabbed the nearest weapon to hand. A rusted chisel, dulled by age and misuse.

A disembodied arm forced the kid back into the room at gunpoint, the gunman blind to Shepard waiting in position behind the door.

Shepard timed the snatch as the Glock passed his eyeline. He caught the barrel in one hand, jerking the holder off balance, and twisting the weapon against the wrist joint. His other hand arced an uppercut with the chisel.

The dull blade penetrated the underside of the man's chin and exited through the roof of his mouth to take root in the cavity behind his nose and eyes. He dropped like a stone and Shepard, using the falling body as cover, sighted a second figure raising a weapon.

Snapping up his aim, Shepard squeezed off a double tap, his rounds striking the second target on the cheek and the bridge of the nose, decorating the wall behind with a gruesome abstract of blood and brain matter.

"Are you going to be a problem?" Shepard pointed the Glock at Barney Murray, who shrank back against the wall.

"He's okay, he helped get us out. Jesus, Tom." Elaine Weir stepped between the raised weapon and Murray. "Are you alright?"

Shepard could feel the spatter on his face, and from the three expressions, he knew he looked horrific. He retrieved his jeans and dressed, laced up his boots and dragged on a tee.

"I'm fine. Are you okay?" he said. Elaine, weary and red eyed, shook her head.

"I don't know where they've taken Freya."

"Do you know?" Shepard turned to the boy.

Murray nodded.

"There's a Portakabin in the main warehouse. We saw them go inside, but you'll need to hurry. The vans were being loaded."

"What vans?" said Shepard.

"The trucks. They were taking the women and kids away in trucks."

Shepard considered his options. Get the three kids out and Beattie would be in the wind. Go after Beattie and there was every chance the three kids and the rest of the trafficking victims would suffer a short future.

He only had one shot at goal, but he wondered if his

conscience could take the thought of abandoning more innocents to their deaths. He stooped and retrieved the second pistol from the man missing the back of his head.

"Take me to the warehouse," he said, hopeful that he still had time to pull off a double.

Murray nodded.

"Then you'll get these two out of here. Understand? If anything happens to them, I'll find you…" Shepard let the words hang, and Barney paled.

"Go on, lead the way."

Barney exited first, followed by Shepard, with the two girls to the rear. They'd gone ten steps when the shots rang out.

## Chapter 87

The two-tone sounder reverberated in the narrow corridor.

"What's going on?" The police officer's discomfort was now more apparent than it had been in the director's office.

"Something's happening," said Beattie without breaking stride.

"Well, what?"

"How the fuck do we know?" snarled Jackson. "Maybe you brought your mates along?"

"I came to warn you!" The police officer halted.

"Will you come on? Whatever is going on Barrett's boys will deal with it," said Beattie, beckoning the man to move.

Shots rang out, forcing the three into the cover of a pallet stack.

"You alright?" said Beattie.

"It came from up ahead," said Jackson, drawing a Beretta from his waistband as they proceeded.

Jackson loosed three shots as the figures walked into view, cement chippings and explosions of dust erupting as the rounds struck the far wall.

A return barrage of rapid doubles stitched close, thunking into the wooden pallet to Jackson's right and the pipes above his head.

"Go. Get out of here. I'll deal with it," shouted Jackson as he unleashed another flurry of shots. Beattie hesitated, glancing around the flimsy cover to meet the glare of a bearded gunman twenty yards away.

Beattie's eyes snapped closed as the wall beside him took the impact of incoming nine-millimetre rounds, splinters and heat peppering his cheek.

"Go!" Jackson leaned low and returned fire.

Beattie grabbed the police officer by the shoulder and turned him around, retreating the way they had come.

❖ ❖ ❖

"Lena!" Taylor ran at full tilt across the gravel roadway formed between the split stacks of shipping containers. Borodenko collapsed under the weight of the man and crashed to the ground as Taylor slid to a stop.

"Has he been shot?"

"Stabbed. He's lost a lot of blood." The woman was panting hard from the exertion.

"How? Who?" Taylor looked up as a dozen women swarmed past them, flitting like moths to light. Away to her right, headlights and strobing blues lit up by the gatehouse as the sound of feet crashed through the gravel towards her.

"There are others inside. Children too," said Lena breathlessly, her chest heaving.

Taylor snagged the first officer who had cautiously approached.

"Ambulance. Now," she ordered.

He nodded and dropped his mouth to his radio. In the same instant, the racket of automatic gunfire erupted from the front of the warehouse.

Whatever they had hoped to achieve. It had all just morphed into a full-blown shit-show.

## Chapter 88

"You'll be outnumbered in a minute. Throw it down and come out. We can talk about the girl." Freaky stood with his back to the corner, reloading.

"Save your breath. Where's Beattie?"

Shepard, holding a similar stance, took a wary glance into twenty yards of nothing. Stalemate.

"You don't stand a chance, soldier boy. You shouldn't have got involved," shouted Jackson.

"You bastards involved me the day you murdered an innocent woman and child."

Jackson slammed his magazine home and drew the slide.

"You'd have been better walking away," he said, trying to see his opponent.

"Not going to happen. I'm going to make sure you pay for what you did."

"Two minutes and you'll be dead."

"That's what MacBride and Millar told me and I'm still here."

Jackson snarled and whipped out, firing blindly.

Shepard allowed the barrage to cease. The time for standing still had long passed, the sirens were singing for a reason and from the garbled three-way explanation he had received from the kids huddled behind him, there were plenty of heavily armed problems scouring the building that gave Jackson's threat credence.

Beattie was escaping, and there was a higher than average chance that they themselves would be captured or killed if he didn't do something quickly.

The mountain tunnels of Tora Bora and storming innumerable compounds of hardened dirt and mud buildings had honed in Shepard a razor-sharp sense of direction. That, and too many years in the surf and sand, had also tuned his other senses so he could smell the salt and the sea in the damp air, which meant a way out.

"We're moving. You all ready to follow me?" He peered down at the frightened faces huddled behind him. "Do as I say, when I say. Ready?"

As the nods turned to frightened glances at the crash of a door against hinges nearby, Shepard reached across the corridor and unhooked a powder fire extinguisher.

"Time to give it up, soldier boy." Jackson's words rang out, other calls and distinct voices now audible above the echo of footfalls.

Shepard heaved the extinguisher around the corner, and the heavy clang of metal on concrete rang out. Gunfire followed the metallic crash as Jackson fired at the distraction.

Shepard eased out low, taking a double grip, aiming and firing one shot.

The pressurised container cannonballed off the walls with the force of the discharge, obscuring the corridor with an impenetrable blanket of white fog as mono-ammonium phosphate and sodium bicarbonate jetted from the ruptured extinguisher.

Above the discharge, Shepard heard Jackson's surprise and panicked coughs.

"Move!"

❖ ❖ ❖

Chaos crashed the network as Taylor double-checked the fastening of her vest and cleared the breach of her weapon, the Glock a reassuring weight as she prepared for her second contact in as many days.

"Ma'am?"

"I'm ready. Say when," said Taylor.

The armed response team leader was the same commander

to whom Taylor had relinquished her weapon at Signal Foods. He raised a gloved hand and drew a circle in the air, signalling his team to move out.

She followed the phalanx of armed tactical officers across the illuminated path to a fire escape door bleeding light from the building. Overhead the clatter and spotlight of a police helicopter crisscrossed the area and fed commentary of the firefight taking place at the front of the building across the net.

Callsign Charlie had entered the gatehouse to find it unlocked and empty, but as the sergeant and inspector leading the search proceeded on foot to the admin area, they received incoming fire. The inspector, who was wounded in the leg, was saved by the quick actions of his colleague, who dragged him behind the security of a low retaining wall which was where the two men remained pinned.

With the rest of Charlie forced back beyond the compound gate, Section One of the armed response team had set up a cordon and was preparing for a retaliatory frontal assault.

Section Two had crashed the rear barrier and Taylor was in the wake of the six-man fire-team as they hurried to the unguarded rear of the building. She spotted Cook and Macpherson ushering the women away to the safety of the Edgeware Road car park where the yellow and green livery and flashing blues of an ambulance screeched in.

The broad avenues between stacked Hoey Shipping containers offered clear sight-lines if those inside put up a defence, making the approach a tactical nightmare. The echoes of distant gunfire and the moan of the wind swirled between the columns of containers that stepped in rows down a shallow bank to a concrete roadway that encircled the property along the water's edge.

Taylor caught movement low and far to the left, spotting a boat low in the water, the rumble of twin outboards lost to her ears but its running lights illuminating a group of figures hoping aboard seconds before they jammed the throttle open and it sped out to the lough.

"Alpha One. All call signs. Ready to breach." The team leader's voice was tinny in her earpiece.

The helicopter swooped away to the west, downdraft and spotlight sweeping over Taylor and the team as it made to illuminate the fleeing vessel.

One after the other the six armed officers entered the fire door, shouldering left and right as they graced the threshold.

No reports. Taylor followed, weapon aimed low. No contact. They were in.

❖ ❖ ❖

Shepard followed his nose. The undercroft corridor ran parallel to the offices which they had passed earlier but was separated by tons of earth and poured concrete. The passage dipped deeper as it ran downhill towards the lough, the creep of moisture on the walls and tang of the sea stronger the farther they ran. The ragtag crew followed in his wake, with Murray hustling the two women along ahead of him.

The corridor broke right through a set of double swing doors and then right again into a space that facilitated the loading and disembarking of cargo direct from the water. Broad painted beams ran overhead to a half mezzanine floor, where mobile cranes were slung between the beams and the upper section ready to net supplies on and off.

Arc lights shone above, illuminating the massive packing crates and hessian wrapped pallets that had been forklifted into neat rows.

Shepard entered slowly, pistol up and ears pinned back. All seemed quiet. A sectional door opposite was framed by a series of emergency exit signs offering a way out and to safety for Elaine and the other two youngsters.

He didn't see the swinging alloy beam until it blasted the

breath from his body and launched him against a crate of steel-rimmed alloy wheels. The gun clattered from his grip and the flimsy wooden protection wrapping a cargo pallet shattered under the beam's backswing.

Shepard flattened himself against the floor, the beam's tapered steel edge singing as it narrowly avoided decapitating him, the slipstream of its passage cool on his cheek.

The world was dark and then bright as he fought to the surface for a breath, vaguely aware over the ringing in his ears of the sonorous clang of footsteps descending the metalled stairwell from the mezzanine level.

A boot struck him heavily on the side of the head as he crawled to his knees. The second strike, meant to render him incapable, he caught at the last desperate second, twisting the foot and striking out at the supporting leg with a weak kick of his own.

Freaky Jackson fell on top of him.

The kids panicked, splitting up and ferreting between the stacks with two of Jackson's men giving spirited chase. Shepard captured it all as a negative image from the corner of his eye.

Two big hands grabbed him by the head, slamming his skull against the floor, the impact sending sparks of hot pain against his already dull vision.

Jackson was a dead weight. His thighs pinning Shepard, lower limbs snaking to close down any attempt to rise from the floor.

Shepard launched a weak headbutt, but it glanced off with little impact. Jackson's left hand gripped his bicep, forcing his arm to the slab as he tugged the Beretta from his waistband.

Shepard launched his left hand up in a palm strike, rocking back Freaky's head and hyper-extending his neck.

Teeth gritted against the strain of popping cartilage,

Jackson scrambled to keep control of the gun, his grip on Shepard's other arm loosening. Relinquishing the hold, he shifted his seat back, reclaiming the dominant position and taking aim.

Shepard rolled his hips fiercely, tossing the larger man aside, the crack of a gunshot sent wide, the report of the near-miss ringing in his ear.

The two lay face to face on their sides for a heartbeat.

Shepard drew up both knees and launched a two-footed kick into Jackson's abdomen. Jackson, fighting to get his gun hand free, slid a foot away, far enough to right himself and to take a quick aim.

The bullet ricocheted with a metallic chime.

Shepard gripped the alloy wheel, scything it through the space to sweep the gun aside, the backswing connecting with Jackson's head with a flat note, and a bloom of blood and teeth spattered across the floor.

Shepard gripped the rim. Raising it above his head to fell an axe blow.

Jackson surged forward in a rugby tackle.

The rim swept down, but the blow was ineffectual, the tackle jarring it from Shepard's hands to hit the ground and spin away on its axis.

The two men cannoned around the square of packing crates, each fighting for a grip on the other, Jackson snarling, blood and snot peppering Shepard's face.

The larger man's weight crushed Shepard against the rough edge of a crate, pinioning him over the lip. Shepard raked a boot down Jackson's shin, leveraging himself upright, using a foot to brace against the wooden frame.

Jackson fell back under the pressure, an inch-thick strip of nylon packing wrap tearing off in his hand as he scrambled to reclaim his advantage.

Shepard drove forward, but Jackson looped the blue strip

around his neck, Shepard's momentary momentum lost as Jackson twisted the binding. Seizing the opportunity, he shouldered Shepard around, forcing a knee into his back.

Shepard tipped headfirst into an open crate, clawing at the garrotte, feeling his already soaring pulse elevate, his vision narrow and his body jackknife in the grip of hypoxia.

Jackson was unrelenting, pulling the binding tighter, twisting the material and shaking off any attempt to let his opponent regain balance or relief.

The two men clattered against a metal stanchion and for a split second Shepard got release; a quarter breath and the means to turn.

Jackson struck out with a knee, head jerking to the side to avoid Shepard's fingers prying for the soft tissue of his eyes.

Darkness descended as his hands scrambled for purchase, but only found the cold links of a chain. Shepard stared up at the overhead bulwark that protected the edge of the mezzanine from the impact of the crane's run.

His sight dulled, and his grip on the chain hanging from the block and tackle only just kept him on his feet. The block's battered lifting hook hung at eye height.

Freaky Jackson roared, his face puce with strain and the wrap cutting into his own hands, blood from his opponent's neck and his own hands starting to prove a disadvantage, his grip slipping.

The blow was sudden and unexpected.

Jackson dropped his hands from the makeshift garrotte and grabbed at the white-hot pain in his cheek, feeling something hard in his mouth. His eyes widened as he found his jaw locked and off-kilter with the lateral pressure of dislocation. He gagged, tasting the metallic tang of blood and something else, panicking at a sudden inability to draw a clean breath.

Shepard gasped, flailing at the machinery until he caught

the lever and slammed home the green mushroom button to engage the motors.

Cogs whirred to life. The chains snapped taught and Jackson was torn up and away, his legs pinwheeling, and gurgling an inhuman moan as he made a futile bid to grab the chains and release the pressure that was pulling at his face. Gravity and his bodyweight pulled him down against the lifting hook that was tearing upwards through the roof of his mouth and the zygomatic bone of his upper jaw, fracturing the eye sockets and maxilla; shattering everything from his nasal cavity to the frontal suture of his skull.

Shepard collapsed, tearing the binding from his neck and sucking in air, squeezing his eyes shut, trying to focus.

When he looked up, Jackson's hands had fallen to his sides, the machinery whirring on until it hit against the stops and cut out.

Jackson swayed above like a side of beef, the hook embedded deep.

As he blinked away Jackson's blood and opened his eyes, he found another gun aimed at his face.

## Chapter 89

Taylor threaded through the dark corridors in the wake of Alpha Team, clearing each cross corridor and room as they went. The continuing stand-off at the front gate was relayed between hisses of static and sporadic gunfire.

"Alpha One. Hold."

Taylor pulled up shy of the last man and watched as the team leader surveyed a fire escape plan pinned to the wall. Looking up, he beckoned Taylor forward.

They stood in a storage space fifty feet square, filled with racking and storage boxes and the smell of salty air. A double swing door stood opposite with two emergency escape doors on each side.

"We're two floors below the main entrance yard and the main warehousing facility. This is a dockside link that leads to the water and several fire escape stairwells." He tapped the fire escape plan as he spoke. Each section was blown up and identified by colour-coded decals. "The area behind the loading ramps looks like the best bet for the holding area, and it makes sense as this corridor links all the way to our entrance point."

Taylor nodded, following his finger from the entrance doorway and down the corridor to a rectangular space about twice the size of the CID suite.

"Given we've had no contact yet, either they are busy up front or they're clearing out the back."

"I saw a boat down by the dock," said Taylor.

He nodded.

"Me too. Our aerial asset was tracking but had to pull back when they came under fire. If we secure this area it establishes a choke point and then we push to support Delta when they come in the front."

Taylor nodded. Strategically, cutting off the route to both the container yard and the lower level dock area made sense. It left the exit at the front gate as the only option for those inside and even if they got through, the cordon would gather up the runners.

"Boss!" The shout came a second before a door flew wide.

"Armed police! Armed police!" Six voices rose in one, G36K rifles snapping up, their underslung Maglite beams picking out the terrified face of a teenager.

She stumbled, scrambling on hands and knees into the cover afforded by the storage boxes as a second figure emerged on her heels. Dark-skinned, wild-eyed and armed.

"Drop the weapon! Drop the weapon!"

The TSG team exploded into motion, seeking cover with all weapons now switched to the imminent threat. The crack of gunfire sounded, shots going wide as the gunman fired on the fly. Two shots from the team, and he dropped.

The crash of a metal crossbar sounded as one of the side doors flung wide. Taylor, sweeping her weapon to track movement, spotted another girl shouldering through.

"Contact! Contact!" she yelled.

Another man emerged through the same door just as the double door opposite also crashed open, admitting another two armed men.

The girl, running for her life, dipped under a rack.

Taylor leapt up and sprinted, sling-shotting around a rack. The poorly erected metal work straining under her momentum, it toppled, the contents of the shelves starting a domino effect spill into the aisle.

The shelving crashed against the near wall creating a tunnel, which she ducked under, following the girl through the fire escape door. The gunfire in her wake muffled as the door slammed shut.

Thirty yards ahead, the corridor turned; she could hear rapid footfalls and set off in pursuit. Rounding the corner, she glimpsed the girl angling around the next.

The gunfight played out over her earpiece as Taylor continued her pursuit, arriving at concrete fire escape stairs, yellow paint on the edges scuffed black, footsteps hammering upwards.

"Police!" she shouted, but the girl paid no heed.

Taylor grabbed the handrail, taking the steps at pace, the screech of a rusty hinge sounding one landing above. Once at the door, Taylor paused, then hauled it open.

Cool air flooded out. The ceiling soared up to a lattice of steel beams, then twenty yards away dropped from the edge of a mezzanine to a long floor space.

Off to the right, a higher balcony ran east to west with doors at each end and a series of rectangular observation windows obscured by closed vertical blinds.

Suspended in the air opposite her, the surprised eyes of a dead man looked down his nose, his head tilted back unnaturally and the gory tip of a lifting hook exiting his mouth.

## Chapter 90

"You took your time."

Shepard blew out a sharp breath, the dull ache in his head complementing the warm burn that lassoed his neck.

"Maybe if you'd mentioned what you were up to, I'd have been in a position to do something sooner," said Taylor, lowering her gun and offering a hand as he tried to rise.

Shepard slumped against a crate, hands on knees.

"That your handiwork?"

Shepard looked up at Jackson, the body spinning on the hook.

"Catch of the day. It's no more than he deserved."

"Remind me not to get on your bad side," said Taylor.

"The bigger beast got away," he said.

"Beattie?"

"Beattie," said Shepard.

"He's here?" An edge of surprise and hope crept into Taylor's voice.

"He was." Shepard jerked his chin at Jackson, "When he brought me in I saw a lot of weapons and drugs. They're trafficking women too, same set up as Signal."

"And children."

"Who are you?" said Taylor, spinning to face the voice. Recognising the figure she had been chasing.

The woman walked up the ramp that led to the loading deck and the sectional doors beyond.

"This is Elaine Weir," said Shepard. "Beattie had her and her daughter snatched to flush me out." He stretched out a palm in introduction.

"My daughter is in here somewhere. You have to help her. Why aren't you storming the place? Where are the rest of the police?" Elaine was hyperventilating, stress tightening around her like a suffocating blanket.

"Elaine, calm down. We have teams in the building. We'll get your daughter," said Taylor.

"When. When can I see her?" Her tears spilt over, accompanied by anguished sobs.

"Soon. You and Mr Shepard are going to come with me and get to safety first, then…"

"I've a job to finish," said Shepard, pushing himself off the crate and stooping to collect Jackson's discarded Beretta.

Taylor kicked it away.

"You're coming with me. The police will handle this."

"I'll respectfully decline, Inspector. Now, can I pick that up or will I just take yours again?"

"Can your conscience cope if you can't finish what you started and more people die? Tom, let us handle this," said Taylor.

"Like the last time?"

"No…"

"That bastard murdered my wife and child. He let them burn to death."

"I know," said Taylor.

"What?"

"I know. Somehow there was an accident the night Beattie murdered Martin Coleman. They couldn't leave any witnesses. I'm so very sorry."

Shepard closed his eyes, chin sinking to his chest.

"My God, Tom. I'm so sorry." Elaine Weir moved to his side, placing her hand on his arm.

"So you see why I have to finish this?" Shepard looked up, his expression bleak.

"You have to let me bring him in," said Taylor, tightening her grip on the Glock.

"You've tried that."

"Not for this? Not for Coleman, and not for what's happening here?"

"He'll never see a courtroom. Killing Coleman is the tip of the iceberg."

"Tom…"

"Look, I've heard enough. We can't stay here. Are you taking her out?"

"I'm going nowhere without Freya," said Elaine Weir, stepping away from the two.

Taylor puffed out her cheeks.

"Here." She collected the Beretta and passed it across grip first into Shepard's hand.

"Right decision," he said with a tight smile.

"No. A practical one. We push on together until we find a way of getting Elaine to safety and then we decide."

Shepard nodded.

"I can live with that."

"Any idea where they're holding the children?" said Taylor.

"Main floor. One of the kids said they were loading up trucks."

"Kids?"

"Young girl. One of the trafficking victims, and a boy from the Fearon Estate."

"Barney Murray," said Elaine.

"Runs with the Webster boys," said Taylor, eyes again drawn to the corpse of Freaky Jackson.

"I think they're both dead." Elaine's gaze followed Taylor's, her tone flat.

"Jesus, this gets better. Do you know the way?"

Shepard cocked his head towards a set of rubberised crash doors.

Racking the Beretta, he led the way up the ramp from the seaward side to where the larger storage and loading bays would face the main access road and rise to the floor above.

One overriding thought was distilling in his head. If Beattie walked into his sights again, Taylor wouldn't get her day in court. She would have to dance on the bastard's grave instead.

❖ ❖ ❖

The boardroom had become claustrophobic. Not from overcrowding, but in the sense it was in the eye of a viciously tightening knot.

While automatic gunfire popped and crackled from inside the building, shots out the front had died to the occasional rifle crack from one of General Sunday's men as they kept down the heads of the gathered police.

The scene through the viewports was now organised chaos as shutters were barricaded with shipping crates, the containers unceremoniously dumped by forklift and pallet truck to make entry as difficult as possible. Outside, the peal of a siren was audible over the commotion, and the gleam of the blue lights catching the high beams and underside of the roof remained a constant presence.

General Sunday, the Venezuelans, and their personnel contingents had been escorted by one of Barrett's trusted security detail to a small jetty out the back of the property. The report that they were clear was one small consolation, however, the presence of the police chopper and a TSG team ruled out a second trip to sea.

Jock Hayes loosed his top button. Sweat beaded his forehead, and he dabbed it away with the cuff of his suit coat.

"We need to go." Gordon Beattie strode into the room. Behind him, his visitor looked ashen.

"Where's Freaky?" said Hayes.

"Out there somewhere. The cops are inside."

"And your captive?" said Barrett.

"Loose." Beattie pulled out his phone. The signal was

blank, so he reached for the spider phone on the conference table.

"They'll have pulled the cell towers. I don't think you'll be able to call out there either," said Hayes.

Beattie tapped the call icon and got an engaged tone.

"Have we a plan C?" he said.

The policeman collected one of the abandoned whiskies and slugged it, wiping the back of his hand across his lips.

"Well?" Barrett looked to the policeman who nodded.

"I have."

Barrett signalled to his tall, suited guardian, jacket unbuttoned, submachine gun slung on a strap in his hands. The bodyguard made for the door as the officer finished speaking.

"I'll warn you now. It won't be pleasant."

## Chapter 91

Taylor pressed the earpiece to her ear and toggled the mic, but the hiss of static remained.

As they had moved through the central corridors linking the dockside to the main storage area, the TSG reports and control communications had become distorted, eventually stalling completely. Ahead of her, Shepard pushed open a fire door.

Peering through the crack, he saw a vast space. At the far end, two sets of metal steps rose to a wraparound mezzanine. Open at the centre of the north wall was another large sectional door through which he could see blue lights dancing across high ceilings.

To get there they would have to cross the space, and he was confident given the shelving, steel packing containers and pallets of goods they would be able to pass in cover, but what they'd find on the other side remained in question.

They only had two guns and a civilian in tow, and Shepard would have preferred to only have himself to worry about. As he eased the door wider and crossed the threshold, he could see a row of charging forklifts and a big red Manitou, their lifting blades retrofitted with broad clamps for hoisting cargo onto the higher shelving. A sudden movement to his left spurred him to duck from sight.

A white box van reversed under a raised shutter into some open floor space, tyres squeaking to a stop on the painted floor. As its front doors popped open, he saw women and children being hustled from a fenced section below the mezzanine, the area reminiscent of a bonded compound or import quarantine area.

"Freya!" yelled Elaine Weir, shoving past.

Shepard winced and pushed her to the ground as the first crack of gunfire zipped in their direction.

Taylor dropped to a knee behind a stack of Maersk Line steel containers, the long narrow boxes of thick seaworthy steel affording greater cover than the stack of flimsy wooden boxes Shepard dragged a screaming Elaine Weir behind.

"Shepard!" Taylor called a warning as sparks from incoming rounds lit the surrounding stanchions.

"I've no shot," he shouted. "Taylor, they're splitting to flank us."

Shepard put a hand on Elaine's back, pinning her as she squirmed and screeched. A glance confirmed they would be fighting for every inch from here on.

As the driver jumped back in the van, the passenger hopped into the rear of the truck, snatching the screaming youngsters from the duo of women who ushered them forward.

"Right. Right. Right," shouted Taylor.

Shepard twisted, popped up from cover, and fired, his two shots striking the sneaking gunman in the upper chest. He ducked as suppressing rounds rained in from nearby.

Peering through a gap in the wood, he caught a muzzle flash thirty feet away, the rat-a-tat-tat of rounds pinning him down.

Stealing a poorly aimed return of fire, he spotted a group of suits exiting the impound area but moving away from the van. He swore as he spotted Beattie among them.

Elaine dragged herself free and to her feet, Shepard lunging to pull her back as more gunfire cracked into the ground around them.

The suits rounded a railing and began to descend a set of concrete steps, their heads disappearing from view.

Shepard rose and fired off his remaining rounds, forcing the rifleman into cover.

Taylor caught the profile of Beattie who, turning at the sound of gunshots, looked straight at her, one hand on the rail and his other pushing the man in front onwards.

The barrage of covering fire from Shepard gave her a window to move, and she sprinted from cover, taking a long slide to the stack where the man Shepard had shot lay gurgling and coughing up a bloody mist. Relieving him of his weapon, a Heckler & Koch UMP, she then dropped, checked and replaced the clip, and tugged free the bandolier of back-up .45 ACP magazines he wore on his waist.

"Shepard!"

As he looked up, Taylor slid the weapon across the twenty feet separating them, tossing the ammunition afterwards. She then helped herself to the man's sidearm, a short-barrelled H&K USP.

"Stop the van," she shouted.

"No, I'm going after Beattie!"

"Stop the van, don't put her through what you went through. Get those kids."

Taylor caught movement. Bracing her weapon, she centred the aiming dots and fired instinctively. She didn't see the impact but saw the mist of blood.

"Taylor!" shouted Shepard in protest. Recovering the submachine gun he slapped the clip and racked the arming slide. He stood, but Taylor was off at a sprint, ducking under shelving and slaloming between boxes.

"Tom. Please." Elaine stared up at him, and he glared across to where the van was parked, the rear doors slamming home as the engine gunned with a roar.

"Stay here. Crawl under that shelf and stay in cover. Do you hear me, Elaine!"

She nodded.

"I mean it. I can't do this if you keep tripping after me," he said, grabbing her by the shoulder and roughly pushing her down.

"I know." Elaine's pretty face was ugly with tears. "Please. Get her back."

He looked to see Taylor make the railing and descend back into the undercroft after Beattie.

He roared a curse into himself.

"Don't come out of there until you see me or the cops." He looped the UMP's strap and the bandolier of spare clips over his shoulder.

"I'll get her, okay. I'll get her back for you."

## Chapter 92

Taylor paused, her senses strained in the gathering gloom.

She had descended two flights of concrete steps and was now faced with a cavernous tunnel that forked in two directions. A ribbon of electrical cable tray, water pipes and trunking threaded down each yawning mouth.

She couldn't hear anything other than her own heavy breathing and the steady drip of water from the overhead expanse of ceiling.

Pulling a small Maglite from a chest pouch, she clicked the narrow beam on. To her right were the closed cage doors of a freight elevator, the call light blinking red and the dull glow from its internal bulkhead lamp offering minimal illumination.

Running the beam across the walls and floor, she spotted a faint set of wet footprints tracking from a puddle and veering into the right tunnel, the walls chipped and scratched from where larger items of cargo had clashed. Weapon up, she followed the tracks until the ground became too damp to decipher the trail.

A cool breeze and the scent of sewage and stagnation grew stronger the deeper she walked.

Above and to her right, the scuffle and high-pitched squeak of rodents, and the creak and rush of fluid through the overhead pipes added to the taut edge of anxiousness she was feeling.

Up ahead she heard the protest of rusted hinges and the teeth-jarring scrape of metal on metal.

Picking up the pace, she hurried deeper into the darkness.

❖ ❖ ❖

Shepard erupted from cover and sprinted the first thirty

yards at full pelt, weaving to his right at the last second as one woman at the rear of the van raised the blued barrel of a Benelli 12 gauge.

She was at the extreme end of the weapon's range, but it blasted the packing crate to the left of Shepard's head to smithereens. He heard the ratchet of the reload and whipped out to the right of the pillar that blocked her view of his movement. A single tap of the UMP's trigger and the blood misted from the back of her skull.

The van sped away, tyres screeching as it cornered the obstacles of the storage bay and took a hard right to put it nose on with the exit shutter. The brake lights flared between the gaps in the shelves and a door opened, footsteps running to open the shutter.

He couldn't see the second woman. Distracted by the appearance of Beattie, and Elaine's attempt to rush for her daughter, he was unsure if she had entered the back of the vehicle with the children.

The rasp of a second tactical shotgun being cocked behind him answered the question.

"Hands," she barked.

Shepard held the UMP at arm's length, his other splayed wide. He could hear the metallic groan of the shutter rising.

"Turn around and kick the gun to me."

He slowly turned.

She was tall and well put together. Broad in the shoulder like a swimmer, with manly features and a brutal bob.

"Armed police!"

Shepard and the woman turned in unison to look at the upper ramp where a team of TSG officers swarmed across the lip of the mezzanine, the integrated headlamps of their Kevlar helmets lancing across the space between.

She raised the Benelli at the nearest officer. Shepard shot her through the heart.

"Contact! Contact!"

He was aware of the voices rising and the motion of weapons weaving towards him.

Ducking back behind the pillar that had obscured him before, he dodged under a shelving unit and rolled into the adjacent aisle. He sprinted a dozen yards then rolled under another until he was two lanes across.

Boots hammered on the stairs. The roller shutter was grinding up, and the van was revving, the driver impatient to get clear.

The grunt of acceleration set off a wail of frightened voices from the vehicle's rear compartment.

A round zipped past Shepard.

Head down, he sprinted to the end of the aisle and rounded the corner into cover, swearing as the van exited far to the right, a quartet of police officers running up the ramp to follow.

He knew the vehicle could only turn to the left and race parallel to the building heading for the rear container yard and the back gate, and if it negotiated the speed control measures and the weaving gravel lanes and got to the access road, its human cargo would be gone.

Swearing again, he veered left, sprinting hard in the same direction and prayed he could get to where he needed to be before the van did.

## Chapter 93

Taylor now realised she had descended into an underground landing station.

The tunnel had dipped into a central channel with a raised walkway on each side. The central channel at first held a small lick of fuel-polluted water but had become deeper as the passage sloped away.

Ahead there was a low glow of electrical light and the walkway opened onto a raised iron dock. The water lapped underneath, slapping on the support beams. Parked and in darkness, water lapping halfway up huge wheels, was a bug-eyed crossbreed of a tractor unit and a flatbed lorry.

Clinging to the shadows, she could hear voices, the words distorted by the echo from the low ceiling and the acoustics of the tunnel. Creeping on, she used the vehicle to mask her approach.

Moving from the walkway up the metal steps to the deck, she caught sight of her quarry.

"Police," she said, her tone authoritative, and the echo returning to her.

A whispered conversation ceased, followed by the sound of retreating footsteps and the harsh grind of steel on steel.

She moved towards two shadows, silhouetted by a set of low lamps mounted along the edge of a fenced boundary.

She could see a lighter shade of darkness beyond, the breeze indicating the mouth of the tunnel and the lough wasn't much farther past this point.

"Step away from the doorway. Slowly and with your hands raised," she said.

The low bubbling grumble of a motorcycle kicked up in the distance.

"Did you give any thought to my offer, Veronica?" said Gordon Beattie, moving away from where he had looped a heavy padlock on the gate, to where the control mechanism of a stubby crane arm and wet riser were mounted on a supporting cross-beam.

The metal platform designed to transfer barge cargo from the water to the deck lay below the waterline and the crane arm was poised above the bed of the tractor-trailer.

"I told you what would happen if our paths crossed again," said Taylor. She held the Glock steady, covering Beattie and the other figure, confident if either made a rash move, she could deal with it.

"And I told you you'd be wasting your time." Beattie tapped a rhythm with the padlock's key against the metalwork.

"I'll take my chances. I hit the post last time but drugs, guns, women and children? Even for you, that's scraping the barrel, Monster."

Beattie shrugged.

"I'll not be tied to any of it. I'm not here. I'm enjoying a very lucrative trade meeting with some of the province's most influential leaders of industry."

Taylor gave a low chuckle at the irony.

"Old dog. Old tricks," she said.

Beattie cocked his head, his expression one of amusement. Taylor moved her aim to the body wreathed in the shadows cast by the dull yellow sodium bulkhead.

"You can step out of the shadows, sir. I know everything."

At first, there was no sign he'd heard, much less was going to comply. Then he did, taking one long stride forward, the stubby barrel of his personal protection weapon aimed back at her.

"Inspector."

His refined accent was hewn rougher by the acoustics and

the tension of the stand-off.

Taylor kept her weapon poised on Assistant Chief Constable Ken Wallace, his position forming the point of a triangle with herself and Gordon Beattie.

## Chapter 94

"Put your gun down, Inspector."

"I don't think you're in a position to be giving orders anymore."

Wallace didn't flinch, his gun hand tucked firmly on his right hip.

"You don't know what's going on here, so I suggest for the sake of your career you stand down."

"Is that how we're going to play it?" Taylor remained focused on Wallace. In her peripheral vision, Beattie had leaned back against the cross-beam, his breath fogging in the chill of the underground tunnel.

The revs of the motorcycle intensified and then droned from earshot.

"This isn't a game, Veronica," said Wallace.

"Who was that?"

"None of your business," said Beattie. "Put the gun down."

"I don't think that would end too well for me," said Taylor. She looked at Wallace, noting a strained expression.

"Veronica, you lost the last time, and I gave you the courtesy of letting you walk away. That can't happen now." Beattie pushed off the barrier, raising his hands as Taylor eased the Glock in his direction.

"I'm supposed to be afraid of your threats?"

"Veronica. Put the gun down." Wallace's tone had become conciliatory. "This is something far beyond what you can comprehend."

"Enlighten me?"

Beattie put his hands back in his pockets and resumed his position, one leg tucked up behind him. Wallace glanced at him.

"Whatever? Jock and the other lads will be down here in a minute." Beattie shrugged, the meaning clear.

"Gordon is a confidential informant."

"Bullshit…"

"He is a confidential informant and as such must retain certain liberties to ensure that any intelligence we act upon does not compromise his position with the people he is doing business with."

"Get out of jail free," said Beattie, grinning.

"You have records and affidavits to corroborate all this, of course?"

"Yes," Wallace said.

"No, you don't."

"Veronica put the fucking gun down or so help me I'll shoot you."

Taylor eased to her right, narrowing her profile, the move only offering her a psychological boost. Wallace couldn't miss.

"The boot's on the other foot." Her disdain for her superior was clear. "You're his informant, same as you were for Martin Coleman. That's how you lured Coleman out to Portmuck."

"Ack, just shoot her," said Beattie.

"Killing me won't stop him, Monster."

"Shepard?" said Wallace.

"You got the memo then? I heard you couldn't be reached."

"He'll not get anywhere near me after this. Your lot know who he is and Kenny will have him lifted or tell me where he is so I can send him off to meet his bloody family."

"Why did you kill them?" said Taylor.

"Because the stupid bitch got in the way," shouted Beattie.

"Veronica, listen to me. Coleman had to go," said Wallace.

"Listen to yourself…"

"We were trying to secure peace among the gangs. Coleman wasn't prepared to come to the table."

"Like Billy McBride?"

"McBride was a raping nut job. I should have killed him too, but he served a purpose." Beattie spat over the rail into the filthy water. "Don't be shedding tears over what happened to him," said Beattie.

"With Coleman eliminated and Gordon in position, we had an opportunity to dismantle the remnants of any dissenters to the peace process quietly. The death of Martin Coleman prevented hundreds more trying to go out in a blaze of glory."

"That justifies nothing, or explains why you burned a woman and child to death in their car."

"Rab's gun jammed and Coleman made a run for it. She knocked him down. There was blood all over the car." Beattie shook his head at the memory. It was farcical, two bullets in the back and then Coleman vaulting over the wooden stile, falling down the verge and bouncing over the bonnet of the passing car.

Taylor's mind strayed back to the old crime scene images. The broken headlamp she'd put down to the heat. The large dip in the bodywork blamed on impact with the verge.

"She'd got out to help him and realised he'd been shot. She saw Ken in his uniform, and then Freaky finished Marty off in front of her. It was him and McBride that torched the car."

"You were an innocent bystander?"

"They begged me to kill my friend for the greater good." He moved from the rail agitated, a finger pointed at Wallace. "Him and more like him."

Taylor covered both men with her gun, her ears straining to hear if any back-up had discovered the tunnels or if Beattie's men were on the approach.

"I did it for my country. For peace," he said, with an emphatic stab into the air.

"You did it to feather your own nest, you narcissistic

bastard."

"And why shouldn't I be rewarded? Do you know what would have happened if the ruling council had found I was behind Marty's death? Have you any idea?"

"It wasn't just Coleman. He let you get away with murder so that you could set up your brothers and when he couldn't get at them legitimately, he enabled you to sort the problem," said Taylor.

"Of course he did. And I'd do it again. Those so-called Loyalists were nothing of the sort. They were only interested in number one rather than keeping this country British, and if you ever thought of putting me in front of a judge, then the world would hear it was men like me who were the real peacemakers."

"Men like you?" Taylor tutted, shaking her head.

"You think the same thing wasn't happening on the other side?"

Taylor held her tongue, unsure if she wanted to believe what Beattie was saying. The expression on Wallace's face was doing nothing to ease the icy dread slipping through her guts.

"Are you even old enough to remember the final days? There wasn't a week went past when a crooked politician or a peeler didn't have a skeleton dragged out and was forced to resign. How many influential members of the security forces were killed in the run-up? Training accidents. House fires. Flat out failures in personal protection. Even that bloody helicopter crash. You ever wonder why?"

Beattie was on a roll, justifying his place in history. His rise and his legacy.

"They didn't buy into the end game, so they had to go. You've no idea how deep this goes, Veronica."

"Beattie," said Wallace, a warning in his voice.

"Fuck off, Kenny. They'd never have let a Fenian join the

club if it wasn't for the results you got from me."

Wallace's face pinched at the insult.

"Aye, and you know it too," said Beattie. "That carry-on up above, Veronica. Your boss here knows the truth of that. I'd no idea I was getting roped into the skin trade. It's not my scene."

"You expect me to believe that, after all you set Rab up to do?" said Taylor.

"Rab should have known better than to get into bed with the bastards. You know, I'm starting to think they were planning the same for me as they did for Marty all them years ago." Beattie pushed off the rail, raising the padlock key.

"I'm walking out of here and shutting that gate behind me. Sort this mess out, Kenny. Either bring her onside or get rid of her."

As Beattie took a step towards the gate the gunshot was deafening in the enclosed space.

## Chapter 95

Erin Reilly thumbed the intercom, the little ring of infrared lights illuminating as the call tone warbled.

"That's Howard's car on the road," announced Chris Walker, putting his phone back in his jacket. The call to confirm the licence plate had returned a positive. "Anything?"

Reilly stepped over the low ornamental hedge and put a hand up to the glass of the front window.

"Not answering. Try the phone again," she said.

The living room was lit by a standing lamp, the room neat but absent sign of the owner, save a bottle of vodka and a couple of glasses on a coffee table, newspapers and paperwork scattered across the surface. A duck-egg blue scatter cushion lay on the floor, matching a throw rumpled from recent use.

The rising triple tone of a landline sounded from inside. Walker let it continue until the answering machine cut in.

"Jane Richards is unavailable at present…" he mimicked.

Reilly thumped the large brass knocker mounted on the red door.

"Can I help you?"

The two detectives turned at the sound of the voice.

"You're not those dreadful energy sales folk, are you?" She was a pinch-faced old matron, the eyeglasses perched on the tip of her nose secured around a chicken thin throat by a necklace of black beads. "If you are, I have to tell you that I've complained. It's a disgrace. And I saw you tramping over those begonias!"

"We're the police, madam," said Walker, rooting out his warrant card.

A rail-thin hand clasped the collar of her Barbour coat.

"My goodness. Is everything alright with Ms Richards?"

Reilly knew the look and caught the archness of the question. This one would have caught the scent of scandal through net curtains at a hundred yards and carried the gossip to the bridge club in the blink of an eye.

"Have you seen Ms Richards today, madam?"

The old woman blinked then looked about, indicating a spot outside the gate.

"She must be in. It's recycling day. She always brings the bin in when she gets home."

Reilly glanced along the path to a cubby sheltering bins and council recycling containers.

"Perhaps she's busy. She has a guest by the look of it." A knowing bob of the head at the big Saab.

"Do you know who this car belongs to?" said Reilly.

"Oh yes. I do indeed. That's the councilman's car."

Reilly turned her back and thumped the brass knocker again.

"I hope there's nothing wrong. Are you sure you don't need my help?"

"I'm sure it's fine, madam," assured Walker.

"I have a key."

Walker looked to Reilly, who moved down the path as the woman continued.

"She's away quite a bit. With the organisation. Sanctuary? Anyway, I tidy up a bit and make sure the cat is taken care of. Mable Thorpe. Number twenty-seven."

"Would you mind? Just to be on the safe side?" said Reilly, giving a polite smile in greeting.

The pinched face brightened, alive at the notion of being involved and the thought of what juice could be squeezed from the meat of such a juicy scandal.

"Absolutely. Absolutely. Just a moment. Give me just a

moment."

Walker watched as she power-walked in spritely delight a few doors down, dipping into a well-tended front garden and through the front door, returning a moment later. A similar run-walk but brandishing a key in the air and a grin that threatened to lop off her ears.

"Here we go, officer. Here we go."

Reilly opened the gate and helped her up to the front door.

"Shall we try once more?" asked Walker.

Mable Thorpe had the key in the lock and glared back.

"Go ahead, ma'am," said Reilly.

Thorpe eased the door open. The low drone from a radio and the occasional electronically elongated bleep of the answer phone announcing messages greeted them.

Thorpe had both feet over the threshold before Reilly could halt her.

"Could you wait here please, ma'am? Please? Just for a moment."

Thorpe began to protest, robbed of the chance to be in the midst of whatever was going on.

"Miss Richards? Councillor Howard?" called Reilly.

She motioned to Walker to stay in the small porch with Thorpe.

The heating was on, the red LED on the thermostat bright. Reilly crossed the living area and noted the bottle of vodka was down to the last half inch. The glasses had left rings of condensation on the table and several sheets of the paperwork; lists, extracted spreadsheet printouts of financial transactions, and email correspondence. To the right a manila envelope. The flap cracked open but empty.

A patterned box of Kleenex lay beside the spilt cushion, several discarded tissues stuffed down the arm of the chair with the trace of smudged mascara.

"Anybody home?"

Reilly carefully negotiated the rest of the ground floor. No one in the small bathroom tucked away under the stair space. The kitchen empty, no dishes on display, kettle cold.

"Does Ms Richards have a car?" she said as she re-entered the living area.

Mable Thorpe nodded.

"Parked around the back. Hasn't moved all day." Thorpe neither had the grace to blush or explain how she knew this. Reilly admired the professional busybody's powers of observation and moved to broaden her search to the upper floor.

The second stair creaked. A misshapen lump on the fourth where the gripper rod was poorly fitted. As Reilly graced the landing, she could hear the soft gurgle of water and then the hiss of a discharging cistern. The bathroom was to her left, door open but no occupancy, the room ahead a well kitted out dressing-room. Her reflection stared back from floor to ceiling slide robes. The door to the right was ajar and the soft glow of a lamp bled out.

"Hello? It's the police, Ms Richards. Is anyone home?"

Reilly used the tip of her shoe to ease the door open.

Malcolm Howard lay on his back, one arm draped off the bed, his face upturned with vomit smearing his cheek. A polished shoe lay on the plush white carpet between the body and the door. His jacket and tie were folded over the arm of a wing-backed chair.

Reilly rushed in, the tone of his complexion and the coolness of his throat telling her he was long gone.

Jane Richards lay beside him. Scattered on the bedside table were a series of explicit photographs of the two and dozens of empty silver pill sleeves and small white tablets of over-the-counter codeine and another bottle of vodka, drained to death.

Reilly reached out for Richards' wrist. Her skin was grey

and clammy. A gurgle escaped the woman's throat, then nothing.

Reilly dragged her from the bed and straddled her, ear to the vomit-scented lips, one hand interlacing the other, settling on the breastbone.

"Chris!" she shouted, urgency in her voice. "Chris!"

His footsteps thundered up the stairs.

"Chris. Ambulance. Send for an ambulance now!"

## Chapter 96

Macpherson barked into the TETRA and watched as one of the ambulances lit up, the blue strobes cascading around the frontage of the business units and the whine of sirens drowning out the response coming through on the handset.

"Aye. One away. Make sure it gets through pronto. The wee bugger has lost a lot of blood."

Carrie Cook slammed home the rear door of a second vehicle and it went through the same routine. Lights and sound, the rumble of rubber on tarmac as it sped away.

She peeled off a pair of bloodstained nitrile gloves, the gore a result of holding pressure on Gary Webster's stab wounds as paramedics had hooked up a temporary line to feed him a paracetamol painkiller on top of a ten cc jag of morphine.

"He make it?" asked Macpherson.

"Touch and go."

"The brother?"

"Didn't say." Cooke indicated a young woman wrapped in a space blanket, sat on the rear step of another ambulance. "She says he got clobbered over the head and wasn't moving when she decided to get the rest of them out."

Macpherson looked across and caught the eye of Lena Borodenko, who raised a hand in recognition, her expression obscured by a mask delivering an oxygen and nitrous oxide mix from a blue Entonox cylinder. He waved back, giving a paternal nod and smile, hoping it was reassuring.

Another crack of gunfire sounded, the quiet scene when the team had arrived now in chaos. A cordon of red and white tape sealed off all exits from Hoey Shipping with another, twenty metres back, enforced by four liveried Land Rovers bumped up two by two on each side of the road.

A command car and a Škoda Octavia from the Armed Response Unit were parked beside the CID Vauxhall. The detective sergeant marched over.

"What's happening inside?" said Macpherson.

A tall and impossibly young-looking inspector in bug helmet and flame-proof coveralls turned from where he and a burly sergeant were poring over a fold-out map.

"Alpha has established a position on the fringe of the main warehouse, and we're about to push Charlie in through the front."

"My inspector is in there too."

The big man shook his head.

"She isn't with the team. They came under contact and she took off after a suspect. No comms since." He put a placating hand up to prevent Macpherson from blowing. "It's a multi-tier concrete and steel structure, so it's probably just the signal. The tunnels that lead down to the dock and into the container yard will play havoc with the short-range."

Macpherson nodded, understanding but far from happy.

"Heads-up."

A flash of headlights illuminated the broad strip of roadway that edged the perimeter of the building. A series of fluorescent barriers bisected the path, ensuring any passing vehicle had to slalom until they passed under a low set of goalposts that signposted the entrance to the narrow road opening to the exit beyond the container yard. The measures prevented anyone gathering enough momentum or loss of control on the tight right turn where the roadway dropped off the precipitous path into the water of the lough below.

"Command One, be advised we have a vehicle moving around the perimeter of the building. It looks like he's trying to make a break for the container yard."

There was an eruption of screeching sound as a section of siding twenty yards ahead of the van was torn asunder, exploding out from the building in an ear-splitting crash of metal and ripping cladding.

Macpherson watched in horrified fascination as the cab of the van, too close to swerve or otherwise avoid the impact, was impaled on the forks of a grunting red Manitou.

❖ ❖ ❖

Shepard pitched against the steering wheel with the force of impact.

Although protected on each side by fastened steel window shutters, the front Plexiglas windscreen shattered as the Manitou's lifting blades skewered the cab of the van.

He felt the collision dwindle the torque of the telehandler's hundred horsepower and gunned the throttle to compensate, stubby tyres and four-wheel drive biting into the rubble and powering the Manitou across the newly created threshold of the building.

In the instant he cleared the breach, the impact, weight and speed of the van tore the rear end clear, shearing the telehandler through forty-five degrees in a series of teeth-jarring bumps.

Shepard's head slammed off the right-hand door column, and he felt the familiar warm rush of blood across his cheek.

Now traversing backwards, he was face to face with what remained of the van cabin and, obscured from his sight in the back, was a payload of petrified children.

He pumped the Manitou's brakes, but the combined weight of the two vehicles and the slope of the roadway saw gravity take over, and in the shattered remnants of the wing mirrors he watched the road running out, glimpsing beyond the edge the flash of a spotlight flickering over white-capped waves.

Reaching forward, he flipped the control toggle for the stabilisers. The lamp blinked once, then was gone, and the big brute stalled.

He reached for the ignition, pumping the gas, and willing the electronics to kick in before it was too late and both vehicles plummeted into the dark, angry sea.

*Chapter 97*

Taylor stared as the blood bloomed across the crisp white Oxford shirt.

Beattie's movement to the gate stopped dead as he comprehended what had just happened. Ken Wallace aimed the still smoking barrel of his weapon at Taylor.

"Drop the gun and kick it away, Veronica."

Taylor watched as Beattie staggered against the bars of the gate leading to the tunnel's exit, one hand clamped over the gut shot. Groaning, he slid to his backside, coming to rest against the bars.

"Veronica!" snapped Wallace.

She let the Glock fall free, giving it a solid kick to clatter across the iron deck between them.

"This is your plan? You're going to shoot the both of us and then disappear back to HQ like you never left?"

Wallace shook his head.

"The man who left through that gate will see I'm covered." He shrugged. "You aren't capable of understanding what is at stake, so why waste my breath." He gave a sad shake of the head. "It didn't have to end like this."

"I was supposed to let you both go?"

"I should have listened to Law," said Wallace, half to himself, and looking down at Beattie who was losing colour.

"Is he in on it too?"

"William Law?" Wallace chuckled, the sound eerie as it echoed in harmony with the slapping of the water. "He can only see in black and white. He wouldn't have the brains or the inclination to acknowledge that the only effective way to make and maintain peace is to operate inside the shades of grey."

"By ridding yourself of the people who get in the way, and then enabling the likes of him," snapped Taylor.

Beattie coughed up a mouthful of blood, face contorted in pain. The entrance wound had saturated his shirt and jacket.

"You have Beattie on a pedestal, Veronica. He's a cog in the wheel, that's all."

"That's all? How can you just turn a blind eye to the misery that he's inflicted?"

"By seeing the bigger picture. I was in Coleman's pocket. Then some influential people needed a shift in the dynamics. The Monster isn't stupid, he spotted the potential, and he's reaped the profits. He should have been on his way to his last big payday but, as is the way of it, in this godforsaken country you can't escape the past. This Shepard wherever he's crawled out from has royally fucked this whole thing up."

Beattie crawled onto his hands and knees, blood pooling under him, a hand clamped to his belly, and bloody drool spilling from his mouth.

"We could have sorted this out… Why didn't you tell me that shite had planned…" His cobalt eyes hadn't lost their gleam, but the shadows underneath had deepened, every movement causing him to bite down in pain.

"Gordon, it's all well and good ensuring you have the means and the security to ship your products. We all get rich. Yes. But there was always going to be room for expansion. All those trips across the Atlantic. Africa to Europe unchallenged. Shipping back empty was such a damn waste of resource."

"So you decided to kick-start a trafficking route?" said Taylor, what she had uncovered in the warehouse callously confirmed.

"Migrants are flooding into the country, and the people that hold the purse strings don't want them. The public had their say and, well," Wallace gave a cold laugh. "Look how that turned out. They were here illegally by and large. A commodity that could be tethered and turned to profit rather than impact on the already significant economic losses being managed to the point of failure."

"They were fucking children." A bloody snarl of snot erupted as Beattie tried to stand.

"How many children's lives have you destroyed, Monster?" sneered Wallace.

Beattie wobbled against the deck and slumped, losing the battle against shock and blood loss.

"I never forced anything on anybody that didn't want it…"

"Shite. You got your hooks into people. The addiction you've pushed all these years has blighted more families and ruined more lives than a few boatloads sent off to please the troops or make a wealthy warlord happy."

"You're sick, Wallace," said Taylor.

Beattie coughed, giving a grin of resignation.

"I told you there was worse than me," he said.

The sound of heavy boots echoed along the tunnel walls, Taylor shot a look over her shoulder, managing a small sidestep before Wallace raised his weapon.

"No rash moves, Veronica. Beattie, give me the key."

"Fuck you!"

"Give me the key!" Wallace marched across and backhanded the barrel across Beattie's face, the dull thwack splitting the skin from the apple of his cheek to the bridge of his nose. Beattie cried out, dropping the keys to the deck for Wallace to snatch them up.

Torchlight flickered in the distance behind them. Taylor heard the dull squelch and warble of a TETRA, but it was too little, too late.

"I wish it could have been different, Veronica. You were a good officer." Wallace offered a single nod of apology and raised the pistol for the final time.

He didn't give her a chance to form a reply before the gunshots rang out, bullets slamming home until the clip emptied, and the slide locked.

The barrage was deafening. Ears ringing, Taylor felt every impact, only vaguely aware of the shouts and the splash and clatter of boots moving up behind her.

She sank to her knees, a fine mist of blood on her lips and in her eyes. She gasped for a breath.

"Armed police! Armed police!"

The beams of light coalesced into a larger pool, the glare dancing across her face, shining in her eyes. Shouts of command and questions.

Time sped up.

"Get the paramedics down here!" she shouted, her hands slick with blood as she pressed down on Beattie's stomach wound. His hand fell to the deck, and he released her Glock, which she pushed away towards the nearest ARO.

Beattie gave a final wheezing cough, his teeth bloody, cobalt eyes narrowing with the flicker of a grin, even as he released a low groan of pain.

"What's going to get you out of bed tomorrow, Veronica?"

"Paramedics!" Taylor's roar echoed off the walls.

The team leader placed his lips to the mic. She heard his rapid report and subsequent request, continuing to apply heavy pressure onto Beattie's wound. Her other hand balled the fabric of his jacket where the round had exited.

She glared at him, gritting her teeth and driving the heel of her hand against the sopping Egyptian cotton.

"Fuck you, Monster. You're not dead yet."

Assistant Chief Constable Kenneth Wallace was though. He lay on his back with the key to freedom in his hand and a surprised look of defeat on his face.

## Chapter 98

Taylor had watched the spotlight as it traversed the dark water for half an hour before Macpherson dragged her away from the railing and over to where triage had been set up. Carrie Cook rustled up three cups of steaming black coffee from nearby a tuck truck.

Above, on the road, the electronic honk and whoop of a siren broke the silence as they sipped. Taylor winced, the coffee hot and bitter.

"He's in a bad way, but he's still breathing," said Cook. Taylor glanced up the hill to the ambulance that would transfer Gordon Beattie to the Royal Hospital.

The coffee tasted like ash, conflict twisting in her guts. He was going to live. She knew it in her heart, knew that she had saved him; the one man whose fingertip grip on life she should have prised free to let him slip off to hell.

"What about Wallace?" said Macpherson.

Taylor looked out to sea again.

"Bent," she said. "He was Coleman's man inside before selling out to a larger organised criminal enterprise. He set Beattie up as the replacement to help his ascent." She bit down on her tongue, the rest of the story she needed to process, not sure how much to accept, and concerned the revelation would put her colleagues in the firing line alongside her.

If Wallace and Beattie were to be believed, this was a poison that could have spread too deep to be cut out, and she would need her wits about her throughout the debrief and the coming days.

"Inspector?"

Taylor looked up. Two paramedics held the weak figure of

Elaine Weir between them, a space blanket wrapped around her shoulders.

"Elaine. Your daughter's okay, she's over there," said Taylor with a tight supportive smile.

Tears of relief fell from Elaine's face.

"Carrie, see her across. Make sure they give them a few moments together."

Cook nodded, taking up the position of one paramedic and leading Elaine to the pop-up tent where the survivors of the trafficking gang were being assessed and treated. Some uniforms snapped pictures on mobile telephones, others took personal details to assist in the huge task that would soon face the Customs and Border Service in identifying and repatriating the victims.

"Did you see him get out?" said Taylor, watching as Elaine was led away.

Macpherson shook his head.

"He came through that opening and rammed the truck," Macpherson pointed to the rent in the siding. "He must have engaged the stabilisers before the Manitou hit the lip of the sea wall, but the impact tore the cab off the chassis. The engine block and the drop bars stopped the van following it into the drink." He puffed out a breath as they surveyed the wreckage. "We had people down there seconds after, but there was no sign anybody got out. The two in the van's cab were dead, and everybody in the back was shaken. Cuts and bruises, but nothing that won't physically heal."

Taylor wanted to walk back down to the sea wall and resume her vigil. The spotlight from the helicopter continued to sweep the surface, and a team of search and rescue divers would arrive soon. An assessment would be carried out, the dive likely suspended until daylight, at which point the grim task of winching out the carcass of the telehandler's cab and Shepard's body would begin.

"It was him then?"

"They botched Coleman's murder, and the wife saw it all. He was striking back."

"How did he find out?"

Taylor had her opinions, but she held onto them.

"We might never know," she said.

All around, the chaos of events continued to burn bright with frenetic energy.

The TSG teams, backed up by uniform were rounding up and loading the remnants of the warehouse crews into the back of liveried wagons for the trip to Musgrave Street for questioning and the subsequent laying of charges.

The small triage area was lit by the glow of flickering blues. Sirens were silent as paramedics tended to cuts and minor injuries, victims faces pale and eyes wary. Rescued, but their ordeal not yet over.

Above, on the road, car doors banged with the arrival of more coordination, figures of seniority making an appearance as the magnitude of what had transpired filtered through the chain of command.

"I'm shattered," said Taylor.

Macpherson looked at her; suit ripped and filthy from the tunnels. Her hair unruly and covered in the blood of Wallace and Beattie.

"Come on. I'll take you to get cleaned up." He put his arms round her shoulder and guided her away from the water.

"Will you do me a favour, Doc?"

"Aye, of course, girl. What is it?" He stopped, paternal concern on his face.

"Can we spin past the Maharaja on the way back? I'm starving all of a sudden."

Macpherson's face lit up brighter than the fifteen million candlepower spotlight that continued to traverse the small patch of white-crested waves sweeping out into the icy blackness of the Irish Sea.

## Chapter 99

"You know we were good at this sort of thing once upon a time," said Michael Keane as the women boarded a bus.

Taylor watched as one girl paused and waved. She raised a hand and smiled, offering goodbye to a girl she never got to know but who had been instrumental in helping piece together some gaps in the story over the last few days.

Rachael Petroskovia had been duped into servitude, applying and turning up to a recruitment weekend in an upmarket hotel in the centre of Sofia, from where it had been a dizzying descent into slavery. Passport removed and attempts at escape brutally punished, Petroskovia found herself gutting beef carcasses in a processing plant on the east coast of the Irish Republic for eighteen hours a day. For the remaining six she was locked with fifteen other women in freezing and putrid conditions in old field accommodation on-site, sharing a single squalid shower and toilet and subsisting on whatever slop was served up in a greasy, rat-infested canteen.

From there she detailed the links to Sanctuary and the systematic exploitation and domestic servitude that had been forced upon her and women like her.

Lena Borodenko corroborated the tale. The beatings, stress, kidnap, and torture miraculously having no detrimental effect on the tiny life in her womb.

Sanctuary had been created to help those who desperately needed assistance, but unfortunately, it had been corrupted and become the antithesis of what it should have stood for. It wasn't the first time an institution with easy access to the vulnerable had been targeted. Children's homes, religious bodies, hospitals, had all fallen victim, each at the mercy of predatory individuals and Sanctuary had just become the latest in a long litany.

Millar, needing a steady stream of flesh to service his brothels and bars, with the assistance of Daphne Morrow had acquired and established a chain of halfway houses that Morrow filled with potential victims by exploiting her links with the charity. Desperate, worn down, and weakened, the victims were easy fodder for the cunning Millar and the men and women he paraded through to take advantage, be it as slave labour, or as nubile flesh to be pawed at and abused.

Both Baxters had succumbed. Bryce, a regular in the orgies that Millar put on, had, with the help of his father bought a 'wife' from the harem. Charles Baxter, enthralled and obsessed by Lena in particular, had yielded to his base desires and been corrupted by his introduction and access to the enviable client list sourced from the Thirty-One Club.

The speed and ease of Millar's accomplishments, and the void afforded by Beattie's arrest and enforced period of absence, was all he needed to trade the women and children further afield, linking up with the Albanians to form a chain of human misery.

When Lena fell pregnant, Baxter had offered assurances, then it had all turned sour. Perhaps he realised the foolishness. Perhaps Millar offered him a new concubine. It didn't matter. At that point, Millar had been murdered, and Lena planned to run, but Daphne Morrow caught up with her first, delivering her to Jackson and Beattie to explain her role, before salvation arrived from an unexpected source. Gary Webster had survived his wounds, although his brother had not regained consciousness and remained in a serious condition.

Their friend and compatriot Barney Murray was singing like a lark, and the seizure of assets and raids on Jackson's stash houses and Millar's properties had provided a massive coup in the quantities of drugs and cash recovered.

"They'll be alright, you know?" Keane laid a hand on Taylor's arm, mistaking her contemplation as concern.

"Where will they go?"

"There's an old convent on the north coast. Oh, nothing like what you're thinking." He shook his head as Taylor's eyes widened. "Modernity comes to us all. Think of it as one of those health retreats. They'll have chalets and the space to heal. The Sisters will welcome them."

Taylor patted the old priest's hand, grateful for his sensitivity and assistance.

"What about you, Inspector?" said Keane.

"What about me?"

The old priest looked at her.

"You've had a tumultuous time, lost colleagues. It can't be easy to be the centre of attention again?"

The wheels of officialdom had rolled into life following the mop-up at Hoag Shipping. The wagons had circled, and the information that made its way to the press had a saccharine taint concerning Wallace's demise in the line of duty.

Chief Superintendent Law, backed by Gillian Reed, had laid out the penalty for non-observance of the party line without room for misinterpretation. For Taylor, receiving plaudits for her work in exposing the Sanctuary ring and the rescue of the trafficking victims was enough to mitigate the criticism that arose out of Malcolm Howard's suicide. Jane Richards, thanks to Reilly's quick actions, had pulled through and was assisting the forensic accounting team in dissecting the fraudulent transactions Howard had deftly handled through her charitable accounts. Havelock Holdings was also proving a rich vein of intelligence into how Millar had laundered his illicit profits, and hopefully, it would only be a matter of time before those transactions opened up wider investigations into members of the Thirty-One Club.

Taylor looked back at the bus which had rumbled to life. A hiss of air brakes and it began to roll away from the front of the old chapel.

"I'll be fine," said Taylor.

"I'll be here if you need to talk. One tragedy is enough to bear without you letting the black dog creep up on you."

"I'll be fine. I've got my sergeant there to keep my mind occupied." She nodded at Macpherson, perched on the front quarter panel of the Vauxhall, his hand buried in a packet of Jelly Babies.

"You should take a few days off."

"That's what he said."

The old priest laughed and Macpherson looked up, the old copper's nouse picking up when his name was being taken in vain.

"I heard they called off the search," said Keane.

"They did. No sign of a body but they tell me it can be weeks sometimes before the sea gives up it's dead."

"I'd like to offer my services, when the time comes." He paused, eyes rheumy, a block of emotion caught in his throat.

"Of course."

"It's a tragic end to a tragic tale," said Keane.

Taylor nodded but said nothing, her own emotions hard to pin down. She couldn't profess to know Tom Shepard, but she felt guilt over his death and for robbing him of his vengeance. Any opportunity to know more about the man who had brought about the end of her quest to shackle Beattie had been redacted. All the files relating to the death of Martin Coleman and Cara Maguire had been collected by a suited and patent-shoed bureaucrat from the Northern Ireland Office. Pleasantries and effusive gratitude aside, Taylor knew a spook when she saw one. The legacy of the Troubles was still reaching out through time to affect those in the present, and those shadowy links, like the mystery of Tom

Shepard and the men who had escaped Hoey International Cargo, would, it seem, remain shrouded in mystery for the time being.

She would have been content if her feelings about Gordon Beattie had disappeared as quickly, but as the days wore on, she was finding those even more difficult to process.

Her nemesis was laid out in a medically induced coma, sepsis raging through his body from a ruptured spleen and shattered bowel. At one stage the medics had reported it was touch and go, but when she'd last phoned, the ICU ward sister had said he was a tough old sod and would likely pull through.

Taylor, closing the call, caught the reflection of a smile on her face. The elation that the bastard who had haunted her dreams was still breathing caught her off balance. Maybe the two of them weren't finished yet, but she pushed the thoughts aside for another day.

The sun broke from behind a veil of clouds and the small forecourt in front of the chapel was bathed in warmth. Macpherson, having broken off from nibbling the heads off his sweeties to take a call, and with his usual gruff grace, slapped a meaty mitt on the horn to gain her attention, jerking his head at the car and clunking open the driver's door.

Taylor let the warmth of the sun bathe her face, feeling a familiar tremor of anticipation rise in the pit of her stomach as she bid the priest goodbye, ready to face whatever the call would bring.

Crime in the city never took a day off, so neither would she.

## *Epilogue*

Father Michael Keane placed his stole upon a hook on the back of the vestry door and unbuttoned his cassock. The familiar practices settled the whirling thoughts and sense of grief that had permeated his mind for the last thirty-six hours.

Gathering the meagre offering and readying to place it in the safe, his heart sank. The small cell door was open, and inside he could see the door of the safe unlocked. He closed his eyes, pushing bitter recrimination aside. It was likely his own fault, but it was a disappointment that the theft of those small offerings of compassion had succumbed to the hands of thieves.

Distracted by arrangements for the women's care, answering the inspector's questions regarding Thomas Shepard and assuaging in his own mind his guilt in the proceedings, he must have failed to secure the room.

Keane frowned as he eased the safe open to find it far from empty.

Crammed inside, a black canvas sack was pulled tight by a drawstring. Beside the bag stood a bottle of Bushmills whiskey, around the neck of which hung a cross set upon a chain of polished beads.

A smile rose from the old man's toes to stretch the sagging skin of his face from ear to ear. Reaching out he picked up the offering of gratitude from a lifetime ago, the beads smooth to the touch.

He struggled to lift the bag, its weight deceptive. A deep whump sounded as it hit the old stone tiles. His arthritic fingers fussed over the tied loop.

Wrapped cash bundles filled it to the brim, with a note in

neat script tucked under the band of the top brick.

*'See some good comes from this.'*

Keane tipped the bag over, the two-inch-thick bundles of used banknotes tumbling out; each stack the proceeds of crime. The profits of misery.

He picked one up, drawing in the heady scent as he ruffled the edges of paper worn smooth by many hands.

Scooping the wads back into the bag, he placed it in the safe and looped the rosary around his neck, walking back to the nave and over to the altar feeling lighter than the last time he had passed.

Kneeling, he bowed his head. Thanking his Lord for mercy and praying for the soul who had cheated death.

## *Afterword*

### THANK-YOU FOR READING 'CODE OF SILENCE'

I sincerely hope you enjoyed my debut novel. If you did, please spare a moment to leave a review it will be very much appreciated and helps immensely in assisting others to find this, and my other books.

Both Veronica Taylor and Tom Shepard will return in:

**THE CROSSED KEYS**
and
**NO GOING BACK**

You can find out about these books and more by signing up at my website:

www.pwjordanauthor.com

## *Acknowledgments*

The writing of this novel has been a long journey, and an ambition which I couldn't have fulfilled if the love of books had not been instilled in me as a child.

For that, I am forever grateful to my parents.

The pandemic of 2020 granted me the opportunity and the time to finally dedicate the hours to writing this book, but I still couldn't have done it without the love and unswerving support of my family who gifted me the time and their encouragement as I spent my early mornings and late nights at the keyboard.

This book is for Donna and Erin. Thank you for helping me chase a childhood dream.

I love you both.

Phillip Jordan
    March 2021

*Also by Phillip Jordan*

## ALSO BY PHILLIP JORDAN

### THE BELFAST CRIME SERIES

CODE OF SILENCE
COMING SOON- THE CROSSED KEYS
COMING SOON- NO GOING BACK

### THE BELFAST CRIME CASE-FILES

BEHIND CLOSED DOORS
COMING SOON- INTO THIN AIR

### THE TASK FORCE TRIDENT MISSION FILES

AGENT IN PLACE
COMING SOON- DOUBLE CROSS

*Get Exclusive Material*

## GET EXCLUSIVE NEWS AND UPDATES FROM THE AUTHOR

Building a relationship with my readers is *the* best thing about writing.

Visit and join up for information on new books and deals and to find out more about my life growing up on the same streets that Detective Inspector Taylor treads and get some exclusive True Crime stories about the flawed but fabulous city that inspired me to write.

You can get this **for free,** by signing up at my website.

Visit at www.pwjordanauthor.com

*About Phillip Jordan*

## ABOUT PHILLIP JORDAN

Phillip Jordan was born in Belfast, Northern Ireland and grew up in the city that holds the dubious double honour of being home to Europe's Most Bombed Hotel and scene of its largest ever bank robbery.

He had a successful career in the Security Industry for twenty years before transitioning into the Telecommunications Sector.

Aside from writing Phillip has competed in Olympic and Ironman Distance Triathlon events both Nationally and Internationally including a European Age-Group Championship and the World Police and Fire Games.

Taking the opportunity afforded by recent world events to write full-time Phillip wrote his Debut Crime Thriller, CODE OF SILENCE, finding inspiration in the dark and tragic history of Northern Ireland but also in the black humour, relentless tenacity and Craic of the people who call the fabulous but flawed City of his birth home.

Phillip now lives on the County Down coast and is currently writing two novel series.
For more information:
www.pwjordanauthor.com
www.facebook.com/phillipjordanauthor/

*Copyright*

A FIVE FOUR PUBLICATION.
First published in Great Britain in 2021 by
FIVE FOUR PUBLISHING LIMITED
*Copyright © 2021 PHILLIP JORDAN*

The moral right of Phillip Jordan to be identified as the author of this work has been asserted by him in accordance with the Copyright, Designs and Patents Act 1988.

All the characters and events in this book are fictitious, and any resemblance to actual entities or persons either living or dead is purely coincidental.

All rights reserved. No part of this publication may be reproduced, stored in a retrieval system or transmitted in any form or by any means, without prior permission in writing of the publisher, nor to be otherwise circulated in any form of binding or cover other than that in which it is published without a similar condition, including this condition, being imposed on the subsequent purchaser.

*Cover Image- Shutterstock

FIVE FOUR PUBLISHING

Printed in Great Britain
by Amazon